LORD OF DARK PLACES

LORD
of
DARK
PLACES

HAL BENNETT

to Owen Laster,
with love

I have not spoken in secret, in a dark place of
the earth: . . . I declare things that are right.
　　　　　　　　　　　　—Isaiah, 45:19

Before a man can be saved, he must be born again
Lord, how can a man be born again?
He must die, motherfucker. He must die.
　　　　　　　　—The Journal of Reverend Cobb

LORD OF DARK PLACES

THE PROLOGUE

WHEN Madame Eudora died of uterine cancer back in 1919, her nephew-husband—his name was Roosevelt, after the one who carried the big stick—tried vainly to continue the religion that she founded. But nobody took Roosevelt seriously, because he lacked the boldness that people had mistaken for divine fire in Madame Eudora. Furthermore, the fact that Madame Eudora had died at all caused some of her followers to wonder whether she really had been inspired From Above. Dying the way she had seemed to some of them that Roosevelt had played in her tail too much—which is how some of them referred to the act of fucking—and that she had lost faith in her own religion, that promised freedom from pain, among a number of other benefits, and everlasting life as well; and they turned to other prophets for sustenance. Even Roosevelt's wild tale about Madame Eudora being taken up into heaven body and soul did not convince many of her followers; and those who did believe him converted to Catholicism, since such a miracle seemed to validate the Virgin Mary more than it did Madame Eudora, who turned so purplish-black and grew so fat before she died that she would have been extremely difficult to levitate.

After several months of traveling back and forth through the South with his son Titus, trying to revive some interest in Madame Eudora's religion, Roosevelt decided to settle down on a place he called a farm, south of Goldsboro in North Carolina. Actually, it was a very small house with a rather large backyard, but like most black people, Roosevelt lived inside a special reality that made everything what he wanted it to be. He called the place a farm; he planted two or three rows of tomatoes and corn there and called it his crop. Titus was in his early twenties then; and he spent most of his time in his room, jerking off and reading Solomon in the Bible, which always got him hot.

They had been on the farm several months when some white people who had known Madame Eudora and had just heard the news of her death, came by the house to tell Roosevelt how sorry they were. Madame Eudora had been very popular among Southern whites. She had called her religion The Church of Stephen Martyr; and she had taught, in a sly, abstract kind of way that niggers ought to stay in their place, and die like dogs. The white people liked that; they stood in the door talking about what a superlatively good nigger Madame Eudora had been. They called her Aunt Eudora, as though they were all her nephews and nieces.

Titus had stood on the upper part of the stairwell and heard Roosevelt actually stand there in the door and tell those white people that he wouldn't be presumptuous enough to invite them in, that they were too *good* to come into his house. Even in the short while he had been in Goldsboro, Roosevelt had achieved something of the status of a wise man by telling white people what a dumb, low-down, no-good nigger he was. The white people liked to hear a nigger talk like that. "Why, your house ain't all *that* bad," one of them said, poking his head democratically through the door.

Respectfully, but firmly, Roosevelt barred his way. "It ain't that the house is all that *bad. . . .* In fact, it's a pretty good house, if I do say so myself. It's bought and paid for, actually. I used the little money my wife left me. But what I mean to say is that you all is too *good* to come inside. Lord knows, I don't mean no lack of respect. But it's just that I knows my place, sir. If I was to cuss a white man, or be disrespectful to a white woman, I'd expect you all to deal with me the way you're supposed to. So you see why I don't want you to come into my house, sir, although you're perfectly welcome to, if you've a mind to. Because it ain't nothing but a poor old dumb nigger's house, it just ain't good enough for white folks, sir."

So they went away, talking about what a fine example of a nigger Roosevelt was, more of them niggers ought to be like that. And when one of the white ladies in town reported that Roosevelt had *winked* at her, or it might have been a tic, the white men came at night and lynched Roosevelt, as he certainly would have preferred they do, if he had only known why they were lynching him in the first place.

Titus had seen the whole thing. Roosevelt was sleeping in one of Madame Eudora's old flowered dresses when the white men came. They greeted him pleasantly and told him to come with them. Roosevelt obeyed at once, even when they told him he didn't need to take off the dress or put his pants on. They escorted him with the greatest courtesy to an oak tree out in the woods. One of the white men was named Mr. Johnson, and he asked Roosevelt how his crops were coming along. "Just fine, Mr. Johnson. Just fine," Roosevelt said. "I suspect I might have an early harvest this year." They tied his hands behind his back and put the noose around his neck. Roosevelt started to cry then. "I'm a good nigger, ain't I, Mr. Johnson?" That was all Roosevelt said, he didn't even ask them why they were killing him, since obviously it was their right to use him as they saw fit. "You're a very good nigger," Mr. Johnson told Roosevelt, touching him on his shoulder with a kind of awkward affection. Then he wiped his hand on his overalls while five white men hauled Roosevelt six feet off the ground by his neck. Mr. Johnson and another white man tried to tear Roosevelt's flowered dress off, but they couldn't disconnect it from his neck, he was hanging that high up. So they left it falling around his body like a cape. "By God, that nigger's got the biggest peter I ever did see," Mr. Johnson said. He reached up and touched it fondly. He said he thought he'd take it home and keep it as a souvenir . . . did anybody bring his knife? Titus flew back through the woods then and went home. He remembered that there had been yellow streamers across the moon, like cattails. He left Goldsboro that night, and went over into Virginia, where he eventually met Ramona and got married. He was determined that no son of his would die like his father had died. He'd do anything to keep that from happening to a son of his.

One

WHEN he was twelve years old, Joe Market was playing naked down in Lee's Creek one Saturday morning in the spring of 1951, trying to trap catfish with his hands. Although the cats were sluggish and bloated this early in spring, the sun made Joe lazy, and he didn't try very hard to catch them. Every time he moved his feet, mud rose up in mushroom clouds from the bottom of the creek, so that Joe kept his eyes peeled in case some moccasin came sneaking out from the bank and tried to bite his legs in the muddy water.

Lee's Creek ran steady as a clock, and Joe enjoyed the lukewarm current lapping between his legs, the slow drift of his tail floating just below the surface of the slate-gray water. Around him, the red dirt hills of Burnside, Virginia, humped like sleeping beasts in the sunshine. Farther up on the hill, Joe could see his own house, blue woodsmoke zigzagging from the chimney to mix with the bluer sky. Then he looked up the creek where the water was clear, and he saw a moccasin about four feet long coming down the creek toward him. Joe took his time about getting out of there, because the rocks were sharp and could cut his feet. Besides, the snake wasn't that close to him anyway; it was about fifty feet away, at least.

But before Joe moved another step, he saw his father Titus standing on the creek bank. "Your Mama's dead, Joe sweetheart." That's what his father said. "Your Mama's dead, Joe sweetheart." Standing there in raggedy blue overalls and a pink shirt on the creek bank, wearing a straw hat he had stolen from a mule in Dillwyn. The hat still had the holes in it from the mule's ears; Titus claimed they kept his brain warm. "Did you hear what

I said, Joe? How come you stand there like a fool? Your Mama's dead, don't you understand?"

"Dead, Daddy?" He tried to move, but his legs wouldn't obey him. "You say Mama is *dead*? She was picking peas when I left the house. How come she dead so fast?" The snake was very close now, long and ugly gray-black in the rippling water. And beautiful, too. Like the sound of music moving down the creek.

Titus took off his hat. His whole head was shaved clean and shaped like a black bullet. "I've always spoke the truth, Joe. And I'm not going to start lying now." He was a tall, stooped man with arms like an ape. His own parents had been very close kin before they were married, and Titus sometimes grinned without meaning to. He was grinning now. "I was riding down in the low ground when my tail got hard. So I went up to the house where your Mama was bending over the stove, stirring in a pot of peas. When I come up behind her, she turned with this agony all over her face. She said, *Honey, I know it's my duty. But I been feeling terribly bad lately. I been having me a terrible pain around my heart.* By this time, my tail was as hard as a rock, so I told your Mama it weren't nothing but gas, that pain she was talking about. I told her to take some baking soda in a little warm water. As soon as she belched, she looked a whole lot better. *I know it's my duty,* she said. She belched some more, and it sounded like that gas was leaving her. Then she took off her apron and went into our room and got on the bed."

Joe stood stock still in the water. From the corner of his eye, he saw the snake glide into the mud blossoming around his legs. But he was paralyzed there in the creek. He couldn't see the snake now. All of a sudden, he felt its long, cool body sliding like slow music against his leg. He was filled with self-loathing, and he thought, *Joe Market, you ain't nothing but a dirty good for nothing black nigger.* A snake touching him like that. He expected to fall down dead in the water. Instead, a hot, happy chill shot through all of him, the snake had felt that good and cool. His head jerked around, and when he saw the snake swim from the muddy water, he thought he heard the echo of its body trilling as the snake disappeared downstream.

"I tried to get your Mama to take off her shoes and the rest of her clothes," Titus Market was saying. He grinned and grinned, twirling the straw hat on his finger like a whirligig. "But she said you'd be coming home for dinner in a little while, son. Besides, she didn't want to take too long because the peas might burn. She said she only wanted to help me out some, that was all, that's what a wife is for. So I just unbuttoned my overalls, and when I was satisfied, your Mama moaned a little and said, *Yes honey, that's what a wife is for, regardless of how much pain been hurting her in her chest.* . . . That was the last thing she said, Joe. I didn't know she was dead then. I lowered my head to kiss her some when my nature come singing out. That's when I knew she was dead. I thought for a minute before I got up. I thought, *You're a real man, Titus, you killed her with your tail.* I was sorry, but I couldn't help feeling a little proud, too, doing something like that. There's very little a man can feel proud of nowadays. . . ."

Joe felt the creek water swirling cold now around his own tail. Startled, he looked down and saw that it had got hard; and he felt almost overwhelmed by his own beauty and the beauty of his tail, as though the snake's touching him had baptized and purified him in some way, making him the most beautiful person in the world. His legs unlocked, and he waded from the creek. Titus dropped his hat. "Sweetheart, your tail's hard at a time like this?" Yeah, his tail was hard. He didn't know why, but it was bone hard. "You ugly black sonofabitch," he said to Titus. It was the first time he had ever cursed his father. "You killed my Mama."

Titus started to cry. "I loved your Mama, that's the honest-to-God truth. It was an accident, that's all. I certainly didn't *mean* to kill her. Now I ain't got me nobody regular to fuck when I feel like it. You think I'd deliberately kill her and leave myself in this kind of predicament? But why ain't you crying like I am, son? Ain't you sorry your Mama's dead?" Joe didn't know why he wasn't crying, but his eyes were completely dry, even after Titus wrapped him in his arms and kissed his eyes, as though his lips could strike water there. When Joe still didn't cry, Titus walked with him up to the house on the hill. Titus sat on the porch and kept on crying. Joe hung around in the yard for a while; then he went into the bedroom where Ramona Market sprawled on the bed with her gingham dress up around her waist and her pink bloomers down to her shoes.

Her large cow eyes were still open and gazed somehow to the left, as though death had surprised her from that side. Sperm markings shone on her wrinkled inner thighs like the dried glitter of a snail. She was forty-six years old, but she looked like a scrawny old woman of nearly a hundred. She had been born and bred in the city of Lynchburg, and when she came to Burnside with Titus Market, she had tried to show that she was not a weak city woman by working three times as hard as any country one. The women of Burnside had openly resented her for that, because they thought that Ramona was setting a bad example for the rest of them by working as hard as she did. Even Titus tried to slow her down some by telling her that she didn't have to be *his* nigger, she was a lot more light-skinned than he was. But Ramona wouldn't stop for a minute. They should have been very well off, all the work she did. But the more Ramona worked, the more Titus did nothing except think of outlandish schemes for making easy money. So that Ramona was doing the work that Titus ought to have done, and they had just enough to live on. Titus wasn't especially surprised when Ramona died; he didn't see how any human being could work as hard as she did and not die. On a typical day, she cooked three meals, cleaned house, milked, churned, plowed, sowed, shod mules, hoed weeds and corn, and taught young Joe the Bible every night before she fell exhausted into bed with Titus Market.

The walls in the old house were paper thin, and Joe had often heard Titus urging Ramona in a loud, desperate whisper to take his tail into her mouth. "Suck it, Ramona baby. Open up your mouth and *suck* it, honey. It ain't going to bite." But Joe never heard Ramona do any sucking, because she'd start talking up a blue streak the more Titus insisted, as though putting her mouth to its proper use would inspire Titus to give up the idea burning his mind. After a while, it seemed to Joe that Ramona rushed around with her thin lips pursed tighter than usual, certainly to throw Titus off by pretending that her mouth was smaller than it really was.

Ramona tried to keep Joe on the run as well. But he was agile enough to stay out of her reach until it came time for Bible studies, when he was too tired to avoid her any longer. Just last week, Joe had been listening drowsily to Ramona reading about the sins of Sodom and Gomorrah, when she stopped in the middle of a sentence and pointed to his mouth, his groin, and the flat of his buttocks where he slouched on the sofa beside her. "Has your father tried to do anything to you here, and here, and *here*?" Ramona whispered. "No ma'am," Joe said. He was so sleepy. He wondered why his mother was whispering, because Titus wasn't even in the house, he was out running around somewhere in his old jalopy. Ramona said "If he ever does try to do something to you, I want you to tell me. You hear?" He nodded. Still, Ramona persisted. "And if I'm not here . . . I mean, if anything happens to me, and he tries something like that with you, I want you to tell Reverend Cobb. You hear?" Joe nodded again. Ramona seemed satisfied then. She put the Bible away. Gratefully, Joe stumbled off to bed.

That was last week. Now, Ramona was dead. A trickle of saliva drained from the corner of her mouth. She seemed like a dead stranger to Joe. He looked at her a while longer. All he could think was, *My Daddy's a real man, he killed her with his tail.* He didn't touch Ramona's bloomers, but he did pull her dress down before he left the room. He went out the back door because he didn't want to see Titus again. The rest of the house smelled like burnt peas. Ramona worrying about the peas burning, and they had burned anyway.

Joe was still naked. He went down to the creek and put on his clothes just as the death bell up at the house began its slow, steady tolling. Titus was summoning the neighbors, which was always the first step in their ritual for burying the dead. It was almost as though a person wasn't really dead in Burnside until the neighbors came to see. Joe was glad he had pulled her dress down. He could only think of the dead woman as "her"; she had been too old and ugly in death to be his mother.

He wanted night to come, but the sun would not go down. Around the whole rim of the sky, clouds hung in white dumpling shapes. He felt a growling in his stomach, and realized that he was hungry. Higher on the hill, there was a tomato patch. From there, Joe could see the first people arriving at the house to mourn the dead woman. There was no more smoke coming from the chimney; the fire must have gone out. Joe ate tomatoes until the last car and buggy had pulled up to the house. After a while, his stomach stopped growling. The sky got dark all at once, as though somebody had blown the sun out.

Then he heard his father calling him. But he did not go up to the house. He went back to the creek and stayed there all night. From time to time he dozed. But mostly, he just listened and watched for snakes to come crawling in the full moon. He propped himself against a tobacco stick that he was going to use to kill any snake that tried to kill him. But he did not see any snake at all; and when morning finally did come, he felt that yesterday had been only a terrible dream.

Until he saw his father Titus coming down the hill to the creek. Joe sat very still, holding the tobacco stick, until Titus came close. "I called you yesterday, Joe." Titus was grinning. "Why didn't you come to the house?" Joe jumped up and hit him with the stick. He tried to hit him in the face, but Titus threw his arm up and caught the blow. "Now what'd you want to do that for? After I come all this way to talk to you. I got a plan to talk to you about, Joe, now that your Mama's dead." Joe stood there with his fists balled up. "You killed her," he said bitterly. Grinning, Titus picked up the tobacco stick and broke it in two. Then he dropped to one knee and grabbed Joe and curved him backwards over his other leg. "I got a plan," Titus said. "For a long time now, I been thinking about starting me a new religion. I used to talk to your Mama about it, but she didn't see nothing wrong at all with the Christian religion. I put my plan away, because your Mama laughed at the idea. But your Mama's dead now, Joe. There's just you and me. We got to think about ourselves and this new religion." Joe struggled in his father's arms, trying to break away. "Easy, Joe sweetheart," Titus said, like talking to a skittish mare. Then Joe felt Titus unbutton his jeans. His heart skidded to a stop and then started again. Twisting, he slumped to the ground, dragging Titus with him. Ramona had warned him not to let Titus do anything to him there. But it felt so good, he sprawled back with his eyes closed. Sweat broke out on him everywhere. The sun was so hot for that time of year. A current of fire raced from his brain down his backbone. Then he felt evil and empty, but relaxed.

Titus Market's mother, Madame Eudora, had been a Christian evangelist who fell deeply in love with one of her nephews and married herself to him. A chesty woman with large gold teeth, Madame Eudora said there was clear evidence that Eve and her daughters had mated with their own sons and fathers to get the human race on its way. She thought that she had shown a certain superior imagination in mating with her nephew. Those other southern Negroes who knew the truth did not find it especially unusual that Madame Eudora and her nephew should have married and begot a son. With the white man on all their tails, their motto was live and let live, they didn't have time exactly to pay attention to what other niggers were doing. Besides, the fact that Madame Eudora was very light-skinned and a preacher in the bargain made them think she knew what she was talking about. The nephew didn't seem to mind, either. He thought he was very lucky, being married to somebody as nice and light-skinned as his aunt was. He was a little scrawny black boy, in the beginning—he got fat and much blacker later on—and he used up most of his energy trying to keep from calling his wife his aunt. In Madame Eudora's religious ceremonies throughout the South, he sat immediately to her right. That was the same position that Christ had given the Disciple He loved. As Madame Eudora preached, the nephew shouted pious things from time to time, and played the tambourine. Sometimes he did slip up, and called his wife his aunt in front of other people. Madame Eudora always enjoyed that, and laughed like a wild woman, showing all her gold teeth.

If white people knew anything about the incestuous relationship, they did not stir themselves to do anything about it. For one thing, the white South almost never mixes with its colored people, except to fuck them, and to lynch them if they get too far out of line. Aside from this, Southern men of both races practice sex regularly with boys and girls, as well as with dogs, goats, sheep, geese, cows, chickens and other animals of the lower order. Incest, then, is hardly a scandalous affair; and any white people who knew about Madame Eudora and her nephew-husband would have applauded her for her good taste and restraint. At least she picked something that didn't bark. Besides, she was teaching her son Titus to be respectful and polite to white people, which was all they cared about in Negroes any way.

At an early age, Titus had shown an unusual, though somewhat bizarre, brilliance, and Madame Eudora schooled him in as many teachings of the Bible as would fit into his egg-shaped head. When he was sixteen, she shipped him off to Hampton Institute for further study. But the fact that he was nearly an idiot sometimes gave Titus Market a super-intelligence that frightened sedate instructors at Hampton. They conspired to eject him from the Institute with the argument that because he grinned most of the time, he was not Institute material and could not possibly be a serious student. Besides, they thought that the shape of his head gave the Institute a bad name; and they were tired of hiding him whenever white folks came to inspect. After his dismissal, Titus traveled through all the South with Madame Eudora and her nephew-husband, and continued his education that way.

It was on these travels that Titus saw what he thought was the failure of the Christian church to meet the real needs of the black man. He thought that the Negro was highly illogical in choosing a first-class religion while he was still subject to second-class citizenship. Furthermore, it seemed to Titus that the main error of the Christian religion is that its central figure is depicted as a white man. And a Jew in the bargain. So that an ideal of racial purity is established that can never be fully realized by black Christians, and a wide, unbridgeable gap is created between the ideas of *black* good and evil and *white* good and evil. Titus saw the true religion of the black man best expressed in the offshoots from Christianity, such as his mother's church and the one he himself intended to found.

Some twenty years passed between the idea and the act. Titus had to wait until both his parents died. Then he married Ramona, hoping that she would help him; but Ramona ridiculed what she called his fool ideas and tried to make a happy farmer out of him. Still, the longer Titus waited, the more he came to believe that black people agonized for a religion based on something more tangible than the white myths and mysteries of the Bible. With Ramona dead now, he set about to build his own church.

He had read about cults that worshipped the tail of a man, and he decided to make that and the naked male black body central parts of his religious symbolism. Furthermore, Joe would be the main figure of the new religion; and at the end of each ceremony, Joe would take off his clothes and show his holy objects to the faithful. Not that Titus thought such a daring innovation would do any real good, but it might be an important first step toward undoing some of the *white-man* evil of Christianity. Because the Christian church certainly didn't have any objects like Joe's to offer. Titus called his religion The Church of the Naked Child.

As for Joe, he was overjoyed with the plan Titus proposed. For one thing, it meant that he wouldn't have to go to school. And he liked the idea of leaving Burnside. But more than any of that, Titus had promised him that eventually the whole blessed world would see him naked. It made his tail itch every time he thought about it. On their last day in Burnside, Joe went to see May Jones at her house on the highway, to tell her the good news.

May was naked and digging in her sweet peas when Joe got there. "I'm always naked at home," May said. "It's more comfortable that way." Aside from selling her tail all the time, May Jones

was the blackest thing in Burnside. Everybody said so, and she herself admitted it with a kind of hurt pride that among so many black
people, she had been singled out to be the blackest. She was tall,
and somewhat round-shouldered from the weight of her breasts.
The rest of her body was lean and slender, and she carried it like a
prowling cat as she dipped into a zinc bucket and spread cow manure around the sweet peas.

Joe worked with her for a while. The sweet peas were only slips
now, but May was getting them ready for the peak of her summer
business, since she had found that men are more passionate in hot,
perfumed weather as she serviced them in her sweet peas. Digging
and spreading cow manure, she handled her hoe delicately; she
cautioned Joe to do the same, so as not to bruise the young plants.

With the two of them working together, they soon finished the
job. "I'm going away," Joe said then. "That's what I come to tell you,
May. I'm going away with Daddy to start a new church." He told
her about the new religion, how he'd take off his clothes after Titus
preached. "That's a wonderful, *nice* idea," May said. Joe had never
really had any doubts, but he felt much better now, knowing what
May thought about it.

"Since you're going away," May said, "I've got something for
you." She went into the house and brought out a gilt-colored candy
box. She kept all the hair from her comb and the parings from her
toes here, so that nobody could use them to conjure her with. The
toenails were little yellow crescent moons, brittle with age. Over
the years, the box had filled up once or twice, and May had destroyed the contents by fire in the middle of the night, when there
was small chance that one of her enemies could trap the smoke in a
bottle and conjure her that way. Now, she gave Joe a gold cross that
opened up in the back. "This belonged to my mother," she said.
Then she chopped a few toenails up and stuffed them into the
cross. "Now you wear this for good luck." The heat from her body
nearly scorched him when he bowed his head and she fastened the
chain around his neck. "May?" She smelled like a hot, lazy cat. He
grabbed her, and they fell to the ground together.

Afterwards, she sat plaiting her hair. Joe sprawled naked with his back against the hedges, scratching his belly. "I was sorry to hear about your Mama," May said. Joe felt very surprised. He might have been spawned by sun and young sweet peas, the two combining in his nose like hot, green manure. He had completely forgotten about his mother. "They buried her day before yesterday," he said. He looked up and saw the sky so blue that it hurt his eyes. The sun was so hot for April, it might have been the middle of summer. Still, the cross felt cold and heavy on Joe's chest, and he started to cry.

"Now now now, I am your mother," May said. "Don't you remember that I was your mother in the Christmas tableau?" He remembered. Some six years ago, May had been elected to play the Virgin Mary in the church's Christmas tableau. Joe had played the Christchild; and as far as he could see now, that did make May Jones his mother. It seemed important and exciting to him that one of his mothers was dead and buried while the other one was still alive. He wondered if anybody else in the world could claim to have two mothers.

Still, he cried and cried. May crawled to him and cupped his butt in her greasy hands. "I am your mother," May said. "Now you stop crying, Joe baby. . . ." Her ears were greasy, too. "I'm going to give you my *blessing*, son." Joe stopped crying while she blessed him so good. She really was his mother and he was her son, born of the Holy Ghost and the scalding, slick spit of her immaculate mouth. After a while, Joe put his clothes on and went home. "Be seeing you," May called, when he got to the highway. Joe waved. From that distance, her black body was a lean silhouette. That same afternoon, Titus finished boarding up his house; and he and Joe left Burnside to spread the true word of the true God to black people.

Titus threw away the yellow straw hat he had stolen from a mule, and hid the shape of his head inside a green turban, indicating a fertile mind. A black suit, pointed-toed black suedes, and one of Madame Eudora's old brocaded capes completed his costume. He called himself Prophet Titus. With Joe at his side, he preached up and down Virginia that spring and summer of 1951. The fighting in Korea was a year old, and Titus sometimes preached against the war, especially when he appeared in a community that had sons fighting in segregated outfits in Korea. But more often than not, he talked about redemption. "How can a black man find redemption in a white man's world? Who can rescue *us* from the penalties of God's violated law? No white man can do that—he's too full of sin himself! So what I say is that we need a *new* Redeemer, a *black* Saviour, someone who will deliver us not only from God's wrath, but from the white man's as well!" He was grinning; his eyes shone like murky lanterns. He unfastened the cape and let it fall in a pile at his feet. That was the sign for Joe to mount the pulpit with Titus; and he did so now, feeling every eye in the gathering fall on him as he climbed the three steps to the wooden stand. He wore skin-hugging white jeans and a white tee shirt that set off his black arms and neck. Hooking his thumbs in his hip pockets, spreading his legs and thrusting his groin forward, he stood a bit to the left and rear of Titus and gazed down into the faces of the people.

There were around a hundred of them in all, but the women in the congregation outnumbered the men two-to-one, because a woman is always alert for news of any religion in which she might become the Virgin Mother and enjoy the ineffable mystery of having her tail played in by the Holy Ghost. These women were no different. They wore clean drawers in case tonight was the night, or in case they got too happy and fainted and their dresses came up. They gazed first at Titus and then at Joe, the kind of expectancy on their faces that people wear when they go applying for an important job. Yes, one of them just might be chosen tonight to have her thighs parted and get herself filled by the forerunners of The Black Messiah.

For Titus made it quite clear that neither he nor Joe was The New Messiah, only The Ones Who Come Before Him. "I say to you that we are not The Chosen One. But we are here to announce to you that a Chosen One is coming, a black man, to redeem us from our sins. He is coming soon, and my son and I are the ones who come before Him."

Craning their necks now, the women shuffled from foot to foot as Titus increased the tempo of his preaching. "A Little Child shall lead you!" Titus cried. "And we *have* found a Redeemer! We *have* found a Saviour!" He reached back and poked Joe in the chest. He had decided against having himself or Joe be the actual Saviour in fact, just in case some nigger asked for a miracle. There were always people like that who tried to put people on the spot by asking the impossible. Once or twice even, some smart nigger had told Titus that his doctrine seemed mixed-up and confusing. "What's confusing about it?" Titus had blazed from the pulpit. "What you need, sir, is *faith*. With faith, it's possible to believe anything." That had shut them niggers up sure enough. "Now I say to you, this child here is *not* our Saviour," Titus stressed again. "Our Saviour comes after him. But our truth and our salvation rest in this child here, who's going to take off his clothes right now. Take off your clothes, son." The crowd got quiet as death. Somebody snickered. And then fell silent as Joe took off his clothes.

He was indeed a beautiful child. Although he was only twelve years old, he might have been a lean young man in his late teens. Serene and handsome, his face shone in the light of a dozen lanterns that Titus had strung in a kind of halo around the pulpit. He had got an unusually early start with the sex practices of Burnside, and his enormous tail showed that fact. Raising his arms, he stretched, and tightened the muscles in his butt. He loved the adoration of the crowd, he wanted everybody to see his tail. "We are all naked before Jehovah!" Titus thundered. The crowd yelled *Amen!* Titus shrilled a gold tambourine. The crowd yelled *Hallelujah!* Carried away by the sight of God's handiwork, some of the sisters fainted. Others shouted *Praise Be the Lord!* and clapped their hands. They were all grateful they had worn clean drawers.

The men stood quietly admiring Joe Market, some of them with a certain envy for his father's bold daring. Others wondered why Titus grinned so much, even when he was praying. "Behold, O God, this Thy most wonderful handiwork, who comes before the Saviour. Through him, bring us a Black Saviour for our sins and a Black Redeemer for us, Thy chosen people. We're going to take up a collection now." He fairly ran down to the back of the crowd, before anybody could get away. Joe always stayed naked in the pulpit until the collection was over. As usual, the women were more generous than the men. Titus collected in his gold-colored tambourine. He even revived the sisters who had fainted and asked them for a donation. "I know you'd be mighty put out, sister, if I didn't wake you up and give you this opportunity to make your donation to The Naked Child." They were especially generous, the sisters who had fainted. "Thank you, Prophet Titus, for giving us this chance to donate." They wondered if he'd seen their clean drawers when they fainted. Titus grinned and grinned. After the collection was over, he blessed the crowd. Joe put on his clothes, and everybody went home.

One night, Titus set up his platform beside James River. "Behold The Naked Child!" Titus cried. Stark naked in the lantern light, so many eyes caressing him, Joe felt his nature rising. Filled with a strange excitement that he had never felt before, he dived into the water. Startled, he grinned down in the muddy river. He'd come before the Saviour, all right. Titus was delighted when Joe told him what had happened. He decided that from then on, he would concentrate only on seacoast towns or places where there was sufficient water, and to end each ceremony with Joe diving into the water. Titus called that The Baptism of The Naked Child. He constructed a portable scaffold for Joe to dive from, and carried it in the trunk of his jalopy when he and Joe left Virginia and fanned out through the coastal South. Adding yet another ritual to his religion, Titus bought a tent, and a folding cot with red satin covering, where Joe could wait after his dive for the closer inspection of the faithful. For this closer look, Titus asked a donation of $2.00 or the equivalent in fatback, tobacco, or chickens. The donation was considerably higher for touching Joe or bedding down with him, and depended on the excitement that Titus could divine in the faithful, men and women alike. With this dramatic new touch, the religion prospered even more over the next three years. But Titus squandered nearly all of their earnings on whores for himself and Joe. "Always give in when you're tempted," he instructed Joe. "That way, you'll never have problems with your conscience."

When Joe turned sixteen, it had become more than obvious

that The Naked Child had become a man. Tall, black, brutally handsome, Joe stood nearly six feet tall. He certainly wasn't a child any longer, and Titus found himself faced with the problem of whether to keep on undressing Joe in public, or to change the name of his religion. After much thought and prayer, he decided on the latter course, and the religion became known as The Church of The Naked Disciple. Titus was very pleased about the way he had steered Joe through the crucial years to manhood. Sometimes, thinking about it, his eyes filled with large tears. Sometimes he wished that his wife Ramona had lived to see all the wonderful things that were happening to their son.

Joe was hit by a throbbing excitement now every time he undressed in front of the crowd. More and more, Titus was taking his time before giving the signal to dive, letting the crowd get a good eyeful of the holy object. Standing erect over the crowd, Joe could feel the pounding in his big tail beating all the way down to his toes and up to his brain. He heard some of the sisters moan. Some of them were sobbing. Some of the rest of them had their mouths wide open. Titus shouted and bobbed up and down in the pulpit like he'd gone completely crazy. *Hallelujah! Amen! Behold the Naked Disciple!* Joe threw his head back and laughed up at the stars. Man, he felt great. Just great. A hundred hands reached out, trying to touch him. His butt quivered. Then Titus shrilled his gold tambourine, and Joe dived into the water. That dive always refreshed him. He dragged himself up on the soft dirt and padded to the tent. He dried himself. Then he smoked some pot and waited for the excitement to begin again. Titus, a great pot smoker himself in recent years, had turned Joe on to the fact that pot made the excitement greater.

One night in Alabama, while Joe was waiting for customers, Titus parted the tent flap and came in with May Jones, all dressed up like a lady. Joe recognized her at once. "Joe honey, is that you, baby?" He felt like crying. He jumped up and hugged her half to death, spinning her around the floor. "May Jones, what you doing down here from Burnside? They run you out or something?"

"No days like that," May said, when she could catch her

breath. "Believe it or not, Joe, I'm down here on vacation. I got an aunt that lives out near Dothan."

"Daddy, you believe this is May Jones? Did you know this was May?"

"I did not," Titus said. He didn't seem to be happy to see May at all. "I didn't recognize you, ma'am," he said formally. He stood there fumbling in his pockets.

May laughed. "I know you didn't, Titus Market. But I recognized you. Why, I nearly *died* when somebody told me you all had a meeting over here tonight. Oh, it's so good to see you, Joe baby! I'm really glad to see you!"

"Joe, there're two or three people waiting," Titus said pointedly.

"Daddy, I can't see no other people now. May's here. I want to talk to her. Why, we ain't seen each other for nearly four years."

But Titus didn't budge until May dug in her pocketbook and gave him ten dollars. "That'll buy you exactly one hour," he said, checking his watch. He dropped the tent flap and disappeared.

"Baldheaded bastard," Joe said. He almost wished that Titus would drop dead, treating May like that.

"Don't worry about it, baby," May said. "I just *had* to see you. What you been doing, honey? When you coming back to Burnside? Lawd, you're really a man now!" she cried. "You got big all over!" She reached out and lifted his tail, letting it fall heavily against his thigh. She had been a grown woman while he was still a little boy, so he wasn't surprised by how old she looked. Not too old, though. But still black, and almost pretty. "Boy, you didn't have no tail like that when you played the Christchild. You remember?"

Joe laughed. "Sure I remember. How could I forget something like that?" He was so glad to see somebody who'd known him before. "You see I still got the cross you gave me?"

May nodded. "Joe honey . . . you can tell me to mind my business if you want to . . . but are you happy, honey?"

"I'm happy," he said quietly.

May drew him to the cot with her. "No you ain't, Joe. I was outside at the meeting. You ain't happy at all."

"I'm happy," he said. "As happy as anybody else. . . . But tell me, what's happening back in Burnside?"

"Oh, the same old thing. People still farming, and playing in each other's tails. I did me a good business while the war was going on. I put some money away, too. That's why I'm able to take a vacation. I've never had a vacation, and I decided it was time I had one." She plucked at the satin cover. "When you had a vacation, Joe?"

"Me?" He was surprised. "I never had no vacation. I don't work hard. I . . . I work here with Daddy. . . . We travel a lot, you understand. Sometimes I go to the movies. I read funny books, I listen to the radio. . . ."

"Joe, honey, this ain't no life for you!" May said bitterly. "Why, I saw you out there on that scaffold, showing yourself to all those people, and I thought, *That boy's not happy, and I'm going to tell him so.* I thought it was a good idea when you told me about this religion thing. But I don't any more. Joe honey, you need yourself a girl friend . . . you need to be around children your own age . . . somebody you can talk to. . . . You ought to go up North maybe, I don't know. But this . . ." —she swept her hand in a broad circle of disdain— ". . . this ain't no kind of life for you, baby."

"I'm happy," he said stubbornly. All at once, he was tired of May. "You paid your money," he said brutally. "You want to get fucked?"

May stared at him a while, but he wouldn't meet her gaze. "Sure I want to get fucked," she said finally. "Why you think I come in here? I'm certainly not one to spend money for nothing." He fucked her.

Afterwards, while she was dressing, he said quietly behind her, "May, I'm glad to see you. I really am."

"I'm glad to see *you*," she said. She didn't even turn around. She walked out without saying good-by.

Titus came grinning in right away. "You handled her real well, Joe. Nothing but a busybody, and a whore in the bargain. Trying to give *you* advice! I must confess, son, I was listening out behind the tent. I didn't want her to do or say anything to harm you. But you handled her real well, son."

Joe gazed at him coldly. Sometimes, he just couldn't stand Titus. "I thought you said there were people waiting."

"That's my boy," Titus said. He went outside and sent the next customer in. A man. Joe lay back and let him suck. He really was glad to see May, he wondered if she knew that. But how could he change now? Man, this was the only thing he knew how to do. He busted his nuts and smoked some pot while he was waiting for the next customer.

This one was an old widow woman. She had paid three fat young hens for Joe to fuck her. Man, she looked like she was ninety years old! But she called him "sir." He sure was glad he'd smoked that pot. He put some vaseline on his tail and nearly fucked her to death. Fucking. That was the only thing he knew how to do. Nobody had taught him anything else. Except how to smoke pot.

And he had been with children his age, he hadn't wanted to tell May that. Several times, Titus had taken him to parties, things like that, where children went with grownups. The children had treated him like he was some kind of freak. He hated children. He was always bigger than they were. Smarter, too. The last time he'd been with some, they'd pissed him off so much that he took out his tail and tried to make them all suck it. And that was the end of that. "I'm happy," he thought, fucking the old widow woman. Her flesh felt like dried death. Then he made his mind a complete blank. It didn't pay to think too much, he knew that.

They always wintered in the deep South. One evening they were on their way through Mississippi to another meeting place near the border with Louisiana when they met five white boys pissing on the road. Titus was driving the jalopy with a banner that read CHURCH OF THE NAKED DISCIPLE taped across the lower windshield. "Roll your window up, Joe. And lock the door." Titus cracked his window some. The brakes cried when he stopped. He kept the car motor running. They were very close to Louisiana. Leaves were falling like stealthy footsteps in the woods.

The white boys stood right in the middle of the road, pissing and laughing. Except one of them. He was on crutches, and wore an old khaki Army uniform. He was very blond, his skin burned the color of cinnamon. His pale blue eyes gazed somewhere beyond everything in a see-nothing stare. Leaning on his crutches, he stared dully while the other boys finished pissing.

"Look at them niggers, J.D." The tallest boy clapped the cripple fondly on the back. "You see, J.D.? Church of the Naked Disciple, that's what the sign says. Nigger, which one of you is The Naked Disciple?"

Titus was grinning and bobbing his head. "My boy here, sir. He's The Naked Disciple, sir."

The tall boy laughed, shaking his shoulders like a peacock. his checkered shirt was open down to his faded blue dungarees. He had curly blond hair even on his chest and at the beginning of his belly. Sullen, handsome, his face was the color of geraniums. "And this here's J.D.," he said, pushing the cripple gently forward. "J.D.'s my baby brother. He got his nerves all shot up in Korea, fighting them Commies so they wouldn't come over here and get you niggers." He chuckled a while at that. It was just before sunset, in October, and the shadows were falling heavily around them now. Except for J.D., the others shuffled and snorted impatiently like quiet horses, waiting to trample something. The four of them wore the same kind of checkered shirts and hobnailed boots and tight-fitting dungarees riding low on their hips. Obviously the tall boy was their leader. He was as slender as a woman. There was a galloping stallion engraved on the brass buckle of his broad black belt. He cleared his throat twice quickly, before he said, "The war's been over more than two years now, and J.D. still ain't come to his senses. We've tried since he come home to get him to talk, to do something." His face turned sad, almost gentle. "I love J.D., I can't hardly stand to see him this way. Lord knows, we've tried just about everything, but J.D. don't respond to nothing."

Titus made a steeple of his fingers on the steering wheel. "That war was a terrible thing, sir . . . a terrible thing. And we colored people are very fortunate that you white people saved us from those Communists. To show my own personal gratitude, I'd be happy to say a prayer for your brother. If you'd like me to, sir. It might do him all the good in the world." The tall boy actually seemed to be considering that. He hooked his thumbs in his belt, smoothing his fingers over the engraved stallion. "Like I say, we've tried everything. . . . We even had him baptized again, in water that somebody brought back from Jerusalem, Mama thought that might do some good."

But when the others snickered behind him—flexing the muscles in their arms and butts—he looked as cruel as he could. "You hear that nigger, J.D.? He wants to *pray* for you. As if Jesus Christ'd pay any attention to a prayer from a nigger. He wants to eat in the same restaurant with you too, J.D. You want to eat at the same table with niggers like these?" J.D. didn't say anything; his blue eyes seemed to be staring at something that none of them could see. But the other three boys shook their heads broadly. The tall one went on. "Now listen to this, J.D. Last year, the Yankee Supreme Court said that separate but equal ain't good enough any more. You hear that, J.D.? Now we got to be *together* and equal. Look at these niggers, J.D. You want to be integrated with them?" He draped a loving arm around the cripple's shoulders, and the others laughed. But J.D. just stared.

Joe and Titus sat as stiff as ice. The car was trembling all over from the idling motor. Titus had his right hand curled around the claw hammer that he carried hidden down between the seats in case of trouble. He said, "It just might do some good for me to pray for him, sir." All at once, the sun went down around them. The tall boy hesitated; the others shuffled uncomfortably. "What good would a nigger prayer do?" one of them said. The tall boy grinned weakly. "Yeah, that's right . . . what good *could* a nigger prayer do for my brother?" Helping J.D. along, all of them went around to the other side of the car.

Joe looked at the broken figure of J.D., then away. He could hear the oppressive chirping of crickets. There were pines on either side of the road, and his nostrils suddenly filled with the evil smell of resin. Everything was bathed in red. Joe sat very still and said nothing. The cripple just stood there, but the other four boys looked at Joe and started laughing. "The Naked Disciple," they said. The tall one opened his dungarees and dragged out his tail. He pissed again. "You want some white meat, nigger?" He whacked his tail against the window, spreading urine. His tail started to swell. "Come on, J.D. Let's give the nigger boy some white peter." He pushed J.D. forward on his crutches, but J.D. crumbled like a scarecrow, staring. The rest of them crowded close to the car, opening their dungarees and trying to get the door open. "*J.D. do something goddamn it motherfucker!*" The tall boy sounded like he was going to cry.

Titus threw the car into gear and took off. The right fender knocked the crippled boy's crutches from under him and sent him sprawling. But Titus kept on, muttering to the car like he was urging on a mule. Joe looked back and saw the white boys in the road, the cripple sprawling, the tall one running to him, the others laughing and shaking their tails at the fleeting car until the trees hid them from view. "Them dirty white boys," Joe said. He was filled with disgust. That dirty thing they wanted to do to him. He did it to other people, but he'd die before he let anybody do anything like that to him. The sky turned dark and starless.

Titus held the hammer in his lap until they crossed the state border. The car was filled with the smell of fear, and neither of them said another word until they crossed over into Louisiana. Then Titus relaxed some, and started to talk. "You were lucky they didn't try to lynch you, son. Like I told you, my own Daddy was lynched. And doing that to a man's much worse than trying to fuck him. When somebody hauls you away and strips you naked and kills you in the night . . . that's a whole lot worse than being fucked." He shook his head, squinting out at the dark road. "I believe that the best way to judge a man is according to the things he *won't* do. So what you have to do, son, is decide which one thing is more evil than the other, and you reject that. You know what them boys wanted to do. But they *didn't* want to lynch you, and I'm glad of that. Because it's a lot worse than what they did want to do."

They were driving through a field of tall grass that nodded to a slow, nocturnal music. Over his shoulder, Joe could see a few stars that had come out, and the full moon, following them. Gently, Titus laid his hand on Joe's leg. "You know, something happens like that thing with the white boys, and I start asking myself questions. I just thought I'd talk about this, Joe, in case you ever have any doubts about . . . well, about the *rightness* of what you're doing. But there's nothing wrong with taking off your clothes in front of people who think you might be a god. And you might be at that. Who's to say for sure? Anything's possible in a place where men still lynch each other. Although I do sometimes think we might both be better off back in Burnside, planting tobacco. You ever think about that, Joe? About going back to Burnside?" Joe shook his head. Those dirty, nasty white boys had frightened him more than he'd ever been frightened in his life. But there was nothing in Burnside for him now, not after all he'd seen and done. "I don't want to go back there," Joe said. "I like what I'm doing."

"Yes, I suppose you would," Titus said, somewhat dryly. "I suppose I'd like it, too, if I was in your pants." There was bitterness in his voice now. "The Naked Disciple," he added, with heavy sarcasm. Joe laughed, the fear and tension leaving him as he rolled down the window and listened to the crickets. They sounded like clear, soft singing over here in Louisiana. "Besides," he said, "if them white boys got too tough, all I had to do was take off my clothes. They would've stopped then."

Titus looked at him sharply. "You think so? Well, you got another think coming, boy." He slowed the car some and peered into Joe's face as though he no longer recognized him. "You really think so?" Titus said. He was certainly amazed. "Why, them white boys would've *fucked* you if you'd taken off your clothes." Joe shrugged, and did not answer. Deeply troubled, Titus drove on.

A few hours later, they came to New Orleans. But Titus did not hold a service that night. He was worried about Joe. He just didn't know what had come over that boy all of a sudden. Or himself, either. It wasn't usual for him to think this way. But he couldn't stop worrying; and he decided that he and Joe ought to get some pussy, maybe that would help straighten things out.

After leaving the car and their equipment at a boarding house where they usually stayed in New Orleans, they went down to St. Peter Street. Joe was eager and smiling, always ready for whores.

"How many women we going to fuck tonight, Daddy?" They had shared as many as a dozen women in monumental orgies; but Titus wanted to have Joe closer to him tonight than a gang of whores would allow. "Let's get just one bitch, son, and fuck her to death."

They strode down St. Peter Street in a mist of shifting shadows and pastel-colored neon lights until Titus spotted a woman who looked like she might do. Black herself, she wore a black satin dress that held her like a glove and left most of her big titties hanging out. "You like her, son? You think you'd like to fuck her while she sucks me?" Joe nodded. "Right now I feel like I could fuck a snake." Grinning, Titus went over to the whore with some money in his fist. "Lady, I'll give you fifty dollars if you fuck my son and me together." The whore looked at the money and Titus' green turban. "*I* certainly ain't no lady," she said, almost indignantly. She half-turned and squinted at Joe where he waited across the street. Her lips were full and dark red, and Titus imagined how they'd feel sucking him. Turning back to him, the whore smiled, as though she'd read his mind. "Things are kind of slow," she said. "I think it might be nice for you and your son to fuck me together." She stashed the money between her titties; and Titus and Joe followed her to a small, dingy room over a storefront on Piety Street.

The whore squirmed out of her dress and kicked off her shoes. "Let's hurry up, darlings. I ain't got all night, you know." She was naked, ready to be fucked right then; but Titus liked for women to kiss and suck on his bald head while Joe was fucking them. When he told the whore what he wanted her to do, she laughed joyously. "I think you must be *crazy*!" she cried. But she didn't seem to object to the idea; nor did she make any comment about Titus' pointed head after he took off his turban.

Titus lit a stick of pot and they all got high. Then he and Joe got naked and stood side by side with their big tails throbbing hard to show the whore what she was letting herself in for. She looked from one to the other, her eyes wide as tea cups. "*Both* you men going to fuck me?" She asked as though she had not known it before. "Lawd, as sure as I'm born, you two men going to fuck me to *death*!" Her lips spread back in a scared, happy grin; and her eyes seemed to cross, she was staring at their tails so hard. Brutally, Joe dragged her down backwards to the smelly bed. Man, he wouldn't wait another minute! Spreading her legs with his knee, he slid his long, thick tail into her pussy from behind. She cried like she'd been stabbed with a knife. Her pussy was hairy and wet and fat. Then she started grinding her ass like crazy. *"Oh fuckmebabyfuckmypussylikeyou-neverfuckedapussybefore . . ."* Joe fucked her.

Grinning, Titus watched awhile. Then he laid against the whore's titties, doubling his knees to her belly as best he could. When he stuck the point of his head against the whore's mouth, she kissed and sucked it greedily. With Joe's tail inside her like that, she'd suck a duck's ass right now, if one happened to be around. Very content, Titus closed his eyes.

But instead of alerting his body and soothing his mind as it usually did, the kissing and sucking had the opposite effect. Titus' brain burned with slow excitement under the whore's hot mouth; and he found that he just couldn't stop thinking. Indeed, he felt like he might have an attack of brilliance. He reached and caught Joe by the cheeks of his butt, mashing the whore tighter between him and his son, thrilling with a flush of hot pride at the precise gyrations of Joe's behind, the flex of muscles in his butt as he slid in and out of the whore with long, steady strokes. Titus rammed his head harder against the whore's mouth. He loved the way she made his skull tingle as she sucked lovingly and with great care, so that it was impossible for him to tell where her mouth and tongue ended and the sensitive point of his own head began. At the same time, he heard the lazy, lonesome horns of ships plying the Mississippi, and he thought, *Does the ship ever start believing that it is the river on which it runs? Does it ever lose sight of the thin line that separates it from the smooth-flowing river?*

Titus was not a sailor; in fact, water frightened him with its slow-moving promise of baptism and a murky kind of salvation inside the ritual of the Church. Any religion, he thought, including his own, could only promise that dying would be a little easier. But none of them could ever change the essential fact of death. What they did do was to put a sugar coating around the bitter pill, and that sugar was what they called salvation. Which to Titus' mind was just another way of saying death.

"Am I doing all right, sugar? Is that the way you like it?" The whore's titties rested against his shoulder like black satin pillows. "You doing just fine, honey. Concentrate on the uppermost part there. That's where it really feels good." Joe was clutching him by his tails and balls, holding him there for support as he piled into the whore. Titus made his tail tremble. *Fuck that black bitch, boy. Fuck her to death.* Joe squeezed, and fucked on. Titus felt a tear wet his eye. That kid. That beautiful fucking kid. He went back to his thoughts.

He was not a man of the earth, either. The trouble with everything that walks or crawls, he thought, is that the greedy earth is always there waiting to receive us. When he was a child, he had tried to fly, because birds made it seem easy. He had often resented the fact that he had not been born some creature of the air that can fly away before death overtakes it. A flying thing lives all its life senseless as an angel, and death for it is nothing more than a graceful fall, like a feather floating down to a solitary niche, instead of the terrible tearing and rending of death on earth.

And aside from death, even the softest, easiest kind, Titus thought that the next greatest tragedy happens when a man loses sight of who he really is, which is what it seemed was the trouble with Joe now. When had Joe started thinking that he was really The Naked Disciple, with some kind of supernatural power in his naked body that could change people like those white boys they had met on the road? *All I had to do was take off my clothes. They would've stopped then.* A fool caught inside his own lie. Other people were supposed to think like that, but certainly not Joe. It reminded Titus of a rabbit he had hunted with his father one day, the two of them crashing through the bushes behind a yelping hound; and he had felt the rabbit's palpitating terror in such a way that he wondered now about the possibility of the rabbit's believing that it was the hound, some combination of fear and desperation stepping down on its fluffy mind like a heavy boot, so that it no longer seemed necessary to run; and it had huddled there inside the bramble until the slavering hound parted the bushes and tore its throat to shreds. Later on, when his father had separated the rabbit from the spit and handed him a hot shank, Titus had eaten it greedily because he had enjoyed the distortions of death that made the rabbit right for roasting.

It seemed to him now that Joe was just about to get himself roasted the same kind of way, because he had fallen head over heels into the trap of confusing reality with what *seems* to be reality, and from which the only possible escape is death. And Titus didn't know what to do about it. That's why he was worried and upset, because he loved that goddamned boy. Fucking that whore to death with his great big tail, holding on to *his* tail for dear life, like he never wanted to let his Daddy go. *Fuck her, Joe baby.*

Titus shifted under the whore's slick mouth; and she turned solicitous at once. "Did I hurt you, honey?" Titus shook his head. The whore slid her lips ecstatically around his bald dome as Titus closed his eyes again. He thought, *Life is a terrifying chase; death is the big hound dog that chews us up and saves us from it.* In other words, if you want to save somebody, then you've got to throw them to the thing that's chasing them.

Titus grinned now, like he sometimes did without meaning to. He felt that he had discovered a great truth. Wasn't that what the Bible was all about? Judas betrayed Christ *because* he loved him. The whore's mouth made a lovely and agreeable mess on the peaked point of his head. Everybody had always thought that he was crazy because his head was shaped that way. But he knew one thing—if a child of his had to die, he'd rather be the one to do the killing. No some dirty white motherfuckers with hard-ons. . . . Slowly, he moved his head under the whore's sweet ministrations. He could hear the leaden ship horns only faintly now—soft, heavy, colored dull gray. Damn it, he loved Joe. But it seemed certain that Joe had started to float along toward disaster, like the sad, receding ships. Titus was filled with confusion; how could he save his son?

Suddenly, he felt a strange sensation surrounding him and a voice speaking to him as from a whirlwind. *If you want to save your son, you've got to destroy your religion.* Startled, Titus jerked away and stared at the whore. She had her eyes closed, a look of inde-scribable joy softening the features of her face as Joe poured tail into her. Joe had his eyes closed too, his head jammed against the whore's back. Still, Titus had heard the voice clearly and unmistak-ably, even if only inside his own head. *Destroy your religion.* Well, he did love Joe; but wouldn't that be going just a little too far?

He didn't know where that damned voice had come from; but it irritated him so much that he unlocked Joe's hand from around his tail and slid out of bed. "You all intend to fuck all night?" he said peevishly. He couldn't help it; he just hated the way they were hav-ing all the fucking fun and he was having none. "It seems to me you all should've come a long time ago," he added sarcastically. But nei-ther Joe nor the whore seemed disturbed by Titus's new attitude. Lazily scratching her head, the whore lifted her leg as Joe pulled out of her. "This boy, he's already come three times. Didn't you know that?"

"How could I know?" Titus said acidly. "He didn't come in me."

"Well, he come in *me*. That's why I know."

Joe went to the sink to wash up. 'Daddy, I think I'll go out for a while," he said. He was very accustomed to rapid changes in his fa-ther's moods, especially where women were concerned. "I'm tired of this stuffy old room."

"So you're running out on me?" Titus cried. "Here I've been wracking my brain about you, and now you're running out!" He knew he was being unreasonable, but he just couldn't help it.

"Lawd, what's the matter with him?" the whore said. "Wasting all this time talking when we could be fucking." She seemed very amused, and that only made Titus angrier. "I'll show you what's wrong with me!" he yelled. Deliberately, he straddled the whore's neck and shoulders and stuffed his soft tail into her mouth. That ought to shut her up. Fondling his balls lovingly, the whore straight-ened out on the bed and sucked. Titus grinned. His tail wasn't soft any more, and he felt just fine now. "You go on out, Joe. But don't you get in no trouble, you hear?"

Joe finished dressing. "I'm going to the boarding house," he said from the doorway. "I want to get me some sleep." But Titus was up on his hands and knees now, fucking the whore deep down her throat, and he was much too busy to hear. "That . . . is . . . *fine* . . . sugar . . . youkeeponsucking . . . me . . . like . . . that . . . I'mgoing . . . tocomerightdownyourfuckingthroat. . . ." It amazed him that she could suck as much of his gigantic tail as she did without gagging or throwing up like other women. And she turned his body on in a way that nobody ever had before, so that he felt as though he was flying somewhere through the emanations of a blue-hot day— soaring, falling down through the dizzying currents, rising again to her flailing tongue. One of her hard, fat nipples stuck straight up his ass; and she sucked him off so superbly that he had to pray to keep from coming right then, although his toes curled up and he nearly shit right on her chest. A sob caught in the back of his throat, and he realized, with a gratifying shock, that he had fallen in love with the whore. He didn't give a damn about Joe or anybody else right now. Nobody had ever sucked him off that beautifully before. "Honey, I *love* you," he said; and he burst into tears, he felt so fucking happy.

When Joe finally woke up in the stuffy boarding house, the day after being with the whore, it was nearly noon. Titus still hadn't come home, but Joe wasn't worried about him, although it was the first time they'd spent a night away from each other since leaving Burnside. Now, a solitary fly buzzed around Joe's head, and he felt the vague beginnings of loneliness. Moving quickly, he caught the fly in his cupped hand. "Shit, I'm not a little boy any longer," he said to the squalid room. "I'm going to do something on my own for a change." He smashed the fly between his fingers. Then, bouncing out of bed, he took a quick shower and went outdoors into a muggy, disagreeable October day. But Joe enjoyed the heat; it made him feel as though he had finally stepped from the cool world of childhood into the burning fire of being a man. Walking with long steps, he felt free for the first time in his life, and unhampered by the towering presence of Titus, which always made him feel small and less than he was. He ate a couple of hot dogs for breakfast, then he hired a truck driver and some day workers from Orleans Street to set up a meeting place down by the Mississippi where Titus had preached before. "Where's that old crazy Daddy of yours?" one of the men said. "He's shacked up with a whore," Joe said. All the men laughed. They were loading equipment from the jalopy onto the truck. "Yeah, well, Titus ain't crazy enough to keep you around no whore with him," the driver said. "He's jealous of that peter you got." The men teased Joe all the way out to the river site.

They worked until early afternoon with the tent and scaffold. The fact that Titus wasn't there to egg them on made them take more time than was really necessary. But Joe didn't care how long the workers took; they treated him like a man among men, and he knew that he'd lose their respect if he chased around screaming after them like Titus did. And speaking of Titus, what the fuck was he doing now anyway? Was he still with that whore? And was Titus really jealous of him like that driver said? No shit, man, he'd never thought about that before; but he decided to keep his eyes peeled from then on, just to make sure.

When the men finished working, Joe paid them off. That was almost all the money he had left, but he'd be able to get more from Titus . . . if Titus ever did show up. "Why *thank* you, sir," the driver said. He touched his cap respectfully. "You be good now." He dropped Joe on Canal Street and drove off.

Joe waved at the men in the truck. The driver had called him sir. Man, that felt good, like a warm hand cupping his balls. He'd have to tell Titus about that. Sir. He walked on. Maybe Titus was waiting for him now at the boarding house. Well fuck it, let Titus wait. He wasn't ready to crawl back inside of Titus' asshole and languish there curled and protected like some baby inside of a shitty womb. He was a *man* now; maybe he never would need Titus anymore. But one thing he knew for sure—when he did see Titus, there were going to be some changes made. He wasn't a kid any longer, and he was going to tell Titus so in no uncertain terms. They'd be men together after that, sharing everything. Money. Women. Work. No more of this horseshit of Titus laying around with some whore while *he* had to do all the work.

Drifting along with the crowds on Canal Street, he thought

that New Orleans smelled stale and corrupt, like a pile of buildings washed up on a river bank and left to rot in the sticky Delta sun. As for the people, they moved past him like listless machines mired down in mud or molasses. Nobody paid any attention to him. Didn't they know that he was The Naked Disciple, the son of Prophet Titus, come with a new joy and word of a Black Messiah? Maybe some of them had even seen him naked on that scaffold. Joe flashed his beautiful smile; but those people who bothered to look at him just stared at him blankly. Man, he ought to drag out his tail and baptize all of them with come, they'd recognize him then. Dumbass niggers.

He stopped to admire his reflection in a store window. Shit, he knew he was the best-looking thing in New Orleans. And all anybody had to do was look at his white jeans to know he had some tail on him. Or peter. That's what those men called his tail. Peter. Joe liked calling it that. A man's word. Like Peter in the Bible. *And I say also unto thee, That thou art Peter, and upon this rock I will build my church; and the gates of hell shall not prevail against it.* His mother Ramona had read that to him from the Bible; and it surprised him that he was thinking about Ramona, because that was something he almost never did any more. Still, he did wonder what she would think about The Church of the Naked Disciple. And about his getting naked in front of all those people. And letting Titus suck his peter, after she had warned him so firmly against it. Joe shook his head. Man, it was stupid to wonder about all of that, because there wouldn't be any Church of the Naked Disciple if Ramona was still living. There wouldn't be anything. Shit. He didn't mind Titus sucking him off every once in a while; in fact, he enjoyed it. Shit. His peter was getting hard right now, he could stand being sucked off. He was almost glad Ramona was dead; if she was alive, he'd be back in Burnside letting her treat him like a baby while he busted his balls out in the fields with all those other dumb niggers.

He walked on happily, throwing his left leg to show off the growing bulge of his peter against his thigh. *Thou art Peter.* Well, he was, wasn't he? And Titus had built a church upon his rock. Joe laughed at that. Maybe it did piss Titus off, the fact that his peter was so big. And rock hard now. But shit man, Titus had a big peter, too. The difference was that Titus was an old man, while he was a young man, and good-looking. That's why people paid him to suck his young sweet peter, his long thick peter, his harder-than-a-rock-peter where Titus had built his goddamned church and kept all the money for himself. Well, that shit was going to be changed from now on. He wanted his fair share of the money, too. Man. He felt like coming, his peter was just that hard. And all them motherfuck-ing people looking now. He wanted to take his raw peter out and show it all to them, let everybody suck it right here in the afternoon sun on Canal Street, everybody, old women, dogs, children, young girls, men, everybody sucking his peter, fighting everybody for his come. . . .

Man. *I am The Naked Discple.* It seemed a very real and beau-tiful thing to be. He didn't care now that nobody knew who he was. *He* knew who he was, and that was knowledge enough. He was the Peter inside his pants. And The Naked Disciple. Before that, he was the Christchild in the Christmas tableau in Burnside. And The Naked Child in the early days of Titus' church. Now he was a man. *When I was a child, I spake as a child, I understood as a child, I thought as a child: but when I became a man, I put away childish things.* A white cop looked at him, but his peter just got harder. *Fuck you, jack. You want to suck my big black peter? You white motherfucker, I know you want to suck my peter.* He wished he was double-jointed so he could suck it himself. Man. He loved his peter just that much. *Look at me, all you peterhungry motherfuckers. Feast your eyes on my peter. Let your mouths run water and your pussies and assholes pop. But don't nobody get none of my peter to-day.* Yeah. He decided then that today ought to be his peter's day off. Today he was going to suck his own peter. All those gaping motherfuckers could look, but none of them could touch. Not to-day. *And now abideth faith, hope, charity, these three; but the greatest of these is my peter and ME.*

Then he glanced over his shoulder and saw that the white cop was following him. Bam! Just like that, he thought about those white boys on the road yesterday. They'd just *wanted* to fuck him. That cop, he looked like he *would* fuck him. Joe sped up. His peter fell soft, and shrivelled against his leg. He wanted to run, but he was afraid that cop would shoot him in the back, crowd or no crowd. Man! That cop, he was a big motherfucker, too. *Titus, where the fuck you at? How come you ain't here to protect me?* He'd gladly crawl inside Titus' asshole right now, to get away from that cop.

But he was trapped; he had come to the docks, and the river lay right in front of him. Threading his way through the crowd, the big white cop was fast closing the distance between them. Just then, Joe saw the ferry boat that went across the river. He burst into a spring and ran up the gangplank.

He paid the fare and then blended in with the other passengers lining the railing. Cautiously, he looked for the cop. Man, he almost he shit for joy! That cop had turned and was walking down the pier. Joe laughed shakily. *Shit man, you so dumb. That cop wasn't following you at all.* Still, he'd had a good scare; and he felt uneasy until the ferry dropped its moorings and backed awkwardly into the muddy river.

The boat's slow, lazy motion calmed him down; and when it docked, he walked off whistling. The air over here was clean and fresh, it was a pleasure just to breathe. He waited until the ferry loaded and started back across the river. Then he followed a winding dirt road far out into the green countryside.

After a while, he stopped to smoke some pot. He hadn't met one person or even seen a house on this road yet. And he was glad of that, because he was tired of people right now. Besides, that cop in New Orleans had scared the shit out of him. He liked being alone. He walked around a bend in the road then and saw a small house set back in a clearing among the tall pines.

The house was painted white and pink; there was a nice front yard with flowers and a wire fence that went all around it. Joe thought it was a very pretty house. Peaceful, too. He almost wished he could live in a house like that. Or lie in those flowers and suck his own peter, he hadn't forgot about that. Then he saw a square, neat sign nailed to a post in the front yard. He went closer to read it:

KEEP OUT!
Niggers, Dogs,
Catholics, Beggars,
Peddlers, & etc.

While he was reading the sign, a young white woman came out of the house. She had on a white cotton dress and white sneakers. Her hair was cut short and dyed platinum like Lana Turner's. She said, "What you looking at, boy?" Joe made his mind a complete blank and shuffled off like he didn't hear that white woman, he certainly didn't want any trouble with *her*. But she scurried to the fence like a spider. "Nigger, I said what you looking at? Didn't you hear me, nigger?"

Joe stopped. "I heard you, ma'am. . . . I was looking at that sign. . . ." *Lawd help me Lawd help me Lawd.* He wished he was back in that boarding house in bed. He wished he could start this day all over again. Because he had an idea now that something terrible was going to happen to him. If not today, then later on, because of this day. And just because he'd gone off by himself without that goddamned grinning Titus. But he couldn't allow himself to hate Titus now, because he could feel a strange kind of hate radiating from that white woman.

Moving closer to the fence, she jerked a thumb across her shoulder at the sign. "Personally, I ain't got nothing against niggers myself. To tell the truth, I *love* niggers. That's why my Daddy keeps me locked up here. That's why he put that sign there." She patted her hair and smiled through thick layers of raspberry-colored lipstick.

She didn't love him. That was bullshit. She hated him. He could feel it. Like a cold hand around his throat. "I think it's a very nasty thing to do," he said. His throat pained him.

She stopped smiling all at once. "*What?*" The hate rose up in waves now, as though she had opened an oven door. Her face turned red as a beet. "What's that you say, nigger?"

He'd never talked to a white woman like that before. Maybe it was the pot he'd smoked that gave him courage. But that sign seemed so *evil* in the middle of those pretty flowers. "It's an ugly sign," he said indignantly. "Comparing colored people to dogs like that."

Frowning, biting her lips, the white woman studied him a while. He kept his eyes respectfully to the ground—in some places down here, it was against the law to even look at a white woman, he knew that. And he looked up only when she went over to the sign and worked it from side to side until it came out of the dirt. She put the sign face down on the bright green grass and sauntered back to the fence. "I reckon that is a whole lot better," she said. "Now I got something here I bet you won't think is ugly." She stepped close to the fence and raised her white dress. Joe's face got very hot. She didn't have any bloomers on at all. He turned away. Behind him, the white woman laughed in a high-pitched voice. "Don't you turn your back on me, nigger! Look at me!" His knees felt locked—*LawdhelpmeLawdhelpme*—but he managed to turn, and looked at her hairy pink pussy.

He'd never seen a white woman's pussy before. She seemed to realize that, because she half-squatted and spread the lips of it with the fingers of her free hand to give him a good look at its rosy inside. He thought it looked like anybody else's pussy, except for the color. "Ain't it *pretty?*" she said. "This here's the prettiest pussy in all Louisiana. Why, even the Governor's wife's pussy ain't any prettier than mine." Her mouth was smiling. Pulled open like that, her pussy seemed to smile, too. Her eyes glittered with hate.

It's the pot, Joe thought. *Everything's exaggerated with pot. Her pussy couldn't be smiling. And she really can't hate me, showing me her pussy like that.* He tried to jam his eyes shut, but they wouldn't close. "I guess I'd better be running along," he stammered. He wanted so hard for her to like him. He started off. But the woman lowered her dress and grabbed the fence so fiercely that all the blood drained from her knuckles. "Nigger, you leave me right now . . . you leave, and I'm going to tell some white men that a nigger looking like you got fresh with me. You know what *that* means, don't you?" Sweat dropped from his armpits, down his sides. "Don't you?" Man. She *hated* him. "You know what that means?"

"Yes, ma'am." He felt hot and dizzy. He didn't know what to do. And that white woman—she looked like a white animal in a cage. Imagine, showing your pussy to somebody just because they happened to walk by! And hating somebody like she did. *Please like me, ma'am. Please.*

She kept on talking. "I don't know if you know where you're at, nigger. But this here's Plaquemines Parish; they boiled a nigger to death here not so long ago. I mean, *in hot water*, the same way you'd boil a lobster. You hear about that?" His mouth was too dry to speak, so he nodded. Everybody knew about the terrible things they did to colored people in the South. Boiling a colored man was kind compared to some of the things he'd heard about. Titus had told him about them roasting a colored man once. And of course he'd heard about them lynching his grandfather. "Nigger?" She was bent almost double, looking into his face. He kept on nodding. He couldn't remember when he'd been called nigger so many times before; and it had an almost purifying effect on him. He wasn't Joe Market any more; he was a nigger, pure and simple. He was *her* nigger. He belonged to her. She could kill him with that pink pussy. Or with a rope. She could fuck him to death if she wanted to. Or boil him like a lobster. Because he was black and she was white and that made him hers. *Lawd if I live through this day I'll never forget it.* He didn't belong to anybody, but he belonged to her. All of him. *White bitch.* So that when she looked at the print of his peter through his pants, it rose obediently to attention.

"I want you to fuck me, nigger."

"Yes, ma'am."

Her nigger, her peter. She could kill him if she wanted to. She had a right to. Or fuck him. Whichever.

"You want to fuck me, nigger?"

". . . Yes . . . yes . . . ma'am. . . ." He wanted to kill her, too. She made him feel like a dog and a man at the same time, degraded and glorified, hot and cold with excitement and fear as she hoisted her dress again. "Then you come here and bring that big peter with you. Nigger. I can see it's hard already through your pants, you ain't fooling me none." She looked at the outline of his peter with love. She hated him. She loved his peter. *Love me, ma'am. Please.* But she loved his peter.

He staggered over to the fence. Those little diamond-shaped openings were just big enough for her to squeeze her hand through; compressing her fingers until her hand looked like the head of a white snake, she worked it through the fence and grabbed his peter through his pants. "Oh . . . I'd *admire* having that hard thing in me. But I can't get out there because my Daddy hates for me to mess around with niggers. That's why he keeps the gate locked. And you can't come in here either, I certainly don't have to tell you why."

"So how we going to do it?" He thought he'd die from excitement.

"Stick it through the fence."

"Huh?"

"*Stick it through the fence!*" Her breath felt like a hot gust of wind in his face.

"I don't think it'll fit. I mean, I think the hole's too small.'

She felt him up and down. "It'll fit all right. And it's certainly long enough, I thank the Lord for that. Sometimes they're not long enough to do me any real good." Her fingers ate into his crotch. "Stick it through the fence!"

"Yes, ma'am . . . anything you say, ma'am. . . ." He was so hard, he couldn't get his peter out through the fly. So he opened his belt and dropped his pants around his knees.

"Good God!" she cried. *"Good God!"* She jammed her other hand through the fence and tried to drag his peter back to her. But she wasn't doing much good, she was too excited.

Joe wanted to get over that fence now. He wanted to fuck that white woman to death in every hole she had . . . both of them naked on the grass, his long black peter rammed to the hairy hilt inside all her whiteness, black ass humping the orange-yellow sun probing like a hot finger down his red asshole. . . . Man. He bet he could get over that fence; he took a step back to see.

But the white woman misunderstood. "Nigger, I *dare* you to run away! I just *dare* you! Now you stick your peter through this fence, you hear me? Don't you know how to act when a white woman tells you to do something?" Her face was red and petulant; and he knew she'd tell that lie on him if he ran away, about his getting fresh with her. Man. He didn't want nobody to boil *him*. Squatting a little, supporting his knees against the fence, he slid his peter into one of those holes. It was a tight fit, his peter was so hard; but he managed to get it through by working it carefully.

"Hurry," she said. "Nigger, you hurry now." She watched his peter inching toward her like it was something good to eat. "Lord, I don't know *what* my poor Daddy would do if he caught us out here like this, he'd probably boil us both. You keep your eyes open, nigger, so we don't get caught." But Joe couldn't look anywhere except at her pink pussy, when she raised her dress again, and his peter stuck through the fence. "Oh . . . I'm so *glad* it's long enough," she said. She dropped spit into her free hand and slipped it around the swollen head of his peter. "You stand just like that," she said. Holding his peter steady, she eased her hot, gummy pussy right down on him.

He thought he would faint. Standing on tip toes, clutching the fence for support, they drove their hips angrily at each other. She was the first white woman he'd ever fucked. All his life he'd thought they carried some special king of jewel around between their legs, the careful way they walked. And the way white men cut your nuts out if you even acted like you wanted to fuck one of their women. Now he was fucking one, and he was a little disappointed to find that her pussy felt and smelled just like any other pussy he'd ever had. *White bitch I ought to fuck you to death I want to fuck you to death.* He was throwing all the slippery peter he could at her now, that wire fence kept him from getting all his peter up inside her. He pulled on the fence, trying to yank it from between them. But she pulled the fence right back to her so that it swayed between them as she slid her deep, tight pussy up and down on Joe's peter; it felt as though she had hired the hot hands of pickaninnies inside her to jack him off at the same time.

Grunting like a hog, she rammed her face to the fence and stuck her tongue through another hole. He was trying to drive all of his peter inside her, he didn't give a shit about her tongue. But she wiggled it at him in a commanding way, and he moved his head closer and sucked her sweet little tongue, it reminded him of a slimy cat's. Spit ran like syrup down his chin to his chest. *White bitch I'm going to kill you with my peter.* Lord! He wished he could ram it down her white fucking throat! He'd kill her that way, all the big black peter he had choking her down her throat. . . .

But the fence swayed sturdily between them. That motherfucking fence. He wanted to drive his peter and balls right out through her white asshole on the other side. Who'd she think she was anyway, hating him? He tightened his butt and fucked her like she was dirt, he had her tongue clamped between his teeth until she moaned and tore her tongue away. *OhniggerImcoming niggerfuckmeniggerpleaseniggerfuckmeniggerfuckmeniggerfuckme nigger!* Driving his peter like a massive ramrod, he came too.

Man. He loved that white woman now. He wanted to throw his arms around her, squeeze her to his chest, smother her face with kisses; he always felt like that when he was coming in a woman. "Oh . . . *baby* . . . bitch . . . *baby.* . . . it feels so motherfucking *good.* . . ." He felt like his whole spine had cracked wide open. "I *love* you, baby." With come pulsating out of him, he didn't see why white people and black people didn't like each other. *"Shit."* But the white woman was ominously quiet now. Shit. It didn't matter to *him* that she was white. He did love her, but he didn't want to look at her. Man, he was still coming. He threw his head back and saw a bluebird flutter into a locust tree. Joe sighed, and the bird flew away. He was sure it was a sign, but he didn't know of what. This pickaninny hands . . . they coaxed the last drop of milk out of him, and he sagged against the fence like somebody dead.

She slid off his peter then. But he was still hard, man, he wanted to fuck some more. "Hey baby, don't go away. Please." He wouldn't look at her, but he could see under his lashes as she walked over to the flowers, arranging her dress. Then she picked up the sign and stuck it back in the ground.

KEEP OUT!
Niggers, Dogs,
Catholics, Beggars,
Peddlers, & etc.

Joe looked at her then. Goddamn it. He knew it. Her face was *twisted* with hate. She had all his come inside her and she still hated him. "Don't . . . please . . . ," he said weakly. He held up his hand as though she had struck him. But she didn't say a word. She went into the house.

Joe really got scared then. He thought she was going to telephone somebody and get him killed. Man! His goddamned peter was still hard, and he tried to drag it back through the fence without hurting himself. *LawdLawdLawd . . . get soft you motherfucker!* But it wouldn't get soft, it got harder; it still wanted some of that white pussy. *They going to roast you, man!* But the more terror he felt, the harder his peter seemed to get. *They going to boil you.* Man! *They going to stick hot knives up your asshole and cut your insides out.* O Lawd. . . . He wiggled his ass powerfully one last time and his peter fell soft and jerked free. He pulled his pants up and ran like hell. *ThankyouLawdthankyouLawdthankyou. . . .*

He was so scared that he finally had to stop running and sit down. Then he got scared just from sitting, so he started running again. Suppose they'd caught him fucking that white woman? Suppose they'd caught him with his hard peter stuck through that fence? Man. For a minute, he felt like *he* was a white man chasing a nigger who had disrespected a white woman. Boy, if he caught that nigger, he'd *boil* him, that's what he'd do. That's the only way you can teach these niggers some respect. He'd cut his nuts out . . . he'd hang him from a tree . . . he'd cut his peter out and take it home for a souvenir. . . .

That brought him up short. *Whoa, man! You a nigger! You ain't chasing nobody. But somebody might be chasing you, if that white woman told on you.* He ran even harder. He didn't want to think about *her*—how she had used him, then turned her back and went into the house like he really was some kind of black dog—and he started cursing Titus because Titus wasn't with him. None of this would have happened if Titus had been with him. Finally, he was so tired and scared at the same time that he didn't care anymore whether anybody caught him or not. He lay right down on the side of the road, where those white people could find him if they did come looking for him.

But nobody came for him at all. He must have slept, because it was dark when he woke up. And chilly. Shit. He walked on down to the ferry. The moon was full, gigantic and orange-colored. Then the moon started getting dark—there was an eclipse of the moon. He was sure now that he'd never forget this day. Shit. He felt almost good again. He wasn't even scared anymore. The only thing he was sorry about was that he hadn't been able to fuck that white woman the way he'd wanted to. Shit. He had about three inches of peter that never did get inside her.

By the time he got back to the boarding house, the moon was completely covered over. He thought it looked kind of scary, that funny light glowing all around the dark disk of the moon. It re-minded him of that white woman . . . she was the sunlight glowing around his moondark peter while he worked on up inside of her . . . but not nearly as much as he wanted to because of that goddamned fence . . . Man, he wanted to tear her pussy into little pieces. . . .

He started to get excited again. But he felt ashamed, too. No-body had ever *used* him that way before. And today was supposed to have been his peter's day off. Shit. That white woman had *raped* him, that's what she did. Well, he was going to get even with her for that. Some day, some kind of way. With all white people.

Titus still hadn't come home. Well fuck him. Baldheaded bas-tard. Joe took a shower. Then he went to bed and drew up into a tight ball, carrying his groin as close to his mouth as he could; but he still couldn't suck his peter. Shit. He thought that being sucked was the most beautiful thing in the world. And he couldn't even do it to himself. Man. It made him pretty fucking suspicious of *God*, that's what it did. If a dog could suck his own peter, why couldn't a man? Shit. That fucking white woman, she didn't even suck him. He went to sleep with a stone hard on. Maybe Titus would come home and suck him. Shit.

But when Titus finally did show up, it was the following afternoon. He and the whore came down to the tent where Joe was waiting to see if there would be evening services. "I want you to meet your new mother," Titus said. 'They told me at the boarding house that you were down here."

"My name's Elizabeth," the whore said. Joe greeted her with a bland kind of interest, as though he'd never seen her before. And he was so glad to see Titus that he forgot to be mad with him for staying gone so long. "You all really get married?" he said. Titus stuck his chest out and grinned; Elizabeth flashed her wedding ring. "Your Daddy, he swept me right off my feet," she said, laughing. "He married us himself. I sure do hope it's legal."

"It's legal right enough," Titus said. "Joe, I bet you're really surprised, boy, me getting married again." But Joe wasn't surprised at all; he'd long since come to expect anything from Titus. "I just wondered where you were, that's all. Some people been waiting all day to see if there're going to be services."

"There'll be services," Titus said. "Then my wife and me, we're going on a honeymoon for a couple more days."

Elizabeth sniffed. "Is that pot I smell?" It was. Joe gave her a joint, and she smoked it the way she was supposed to, sucking in air at the same time. Joe smoked some more; Titus smoked, too. He was proud of the way Elizabeth was winning over Joe. She asked him about the cross he wore around his neck, the one that May Jones had filled with bits of her toenails nearly five years ago in Burnside. Joe told her it was a good-luck piece. Elizabeth nodded; she seemed interested in everything. There was a chamber pot in the tent that Joe had peed in; Elizabeth poked it with the toe of her new white pump. "That's a *pretty* pot," she said. "Where'd you all get that?" Titus told her they'd stolen it from a whorehouse in Montgomery, and the three of them laughed amiably. They chatted

about the weather, how hot it was in New Orleans. Then Elizabeth
went out front to let Titus and Joe get ready for the evening's
service.

As soon as the flap closed behind Elizabeth, Titus stopped
grinning. "You all right, Joe? You look . . . *funny* . . . in the face. Boy,
is there something you want to tell me?"

"No." But Joe wanted to tell him everything—how that white
woman had raped him, how scared he'd been, and how absolutely
lonely he'd felt without Titus there with him. But he thought that to
talk about those things would make him seem like a child again.
And he had definitely put away childish things.

"I missed you," Titus said. "I missed you like the devil." Joe
said nothing, and Titus tried another tack. "I've been thinking
about using Elizabeth in the services with you. I thought I might
call her The Naked Virgin. The Naked Disciple and The Naked Virgin together. You like that idea?" Joe shrugged. "It sounds all right.
She didn't look like no virgin, but she's got nice titties. You going to
let me fuck her again some time?"

Titus was shaving. His hand paused in mid-air; his eyes turned
red and mean as a pig's. "No I'm not going to let you fuck her! She's
married to *me*, and that means she's a decent, respectable woman!
Furthermore, she's your mother now! What's the matter with you,
boy? You crazy or something?" Joe stepped in front of Titus at the
mirror to brush his hair. "She's not my real mother, you know that.
Besides, it don't make me no difference. I've already fucked her
anyway. Or don't you remember?" Titus felt like striking him. "She
wasn't your mother then," he said hotly. "She's not my mother now,"
Joe countered. He pulled on a fresh pair of white jeans, making a
big to-do about stuffing his peter inside them. *He's really jealous*,
Joe thought. *Just like that truck driver said.* No shit. He got a kick
out of that, Titus being jealous of him. Swaggering, he went
outside.

Titus finished shaving somehow, although his hand was
trembling. That fucking Joe, talking about Elizabeth like that. He
was very upset, and he hurried and dressed and went out front.
Composed and smiling, as befitted a preacher's wife, Elizabeth was

sitting on the front row in her new white dress. "Titus honey, you look upset. You want me to suck you or something before you start preaching?"

"No . . . no . . . I'm all right. Besides, there's no time." He saw Joe lounging against the scaffold. God, he had to admit that boy was beautiful! And he certainly did love him. But goddamn it, why'd he have to act so smart, talking about fucking Elizabeth that way? She was watching Joe, too; and it seemed to Titus that her titties were rising and falling faster than usual. "What you think about my boy Joe?" he asked casually.

"He's a *handsome* boy," Elizabeth said. "And he might as well be naked in them pants, he's got the biggest tail I ever did see, next to yours. You can tell he took after his Daddy."

Titus started sweating now. The area was gradually filling up with people who had come for the services. "Listen," Titus said urgently, "Joe's your son now, I want you to forget you ever had anything to do with him before. You know what I mean?" Elizabeth seemed surprised. "Forget? You mean, forget that he *fucked* me? Honey, how could I forget something like that? Besides, he's not my son. He's your son. Anyway, are you sure we're really married? I didn't know that people could just marry themselves to each other." Titus started pouting. "We're married," he said. "I'm a preacher, and I married us. That's as legal as you can get. Besides, it's the same way my mother married my father." Elizabeth seemed satisfied with that. "Well, as long as it's *legal*," she said. "I sure don't want to be living in sin with no man." He couldn't really blame Elizabeth for the way she felt about things; he loved her, but she wasn't exactly the brightest thing in the world. But he'd fix that little smart Joe motherfucker, trying to steal his wife right from under his very nose. Asking if he could *fuck* her. Well, he was going to get fucked, all right.

His jalopy was parked out behind the tent, and he managed to get in it and make off without being seen. He drove a ways down the road to a telephone booth and dialed police headquarters. When a voice answered, Titus said, "By God now, I'm a white man, sir, and I want to report that a bunch of niggers are getting ready to take their clothes off at some kind of religious meeting down by the Mississippi." The policeman sounded very interested. "Nigger women or nigger men?" he said. Titus cleared his throat. "Actually, it's a nigger *boy*, sir. Why, he's got people thinking he's some kind of black Jesus Christ. We white folks can't allow that kind of thinking down here in the South." The policeman seemed to understand. "You sure there ain't going to be no naked nigger women?" Titus assured him there wouldn't be. The policeman asked for further details, and Titus gave him the exact location of the meeting place. "Now listen here, I want you boys to do something about them niggers," Titus said. He was so full of indignation that he really felt like a white man. Hell, he'd only been married just a few hours, and already his own son was trying to put him and Elizabeth asunder. Ungrateful bastard. Well, he'd fix Joe all right. "We'll take care of it, sir. Don't you worry about them niggers none." Titus hung up and drove back to the meeting ground. Hunched over the wheel, he started grinning at the fact that it had been left for him to call the law's attention to something he'd been doing in the South for nearly five years. And he was filled with a kind of wonderment that nobody black or white had reported him to the police before.

When he got back to the tent, he went inside and smoked some more pot. Shit, those white cops wouldn't do a thing to him; they'd probably give him a month or so in the work house. Elizabeth could come to see him every day; and if he played his cards right, he might even get off with a suspended sentence, nobody liked to put preachers in jail. But they'd throw the book at Joe, especially here in Louisiana. Didn't he know there was a law against showing yourself to people naked?

Joe came in then, and Titus gave him some pot. "You ready, Daddy? There's a whole crowd of people. Seems to me there's more than usual. We really getting to be something big." Titus was very dry. "Maybe we're getting to be too big. That sometimes happens to people, you know."

Joe had been holding the pot smoke inside his lungs, to get its full effect. He let it out noisily. "Daddy, you been acting very strange today. You sorry you got married again?" Titus shook his head. "There's nothing wrong. And I'm happy I'm married." He noticed that Joe had taken off the cross May Jones gave him. "What happened to the cross?" he said. Joe stubbed the roach out. "Elizabeth liked it, so I gave it to her."

Titus was high now beyond the point of feeling further jealousy. He knew that in a little while, one part of this drama would come to a resounding close, and another part would begin. He threw his arms around Joe and kissed him on the lips. But Joe drew away. "Daddy, you know we ain't got time for nothing like that now. There's all them people waiting." Titus sighed, almost regretfully. Jerusalem had been full of people, too, when Jesus was crucified. Still, he played with Joe's tail some. "I know, son. I just wanted you to know that I love you, that's all. No matter what happens, I want you to know I love you." The marvelous swelling in the jeans excited him as it always did. At the same time, he felt a slicing fear.

Suppose Joe was The Black Messiah? If he himself was Judas the Betrayer, then what else was left for Joe except the role of Jesus Christ. Titus started grinning. He liked that idea, he liked it very much. Being father to Christ, they'd probably make him the Pope, or something like that. With all the people he wanted, to fuck, to have his head sucked. And other things. Kneeling, he opened Joe's zipper and pulled down his jeans. "Daddy, we ain't got time. . . ." But Joe held his head firmly, and Titus started thinking, *If I am Judas and we are here in the Jerusalem of the betrayal, then those white boys on the road were the multitude proclaiming His entrance into the city of sacrifice on a white ass. . . .*

Which meant that the Jewish prophets had been mistaken with their neat little package of predictions about the Christ. For one thing, they left no room for the black man, no possibility that a black man as well as a white one might turn out to be Judas or the Messiah. Aside from that, the prophets made Judas the chief villain in the Bible drama, while it seemed perfectly obvious that Judas had to be the only hero. Because, if the prophecies were true, then somebody had to betray Christ in order to fulfill them.

"Daddy. . . ." Joe's butt trembled in his hands. "Daddy, I shouldn't let you do this. . . . You didn't say nothing about the way I

put up the tent. . . . You went away all that time and left me by myself. . . . I met a white woman yesterday . . . she made me fuck her
. . . I could have been killed. . . . Daddy. . . ." His butt trembled
again, and Titus found it hard to breathe for a while, his whole insides flooded with the hot, sticky promised new life. "Daddy, you
shouldn't have done that now," Joe said. But he didn't sound upset
at all. Titus stood up. "I just wanted you to know I love you, son.
And I like the way you carried on while I was gone. I think you did
a good job."

Joe laughed dryly. "Did you hear what I said about that white
woman?"

"I heard."

"Well, I didn't do a good job with her. She made me fuck her
through a *fence*. She scared the shit out of me."

He could feel Joe's indignation about what had happened. And
the emerging fear as he remembered. *Don't be afraid, son. You're
going to be safe soon.* "She made you fuck her? Did you fuck her
good?"

Joe looked surprised. Then he laughed. "I fucked her good. I
couldn't get it all the way in, though, because of that fence. But I
did the best I could."

"I know you did, son." Titus felt better now; he had done right,
calling in the law. His eyes misted. "Now, Joe there's a new idea I
want to try. I want you to go up on the scaffold tonight and take off
your clothes as soon as I go into the pulpit." Joe was agreeable to
that, because it meant people would have a longer time to see him
naked. Titus grinned. It also meant that Joe would be up there naked whenever the policemen came.

Titus draped his arm around Joe's shoulders, and they went
outside together. Titus was walking on the tips of his toes, he was
just that high. He thought that he felt now as Judas must have felt
after he betrayed Christ. He mounted the pulpit; Joe climbed to
the highest part of the scaffold and took off his jeans.

The crowd became excited at once. Titus could smell their excitement, and his nose and eyes snapped open like a hound's that
has picked up the scent of its prey. Farmers with their women and

children, the crowd ignored Titus. They were looking at the naked figure of Joe above them. Titus leaned back and looked, too. Joe had given his small golden cross to Elizabeth . . . but didn't he know that he had just mounted another one? Because the scaffold was in the form of a cross, a tall oak pole that came apart in sections, with a crossbeam nailed some six feet from the top. It was certainly a cross all right. Titus cleared his throat with satisfaction. He knew what a cross was when he saw one. Hadn't he recognized Ramona's cross? That she was sick, and working too hard? And hadn't he managed to save her? Hadn't he got rid of her so that he could work with Joe alone before the boy got too old to be trained? Titus looked around slyly. He wasn't going to admit that. He was never going to admit that. His problem now had to do with trying to save Joe.

For some reason, his tail was getting hard. He looked at Elizabeth where she sat in a kind of serene dignity in the front row. She was smiling, as though she knew his tail was getting hard. Titus nodded, and winked at Elizabeth; but she had already craned her head back again and was looking at Joe where he posed naked on the high scaffold.

Titus stomped his foot. "I'm going to start preaching now," he cried, in a loud voice. "That is, if you all folks is tired of looking at The Naked Disciple." He was aware that pot and jealousy and indignation were causing his mind to run away with him. He loved Joe, he hated Joe; he felt extremely lucid and bogged down in confusion at the same time. Still, everything was as it should be, he thought. Was it not true that extremes such as love and hate, good and evil, madness and sanity, stand back to back like two duelers about to walk their paces, and fire as they turn, contaminating one another? That would certainly explain why he had called the cops on Joe. *I have enjoyed thee in our love; yea, now even into the hands of death do I deliver thee for love.* Mopping his forehead, he forced himself to calm down some. Then he stretched out his long arms and began his sermon.

"My children," he said in a strong, firm voice, "I am troubled today because I have seen that the problem of white and black together can never be solved by what we have tried to do. We have prayed. We have reasoned. We have begged. We keep talking to the white man. We keep telling him, *Mister White Man, sir, we are dying. Do you understand that, sir? We are dying.* And you know what he says, *Good riddance, nigger. Go on and die.* So we accommodate him. We wait and do nothing. And we die. And death seems sweet because we have spent all our lives waiting for death." Titus shook his head sorrowfully. High on the scaffold above him, Joe's whole body went tense. What the fuck had got into Titus? He'd never heard his father talk like this before, and he listened with both ears. "Well, we old folks, we might be willing to wait," Titus went on, "because we don't have much time left to wait in. But the winds of change are sweeping everything now, and there's a new generation of black young people that is not willing to wait. They want action now! They want change now! They are tired of talking and complaining and dying. They want to live now and hold their heads up now and be treated like men and women now. There is a new generation, I tell you, and they are asking questions and demanding answers. *Why* can't I be equal to you, Mr. White Man? *Why* do I have to wait? *Why* should I lick your boots? But although our young people can question and demand, they will not be heard. We old people know that. They will not be heard. They will be dragged from their beds and lynched in the middle of the night. They will be accosted on lonely roads and killed in the most despicable manner. But they will not be heard. Inside the climate of America, then, is there any salvation for the black man? Certainly there is none for him inside the Christian church. And there is none for him in the Bible. So, if no provision has been made for us to save our souls, we are perfectly free to seek salvation any way we can. My way always has been to be as *contrary* to everything as I can be. When the Bible says black, I say white. When it says good, I say evil. When it says, *Behold, Jehovah is a God of Light,* I say, *Behold, He is the Lord of dark places, for his children gnash their teeth and cry unto Him and are not heard.*"

Titus started to grin. Half the time, he didn't know whether he was coming or going; but he felt positively brilliant now. This was certainly the best sermon he had ever preached. If you could call it a sermon. *You listen to me, Joe baby, I'm talking directly to you. Fuck all these other niggers. I'm talking to you, Joe baby.* "What I am saying, then, is that salvation *might* be possible if slavery itself does not drive the black man into the hell of madness. And if he can distort the Christian values until they are clearly seen to be just another way of holding him satisfied in bondage. And if he can manage *not* to become the sum total of his surroundings, which is the ghetto rung in by bristling steel hatred. And—finally—if he can raise a man from among his own ranks who has sufficient courage and strength to be the black man's king and deliverer."

Titus paused, and wiped his forehead. Where were those policemen? He searched the crowd, but saw only black, frightened faces. Yeah, he knew he was scaring those niggers. They'd come to hear the usual lies about God, and here he was talking against the white man. No wonder they looked scared—the kind of talking he was doing was the best way to wind up on the end of a rope here in the South. Shit, he knew that. Funny, he thought, that those policemen he'd called hadn't shown up yet. Then his eyes fell on four young white men almost hidden down in the last row of seats.

Titus' heart thumped with a new kind of joy. They were policemen, all right. No white people had ever come to his meetings before. He looked at Elizabeth with great love and yearning. He wished he could tell her about the exciting thing that was about to take place. But she was still looking at Joe, and Titus couldn't really blame her for that, because Joe was beautiful and godlike on his high perch.

Then something happened that sent a cold chill through Titus. He was still looking at the policemen when one of them nudged the other and grinned. A simple thing, and yet, Titus was able to see himself as they saw him—a tall, almost cadaverous black man in a green cape and turban and a tattered black suit, something like an animated scarecrow in a green crown, squinting against the dying sun where it fell on him through a ring of pines around the meeting place. As he saw himself through their eyes, he looked completely ridiculous. As Jesus Christ must have looked to the Roman soldiers who came to arrest him. . . .

Titus thought he would die of fear. *He* was the sacrifice, not Joe. The distinction had been nagging him all the time, but he saw it very clearly now. *He* was the Lamb of God, betrayed by the Judas of his country and his generation, tolerated inside a system of segregation where a man could be God if he wanted to, or mad if he wanted to, nobody cared what went on inside the isolation of the black community. . . . The turban on his head was a crown of thorns. His cape was the cape that they would cast lots for after he was crucified. He trembled from head to toe with delicious fear. The policeman who had been nudged grinned back; and then the four of them stood up in the last row, two of them looking at Titus, the other two looking at Joe.

Why had he thought they'd do more to Joe than they would to him? Slowly, deliberately, the policemen moved out into the aisle and sauntered toward the pulpit. At the same time, all the tension released itself in Titus, and he sprang into action. "Joe!" He threw his head back and howled like a dog. "Joe baby, here come the *police*! Save yourself, baby! *Save* yourself, sweetheart!" Joe hesitated only a moment. Then, stark naked, he jumped into the river. His jeans dislodged from the cross bar where he'd held them under his feet, and dropped to the ground like a heavy white bird.

Guns in hand, two of the policemen scrambled to the river's edge. But a third one called them back. "Let him go, he ain't nothing but a boy. This old nigger's the one we want." He and the other policeman grabbed Titus by the arms. Putting their guns away, the other policemen came back from the river bank. "If he ain't come up by now, he's probably drowned anyway," one of them said.

The crowd had watched in a kind of fascinated terror. But when the policemen grabbed Titus, they broke up. Screaming, tumbling over chairs and each other, they fled like sheep. Only Elizabeth sat still. Titus called her to help him. But she looked right through him, with the kind of blank stare she would offer a perfect stranger. And to think that he'd wanted her to be The Naked Virgin. Well, he'd made a lot of mistakes, he had to admit that.

A fifth policeman, one Titus hadn't seen before, came around from the tent. He was carrying the tobacco pouch that Titus kept his pot in.

"I'm a preacher of the gospel!" Titus cried. "I'm a prophet!" His voice sounded sharp as a woman's. "Let go of me! I believe in God! I do! *I do!*" The five policemen started grinning all together. They were going to fuck him, he knew they were going to fuck him, and he started to fight for his life. But one of them kicked him neatly in the nuts, and he collapsed against the policeman behind him.

"Let's take these niggers into the tent and see what else we can find." Titus shuddered with horror. They were going to fuck him in the tent. And Elizabeth, too. One of them had already gone over and was talking to her. She had obviously been waiting for that, because everybody else had already gone. She squirmed in her seat and patted her large bosom as the white man talked. The cross that Joe had given her rested comfortably down in the crevice between her breasts.

Titus started to cry. And remembered the white boys on the road. And how he had told Joe that being lynched is a whole lot worse than being fucked. Well, he wasn't so sure about that now. Because the tail of the policeman behind him was hard as a motherfucker, jammed to his butt. "I believe in God!" Titus cried; and he found, to his great annoyance, that he really did. He always had.

He felt the taint of Madame Eudora and her nephew-husband foaming on his lips. He moved his butt away some, and the policeman's tail followed him, as sure as a cobra's head. "We believe in God too, nigger. What's that got to do with anything?" His voice was a hot, moist whisper in Titus' ear. But Titus was almost happy now. They believed in God, they would sacrifice him as they should.

Then they lifted him up and carried him into the tent, two of them carrying his feet, the other two carrying him by the arms. *I have fought the good fight*, he thought. In his own way. Ass-backwards and sometimes very ugly and evil. But still a fight. And he had destroyed his religion and saved his son, just as the voice had told him to do. Still, he felt genuinely sorry that he had not been born a bird, so that there would be less of him to torture in the name of God, less of him to die. And no way at all for anybody to fuck him in the ass. Who ever heard of anybody fucking a bird in the ass?

The fifth policeman escorted Elizabeth with his hand resting on her elbow. She moved along beside him slowly, the curves and ripples in her body jiggling in a quiet, complacent way. "He pretended we were married," she complained to the policeman. "But I know my place, sir. Honey, I know what *I'm* supposed to do when a white man tell me to."

When all of them were inside the tent, the fifth policeman ducked through the flap and arranged it carefully behind him. Elizabeth was already taking off her clothes. The other policeman started undressing Titus. He opened his mouth and screamed, he couldn't help it. And he kept on screaming until the policeman who'd been holding his arms behind him twisted him around to his knees *I have sacrificed myself for others so that they might live* and grinned *Joe sweetheart I know you're not dead you're on your own now* and rammed something into his mouth to shut him up.

TWO

THE WATER HIT Joe like a cold fist, and he thought that he would die there airless and entombed in the muddy river. Then a vital energy that he could not ignore set his arms and legs flailing and carried him farther downstream until his lungs screamed for air. He broke surface; paddling weakly to shore, he collapsed on his belly in the mud and weeds. His heart thundered, and his mind felt strangely disoriented, as though he'd picked up things where they left off yesterday when he ran away from that white woman. Maybe he had died after all, and was being resurrected now from a watery grave. Or was this the creek in Burnside he'd just crawled naked from? And was Titus grinning there beyond him on the bank with the news of his mother's death? Joe raised his head cautiously.

As far as he could see, the whole Mississippi was colored red, the dying sun reflected like oil slick on the slow-moving river, red on the distant ships, and shore, and piney-wood shanties knee-deep down in red mud. He saw buzzards moving in slow circles overhead. Were they waiting for Titus to die? A tremor went through all of him, because he knew how vicious policemen can be. Titus might be beaten half to death by now, thrown out along-side some country road for those filthy buzzards to fight over his carcass. Still, he felt only a twinge of regret about the possibility of Titus dead or dying. He must have known he'd get arrested, talking some shit about the white man like that. Besides, Joe had never forgiven Titus altogether for killing his mother the way he had. He hoped those policemen did the same thing to Titus, so he'd know how it felt to be fucked to death. . . . And he was very pissed off about Titus marrying a whore like Elizabeth. Had he really expected Joe to accept her as his mother. Especially after

he'd fucked her only two or three days ago? No, he didn't feel
sorry about Titus. Lying there naked in the mud, it seemed that
he had just fucked a white woman through a wire fence; today
was yesterday; Titus was still shacked up in that room with the
whore. There had been no meeting and no policemen, other than
the one he'd fancied had followed him down to the ferry. He had
just freed his peter from that fence and then, magically, he had
transferred himself here from the other side of the Mississippi
River. . . .

His body seemed on fire from the sweat bees, and he jumped
in the river to wash them off. Splashing in the green-gray water,
he washed away the sweat bees and mud; and he pushed all
thoughts of Titus back into the dark places of his mind. There
were railroad tracks that followed the river, and he ran on these,
bounding from rail to rail and tie to tie. He felt that he had somehow been born again, but this time without earthly parents, a naked child of sun setting in the last agony of day, and flat fields,
and the twilight wind where it blew across the Mississippi, bringing with it the medicinal stench of fish. The sun was on the right
side of him, and he realized that he was walking deeper South.
He made an abrupt turn and went the other way. Shit man, he
wanted to go North to escape from those cops. He bet they were
looking for him right now with their peters all hard and everything. Man. And he was *naked*! A trembling spread through his
chest and belly as though he had swallowed butterflies, and he
ducked into the bushes.

Now he didn't feel so happy anymore. He was naked, and
hungry and broke. And all alone in the world. With white policemen looking for him, to fuck him in the ass, probably, the same
way those white boys had wanted to do to him on the road. His
whole body was trembling now, as much from fear as from a
heavy chill that moved in the air, because the sun had completely
disappeared in a dazzling display of reds and golds. Man. He bit
his lips to keep from crying. Them people that said it never got
cold in Louisiana didn't know what they were talking about.

He could hear the metallic commotion of trains coupling

and uncoupling at a nearby depot. It was completely dark now, and he felt safe enough to return to the tracks. But he had to get him some clothes. He walked about fifteen minutes until he came to the train yard. There were a lot of white men in overalls standing around talking, and he didn't see any way here to get some clothes. He thought about jumping on a train, but he didn't know the first thing about hoboing trains. Sticking to the shadows, he walked on, following the railroad tracks with his arms wrapped around himself to keep warm.

The longer he walked, the colder it got. It went through him right to the bone. He felt like a cold, ugly black dog, shivering the way he was. And he was hungry, too, he could eat a raw polecat right now, that's how hungry he was. He tried to get hold of himself, but all he succeeded in doing was crying. The moon was full and in harvest, orange streaked with yellow as it rose behind the pines.

Farther along the road, he saw a woman's dress hanging on somebody's back fence. Man, that was something. It was a white dress with red design, and the idea of putting it on filled him with disgust. But he couldn't go much longer, cold as he was. He snatched the dress and ran like a rickety old man, he was just that cold. But the dress did warm him some, although he felt ridiculous. He just hoped nobody saw him in it.

After a while, he came to a clearing where some Negroes were husking corn. They were laughing and talking among themselves. A young pig was roasting over the fire. Joe stood at the edge of the clearing and quietly took off the dress. Then he went right up to the people. It was safe to tell who he was, now that he was out of town. "I am The Naked Disciple," he said, smiling his beautiful smile.

Some of the women screamed. "Lawd look at the crazy nekkid mans!" They threw rocks and corn husks at him. He just stood there looking at the roasting pig until one of the men got up real leisurely like, hitching up his overalls and slapped him right in the face. "Get outta here, crazy man!" He turned Joe around roughly by the shoulder and kicked him in the butt. "Get outta here, crazy!" Joe grabbed up his dress and ran as hard as he could.

He started to cry again. And he was very bewildered. Nobody had ever not wanted to see him naked. He was so cold. He stopped and put the dress on again, and continued at a slow jog. Crazy man, they called him. He wondered if he was crazy. But he was only sixteen, he'd never heard tell of anybody going crazy that young. He knew that he certainly was cold.

Soon after that, he met some hoboes sitting by the railroad tracks. The moon had turned silver now, and their faces looked gray to him in the ghost light. "I'm cold," he said. "And I'm hungry. I need me a jacket and some shoes, this is a dress I stole off a fence. And I need me some food." Nobody said a word. There were five of those hoboes. They just looked at him, they didn't even seem surprised to see him wearing a dress. Joe thought about taking off the dress, they'd have to give him what he wanted then. But he remembered what had happened to him at the corn-husking. His jaw and his butt still hurt where that man had hit him. "I need me some food and clothes," Joe said in a pitiful whine. The hoboes just looked at him. Joe turned and walked away.

He had gone only a short distance before he realized that one of them had left the railroad track and was following him. He lifted his dress and pissed against a pine tree. The moon was shining directly down on him; he could see all of his tail bathed in the silver light. And he was standing like that when the hobo came up to him under the pine tree and gave him a pair of old shoes and some smelly clothes. "Hope they fit you, man. My name's Pee Wee. I couldn't do nothing back there, you understand? But I been hard up myself, I know how it feels."

Joe put on the pants and shirt, both of which were very tight. The shoes were a little too big for him, but they had soles and the heels were good. The jacket was tight around the shoulders. But he didn't care, he wasn't cold any more. He had left the pants open at the crotch; he took Pee Wee's hand and put it there. He was grateful for the big favor Pee Wee had done him. "You want

me, man, you can have me," he said kindly. Pee Wee jumped like
he'd grabbed a snake. "I'm no queer, man," he said indignantly.
"Just for that, I'm not going to give you the piece of bread I
brought." Joe shrugged. "Anyway, I owe you a favor," he said.
"You can collect on me any time you want to."

The hoboes were going North, and Joe decided to go with
them. They jumped a train and went to sleep in one of the empty
boxcars. Joe woke up during the night and found that somebody
was collecting on him. He wondered if it was Pee Wee after all.
But then he remembered how Pee Wee had carried on when he'd
offered himself in the woods, and he wondered which of the
other hoboes it was. But he couldn't really tell, it was pitch dark
inside the boxcar. And it really didn't matter any way. He'd got
some shoes and some clothes. And Pee Wee had given him the
bread after all. He felt warm all over now. He closed his eyes, and
came, and went back to sleep.

A couple of days later, he separated from the hoboes. Somebody was collecting on him regularly in the dark, and he got tired
of not knowing who it was. Pee Wee came with him, and he figured that it was Pee Wee after all. Pee Wee was a short, black little bow-legged man, with some gold teeth in front. Joe figured
that he must be at least twenty years old, and he wondered why
Pee Wee was tagging along behind a sixteen-year-old kid like
himself. He bet it was Pee Wee who'd been doing all that collecting. But when they jumped a train in Georgia and kept on head-
ing North, Pee Wee just slept curled up against Joe like a little
mangy dog. One night, Joe even found himself halfway hoping
that it had been Pee Wee who was collecting. He'd like somebody to collect on him right now, right this minute. But Pee Wee
slept on like a little dog, breaking wind sometimes, there was
something about his farts that smelled almost sweet.

After a while, Joe woke Pee Wee up. He couldn't stand being
awake all by himself. "My father says that I'm a god," he told Pee
Wee. Maybe Pee Wee would collect on him if he knew something like that. It was so dark in the boxcar. He thought he heard
Pee Wee snicker. "What you laughing at?" he said. "You're about

as much god as I am," Pee Wee said. "Your father was putting you on." Well, he'd figured something like that, too. Still, he was disappointed. He told Pee Wee about himself and Titus and The Church of the Naked Disciple. Something warned him not to say anything about the way Titus sucked him all the time. When Joe finished talking, Pee Wee asked him, "How'd you feel, getting naked in front of all those people?"

"I felt good. They liked me. They liked to look at me." Pee Wee rolled over on his back so that his thigh was touching Joe's. "Your old man sounds like a real slick cat. That was a very nice hustle." Joe didn't understand, and Pee Wee explained. "Your father was *conning* people, you know what that means? He was using religion to get money out of people, that's all. When he called you god, it was the same way that somebody else would call you honey or sweetheart."

Joe thought about that. Was that all there had been to it, then? The outstanding thing in his mind now had to do with those hours he'd spent naked on the road before he stole that dress and found Pee Wee. If he'd really been The Naked Disciple—if there was anything magic or powerful about being The Naked Disciple—, all he would have had to do was to snap his fingers, something like that, and clothes would have come to him from nowhere. And that sure hadn't happened. The Naked Disciple. Shit. No wonder those people had thrown corn husks and rocks at him. And that man had slapped and kicked him.

Still, he felt sad. He had never seriously thought that he was a god; but now that the evidence all seemed to be against such a thing, he desperately wanted to be one. *If I am a god*, he thought, *let this train turn into a white chariot filled with some sharp clothes for me, and good things to eat*. The train wheels sounded lonesome and hollow beneath his head. Pee Wee farted, and that was all that happened. Shit. "Man, I ain't got nobody in the world to look out for me," Joe said mournfully.

Pee Wee was quiet for a while. Then he said, "You think you bad off? Man, you ought to hear my story." He said he came from Alabama, that he'd been riding the rails for a year or so, after some trouble with his wife back in Alabama. "Man, the police looking for me, too. I damn near stomped my old lady to death, she was fucking around with my baby brother. I don't blame my brother, though, he's just a baby. I blame that black bitch, they always manage to spoil something between men." He was curled up into Joe like a fetus now, head against Joe's chest, knees gouged into Joe's groin, mashing his hard tail. "I guess that's why I took a liking to you right away, Joe. You remind me of my brother, he ain't nothing but a great big baby." Joe felt his tail getting harder, and he pushed it deliberately against Pee Wee's knees. Pee Wee didn't move; he left his knees where they were. And after a while, he cleared his throat. "I'll look out for you, baby. I ain't got me nobody, either. I think you and me could get a good thing going." Joe felt so relieved, he almost cried. Man, he was nobody's god, he could hardly bear the thought of being alone in this motherfucker world. Pee Wee slept with his knees against Joe's tail for the rest of that night; but he never would collect on him.

They came to Newark the next morning, and Pee Wee decided that they should stay there. "It's a good town for hustling," Pee Wee said. "Besides, there's a place near here called Cousinsville. A lot of downhome people live there, in case you ever get homesick." Pee Wee hustled a few dollars, Joe hustled a few more. Then Pee Wee rented a room on West Market Street and started bringing clients home for Joe, men or women, it was all the same to Joe, he wasn't prejudiced a bit. In a few months, business was so good that they moved into a furnished apartment on Belmont Avenue. It was even better than the old days with Titus. Pee Wee gave Joe massages to keep him in shape. He also did the pimping. Joe stayed home, smoking pot, watching television, waiting for Pee Wee to come back with people who wanted his dick. That was what they called peter up here. Dick. And a lot of people wanted his dick.

When Joe turned seventeen, Pee Wee brought home a bunch of people and told them that Joe was the cake. Everybody got a chance to eat some of his icing at ten dollars a head. The same thing happened on his eighteenth and nineteenth birth-days. But when Joe turned twenty, Pee Wee upped the birthday price to twenty dollars a head. Man, everybody wanted some of him, his balls were swollen afterwards from coming so much. "Hey man, where you get all them people from?" he asked Pee Wee. "They belong to a fag club down the street," Pee Wee said, counting money. "Why, you got any complaints?" Joe shook his head. "Naw, man. I'm happy, me." That was a damn lie. But he certainly did enjoy those parties, being the candle, the cake, and the guest-of-honor all rolled into one. And Pee Wee really did take good care of him, Joe liked that.

Then one day, Joe woke up and decided to cut his dick off, he was just that disgusted with himself. Man! He'd been here in the North for *five years*, and he hadn't done a damn thing but fuck and get sucked! He had gone to Cousinsville several times and talked to some people from down home. Nobody there had heard anything about Titus. Reverend Cobb was supposed to be hiding up here in the North somewhere, people said. "I hear tell he burned the house down on his wife and escaped up here. You ever heard of a preacher doing something like that, burning up his wife?" Joe shrugged. He expected preachers to do anything, that's how much he thought of them. "What do you hear about May Jones?" he had asked. "Oh, she's still out there on the highway, selling tail as usual." So, she had gone back to Burnside after her vacation. He remem-bered meeting her in that tent in Alabama. She had told him he ought to come North. Well, he was here, and it wasn't too damned different from being in that tent down South. White people were just *sneakier*, that was all. They hated you the same way they hated you down South; but up here, they were sneaky motherfuckers. Joe went back to Newark and sold some dick. The North didn't show him much, but North or South, he was always doing the same thing. Selling dick. Right now, he wished he had a knife, he'd cut that motherfucker right off. He honestly would.

But he didn't really want to cut his dick off, and it scared the shit out of him that he'd even thought about something like that.

This apartment was bugging the hell out of him, that's what it was. He decided to go out for a while. He almost never went anywhere, because he didn't know when Pee Wee might show up with a client. Well, fuck Pee Wee and his clients. Let *him* do some fucking for a change. He put on sneakers, white jeans and a white tee shirt, and went out on the street.

Such a long time had passed since he was last out that he felt like a prisoner released from jail. After a hot summer, fall had come to Belmont Avenue, and the rickety old houses leaned this way and that to a mellow sun. Black children played ball, or marbles, or skipped rope; and Joe felt like getting down and playing with them. But when a stray ball bounced near him and he threw it back to the boy who came running after it, he realized that he was already an old man of twenty-one, the way children parted to let him through their games instead of making him a part of them.

Twenty-one! Man, it seemed like only yesterday when he was playing in the creek down in Burnside. It seemed impossible that ten years had passed so soon—five of them spent here in Newark— and he had the desperate feeling that he was somehow doomed to grow old and die without ever having lived at all. He depended on television for news about events in the world outside of the apartment on Belmont Avenue. But what came to him on television was condensed and glamorized to the point of being almost totally unreal, so that he was able to file actual events away in his mind alongside old Baby Snooks and Shirley Temple movies that he watched every night on the Late Late Show. Now, walking down Belmont Avenue, he felt like a stranger who has come to an exciting but alien new world. and he vowed to change his life. He was going to get out more. And even read the newspapers. Maybe he'd get a job like everybody else. Shit. Hard work never killed anybody. He was twenty-one years old, and he hadn't done an honest day's work in his life.

But the idea of working—that kind of work—exhausted him just thinking about it. And he felt very depressed. He went back to the apartment and turned on television. There was a news report about sit-ins in the South; Joe was watching that when Pee Wee came home and gave him a massage. "Man, that thing is going to explode any day now," Pee Wee said. "All them niggers down there is getting mad. And either the white man is going to kill them, or they going to kill them some white men." Pee Wee went out after a while; Joe kept on watching television. He didn't think those Negroes were going to do much. He hoped they would, but he didn't think so. He switched the channel to a Shirley Temple movie; and he was watching that when Pee Wee came back with some cat who wanted to suck Joe. All dimples and curls, Shirley Temple sang "On the Good Ship Lollipop." Joe busted his nuts, and went to sleep. But Pee Wee woke him up after what seemed a very short while. "You ready to work, baby? House rent's due, and we got to make us some more bread. I'm going out again and see what I can pick up." He slapped Joe lovingly on the butt. They smoked some pot together. Then, Pee Wee went downstairs whistling.

Joe wondered from time to time about Pee Wee, he couldn't help it. After all, you had to be suspicious about a guy who kissed the very ground you walked on. Pee Wee was like that, and he wasn't queer either, Joe could vouch for that. At least, Pee Wee didn't come on queer, grabbing, looking, things like that. Still, there was something funny about Pee Wee that bothered Joe from time to time. He just couldn't put his finger on what it was. But there was something strange about Pee Wee, he was sure of that.

The pot made him feel groggy, and he went into the shower. His head cleared some under the cool water, and he thought, *Man, I just got to change my way of living, I'm twenty-one years old now and I been high on pot since I was thirteen*. Not to mention all the people he'd fucked. Man, there must have been thousands, if not millions, it seemed to him that he'd been fucking and getting sucked all his life.

It depressed him, thinking about things like that. He left the shower and dried on a large fluffy towel with his initials on it. Then he took out a joint from the bedside table and smoked it. He put on a white terry cloth robe. Man, he'd heard too many of Titus' sermons not to be concerned about some of the things Titus had preached about, even if Titus had been a screwball. And there were some things Titus said that Joe had thought about from time to time over the past five years. He'd read a few books, too. Nothing deep and heavy, you understand, but just nice enough to help him ask and answer a few questions. And the pot helped a whole lot. He smoked some more and thought, *What am I supposed to be redeemed from if I ain't never sinned*? He'd never done nothing bad to anybody. The way he figured, it was the other way around. Because Titus had told him once that black people are a nightmare in the sleep of a white man, and when that white man wakes up, all black people disappear. Until the white man goes to sleep, to dream disturbing dreams again. . . . Now, wasn't *that* a big sin, just being a dream—a nightmare—in somebody's head? Man, there was no percentage at all in that. Just thinking about it made him feel all fucked up, and he sucked deeply on the joint. Shit, so what the fuck if nobody knew that he didn't want to be a dream? He wanted to be . . . a summer white bird in a wild cherry tree. But he was too high now to really say what he wanted to be. He heard the key turn in the door then, and Pee Wee came in with a tall, lean Italian stud.

He was a real good-looking guy around twenty-two or -three, dressed completely in black—suit, shirt, shoes, snap-brim hat—except for a yellow tie. His eyes were black, and his hair, and the five o'clock shadow on his chin. Standing behind him, Pee Wee showed Joe the edge of a fifty-dollar bill. Man, that was some bread this guy had paid all right. Standard fee was twenty dollars, he had to be loaded. Or one of those real sick queers that paid big money to have some colored guy beat him up or shit in his face, things like that. But he didn't even look like a client to Joe, although you never could tell about those people just by looking at them. After Pee Wee left, Joe asked the guy, "What's your pleasure?" The Italian shrugged. "You name it." That made Joe feel even stranger. But the guy had paid his money, and that meant he could call the cards. Joe turned his back and took off his robe. It was the first time he'd ever been ashamed to undress in front of anybody. But there was something about the Italian that bothered him. When he was naked, he turned around. The Italian was holding a goddamned gun the size of a cannon. "Vice squad," he said, flashing a badge.

Wham! Joe staggered back and sat on the bed. He could see his reflection in the mirror on the dresser, and he thought that he must be the prettiest black whore to get busted all year long. The cop was looking at him too; and Joe's body turned warm the way it did when people who were looking at him liked him. The cop liked him; he wasn't queer, but he did like him. *Use it, baby. You want your black ass to be in jail? All them cats there and not a nickel between them.* There was a joint in the ashtray beside the bed. Hell, he might as well smoke it. He took three drags, then he started to cop a plea with the policeman. "Give me a break, man. I never had me no education. I never had me nothing, except this body." He stood up, and felt his muscles ripple out like slow jazz through the room. His dick started to swell, and then unswelled, the cop was looking at his dick, that's why it was doing that. He wasn't queer, but he was definitely interested in something that had to do with Joe's dick. Almost casually, Joe scratched himself there, and the cop's eyes followed his fingers. "Baby, this hustling bit . . . this is all I know how to do to stay alive," Joe said. "A man like me, without an education, he got to make a living the best way he can." He sucked again on the joint and offered it to the cop. But the cop just looked at Joe. The gun didn't move, the cop's eyes didn't move, either. Almost black as a nigger, he gave the impression that down inside him somewhere were nigger things, nigger excitement, a long nigger dick hanging down beside his thigh. He was like a nigger and he was interested, all right. But in what? Joe kept both eyes glued to the cop, trying to figure him out.

Just then, he heard the faraway clatter of familiar high heels moving down the hall outside, and he decided on a last, desperate try. Man, he didn't want his ass to have to go to jail. He put on a broad, beautiful grin. "Baby . . . baby, don't shoot me now," he said to the cop. "I know what it is you want to do, baby. You want to fuck a colored chick with me, baby, that's what you want to do." The high heels were almost outside the door now. Joe took a deep breath and moved a step. He kept his eyes on the white man like a snake, and the gun muzzle followed him with the same kind of slow, hypnotic intensity. "I'm going to get us a chick we can fuck right now," Joe said. He moved slowly, carefully, to open the door. "Well, there's a chick going by right now. Her name is Mavis Lee, I recognize her walk. She's a fine colored chick, man . . . you and me could fuck her together. . . . You want that, man . . . ?"

But before he opened the door, the cop said, "Leave it!" Joe's mouth dropped open. "Huh? What you mean, man?" He thought he had this guy all figured out; but the cop kept the gun right on him. "I said *leave it* . . . don't open that door. And put some clothes on. You've got an appointment downtown."

"Man, give me a *break*!" He heard Mavis Lee's footsteps disappearing downstairs. And he was really scared now, this cat meant business. Well, he did, too. If the chips really were down, he had no intention of going to anybody's goddamn jail, he'd rather die first. Everybody knew what cops did to colored people once they got them in jail. "Man, you might as well shoot me now," Joe said quietly. "Because I ain't going to jail, so some white people can beat me up and fuck me in the ass."

"They don't do that," the cop said harshly.

"Well, whether they do or not, I *still* ain't going." His voice was dead cool, and his body was dry; but he was hot and sweating inside. "Man, I mean every word I say. I'd rather die first. Can you see somebody like me being cooped up in jail?"

Then, a strange thing happened. The cop took a step toward Joe and looked him full in the eyes. Joe had never looked a white person full in the eyes before, and so close. At first, he thought about running out of that room and never coming back, it was that much of a surprise, like gazing into a completely new world, the cop's black eyes with the heavy lids partly closed—lazy, almost sleepy, almost satisfied—the bushy brows, the long curling lashes, like looking inside of another world flavored with garlic and the mild bitterness of beer, looking through another dimension, to see inside the convoluted soul of a white man. Joe tried to move away, but the cop's eyes held him in a steady grip, and he felt compelled to speak. "I . . . I can see completely inside you," he said thickly. It seemed to him a strange thing to say to somebody who was about to take you to jail, or shoot you down like a sick dog for resisting arrest.

The cop did not speak, nor did his eyes flicker. Imbedded inside of slits, they held the cold, unyielding stare of a snake. But the answer was plainly there. *It's all right baby I can see inside of you too*.

The cop shrugged, and put his gun away. "Get dressed," he said, almost gruffly. "You asked for a break, so I'm going to give you one. I won't turn you in providing you do one thing."

"What's that?" Joe was suspicious again. Maybe this guy was queer after all, maybe he was looking for a full-time cocksman. For free. Well, Joe thought, he'd rather go to jail than go through with some shit like that, for free. "What you want me to do?"

"I want you to go to school," the cop said.

Wham again! Just like that. Man, this guy really was turning him on something terrible! "*Me* go to school? Man, you must be kidding! You a *evangelist* or something? What a big monkey like me look like sitting up in school with little girls in the seventh grade?"

"You'd look a whole lot better sitting up in school than you would dead . . . or sitting up in jail." He patted the gun in his belt. "Don't you think so?"

Joe smiled his beautiful smile. "Man, you so right," he said. School! He'd already made up his mind to piss over all them polished seats.

"And another thing," the cop said. "Don't think I chickened out just because you said you weren't going to jail. I'd just as soon shoot you as look at you."

Joe grunted. "What's your name, man? I bet they call you Dick Tracy downtown."

The cop smiled. He was really a very good-looking guy when he smiled. "My name's Tony Brenzo. And don't blame me for this school thing. I got the idea when you mentioned that bit about not having an education."

"Tell me anything," Joe said. But he felt there was some truth in what the cop was saying, he really did seem like an all right guy. Another kind of cop would have gun-whipped him and dragged him off to jail in handcuffs. Yeah, going to school would be a whole lot better than dying, or going to jail. But man, he was *twenty-one years old*, that was no time to be going back to school again!

Pee Wee came in while Joe was putting on his clothes. "Hope you all enjoyed yourselves," he said. He smiled like the cat that swallowed the choicest canary, like he was the cutest, the sharpest, the most discreet black little motherfucking pimp in all the world. "Yeah, we had a ball, baby," Joe said dryly. He had to do something with his hands to keep them from hitting Pee Wee, so he piled them on top of his head.

Pee Wee seemed to get the idea then. "What's the matter, Joe? Something wrong, baby?" Joe exploded like a bomb. He grabbed Pee Wee by the collar and shouted right in his face. "Everything's wrong, you dumb sonofabitch! This guy's a *cop*! He *arrested* me! He wants me to go to *school*!" He shook Pee Wee two or three times, like he was a small, wet dog, then threw him away with contempt.

Pee Wee got up trembling. "You a cop, Mister?" Tony Brenzo showed him his badge. "I'm a cop." Pee Wee started moaning. "LordhavemercyLordhavemercyLordhavemercy." Joe felt like kicking him right in his nuts. "The Lord ain't got a thing to do with this! How could you be so *stupid*, Pee Wee, picking up a cop?"

"How'd I know he was a cop?" Pee Wee was mad as a wet hen now. "You think I would've picked him up if I'd known he was a cop?"

"I think you would! You just that stupid! You the one that needs to go to school, not me!"

They were shouting at the top of their voices, and Tony Brenzo stepped in between them. "Hey, you boys take it easy. . . ." But Pee Wee darted around him and thrust his jaw into Joe's face. "That's twice you called me stupid! Well you were so stupid when I met you, you were *barefoot*, wearing a girl's *dress*, child. I guess you must've thought you was *Miss Shirley Temple*."

"You bring that up, huh?" Joe towered over him in a rage. "Well, I'll tell you this, baby! You been living off the fat of the land *for five years*! Without my dick in someone's ass or mouth, you'd starve to death, baby! You just too stupid to realize it! You dumb, you stupid, you *ignorant*. . . ." He ran out of names to call Pee Wee in that category; and while he was trying to think of some, Pee Wee went into the toilet and got his toothbrush and Nu-Nile. "Well, if that's the way you feel about it, Joe, then we ain't got nothing more to say. I know when my friendship's not wanted." He closed his eyes and held his wrists out for Tony to handcuff them. "I got my toothbrush and my hair grease, Mister. You can take me on to jail."

"I'm not interested in taking anybody to jail," Tony said. "All I'm trying to do is to get this big monkey to go to school so he won't have to be a whore all his life."

Pee Wee opened his eyes, blinking like Miss Bette Davis. "Say *what*? You want Miss Joe here to go to *school*? You don't want to put him in *jail*? Well, why didn't you say so, honey?" He was talking like a fag just to put everybody on. But he was still angry, and he looked at Joe with complete disgust. "Honey, that's exactly what Miss Joe here needs, child, an *education*, you hit the nail right on the head. Maybe it'll teach him who his friends really are."

"I know who my friend are," Joe cut in. "Like I say, you wouldn't be *shit* without my dick. Listen, Tony . . . you make him go to school, too, he thinks he's so goddamned cute."

"I *been* to school," Pee Wee said archly.

"What school?" Joe laughed. "To learn how to be dumb and stupid?"

But Pee Wee was dead serious. "I graduated from Memphis Colored High School. I got my diploma to prove it."

Joe couldn't believe his ears. "You a high school graduate?" Very pleased with himself, Pee Wee dug in his hip pocket and brought out a tattered wallet. From that, he took out a chewed-looking piece of paper that was a photostatic copy of a Memphis Colored High School diploma issued to Clarence P. Weeks. "That's me," Pee Wee said. "I carry this around to prove to people like you that I'm not really an *ignoramus*."

Joe just couldn't believe that Pee Wee was a high school graduate. He bet that Pee Wee had found that diploma on the street in the nigger section of Memphis, and had changed his name to fit the diploma. Yeah, that was it; and he was about to tell Pee Wee so. But Pee Wee was talking to Tony now, mad as a hornet, shrill as any woman. "Come to think of it, man, it ain't no cop's job to make nobody go to school. Why you do that? Why don't you just put us in jail like you supposed to? If we done wrong, then you *supposed* to lock us up. I'd gladly go to jail just to make sure Miss Joe Market goes too, calling me stupid like that."

Tony Brenzo threw up his hands. "Fuck all this noise! Man, you guys are going to drive me crazy! I'm sorry I ever saw you! Just forget I'm a cop, forget everything! Nobody's under arrest, nobody has to go to school, nobody has to do anything. . . !"

"I want to go to school," Joe said. He couldn't bear the idea of somebody as black and dumb as Pee Wee having a high school education when he didn't . "I want to go to school, Tony, and I want you to put my ass in jail if I don't go."

Tony Brenzo calmed down at once. "It's a deal, baby. We start tomorrow."

But Pee Wee was still very angry. "As much education as *he* needs, child, you should have started *yesterday*." Joe swung at him, but he ducked and went outdoors, still mad.

The next day, Tony Brenzo took Joe to Barringer High School and registered him there for night classes on the eighth-grade level. Because he did not work at a regular job, Joe signed up to take more classes than the other students. Going to school from seven o'clock to eleven, on an accelerated schedule, he would be able to finish eighth and ninth grades both in one year.

Tony Brenzo had set up the schedule like that. He was full of excitement about the idea of Joe getting an education. Driving Joe home from school, he said that being so black himself, white people sometimes called him nigger in an affectionate way. So he thought he knew how it must feel to be called that for real, if it bothered him so much when somebody just said it affectionately. "Aside from that," he said, "I think the whole racial thing is lousy anyway."

"You sound just like a record," Joe said, with some scorn. He thought he saw a shadow pass over the Italian's face. "Man, I want to get something straight once and for all," Tony said. "I don't think anybody's ever liked you for yourself before, for the simple fact that you've probably got a very good brain inside that skull of yours. And we'd get along a lot better if you stopped acting like you're nothing but a big, dumb dick." They had come to Belmont Avenue now, and

Tony parked the car. "Shit, I've got dick, too." He tapped his fore-head. "But it's what's up here that really counts. Do I make myself clear, man? Do you dig what I'm saying?"

Joe nodded. No white man had ever talked to him like that be-fore, and he felt shy and embarrassed. But he did manage to get out of the car; then he stuck his head back inside. "You remember now . . . you put me in jail if I don't go to school and get good marks." He couldn't even look at Tony, but he saw Tony nod. "I'll put you in jail," Tony said. He drove off.

Pee Wee was waiting for Joe when he got upstairs. He was sub-dued and very sheepish-looking. "Man, you know I can't stay mad with you," Pee Wee said, showing his gold teeth. "We still friends, baby?"

"We still friends."

"You want some food?"

"No." His head was buzzing with a new kind of excitement.

"A drink?"

"No."

"A rubdown?'"

"All right . . . a rubdown, then."

"Where you been?" Joe kicked off his shoes and took off his pants; Pee Wee folded them nicely for him and hung them over the back of a chair. "I went to register at school with that cop."

Pee Wee grunted. "You still going through with that? Man, that cat can't force you to go to school. Besides, what about our little deal?" He was talking about being a pimp for Joe.

"We'll keep on with that," Joe said. "Only, we got to cut down some, now that I'm in school." He took off his shirt and socks and lay on the bed; Pee Wee's hands commenced a slow, soothing mas-sage on his body. "I want to go to school," Joe said. "And if I don't go and make good grades, that cop's going to bust me . . . I want him to bust me." Pee Wee sounded very jealous. "Man, I bet that guy ain't nothing but a masquerading fag. He don't really care whether you get an education or not, you don't have to pay no attention to him at all. And you don't need to go to no school, man, not with this equip-ment you got." His hands brushed Joe's dick as though by accident;

and Joe started thinking about what Tony Brenzo had said. Was it true that nobody had ever liked him for himself before? He couldn't remember one single person, except his mother, who hadn't liked him because of *how* he was—his dick, his body, his looks—instead of *who* he was. Not even Pee Wee. He didn't even know whether Pee Wee liked the real him or not. "Pee Wee, do you like me, man?" Pee Wee seemed surprised. "Sure I like you, man. Can't you tell that?" His hands brushed Joe's dick again. "We're friends, ain't we? Or you still remembering what went on last night? Man, don't pay no attention to that. We was both just a little upset, that's all."

But the way Pee Wee's hands moved on him, they felt more like the hands of lust—Titus Market used to preach sermons about the sin of lust—and Joe knew that that had been the story of his life up until yesterday when he met Tony Brenzo, who liked him for himself rather than for his dick, who thought that he had a good brain, who thought that he should get an education. Joe noted the date in his head: September 20, 1960. He was 21 years old. Well, starting tomorrow, he was going to turn over a new leaf. He was going to go to school, to bring out the other part of him that only Tony Brenzo had recognized so far.

His first night at school, Joe wore an off-color purple tailor-made suit with chalk stripes, his Puerto Rican–toe patent leather shoes, and a yellow shirt with a wing collar that he had bought just for the occasion. His tie was pale blue with his initials embroidered in white inside a rectangle of pink flowers. Man, he could tell he was sharp, the way everybody paid more attention to him than they did to the teacher. He bet they thought he was Harry Belafonte, he looked a little bit like Harry Belafonte. When people stared at him too hard, he said kindly, "I'm Joe Market," just so they wouldn't think they'd met Harry.

After a few nights of this, the history teacher took Joe aside at the end of her class. Her name was Mrs. Tate, she was a white woman. "Mr. Market, you're an extremely attractive man. And the fact that you dress so . . . so *well* makes you even more attractive.

The other teachers and I have been wondering if you'd mind wearing something a little less stylish so that the students will pay some attention to us." Joe felt very complimented. "I'll see what I can do," he said. He stopped being so sharp, and all his classes settled down into a stiff routine.

Mrs. Tate made American history vivid and exciting. She talked about Negro slavery and American democracy. And about General Eisenhower in a very nice way, he was President then. Joe understood everything she said. He knew that everybody thought he was just a country bumpkin, after he started dressing ordinary, just because he talked with that sprawling downhome accent. But he had gone to seventh grade in Burnside, and those Burnside schools weren't all that bad.

He actually enjoyed learning. He was taking classes in English, history, literature, and mathematics. But when he went home at night, he had terrible dreams in which his dead mother Ramona ridiculed him for getting an education. In one of these dreams, he saw Ramona sitting down in hell in a pea patch. She said, "Joe darling, did you really come all this way just to go to school? And when you going to judge me, sugar lump? When you going to *save* me?" She laughed so largely that he saw all her teeth. At the same time, her arms were making signs of the cross backwards, because she thought he was some kind of crucified black saviour, he saw all this in her mind, that he only had three days to judge all the black men and women who died before he came, like she had died suffocated under his father Titus while Joe had been farting around down in the creek in Burnside. "And now you're fucking around in school," his mother said bitterly, "while I'm sitting in hell in a pea patch." Three days to judge all black souls. "And to save them," Ramona said, laughing in a most ridiculous way. "And to save them. And to save them. . . ."

Joe woke up in a cold sweat. He and Pee Wee shared the same bed, and Pee Wee woke up, too. "What's wrong, baby?" Pee Wee said. He snapped on the light when Joe didn't answer. Pee Wee brought out a joint and lit it. He gave it to Joe, then smoked some himself. "What's wrong, Joe?"

"I just had a dream, that's all." Was it wrong for him to be going to school? Was that what his mother was trying to tell him? Why shouldn't he go to school? And why was he dreaming about Ramona and Titus after all this time?

"Pee Wee?"

"Yeah, baby."

"Pee Wee, you remember me talking about my mother and father, about that religion we had? You remember, that night in the boxcar when we were coming up here from Georgia?"

"I remember. I just thought you was lying, that's all."

Joe nodded. Perhaps it had been a lie. Furthermore, how could he save his mother if she was already in hell? It surprised him that Ramona was in hell. She had been one of the best churchwomen in Burnside, and she'd still wound up in hell.

Pee Wee could see that something was troubling Joe. "Don't worry about nothing, baby. You know it's nearly four o'clock in the morning? I'll give you a quick rubdown. Then you'll be able to go back to sleep."

He fell asleep while Pee Wee was massaging him. But this time he dreamed of May Jones and when he was the Christchild in the Christmas tableau. May was sucking him in the manger while Reverend Cobb preached about Christian love. Then his father Titus came to the front of the church. Grinning, he shoved May aside. . . .

Joe woke up again. He half-expected to find that Pee Wee was sucking him. But Pee Wee was asleep now, and Joe was almost sorry about that. Because his dick was hard as hell, he thought about waking Pee Wee up and asking him to suck him just for old time's sake. How would Pee Wee react to that? Joe didn't know, but he found it interesting to think about, because sometimes he was just as convinced that Pee Wee was queer as he was convinced other times that Pee Wee was not queer.

Joe got up and took a shower. It was nearly daybreak, he thought he might go out in the streets and walk some. Maybe he'd find somebody to suck him out there. Then he started wondering if he might not be turning queer himself, having so much to do with queers. Man, he couldn't dig that shit. He was going to prove that he still liked women. He dried himself, dusted powder under his armpits and all over his groin. Then, stark naked, he went out into the hall and upstairs to Mavis Lee's apartment.

She was still sleeping this early in the morning. "Joe, what's wrong with you? What you doing here naked this hour of the day?" He went in and closed the door behind him. "Nobody saw me," he said. Mavis was looking at him strangely. She was a pretty brown-skinned girl of around twenty. "What you want?" she said, wrinkling her nose. "All that powder on you, you smell like a woman." He didn't say a word. He picked her up and carried her to the bedroom. "What you *want*?" Mavis said. He took off the robe she was wearing. She was naked underneath. Her body was the color of caramel all over. She had nice hard titties, the beginnings of a belly, a round, firm butt, and a thatch of silk-looking hair at the juncture of her smooth thighs. "Oh, you want to *fuck* me?" Mavis said. She sounded half-sleepy, and a little bit surprised. He threw her on the bed and piled into her so hard he almost knocked her off the bed. Then, lifting her head and shoulders up, he wrapped his long arms around her and settled down into a cruel, grinding fuck. She was humming like a spinning machine. Who said he smelled like a woman? Shit. He almost fucked her to death.

He found himself thinking about women almost all the time after that. Even when he was with queers—because he had to go on hustling queers to make his living—he told himself, "Man, this is a real fine chick you're with. She so fine, she might even be a white woman." Shit man, there wasn't a thing queer about him. Then one night in history class, he found himself more excited and alert than usual. Mrs. Tate was talking about America, and Joe got the idea right then that America also was a woman he could love, a large and beautiful white woman, he felt such a warm, spontaneous excitement for her monuments and parks and cities, her *amber waves of grain*. "Since Columbus discovered America on October 12, 1492," Mrs. Tate said, "this country has rapidly grown to become the richest and most powerful nation in the world." Man, that Christopher Columbus must have been a really swinging cat, discovering America like he had. Joe started calling his dick *Christopher*, and he addressed it quietly in the third person whenever it tried to make discoveries on its own. *Now Christopher, I know you dig women, there ain't nothing queer about you. You big beautiful motherfucker. But you don't want that woman. Man, she too old, she ain't shit. You behave yourself. You lay down. You hear me, Christopher?* Sometimes between classes he had to limp to the toilet with Christopher and whip him to death with spit, just so Christopher would let him walk without everybody in school having a fit, all that dick he had.

He certainly didn't know what was wrong with Christopher, because those people at night school didn't move *him* at all. With the exception of a few white people, all of the students were colored, and most of the teachers, too. But it wasn't the fact of their color that bothered Joe about the Negroes. Men and women alike, most of them were much older than he was. And wore the masks of bitter, disinherited people, as though when Columbus died, he left everything to everybody else except them. They acted like bitter little boys and girls in grammar school. "Teacher! Teacher! Teacher!" they hissed angrily, waving their wrinkled old hands, squirming to show how much they knew. Or sometimes, they just wanted to ask permission to go to the basement; being so old, they all had weak bladders. They had all gone to school before, when toilets had been built in the basement. And now when they wanted to pee, they waved their hands like long-suffering children and said, "Teacher, may I please go to the *basement*?" Sometimes, Joe got the idea that they might go downstairs and never come back. Well, they could hide from America all they wanted to, that's what it amounted to, he could see it on their faces. But he thought America was a beautiful white woman, he didn't see why they couldn't think the same thing. He thought they were all very silly. And not very attractive, either. Still, Christopher stayed hard most of the time he was in school. *Down, Christopher. What is the matter with you, man?*

Then Joe realized that it was Miss Barton that Christopher was after. She sat in front of him in history class. Her behind was shaped like a mellow-ripe pear, he was surprised that he hadn't noticed before. He could smell the woman smell about her, like an orchard of ripe fruit in a mellow autumn. It almost drove him wild, once he started paying attention to it. He kept talking to Christopher all the time now, trying to keep him cool. Miss Barton just patting the back of her neck from time to time was almost enough to make him come. She wore her black hair pulled back in a little greasy pony tail. She looked like Jackie Kennedy, without Jackie's great big jaw, that's who she looked like. She seemed not to notice Joe at all. The backs of her ears shone pleasantly in the grooves where they joined her head. *Cool it, Christopher. I see now what you been excited about.*

One night, he got up the nerve to ask Miss Barton to have coffee with him in the cafeteria. She had very large black eyes like a cinnamon deer, and they opened now like he'd shined a light in them instead of just asking her to have a cup of coffee. "I don't drink coffee, Mr. Market. It's bad for the complexion."

"Well, how about milk?" he started to suggest. But Miss Barton had already walked away. She went to a table in the corner where she opened her American History and seemed to be studying very hard, her pretty forehead was wrinkled like a prune. She had the longest, smoothest legs he'd ever seen on a chick. He bet she really had a *Tan Confessions* spread out inside that history book.

Several weeks later, he got around to asking her to have a glass of milk, then. But it seemed that milk gave her diarrhea. "A Coke, then?" Miss Barton took a deep breath. "Mr. Market, I have some studying to do. If you don't mind?" She went to her favorite corner and opened her history book.

This went on for several months. Until one night in class while Joe was carrying on a quiet but intense conversation with Christopher about Miss Barton's behind, the teacher asked him, "Mr. Market, in what year did Abraham Lincoln sign the Emancipation Proclamation?" She had caught him completely off-guard. "Eighteen-hundred-and-sixty," he guessed. Mrs. Tate shook her head and pursed her lips. "Miss Barton," she said. Miss Barton turned and looked over her shoulder at Joe. "It was eighteen-hundred-and-sixty-*one*," she said, with the greatest of satisfaction, and let her eyelids drop like to shield herself from his ignorance. He made up his mind right then to marry the bitch.

After Miss Barton had ignored him for another six months, Joe got desperate. He had been wondering for a long time now why she didn't flip over him like everybody else did. He followed her to the basement one night and nearly broke her damned neck. "Miss Barton, where you think you get off, acting like you don't want to marry me?" he said in a low hiss. He was pulling her neck backwards by her pony tail. He knew it was dangerous; all she had to do was scream and they could put him away for attempted rape. But anything was better than him and Christopher walking around all the time like two dogs in heat.

He wanted to give her a karate chop across her throat the way it was curved back, he was just that mad. "Everybody else in school wants to give me some tail and marry me, where you think you get off, acting like you think I don't even exist? How come you think you so different?" He grabbed Miss Barton's hand and made her feel his dick. She wasn't so cool now. He used his body like a sting ray, he was all over her against the basement wall, and she jumped every time he touched her. After a while, she slumped half down and pulled her head away from him. "You dumb black nigger," she said. She was breathing very hard, and laughing at the same time. "Sure I want to give you some tail, you dumb black nigger. I want to marry you, too." He was so relieved he almost cried. He really did want to marry her. And he was about to get some of her tail right there, he knew that. But they had to break it up, some of those old people were coming down to use the basement. They had time for just a quick kiss, and she used her mouth over his like he had used his body over hers. He heard himself moaning like a woman. "Miss . . . Miss Barton. . . ." She laughed some more. "My name's Odessa," she said. She brushed herself off and straightened her pony tail, and then went up to the cafeteria and had tea, that was her favorite drink. "When I first saw you," she said to Joe, "I thought you were Harry Belafonte. I told my mother so, too. What happened to that purple suit you wore?"

Joe smiled. "I hocked it." Which was true. He had a lot more taste now. Education had done that for him, he was getting ready to go on to tenth grade. He always smiled when he thought of himself in that purple suit. And those Puerto Rican shoes, with the toes pointed so Puerto Ricans could mash up roaches in corners.

When Joe told Pee Wee that he was going to get married, Pee Wee didn't like the idea at all. "How come you don't like the idea, Pee Wee?" Joe looked at him hard. Sometimes he had a real strong feeling that Pee Wee had done that collecting on him. "Buddy, we're a *team*," Pee Wee said. "What I'm going to do without you?"

"You can get yourself a job," Joe said. It surprised him, saying something like that. But he guessed he'd have to get a job, too. Married men don't make out too good as dick hustlers. So Pee Wee got a job driving a taxi. And Joe got a job driving the truck at the laundry in Cousinsville where Odessa worked. Joe was anxious to get married right away, but Odessa kept putting it off until another six months went by. She said that her mother wanted her to get an education and to become a nurse or something, to help ease some of the suffering in the world.

"Speaking of suffering," Joe said, "what about me and Christopher?" He had told her what the pet name stood for; and she laughed with delight that he wanted to go to bed with her all that bad. "Joe, I'm not going to have sex with you until we're married!" she cried, evading his arms and Christopher aimed straight at her. "I know it might be old-fashioned, but Mama and I both think a girl ought to be a virgin when she gets married." So, he figured it was her mother's idea, and he kept on pushing the issue until Odessa finally admitted that her mother had her dominated. She wasn't even interested in being a nurse, not really; and she told Joe that she'd marry him as soon as he could work three months straight without missing a day, no matter what her mother said. "I just want to know that you're stable," Odessa said. Up until then, Joe had averaged about one day a week not working. If he missed one day during three months, Odessa would put the wedding off for three months more. She still wouldn't go to bed with Joe, and he didn't have anything to do with sex all that time. He was saving up for Odessa.

At first, Tony Brenzo didn't think too much of Joe's getting married, either. Joe had gotten over his shyness with the cop a long time ago, and they had become very good friends over the past two years. From time to time, until Joe met Odessa, they made a Triple-S scene with Mavis Lee or some other colored chick. In the Triple-S scene, Tony and Joe both entered Mavis at the same time, one from the front and one from the back, but both of them socked up inside her pussy. Tony had never offered any white girls, and Joe hadn't even bothered to ask for any. He didn't think that a white girl could take the two of them at the same time, Tony had just as much dick as he did.

Tony smoked pot, too, and sometimes they smoked together. But Joe was even getting away from that habit, he didn't feel the need for it. Tony said that he was smoking less pot, too; but when Joe told him about Odessa, the first thing Tony did was to get high. Joe smiled; he'd gotten to know the big Italian very well in two years. "We're still going to be good friends, Tony. We're going to make the Triple-S scene with chicks whenever we want to. Nothing's going to change between us. Don't you worry none, man." Tony handed Joe the joint. "What I want to know," Tony said, "is whether you're still going to school. Is getting married going to change that?"

"No, man. Is that what's bugging you?" Well don't you worry about that. I'm still going to school." They both felt better after that, and they smoked some more pot. "Man, I want you to meet this chick," Joe said. "She looks a little bit like Jackie Kennedy." He took Tony to meet Odessa at an Italian restaurant in Newark. They were on their second bottle of red wine when Tony looked up from his spaghetti. "You don't look like Jackie Kennedy at all," he told Odessa, laughing. "Joe said you look like Jackie, but I think you look like Osa Massey. You know who she is? She's an old-time movie star, that's who you look like." Handsome, tanned, his thick black hair streaked more and more with white over the past two years, Tony looked like a movie star himself. He smiled easily, and treated Odessa with a light kind of charm. But it was obvious that she saw him as some kind of threat to her marriage with Joe. At one point, Tony said, "You lovebirds make me think of getting married, too." Odessa drew closer to Joe. "Why don't you?" she said, somewhat cooly. Tony looked away. For a second, the muscles knotted along the ridge of his jaw. 'I was married. My wife was a teacher. She died of cancer. It was pretty terrible." Odessa reached across the table and covered Tony's hand with both of hers. "I'm so sorry," she said quietly. "About everything." Joe liked that; he sat back and filled his belly with spaghetti while Tony and Odessa settled down to talking warmly about why he should continue his education after he and Odessa got married.

The wedding was scheduled for the same day that John Kennedy got shot in Dallas. Odessa still wanted to go through with the ceremony; but Joe thought they should put it off, at least for a while, he really liked John Kennedy. They waited a week and got married on November 29, 1963, at the Baptist church on Oakwood Avenue, where Odessa and her mother, Miss Lavinia, were both good members. Tony was Joe's best man, which Odessa thought lent a certain elegance to the small ceremony, the fact that Tony was white and so good-looking, and also made up for the fact that Miss Lavinia didn't come to the wedding at all, she was sulking at home. Odessa wore a plain white dress and had her hair combed just like Jackie Kennedy combed hers, that was the style then. But Joe didn't even comment about it, he never compared her to Jackie again after President Kennedy died. When he took Odessa to bed that night—Christopher, that motherfucker hummed like a well-oiled piston—he thought it was the most beautiful thing that had ever happened to him, the shy, innocent way Odessa gave herself to him. He was surprised to find that she really was a virgin, that she'd been keeping herself pure for her husband just like she'd said. Afterwards, Odessa snuggled up to him. "Joe, you happy, honey?" He just nodded in the dark, he was too full to speak. He was happy for the first time in his life. And he was a real man after all.

Miss Lavinia came to see them about a week later. She clearly disapproved of Joe, and told him so. "I had other plans for my daughter," she said. "I was hoping she'd marry a doctor, or become a nurse, all the suffering there is in the world." She wouldn't even look Joe in the eye, he wondered how she even knew what he looked like. She looked like Aunt Jemima to him, and he paid as little attention to her as he could.

With Odessa and Tony both nagging him now, Joe finished twelfth grade in less than a year, and went on to college at night. Odessa stopped going to school as soon as they got married, which was all right with Joe, he didn't want a wife that was too smart. They both worked in the China Doll Hand Laundry next door to where they settled down on lower Decatur Street. The laundry was owned by an old Chinese guy named Mr. Yen. He made his own wine from grapes that he cultivated in his back yard. He also had a pet turkey that he called Ming, and a liking for colored women that Joe tried to satisfy by picking them up for him. One day, Joe took Mr. Yen down to Mavis Lee's apartment on Belmont Avenue, she wouldn't come to Cousinsville to fuck him like all the other girls. Joe was driving the truck from the laundry; Mr. Yen, who was nearly sixty years old, was dressed in a black silk suit, a Panama hat, and a bow tie. He was as excited as a schoolboy. "You're sure she's pretty, Joe? You know I don't like ugly women." Joe laughed. He really liked Mr. Yen, he thought it was an honor for his race that the little Chinaman could be so hung up on colored women. "Don't you worry, Mr. Yen. She's pretty, all right." He parked the truck and went to help Mr. Yen out. But Mr. Yen leapt to the curb before Joe got to him. Joe shook his head; he sure hoped Mavis wouldn't fuck all the starch out of little Mr. Yen, he was trying so hard to act young. He practically ran up the two flights of stairs to Mavis' apartment. Joe felt sorry for him and a little worried, too, because Mr. Yen's face was an ashy-gray color when they got to Mavis' door. "Why don't we rest a while?" Joe said. Mr. Yen nodded; he was too tired even to speak. They waited in front of Mavis' door until Mr. Yen's color came back and his breathing fell to normal. When Joe knocked, Mavis opened the door at once. "Hi, Joe." She wore a print dress that showed her figure to good advantage. She had on just a dab of make-up, and her hair was brushed back and held in a small pony tail. Looking that way, she might have been anybody's kid sister. She nodded pleasantly to Mr. Yen, and took his hat. "I've got Chinese tea brewing," she said. "When Joe told me who he was bringing by, I bought some just in case you wanted a cup." Mr. Yen dropped into the first chair he saw. "I'd love a cup," he said. His color had turned ashy again, and Joe asked him, "Mr. Yen, you sure you feeling all right?" He took the Chinaman's hat and fanned him until Mr. Yen laughed. "I feel fine now," he said. "A pretty woman always makes me feel fine, Joe. And your friend is very pretty indeed." Mavis was coming on like a perfect lady. "Why, thank you, kind sir," she said.

Joe left after she'd served tea and almond cookies. "Don't worry about Mr. Yen. I'll take very good care of him," she whispered to Joe at the door. She grinned like an imp. "He's the first Chinese customer I ever had. I want to see if it's true what they say about Chinese men."

"It's Chinese women they say that about, " Joe said. When he went back a few hours later to pick up Mr. Yen, Mavis wouldn't let him in, she talked to him through the door. "Mr. Yen says he's not ready to go yet. He says to come back later tonight." But when Joe went back later, there was no answer at all, although he nearly kicked the door in. The same thing happened the next morning and afternoon—Joe banging and kicking on the door, calling Mavis and Mr. Yen. But nobody answered in Mavis' apartment, and nobody in the other apartments even bothered to look out, everybody minded his own business in a building like this, it might be dangerous not to.

Joe went back every day for five days looking for Mr. Yen and Mavis, but there was not a trace of either of them. Joe was really worried; he even thought about getting in touch with Tony Brenzo and having the cops look for them. But he didn't like that idea very much, maybe Mavis and Mr. Yen were involved in something that the cops shouldn't know about. So he just kept quiet and waited.

Then, on the sixth night, Mavis and Mr. Yen showed up at Joe's house on lower Decatur Street after he and Odessa had gone to bed. Joe put a robe on and let them in. He was mad enough to die.

"Where the fuck you all been?" he asked. Mavis showed him a large diamond ring. "To Niagara Falls on our honeymoon, Joe darling. Mr. Yen and me got married three days ago." She seemed excited and happy. Mr. Yen, too. In fact, he looked younger and healthier than Joe had ever seen him. "Well, ain't you going to congratulate me, Joe?" Mr. Yen said. He sounded like he was a little afraid of what Joe's reaction might be; after all, Joe had introduced him to Mavis, and now he might be mad or jealous or something. But Joe just hugged the little old Chinaman for sheer joy, he was so glad that nothing bad had happened to them.

Odessa came then to see what all the commotion was about. When Joe told her about Mavis and Mr. Yen, Odessa invited them both in. "You sly old dog," she said to Mr. Yen. "What'd you say your wife's name was?" Mr. Yen was grinning from ear to ear. "Her name's Mavis, but I'm going to call her China Doll from now on, after my laundry." They all laughed at that. Joe opened a bottle of wine and they started to drink. All except Odessa. She didn't drink, all she did was gossip with her mother. So of course she had to throw something on and run out to tell Miss Lavinia. She told her mother everything, as though nothing was true that happened to her unless old Miss Lavinia knew about it. She stayed only about twenty minutes, and Joe was thankful that she came back without her mother, he didn't want to see that funky black bitch tonight. But Odessa was a lot less excited about the marriage when she came back than when she left, and that was probably because Miss Lavinia had put the bad mouth on somebody as young and pretty as Mavis marrying somebody as old as Mr. Yen was. Joe became more certain of that when Odessa slid next to Mavis and asked in her nice-nasty way, "Tell me something about yourself, Mavis. I'm just dying to know how you and Mr. Yen met." He was sleeping with his head on Mavis' shoulder, so it seemed all right to ask questions like that. But Mavis was nobody's fool. "My own grandmother was Chinese on my mother's side," she said. "When Grandma died last week, I went to her funeral. Mr. Yen was there, too, and it was a case of love at first sight, I guess."

Odessa squirmed in her seat. It was clear to Joe that she didn't know whether she was being put on or not. "Well . . . what was Mr. Yen doing at your grandmother's funeral?" Odessa wanted to know. "Were they related?" Mavis shook her head. "No, dear. Every time one Chinese dies, all the Chinese from fifty miles around go to his funeral. Didn't you know that ? That's so people will think that dead Chinese have a lot of live Chinese friends."

Joe served more wine. "Mavis, quit your lying," he said with a grin. "Call me China Doll," Mavis said. She turned to Odessa with a pleasant smile, but her voice was as hard as nails. "The only thing you have to know about me, honey, is that I'm going to make Mr. Yen happy, I'm going to be a very good wife to him." There was a kind of fierce determination in her voice that seemed all too real. Odessa backed down at once. "Why, I'm sure you *will*," she said to Mavis, with that half-shitty smile she used sometimes, the one she copied from her mother. Looking at Mr. Yen sitting next to Mavis, dozing from time to time, Joe saw that the old man's face had turned that sick color again, probably from being so tired. And he wondered whether Mr. Yen would be around long enough for Mavis to be any kind of a wife to him. Still, he was happy they had got married. And when Mr. Yen went home yawning and staggering late that night with his new bride, all Joe could do was grin. Good old Mavis. China Doll. He bet she would make Mr. Yen happy. And he would call her China Doll from now on. Anyway, he was glad that she was going to be living right next door, so that he could fuck her from time to time without having to go all the way to Newark. Not that he was really tired of Odessa. He'd already been married to her going on three years, and they were the happiest years he'd ever spent. It was just that a man needed a different piece of tail every now and then. Although there were certain things about Odessa that did bother him, and mainly, the fact that she let her mother Miss Lavinia shit all over her the way she did.

Odessa and her mother were both very religious. Odessa's favorite hymn was *That Old Rugged Cross*. Sometimes on Sunday mornings and whenever she was working around the house, she used to sing it in a pinched little whine, as though singing about her Jesus constricted her nasal passages. Joe never told her much about

his own early life and Titus Market's religion; but it used to gripe
hell out of him, the way Odessa was always whining that hymn and
trying to drag him off to church with her mother. Finally, he got in
the habit of fucking her nearly to death on Sunday mornings, and
she wasn't too interested in getting up and going to church when
Miss Lavinia came by for her, scratching at the door like a pious cat.
"Odessa sugar, you going to church this morning?" Joe wouldn't
even let Odessa talk, he'd shove so much dick up inside her that she
couldn't even breathe, much less talk. Miss Lavinia scratched again.
"Odessa . . . sugar . . . *I* know what you all doing in there when you
ought to be getting ready for church. *God* know what you doing,
too. God don't like sinners and backsliders, Odessa. Now why don't
you make that husband of yours let you get up, and then come on
and go to church with me, honey?" Joe kept right on fucking. He
could see that Odessa wanted to go to church, and she wanted to be
fucking him, too. Well, that was her problem and her mother's, not
his. Sometimes while he was operating, he could hear the church
bell ringing. Then Miss Lavinia would stop scratching and hightail
it to church; she hated worse than anything to be late for church,
she said it looked so niggerish and common. Listening to her heavy
footsteps running down the hallway, Joe would grin and throw
some more Christopher into Odessa. He was competing with God
and Miss Lavinia both, and he was winning. "Now, you didn't really
want to go to church, did you?" he'd ask Odessa. "No, Joe . . . you
know better than that, baby. . . ." But he could tell that she was lying and telling the truth at the same time. He just kept on fucking;
but he wished he could get his dick up inside of Miss Lavinia, he'd
teach her to fuck with Odessa's head the way she was always doing.
After a while, Odessa stopped talking to him about church altogether, and Joe was very glad of that.

Another thing that bothered him was that Odessa did not want
to have children. She never did come right out and say it, but it was
obvious to Joe after a while that Odessa was doing something to
keep from having a child, since he wasn't doing something to keep
from having one. Joe went with Odessa to a doctor, who said there
was no reason that he could see why they shouldn't have babies.

Odessa smiled in a nervous way and twisted her wedding ring. "Doctor ... maybe ... maybe *God* don't want us to have no babies. ... I mean, that happens sometimes, don't it?" Smiling, the doctor assured her that God wanted everybody to have babies, that was why He created sex. But it was that remark of Odessa's that really put Joe on the track, it sounded so goddamned much like her mother. And he started watching Odessa like a hawk. One time he asked her, "Odessa honey, you do want some babies, don't you?" He was dying to have some; he wanted to see what his children were going to look like, what with Odessa looking like who she looked like, and him looking like Harry Belafonte. He already had the name picked out for the first one, if it was a boy. Christopher. That's what he'd call him. "Sure I want babies, Joe. You know that. Ain't I always told you that?" But three years went by, and not a blessed thing happened.

Some of the guys on the block started to tease Joe. "You need some help, baby?" Pee Wee moved to Cousinsville to be closer to Joe. He said that Odessa had done something to Joe's manhood. Pee Wee was very bitter because Joe had stopped hustling after he got married. He treated Joe like a prize racehorse that he was groom to. He rubbed Joe down now with perfumed alcohol and warm oil when Joe got stiff from working on the delivery truck. "That woman's making a physical wreck out of you, Joe. Your body don't seem the same, since you got married. That's why I'm using this special mixture." Joe loved the way Pee Wee massaged him. He lay on his back with his eyes closed. "Odessa ain't done nothing to me, Pee Wee. Why don't you like her?" He enjoyed the small feud that Odessa and Pee Wee kept up over him. They were together in Pee Wee's bedroom. Joe could smell sweaty socks and the funk of an old man all down in the sheets and covers underneath him. Although Pee Wee wasn't really that old, there was just something old about him. Every time Joe left Pee Wee's place, he went home and took a scalding hot shower. Not to wash off the feeling of Pee Wee's hands, but to wash off the smell of Pee Wee's apartment. Joe thought it was a smell that went right down into the pores. He wondered if Pee Wee had always smelled like that, even when they had been living together. "Naw, I ain't got nothing against Odessa," Pee Wee was saying. "She just another nigger woman, that's all. And you got to watch nigger women like a hawk, or one day you wake up and find them big balls been cut right out." Eagerly, his oily hands went to work on the muscles in Joe's thighs; and Joe tried to forget the fact that he had never seen Pee Wee with a woman. Or with a man, either, except with himself. Pee Wee's hands were soft and supple as a woman's; they did great things to Joe's muscles. "Furthermore, if you all ain't got no babies," Pee Wee said, with biting indignation, "it's because Odessa don't want none. You could give a baby to anybody." Joe concentrated on something else to keep from getting excited. He was almost sorry that Pee Wee wasn't a woman. He'd give him lots of babies.

After that, Joe began to watch Odessa extra carefully, because he didn't want what Pee Wee had said to come true. And he began to notice how Odessa always leaped up from the bed as soon as they had finished fucking and her breathing settled down. She'd disappear into the toilet, and Joe could hear water there sloshing and flushing in a dark, mysterious way. He had hardly paid attention before; but now it always seemed to him that Odessa was destroying the most vital part of him when she really should be trying to convert it into flesh. But he kept quiet, something in him rebelling at trying to force a baby on Odessa if she didn't want one. After all, she had to carry it for nine months, not him. Although he did think that her not wanting to have a child was not at all in keeping with her Jesus bit. Because it was still there, all her religious thing, even if she didn't go to church anymore.

Then he found some pills that Odessa was taking, and he asked Tony Brenzo about them. "They're to keep from getting pregnant," Tony told him. But when he asked Odessa, she said they weren't for that at all, they were for some kind of female trouble, that's what her mother Miss Lavinia had told her.

A few days later, Joe went to talk to Miss Lavinia about Odessa. He was going to talk to Miss Lavinia about something very important, and he paid attention to her really for the first time. She was a large black mountain of a woman who thought that God had put

Negroes on earth for the express purpose of suffering. Her forehead and fat cheeks were wrinkled with almost professional lines of
misery, as though she had received the deepest mandate from God.
She wore a polka-dot Jemina rag around her head, like some nigger
from the cotton field. And she never looked anybody straight in the
eye, as though there was some inherent danger in being able to see
a speaker too clearly. Her favorite hymn was *O Lord, What a Morning*, a song of suffering, and she hummed it under her breath whenever things got quiet. Her arms were large hickory-smoked hams,
and she carried them folded across her belly as though she always
ached there. Joe's favorite picture of her was when she stood on the
high porch every evening except Sunday of course, arms folded,
craning her neck and tilting her large body over the rail to catch
sight of the boy who came to tell what number had come out. That
was another part of her suffering, playing the numbers every day.

When Joe asked Miss Lavinia why Odessa didn't want to have
babies, Miss Lavinia was very surprised, and showed it by staring
harder at the floor. "Joe honey, Odessa told me *you* the one didn't
want no babies, that's why I recommended that pill. I certainly
don't believe in nobody bringing nobody else into this suffering
world."

Joe laid into Odessa that night after school. He slapped her so
hard she hit the wall and knocked down the framed copy of his high
school diploma. "You lying bitch, what you mean telling your Mama
I don't want no babies? I'm *dying* for some babies. And I'm going to
make me some right now." Odessa ran to the bedroom and tried to
crawl under the bed. But Joe dragged her back by the heels. She
screamed at the top of her lungs. "*Joe, what kind of world is this to
be having babies in?*" Joe was so surprised he just sat still on the
floor with her feet trapped in his hands. "What you mean, what
kind of world? It's the same world we always had. Ain't it? I can see
somebody like Miss Lavinia talking like that. But not a pretty
young woman like you. Odessa, this is 1967, we ain't back in no slavery time. You believe that stuff Miss Lavinia talk about? I don't see
nothing wrong with having babies."

He dragged her from under the bed by her heels, and she

came out shaking her head. "They killing colored people all over this country, Joe. They hanging them, and shooting them, and killing them with bombs, and running over them with cars. I don't want them things to happen to no child of mine, Joe. I just don't think I could stand it."

He opened his pants and her legs and moved on up inside her with all his clothes on and hers, too. "Nobody's going to lynch a child of mine," he said, remembering that his own grandfather had been lynched. "You think I'm going to all the trouble of giving somebody a baby, and then let somebody come along and lynch it?"

She was almost choking him to death with her arm around his neck. "Is that right, Joe? Is that right, Joe honey?"

"We can't stop having babies just because people getting killed."

"You right, Joe. You right, honey."

"I didn't know that's why you didn't want no babies. You should've told me before, Odessa. We could've had us a three- or four-year-old son by now."

"I always wanted me a daughter, Joe."

He grunted. It was getting pretty goddamned hard to talk now. "You . . . just . . . got . . . yourself . . . a . . . son," he said. He held her to the floor a long time after that, just in case she did want to go wash the boy out. But Odessa seemed all right now, she bet him five dollars it was a girl baby she said she felt already taking root inside her.

Next day, Joe made up his mind to quit college. He was only in his first year; but Odessa's attitude had started him thinking in a very different way. If his wife didn't want a baby in the kind of world they lived in, he looked around to see why she didn't.

Cousinsville was their world, and Cousinsville was the slums. Plus everything that goes with slums. The filth and overcrowding. Drugs. Crime. Never enough sun to get all the vitamins you needed, it was a good thing they were all colored, they didn't have to worry about getting tanned. But that didn't bother Joe too much, the lack of sunlight. He was a man who needed dark corners to operate in. He knew that. He sometimes still thought about when he'd been The Naked Disciple and those humid southern nights, the gloomy lanterns that were all the light they'd had. He looked good in that kind of light. Maybe it was like an old lady trying to hide her wrinkles—he was only twenty-eight—but up at Seton Hall, where he went to school, everything seemed too stark and somehow unreal in the plain light of day. Outside of Cousinsville was the white world; Joe felt safe and infinitely secure inside the colored world of Cousinsville because it was still a part of the United States. You couldn't find rats that big and healthy anywhere else, he thought with a smile.

Seriously, though, he couldn't see why anybody wouldn't want to have a baby in the United States. It was the greatest country in the world. Everybody knew that. Where else could you find somebody like him, for example? He thought that he was somebody pretty special. And wasn't he a direct product of discrimination, of Titus Market's idea that a colored man needed a colored religion, a colored way of life? He had never forgot Titus Market's talk about every man having to find his own salvation. Joe had the feeling that there was no salvation for him anywhere in the white world. It might not be in Cousinsville, either. But he was sure it wasn't in the clean, orderly streets around Seton Hall, where some people had small statues of nigger stable boys holding lanterns as an ornament to light their lawns.

As for college, he'd have to wait too long before an education really started paying off. With the baby coming, he couldn't afford to wait that long. Besides, he just wasn't the kind of guy to go to college, he'd already seen and done more than most other people would ever see or do. He had learned to think a little bit, and to talk like everybody else when he wanted to; and he was straight all the time. That was enough for him to get out of education. It didn't even occur to him to take off his clothes now, except at night to go to bed with Odessa. The earlier years with his father seemed like part of a distant dream.

Tony Brenzo got very angry when Joe told him that he was going to quit college. "You quit, and I'm going to put your ass in jail."

Joe was dead cool. "You'd better start putting, then. I'm quitting tomorrow. Besides, I don't hustle anymore. You know that."

"You still smoke pot."

"So do you."

Tony sighed. "Why, Joe? Why you want to quit college? Man, you've got a future to think about."

"I got a family coming now, Tony. I got to think about them now, not the future."

"Your family, your future . . . they're one and the same thing."

"And who's going to feed my family right now, Tony? The future? I got to worry about things right now. For all we know, there's not going to be any future." He had a special way of talking to Tony Brenzo. He was very careful to use good English most of the time, and to sound intelligent, to show Tony that the seven years spent in northern schools had been well spent. When he was with colored people, he didn't care how he talked. All he tried to do was get the idea across.

"Look around you, Joe. How can you say there's no future?'" Tony had come by the college for him, and they were walking along Decatur Street now in the middle of spring. The moon was in crescent, the maples along Decatur were fat with buds.

"You mean the trees, Tony?" He had to laugh. "For them, maybe there is a future. I'm talking about flesh and blood . . . about people that can feel, that get hungry, and die." It surprised him, saying something like that. He had never paid too much attention to people one way or another. But now he realized that people were very important to him. America was people. He told Tony so. "Maybe it's because Odessa's going to have a baby, I don't know. But I got this feeling about people that I never had before. There may be a future after all." He found that he could believe in more than the present, as long as there were people involved, and America, and a child of his own among them.

Tony walked a few minutes more in silence. "I'm tired of all this police crap," he said after a while. "Busting people, riding herd on a lot of laws that don't make sense anyway. I like people too, Joe. I like them too damned much to be crapping on them all the time in the name of the law. I've been thinking about joining the Army, just to get away from all this bullshit."

"*You* join the Army? What for? Man, you got it made as it is."

"Believe it or not, this is still a country where some men do patriotic things."

Joe shrugged. "Have fun, man. But I think you ought to make up your mind. First you want to join the Army to get away from all this bullshit. Now you want to join because you're patriotic." He started to whistle *My Country, 'Tis of Thee* in a lewd off-key.

"Getting away and being patriotic might just be the same thing," Tony said.

"That's sure stretching logic," Joe said skeptically. "I think you ought to go get some pussy, I bet you'll see things a whole lot different after that." But he saw that Tony was dead serious, and he stopped joking and draped his arm around Tony's shoulders. "Look, man, go ahead and join the Army if you have to. But don't go over there and get yourself killed in Vietnam, O.K.?"

"Who said anything about Vietnam? I just said I was going to join the Army."

"It's the same thing nowadays," Joe said. They had come to his house. He could see Odessa's shadow moving back and forth across the shades where they were pulled down. He felt a great need for Odessa right now, to pull her close to his chest and to protect her from the possibility of no future at all. "I'll be seeing you, Tony." Tony's face was agonized in the half-light. "Joe, buddy . . . *shit* . . . I wish you'd think some more before you quit school. I think you're making a big mistake."

"It's no mistake, Tony. I'm just not college material," Joe said flatly. Tony shrugged, and clapped him on the shoulder. "Give my regards to Odessa, then. Tell her I'll see her the next time I drop by."

Joe barely waited until Tony drove off before he bounded up the stairs and into the house. Odessa was dusting and arranging things in the living room, something to do until Joe came home from school. He dropped his books on the floor and walked over to her and wrapped his long arms all around her. He imagined that he could already feel the lump in her stomach where the baby was growing. "Let's go to bed," he said hoarsely. Odessa mashed herself closer to him. "All right, honey. I was here walking back and forth, not knowing what I really wanted to do. But this is what I want to do. I want to go to bed with you." For some reason, he felt like crying. It was spring. The trees were budding. And so was Odessa. What a pity that America wasn't a large and beautiful black woman, budding all the time.

Later on, Odessa asked him, "Did you see Tony? I saw his car parked outside. I thought he must've walked up to the school."

"He did. He sent you his regards. He said he'd see you the next time he dropped by." Joe was smoking pot, he did that now from time to time when he felt under a lot of pressure. Odessa didn't mind his smoking pot, but she didn't like to smoke it herself. She said it made her too silly. Releasing the smoke from his chest, Joe opened his eyes and stared straight up at the ceiling. There was something full and expectant about the night, like a dark flower about to burst into satisfying bloom. He put his hand on Odessa's belly and massaged the mound there. "You're getting fat."

"Not yet, silly! But pretty soon. I'm going to have to start letting out my dresses."

He lit a straight cigarette. "What would you say if I told you I was going to join the Army?"

Odessa raised up on one elbow. She was quiet a long while, running her finger up and down his chest to show that she was thinking. "What about school? You going to finish school?"

"I can study in the Army and get through a lot quicker. There was a recruiting sergeant out at the school one day, and I asked him some questions. Besides, with you and the baby as dependents, and if I can make some rank, I could make the same money now that I'd make if I waited to graduate from college in three more years."

Odessa was very quiet. "I'd miss you if you went."

"I'd miss you, too. You know that." Something in his voice told them both that he had definitely made up his mind to go.

"It's going to be hard having the baby without you here to help me."

"Your mother would help you. It's the baby I'm thinking of. That's why I want to go in. Odessa . . . you understand, honey?" She nodded against his shoulder. She was quiet again.

"Suppose they send you to Vietnam?"

"Everybody in the Army ain't in Vietnam."

"But suppose they send you?"

He was getting tired of all this talk. "Suppose they don't? Anyway, it'd mean more money. And that's why I'm going in. For the money." He threw his body at Odessa, just to make her shut up. But Odessa rolled over and started to love him up. She went all over his body like a slobbering wet dog, that was the kind of sex he really liked. It made him feel like a god, somebody loving him up that way.

He would go join the Army and help win the war, like that recruiting sergeant had said. That way, things would be safe and very good for his son. And for himself and Odessa, with the money he'd make. He'd join the Army with Tony Brenzo. Suppose they did send him to Vietnam? He sprawled and lit a joint. Hell, you had to die sometime. Might as well die and get a medal for it.

Two days later, he telephoned Tony Brenzo at Police Headquarters. They chatted about a couple of other things before Joe said, "Look, man, I want to join the Army with you. When you going for the examination?"

"I've already been," Tony said. "I went yesterday." He sounded as though he didn't believe that Joe wanted to join the Army. "Anyway, they turned me down. I've got a busted eardrum that I didn't know a thing about." Joe was very disappointed. "I'm sorry to hear that, man." But Tony still did not take him seriously. "Quit your clowning," he said, laughing. "I think *you* need some pussy to clear your head." In a little while, he hung up.

Joe stayed in the telephone booth a few minutes more. Shit man, the only reason he'd wanted to join the Army in the first place was because Tony had said that he was going to join. Now he felt like he'd walked right into some kind of a trap, because he certainly didn't want to go to the Army all by himself.

He had telephoned from Cheap Mary's, a notions store owned

by an old Jewish woman on the corner of Hickory and Decatur Streets. The cab stand where Pee Wee worked was right outside the store. But Pee Wee's cab wasn't there, and Joe decided to cross Hickory Street to have a beer at Roscoe's Tavern. Maybe he'd find somebody there who'd join the Army with him. But just as he was crossing Hickory Street, Pee Wee pulled up and blew his horn noisily at Joe. "Hey baby, what's happening?" Pee Wee bounced around behind the steering wheel like a monkey on a string, he always seemed happy to see Joe. "Everything's cool, baby." Joe got in the cab with Pee Wee. The Jewish woman they called Cheap Mary was peering out the window of her store to see why the cab horn had been blowing. She seemed annoyed, and Joe told Pee Wee so. Pee Wee laughed. "Man, that old white woman's mad just because she's been living too long." He took out a joint, lit it, and gave it to Joe. They smoked quietly for a while, passing the joint back and forth until it had burned down to a small roach that Pee Wee chewed up to keep anybody from finding it lying around in his cab.

Joe had got very high. "Man, that was some cool grass," he said. It had been a long time since he smoked that much pot at one time. His eyeballs felt scorched in their sockets, but he felt good just being here high with Pee Wee on the corner of Hickory and Decatur, a spring day like this one—man, it was April, he'd just turned twenty-eight last week and Easter was the day after tomorrow, so this was Good Friday, Jesus Christ was going to resurrect himself come Sunday. "Up from the dead he arose, he arose from the dead." Joe sang that softly, a good old Easter hymn. But he believed that Jesus Christ was springtime, a real kind of god that came from the ground each year—the green grass, budding trees, growing things. Titus had made that comparison in a sermon once, and Joe liked the idea of Jesus as springtime. His resurrection was nothing more or less than the coming of spring. Joe sang, "Up from the dead he arose. . . ."

Pee Wee half-smiled; his eyes were blood red from the pot. "How come you ain't working today?" he asked Joe. "I didn't feel like it," Joe said. Man, he didn't give a shit for Easter the way other people celebrated it. That was the only reason everybody was knocking himself out to work, so they'd have money to spend for Easter. Well, Joe wasn't interested in spending or working, because he knew that Easter was nothing more than springtime. Besides, Mr. Yen never said anything to him when he took a day off, because he always made up for it the next day by working extra hard. And he was screwing China Doll from time to time, which meant that she'd keep Mr. Yen from firing him, if the thought ever came to the old man's head. It was around ten o'clock in the morning, and the streets of Cousinsville were quiet and unhurried. A balmy sun shone at a quiet, discreet distance above the top of the slum.

"Pee Wee?"

"Yeah, man?"

"You my friend, Pee Wee?"

Pee Wee sighed. "You going back to that again? Man, you ask me that every week or two. Sure I'm your friend, you know that."

Joe smiled. Good old Pee Wee, he could always depend on him. "Man, I want you to join the Army with me," Joe said. He was so glad that he wouldn't have to go alone.

"*What?* Join the *Army? Me?* Man, you sick in the head or something?"

Well. He certainly hadn't expected that reaction from Pee Wee, not from a friend. "Believe it or not," he said, recalling Tony Brenzo's words with a small display of indignation, "this still is a country in which some men do patriotic things."

"Well, you be as patriotic as you want," Pee Wee said, like a perfect little coward. "I'm going to stay right here and drive my cab. Besides, I got flat feet."

"I don't believe it," Joe said. Man, who would've thought that Pee Wee was such a whining coward? He turned his head delicately away while Pee Wee took off his shoes and socks, because Pee Wee had the stinkingest feet in the whole Decatur section of Cousinsville. "You see?" Pee Wee said. Cautiously, Joe looked. Aside from being dirty, Pee Wee's feet were as flat as two pancakes. And stinking like two skunks. Joe scrambled from the cab; he didn't want to hold his nose because Pee Wee would be insulted. But he couldn't stand it in that cab a minute longer. Pee Wee had never smelled like that when they lived together, this was a real new thing, his stinking so much. "Well, thanks man . . . I'll see you around," Joe said. He was already halfway across Hickory Street. "You serious about joining the Army?" Pee Wee said from the cab window. "I'll talk to you about that later," Joe said. He ducked into Roscoe's Tavern. There was a half-curtain stretched across the window, and Joe could see Pee Wee struggling to get his shoes and socks back on. He was afraid that Pee Wee might follow him here into the tavern, and he was relieved when Pee Wee stopped struggling and rested his head back on the seat, yawning as if he was going to sleep.

The tavern was empty except for Roscoe. He was the owner, but he sometimes worked as bartender. He was short and light-skinned, with freckles the size of huckleberries all over his face and hands. "Roscoe, gimme a drink," Joe said. Roscoe was watching television. The Gale Storm Show. He wiped his hands on his apron and started to fill a glass with draft beer while Joe went to the bathroom. He felt dirty after smelling Pee Wee's feet, and he wanted to wash his hands; but the bathroom was too dirty for that. It was almost too dirty to take a leak in. But Joe did manage to pee; then he went back to the bar and saw that a guy named Lamont Cranston Jones had come in. "Hello, Joe," Lamont said. He sounded just like Pearl Bailey. Joe looked Lamont up and down, sizing him up all over. Lamont was around Joe's age, extremely handsome in a pretty kind of way, with processed hair and one gold tooth that shone like a beacon through his thick, smiling lips. *I'm going to make this monkey join the Army with me*, Joe thought. He said, "Lamont baby, what's happening, Daddy-O?" He wrapped his arm around Lamont's shoulders and told Roscoe to give his *good* friend a drink. "Well, I'm flattered," Lamont said. He ordered Scotch for himself; Joe sipped his beer.

Lamont was an old friend of China Doll's, and Joe had met him that way. But he didn't especially like Lamont. For one thing, there was something very sissified about him that went against Joe's grain. He certainly didn't have anything against sissies, although they were very different from out-and-out queers. Joe defined a sissy as an undeclared queer; and he felt somewhat uncomfortable even being with Lamont. Not that he was afraid that Lamont would declare himself with him—that didn't bother Joe at all; in fact, he was waiting for it—but because Lamont was such a sissy that he did his best to come on like a real he-man. Which just made him sound like Pearl Bailey most of the time.

He always drank top-shelf Scotch, he said he thought beer was weak. He sat with his legs spread open so you could see he had a little dick. His nails were nicely manicured, but he wore male-looking rings—a zircon on each hand in a massive false gold setting—that he ordered from coupons on the backs of comic books. Delicately, with his little finger poked out like he might have been picking his nose or drinking a cup of tea, he scratched his tiny balls from time to time, as though to make sure they hadn't vanished in the intervals between.

Joe only had a few dollars, and they disappeared very rapidly, what with Lamont gulping down double Scotches now, he felt that much of a man. After two or three of those doubles, Lamont started talking about his secret ambitions. "I've always wanted to exercise an influence over a large number of people," he said, flashing both zircons at once. He'd been working in the public relations office at Seton Hall University, he said, although he was collecting unemployment now. The University had asked him to leave because he kept writing things that were too way out for Seton Hall. "Like the time I sent a release out saying that the University was designing a special stamp for the Post Office Department to commemorate the eating of the first hog chitterlings in America." Joe laughed, and Lamont's eyes bubbled with mirth. He gulped the second half of his Scotch and banged, man-like, on the bar for another. "Or the time I wrote a release saying that Seton Hall was backing a movement to re-elect John Kennedy President of the United States posthumously." But when Joe didn't laugh at that, Lamont said, "Well, anything's possible in America, you know." And when Joe still didn't laugh, he said, looking at his polished nails, "In case you don't know, *posthumously* means *after death*." Joe ordered another beer. "I know what it means. It's just that I liked President Kennedy, and I don't see any reason for making jokes about the fact that he got shot." There was an uncomfortable silence between them for a few seconds. Then Lamont laughed in what he must have thought was a masculine way, scratching his balls at the same time to make sure they were still there, and dragged out a twenty-dollar bill from his pants pocket. "Man, all I was doing was trying to influence people, that's why I was so way out. Listen . . . I been saving this money to buy my mother a ham for Easter Sunday. But I feel like we ought to drink it up, you and me, being that we're such good buddies." Joe thought that Lamont was a first-class prick, but he came on like he agreed. After all, he needed somebody to join the Army with him. And shit, man, after he'd already told Odessa he was going, he didn't want to go back on his word. Even if it meant joining up with a sissy like Lamont Cranston Jones. Of all the dumb goddamned names he'd ever heard, that one took the cake.

Joe lit a joint and smoked it. "Here's to you," he said to Lamont. But Lamont grinned timidly. "Pot makes me do crazy things," he said. "Liquor's my poison." Roscoe moved down the bar and took a few drags. Then Joe and Lamont took a booth and settled down to what Lamont called the *serious* business of drinking. After a while, he started talking again about his personal ambitions.

"I've thought that someday I would write a book," he said. Joe asked him about what. "About my life. About my stupid, silly, fucked-up life." His voice dropped to a scared whisper. "You know my mother, don't you?" Now he rolled his eyes around to see who else might hear. "Well, she's trying to kill me. Or make me commit suicide, which is the same thing." Joe just grinned. The pot and liquor had him very high now, and he thought that was the funniest thing he'd ever heard, Lamont talking about his own mother trying to kill him. "Mothers don't do that," Joe said. "Fathers, maybe. But not mothers. . . ." Lamont wasn't even listening, the way he cut in bitterly. "I know you think my name is stupid," he said. "Everybody thinks so, except my mother. You know who Lamont Cranston is? He's The Shadow, you remember that old radio program? *Who knows what evil lurks in the hearts of men? The Shadow knows.*" He laughed diabolically, just like the program. "My mother fell in love with The Shadow's voice, and she named me after him. She wanted me to sound like The Shadow when I grew up. And I grew up sounding like Pearl Bailey. That was a great disappointment to my mother. She wanted me to be greater than Jesus Christ and Frederick Douglass combined, a real leader of my people, making speeches everywhere with my voice sounding like The Shadow's. So that's why I make an ass of myself doing the kind of crap that got me fired from Seton Hall." He was very drunk now, because Roscoe was keeping them both supplied. "You know what I mean, Joe? I didn't turn out to be the kind of man my mother wanted me to be. And that's why she's trying to kill me. She's disappointed in me, she's ashamed of me. She's always telling me I ought to get married and have children." His mouth puckered like he was going to cry. "I think she thinks I'm *queer*. I can see it in her eyes, and that's the main reason she wants to kill me. She thinks I'm queer. And that makes her boiling mad, and she wants to kill me because she gave me The Shadow's name, and I turned out talking like Pearl Bailey. . . ."

One part of Joe wanted to laugh at Lamont's story. But another part of him believed it. He knew Mrs. Jones very well—a fierce old black woman with hollow eyes, eternally frowning, and in a hurry to get from one place to another—and he had a sneaking suspicion that she did want to kill Lamont. Because she had two favorite subjects: how much better off dead people were than live people, she was so tired of living in all this mess; and how much of a real man her dead husband had been, she knew *he* had gone to heaven, no doubt about that. Joe shook his head. Suggestion is a powerful thing, and it did seem to be working on Lamont. Right now, he looked like he was trying to drink himself to death because he couldn't live up to what his mother wanted him to be.

"That's why I want to do something really big," Lamont said, "something to impress my mother so much that she'll have to respect me." He examined his polished nails. "It upsets her that I want to be a writer, that I get my nails polished. I know she thinks I'm queer. And I know she wants me to die. Oh, she's subtle, all right. But she wants it." There were a few dollars left from the twenty; he pushed them aimlessly around the table. "I even try to buy her nice things so she'll lighten up on me, so she won't always be hinting that maybe I'd be better off dead. That's why I was going to buy her a ham for Easter, so maybe she'd say, *Why thank you, son, I know my baby's a real man now*." His mouth puckered, and this time he actually did cry. "Now I can't buy her a ham for Easter, I can't buy her a goddamned thing. And she's just going to keep all that shit up, picking, needling, pushing, trying to make me blow my brains out."

Joe felt very sorry for Lamont. Shit man, that must really be a drag, having a mother that kept trying to make you kill yourself. "Lamont, don't you worry about that ham. I've got another idea. People eat turkey for Easter too, don't they?" Lamont nodded, and Joe said, "Well, don't you worry none, I just got me a good idea. I'm going to get you a turkey for your mother for Easter." He gazed at Lamont with a shrewd eye. "Only, you got to do me a favor in return. Is that agreed?"

Lamont was very happy now, he was smiling like a wet-cheeked girl. "Agreed, Joe. Man, I'd do *anything* for you if you just help me out right now."

Anything? Getting up to take a leak, Joe smiled. He had somebody to join the Army with him after all, because he damned sure didn't want to go there by himself.

Lamont was half-dozing at the table when Joe got back. He helped Lamont up and settled with Roscoe at the bar. By the time they got through paying, Lamont had about sixty cents left out of the twenty dollars; he gave that to Roscoe for a tip. "See you boys around," Roscoe said. He went back to watching television. The Flintstones. Joe steered Lamont out the door. Pee Wee's cab was gone and Joe was glad of that, he didn't want to be messing with Pee Wee right now.

"Where we going?" Lamont said. He had his arm wrapped heavily around Joe's shoulders, his body moulded to Joe's in an intimate way. "We have to hop some fences," Joe said. He was going to steal Mr. Yen's pet turkey so Lamont could give that to his mother for Easter. But Mr. Yen's backyard was halfway up the block, and they'd have to hop about ten or twelve fences starting with Cheap

Mary's here on the corner, if the old Jew woman didn't see them. Joe peered at the store, but he could not see her there. Which was worse, since it meant that she might be out farting around in her backyard. But he felt they had to take the chance, that turkey was really important to Lamont, Joe could see that now. "Come on, let's go, man." He ducked across Hickory Street and up the alley beside Cheap Mary's; Lamont followed him in a drunken wobble.

When Joe got to the end of the alley, he hunkered down in a tight crouch. The alley turned at a right angle and went up to Cheap Mary's back door. Straight ahead of them was Mary's yard, bounded on this side and that by a low wire fence. There were about six or seven yards like this one between them and Mr. Yen's. Craning his neck some, looking over and around the clotheslines and fences between, Joe could see Mr. Yen's grape arbors and the curling vines already in the first stages of turning green.

Lamont was jammed right behind him. "Shhhhh!" Joe warned. He sneaked an eye around the corner, but Cheap Mary's yard was bare. Joe raised up and took the fence in a broad, graceful jump. Lamont followed him, scrambling over with a look of wild glee on his pretty face.

It was around one o'clock in the afternoon now. While the sun did not shine down into those yards, it did hover overhead as a kind of reminder that day was still there. Joe thought there was something very daring about their daytime raid on Mr. Yen's backyard. He took the next fence, and the next, with a growing sense of excitement. Lamont puffed along behind him, panting, sweating and happy. "You're a real friend," he whispered to Joe once. "Nobody's ever been this good to me before." Joe nodded. "Just you remember," he said, "that one good turn deserves another." They dropped together into Mr. Yen's backyard. Ming, Mr. Yen's large pet turkey, looked at them with a kind of mild surprise in his round, bright eyes. "I'll remember," Lamont said. Joe held up his hand for silence.

His own house was next door, but he knew that Odessa was at work behind the counter in Mr. Yen's laundry out front. At this hour, China Doll and Mr. Yen were probably having lunch in the large dining room toward the front of the house on the second floor. Most of the backyard was given over to the grape arbors, and the windows overlooking them in Mr. Yen's apartment belonged to the kitchen and the pantry. If the turkey didn't make too much noise, Joe figured, there was very little chance of anybody seeing them down here.

"The turkey's name is Ming," Joe said. He didn't want Lamont to steal something he didn't know the name of. Lamont nodded and half-bowed toward the bird, as though they had been formally introduced. Joe took a cautious step forward; bright eyes staring straight at them, wattles hanging in red wrinkles, Ming took a precise step away.

He was tied to a wooden stob by a length of twine up under the sheltering vines. He had been Mr. Yen's pet for a long time, and he had grown large and fat; he must have weighed a good thirty pounds. As Joe and Lamont crept toward him, Ming raised his long neck and gobbled two or three times.

Then, Joe pounced. He wrapped both hands around the turkey's neck, but he couldn't stop it from gobbling. Lamont was right there with him, hanging on to the turkey's feet. But Ming was putting up one hell of a commotion, flapping his wings so hard that dirt rose up in clouds underneath the arbor. Every now and then, a gobble escaped from his throat, although Joe was squeezing with all his might.

"This motherfucker won't die!" Joe growled. That seemed to make Lamont very mad, and he started kicking Ming in the butt with the delicate point of his shoe, as though that would help kill him. Then Joe realized what was wrong—that turkey had some kind of powerful windpipe that you couldn't just choke, you had to wring his neck. Joe shifted his hands, and in the second it took him to do that, Ming let out an agonized screech that sounded almost human. "Turkey, you shut up!" Joe hissed. He doubled the turkey's neck back and twisted it until it broke.

An ominous silence settled over everything. Then, in the next minute, they heard the window upstairs slam open, and Mr. Yen's voice jabbering in excited Chinese. That surprised Joe, the fact that

Mr. Yen was speaking Chinese, because he had only heard the old Chinaman speak English. "Man, we better get out of here!" Lamont whispered. He was going all to pieces, and that made Joe determined that he was going to be very cool. Almost leisurely, he picked the dead turkey up in his arms and went to the cellar door. "I'm going to hide out here with the turkey until things quiet down," he told Lamont. "You beat it. If I go with the turkey now, somebody's going to see me. I'll get in touch with you later on." He could hear footsteps rattling inside the building, and two or three more voices now mixed with Mr. Yen's. Lamont darted under the arbor to the fence and sprang over into the next yard. Calmly, Joe opened the cellar door; he broke the twine from the turkey's neck and stuffed it into his pocket. Then he stepped inside the cool cellar. He moved down a few steps and sat there with the turkey in his arms. He could hear Mr. Yen jabbering outside now. Then he heard China Doll say crossly, "Why don't you speak English? Who the devil you think understand Chinese here but you?" And Mr. Yen switched to English right in the middle of a sentence. ". . . *is gone!* My turkey *is gone*! My turkey . . . !"

"I know that," China said. She sounded somewhat bored. "I can see that. The question is, who stole it?"

Surprisingly, Joe heard Odessa's voice; he had been sure that she'd stay out front and tend the register. "Probably some little mannish boys," she said.

"Well, I guess there's not too much we can do about it," China said. Joe could almost see her shrug.

"Odessa, I want you to call the police," Mr. Yen said. His voice was dead calm now.

"What?" Both women sounded surprised. Joe was surprised, too. He'd never even thought about Mr. Yen calling the police; that showed he was a cheap Chinaman, Mr. Yen, because no American would ever think of calling the police about somebody stealing his turkey.

"Man, you must be kidding!" China said. "With all the police got to do, you think they interested in who stole your turkey?"

"Odessa, call the police," Mr. Yen said firmly.

"I'm almost ashamed to," Odessa said. "And the only reason I'll call them is because I work for you. But this is Good Friday, honey, I sure hope them policemen don't crucify *you*." Joe heard her high heels clicking down the alley, and he could tell that she was deliberately shaking her behind from the way her heels sounded.

"Well, we might as well go on back upstairs," China said. "Besides, you look terrible, Mr. Yen. You shouldn't let things affect you so. Come on now, sugar. Let's go back upstairs."

"I loved that turkey," Mr. Yen said. His voice sounded extremely feeble. "Who would be mean enough to steal something I care so much about?"

China's voice was very soothing now. "There's a lot of mean folks about," she said. "I caught sight of somebody jumping over the fence just when we got downstairs. Maybe the police will find out who did it. I'm sure it was just some little mannish boys, like Odessa said. But you got to go upstairs and rest now, sugar. Your color don't look exactly right."

The turkey was warm and heavy on Joe's lap. He shifted the body some and looked for a joint in his sock where he carried them. There was one left, and he was about to light it there at the door. But then he decided to move farther inside the cellar, just so the cops wouldn't smell pot smoke right there if they decided to open the door.

The cellar was very dark, and he dared not put on the light. Feeling with his feet, carrying the dead turkey in both arms, he moved over to where Mr. Yen kept several barrels of wine. He climbed up on the last of the barrels, resting his back against the cool wall. The turkey felt very warm and comfortable across his thighs and crotch. He lighted the joint now and sucked smoke into his lungs. His head was filled with the odor of pot and must and wine.

When he started to see stars spinning on the back part of his eyeballs, he let the pot smoke out. His heart was beating wildly. He thought, *Today is Good Friday and this turkey or me, one of us is Christ in the tomb*. That surprised him, as though the apparatus of his thinking had been taken over by other hands, because he had never thought like that before. But today was Good Friday. And he had killed the turkey. And the cellar was as dark and enclosing as a tomb. The idea tickled him of Christ being a dead turkey, or of a dead turkey being Christ. It sounded just as silly as when he had been The Naked Child and The Naked Disciple. Or when May had been the Virgin Mary and he had been the Christchild in the Christmas tableau back in Burnside.

But he had never believed that he was anybody's Saviour. He had wondered sometimes if he might not be a god. With all that Titus had put him through, he had thought that was possible. And he had thought so right up until that farmer kicked him in the butt in Louisiana. Talking with Pee Wee later on in the boxcar had only convinced him of what he had already found out, how much bullshit their religion had been. As for that other bullshit, about his being a god, he'd got that idea from Titus anyway. He hadn't even known then what a god was, except that it was somebody Titus sucked on whenever he had the appetite. Considering that, and the fact that he'd been showing himself naked to people every day from the time he was twelve until he was sixteen, he didn't think he'd turned out so peculiar after all.

And as for being the Saviour, he'd heard enough talk about Jesus Christ to know that a Saviour is somebody you love and worship and respect. In case some of his believers want to be fucked by him, all the Saviour has to do is make something like a hypnotic gesture, and that person is immediately filled with magic dick. But never with the Saviour's. Joe had figured that out one night a long time ago when he was just plain tired of fucking, and he had tried to fill two or three people with magic dick by gesturing. But those people had paid their money, and they wanted his good hard dick rammed up inside them, none of that magic shit. Which was the best way in the world for him to understand that he was flesh and blood like everybody else, having to fuck men and women who can't feel that they're sucking you or being fucked by you just by looking at you or being in your presence. Joe had worked this out by himself; but he had never complained to Titus because he had actually liked what he was doing, although it had tired him out sometimes. But he had certainly never thought that he was anybody's Saviour or even "the one who comes before Him," that was some more bullshit of Titus'. In fact, now that he'd gotten older, he was looking for a Saviour himself, if he could ever convince himself that he had done evil, or sinned against anybody. And to save him from all the noisy shit that a black man has to put up with in America, no matter that he did love her.

Joe shifted the turkey's weight on his lap. So, this turkey had to be Christ, because he knew damn well that *he* wasn't. He was just plain Joe Market, black, age twenty-eight, trying like hell to get somebody to join the Army with him. That's why he was sitting here high out of his mind on a wine barrel, holding a dead turkey across his lap. To give Lamont for his mother, so that Lamont would feel indebted to him and join the fucking Army with him.

He almost laughed out loud then. Because it struck him that Lamont was the perfect sacrifice for this Good Friday. All that stuff he'd told Joe about his mother, he might have been Jesus Christ complaining to some of his cronies in a Nazarene bar. *Brethren, my mother wants me to be Christ, and I can't even talk right, I sound like Pearl Bailey.* Man, wouldn't that be something, Christ bitching because his mother wanted him to have enough balls to die on the cross according to the prophecies. . . .

Still, he was glad that he had found Lamont to go to the Army with him. Not that he was afraid to go alone, he just wanted somebody there who knew him when he won all those medals and promotions he planned to get, fighting for America. He'd had a secret desire to be a soldier ever since he'd seen some of them leaving May Jones' house down in Burnside. Laughing and talking in a carefree way, ties loose and uniforms wrinkled after a session with May in her sweet peas, they had seemed the highest example of hardy manhood, ready to fight for their country and their loved ones. Joe felt the same way when he saw a war picture, a sense of the spirit and glory of war between men—killing because you had to, drinking hard, fighting hard, fucking hard . . . dying hard, if you had to. . . . Lost inside his fantasy, he imagined that the turkey in his arms was a dead buddy shot to death on the battlefield of righteousness. And he was a good buddy holding back tears, cradling his dead friend's body in a shining display of duty and devotion to that beautiful, irresistible white woman, America. . . .

He heard footsteps then coming up the alley, and all his senses turned on. That heavy, arrogant way of walking could only belong to cops. Joe stubbed out the joint and drew up his legs, squatting there on the wine barrel like an Indian statue, the turkey resting on both his extended arms as though in offering to the cellar's all-consuming darkness. He sat very still and listened.

"What time did the crime occur?" This cop sounded very sarcastic.

"It must have been around one thirty or quarter to two," China said. "My husband could probably tell you more exactly, but he's indisposed at the moment."

"Was he the one that called the cops?" He sounded menacing and very pissed-off, and China coughed in a way that was obviously intended to be apologetic. "My husband is Chinese, gentlemen. Although he's lived in this country a number of years, he's not yet up on American ways. No, he didn't call the police. But he did tell one of our employees to do so. . . ."

"It's the same thing," another police voice said, different from the first. "Sure we're interested in stolen property. . . ."

"But a *turkey*," the first police voice said. He sounded completely disgusted.

"My sentiments exactly," China said. "I'm sorry you gentlemen went to all this trouble. But I will tell my husband that you all are investigating the case. I gave him a mild sedative and he's sleeping now, but he'll be very happy to know that you gentlemen responded so quickly. . . ."

"Yeah, yeah, sure. . . ."

"Yeah. They wouldn't do the same thing in China, I guarantee you that."

"I'm certain you're right," China said sweetly. Joe heard them all going down the alley, and he couldn't help but grin. That China was really something, the way she'd handled those policemen. Still, who did give a damn about a turkey? The only reason Mr. Yen was carrying on so was because he was Chinese. Lord, no real American would care one way or the other.

Joe was tired of being in the cellar, but it was still broad daylight outdoors, and he would be caught if he left now. Then everybody would care about Mr. Yen's turkey, seeing him with it in broad daylight. He decided to go to sleep. He climbed down off the barrel and found a clear place on the floor with his feet. Using the turkey as a pillow, he lay down and soon fell into a deep sleep.

When he finally did wake up, it was dark outside. Carrying the turkey, Joe picked his way over to the cellar door and crept into the backyard. He figured that it must be around seven or eight o'clock, being as dark as it was. Man, that pot really had knocked him out. Hefting the turkey, he went back over the fences the same way that he had come with Lamont. Quietly, he went down the alley beside Cheap Mary's to Hickory Street. Pee Wee's cab wasn't on the corner, and that annoyed Joe. So he walked to Lamont's house on Pierson Street. There were a few people out, but none of them paid any attention to the fact that he was carrying a dead turkey, now that it was night.

Lamont was reading *Ebony* when Joe got there. He looked a mess, but his whole face lit up when he opened the door and saw Joe standing there with the turkey. "Ohhhhhh. . . ." He cooed like a woman getting fucked. Holding his finger to his lips, he took the turkey from Joe and stashed it behind the sofa. "I'll get up early tomorrow morning and pick it," he said. "Ohhhhhh. . . ."

Just then, Lamont's mother called from her bedroom. "Lamont! Lamont! Is that one of your *men* friends?" She put so much emphasis on the word that anybody would have known what she meant.

"Yes, mother . . . but there's nothing going on, I assure you," Lamont said indignantly. "You don't have to stop watching television, you can stay right there." His voice dropped to a whisper again. "Joe, man, I *knew* you wouldn't let me down. You really have done me a big favor."

"I'm glad to hear that, Lamont. Now I want you to do me one."

"What's that? I'd do *anything* for you now." Joe would have sworn that Lamont looked at his dick. Well, not that kind of favor, baby. At least, not now, anyway.

"Lamont?" His mother again.

Joe took a deep breath. "I want you to join the Army with me, man." Lamont's eyes bugged out of his head, but he didn't say a word.

"Lamont, why you and your man friend whispering so quiet out there? Lamont, you doing something *you're not supposed to*?"

Joe nodded toward the bedroom door. "It'd make her think that you're really a man. And it's a chance for glory, Lamont, for the big things you said you wanted to do. You could win medals. . . ."

"Lamont?"

Both of them could hear the old woman's feet hit the floor.

"Lamont!"

Hurriedly, Lamont pushed Joe toward the door. "I'll do it," he said. "Monday morning, after Easter's over, I'll join the Army with you." He closed the door.

And on Monday morning, Joe and Lamont did go to join the Army. They passed both the mental and physical tests, and were sent to Fort Hood, Texas, for three months' basic training. Their fourth month, without even a furlough home, they were shipped off to Vietnam.

After his self-assured bragging to the contrary, propped up by the fact that Odessa was well into her third month of pregnancy, Joe was surprised and offended to find out that the Army really was go-ing to send him to Vietnam. And before the baby was born, even. He would have thought that it was something they were doing to him just because he was colored, except that a lot of white boys were on the same ship with him and Lamont out of San Francisco. Man, he hated the Army. Five minutes after he joined he knew it was the biggest mistake he'd ever made in his life. He thought that military crap was the coldest shit in town, and he was surly and in-different all through basic training. Some monkeys kept trying to make a boxer or a football player out of him, just because they thought he was as dumb as he was big, but he told them what they could do with their footballs and boxing gloves, if their assholes were big enough. He hadn't been home in all the time he'd been in the Army, which he thought was somebody's way of being very clever. Because if they were dumb enough to give him leave, he certainly was smart enough never to come back to the Army. He could desert, he knew that; but it just seemed too much trouble to go through. Besides, they could shoot you for doing that. But he'd desert as sure as hell if they gave him five minutes outside of camp. And while it did fuck him up that the Army was sending him to Vietnam, he'd reached the point by that time where he expected anything from something so childish and absurdly chickenshit.

As for Lamont, he took to the Army like a sissy to a dick. It was like he'd been born for all those rules and regulations. He was the sharpest thing in camp, always polished and pressed, a real military example. But it was true that four months in the Army away from his mother had done wonders for Lamont. He still talked like Pearl Bailey from time to time, mostly when he was excited. But the Army routine had flattened down and leaned out his body so that he looked less like a cunt when he walked. While Joe remained a private, Lamont was promoted to corporal after only a month or two in Vietnam. And when the Army found out about his public relations work at Seton Hall, they tried to assign him to a public information job in Vietnam. But Lamont thought that didn't sound *man* enough; what he preferred was to be in the same company with Joe. He sucked somebody's ass, which is what you always have to do in the Army to get something done; and he and Joe both wound up doing long-range reconnaissance patrols in Vietnam for an airborne brigade.

There were six men on a team, three of them white and three colored, just in case any question came up about integration. The patrol leader was a big Italian guy from New York named Mike Martucci. He reminded Joe of Tony Brenzo, the fact that Tony and Mike were both black Italians. But the resemblance stopped right there. Because Sgt. Martucci was Army all the way. He played football and boxed—he was another guy who tried to recruit Joe for sports—and he seemed to think that everybody who didn't go out for sports was a faggot. But he was a good leader, and the other white boys were all right, too, which made for a good working team. Lamont stuck so close to Mike's tail that Mike made him assistant patrol leader after the other assistant got killed on punji sticks. Those were sharp-tipped bamboo sticks smeared with human shit that the Viet Cong left camouflaged in traps. You fell or stepped on one of those sticks, the shit went right into your body and caused an infection. It was a slow, evil way to die. The assistant patrol leader died that way, and Mike named Lamont to take his place. Which was all right with the other guys, because the Army didn't pay one cent more for the job. Lamont wrote his mother excitedly and told her about his new honor. But Mrs. Jones apparently remained unyielding in her distaste for him, although he wrote her regularly twice a week, and sent her a large allotment check each month.

The patrol's job was to seek out the Viet Cong for their brigade. Like every other scout, Joe Market carried a Claymore mine, 240 rounds of ammunition for his M-16 automatic rifle, four canteens of water and three meals of dried meat with rice. He also had a flare gun, compass, signal mirror, anti-dysentery pills, pep pills for drowsiness, codeine to stop coughs that might give away a position, and tape to close off the wrists and ankles of his uniform to keep out leeches. He kept his M-16 rifle always at the ready. He wore a black-and-green tiger suit that made him blend into the foliage. Sometimes he'd think about all the snazzy clothes he used to wear back home, and he'd smile at how damn far he was away from all that now. He also had morphine for wounds, as well as some pot—which was not Government issue—to make everything seem unreal when reality threatened to overwhelm him. As far as he could see, every American in Vietnam smoked pot. Or almost every American. You could buy it in any cabaret or back alley in Hue or Saigon. Everybody in Joe's patrol used it, except for Lamont, who was high on just being in the Army. Even Sgt. Martucci used pot, and that made everything very cool, since nobody had to hide or sneak around in order to turn on.

When Thanksgiving came, the Army filled them up on turkey, which reminded Lamont of the turkey that Joe had stolen for his mother. "Man, I never told you," Lamont said, leaning intimately over the mess table, "but my mother didn't even eat that turkey, she said it was too tough. So she cut it up in pieces that she wrapped in tinfoil and kept in the icebox for the cat. Man, there was enough turkey there to last that cat for a year." He laughed with a sudden heavy vigor. Then he started telling everybody at the table about how he and his good buddy Joe had stolen that turkey just last Easter, it sounded like such a man thing to do. Joe left the table and went to see if there was any mail.

Odessa was in her seventh month of pregnancy; she wrote him that she was as big as a barn. Joe was glad to hear that. He couldn't stop thinking about the coming baby, and he even wrote to Odessa that the only reason he didn't desert the fucking Army was because they were going to have a baby. All the money he could send her was a few measly dollars a month, which he thought was a disgrace; but that was all he could afford out of what he made. "Now don't you keep on talking like that," Odessa wrote him back. "We're all very proud of you, what you're doing for your country, fighting over there in Vietnam." Shit. It galled him that he used to talk the same way, before he joined the Army.

Sometimes he felt like telling Odessa what the score really was in Vietnam, because most of her letters sounded like propaganda from the Defense Department. He'd write, *Odessa honey, don't write me any more of that shit. Somebody over here's trying to kill me. And that makes all the difference in the world.* He was in a movie one day when the damn thing blew up. Another time, a VC sniper almost shot him in the street. He heard the bullets peppering around him with a kind of lip-smacking delight, and he stood there trying to figure out where they were coming from until somebody shouted *Run you damn fool!* and he dived head-first into a wagon of cabbages that was standing nearby. Yeah man, that Vietnam was out to get him, and he even started becoming suspicious of America for sending him there in the first place. He didn't know whether he still loved the white bitch or not. He certainly didn't think she was beautiful anymore, and he stayed high all the time. If death did come, it sure wouldn't find him in his right mind. But he couldn't tell Odessa things like that, because it might have a bad effect on the baby she was carrying.

Sometimes Odessa told him, in her shy way, how much she missed Christopher, she still called his dick that. And he thought it was sweet of her to keep on doing so, because it meant that he had Christopher here, but she still had Christopher growing inside her in Cousinsville, since he had bet her five dollars that the baby was going to be a boy. When she talked about Christopher, he got so excited that he'd go somewhere and give Christopher a good beating, he didn't like those Vietnam women too much.

In another one of her letters, Odessa told him that Mr. Yen had died of a heart attack, which didn't surprise Joe too much. He bet that China wasn't too sorry, either, although Odessa said that China had taken Mr. Yen's death "real hard." China was a rich woman now, and Joe could just hear those other nigger women's tongues in Decatur, wagging a mile a minute. But China was tough enough to tell all of them to kiss her ass, she couldn't help it if she'd married a rich old man with a weak heart.

Around that Thanksgiving, Joe also got a letter from Tony Brenzo, who said that he had been transferred to a special unit investigating summer riots in places like Newark and Cousinsville. "I'm sorry I can't be there with you," Tony said. "I'm sure it's a very shitty scene, and I have a notion that you wouldn't be there at all if I hadn't planted the idea in your head. So stay well and hurry home. I miss you like hell."

For another month until Christmas, they slogged up and down Vietnam. They had gone for days without seeing one Viet Cong. Walking across the lowlands with his patrol, Joe looked up and saw the slow drift of clouds across an Air Force blue sky. Then, into the jungle, something sweaty and secretive about the eternal twilight of towering trees and tangles of thorn and vines that reached out and touched and tried to detain like the hands of greedy women. Bamboo thickets shot up like prison bars.

Then all of a sudden, they happened on this Viet Cong guy with his head stuck up like a turkey from some wait-a-minute vines.

Somebody had to kill him so that they could move on. "Take him, Joe." It was Mike Martucci whispering into his ear. The patrol crowded up behind him on their bellies. Squinting, Joe aimed his M-16. That guy wore a uniform that looked like black pajamas, as though he were getting ready to go to bed instead of waiting to kill somebody. Joe remembered that back in Cousinsville, he had thought it would be glorious to kill on the field of battle, and war it-self had seemed a kind of ecstasy between enraptured adversaries. Well, Vietnam had shown him better than that. *I'm certainly not going to kill that guy, I don't want to kill nobody. I'm just going to scare him out of our way.* He didn't even aim all that carefully. He milked the trigger and shot the Viet Cong straight through the head.

Joe thought he felt that bullet go right through his own head. Man, how'd he done a thing like that? It was the first person he'd ever killed in his life, and he hadn't even aimed for that guy! He looked around to see if somebody else might have shot him, but they were just starting to get up from the ground, and he was the only one who had his rifle ready. God *damn* it! Mother*fucking* son-ofabitch, he felt like he was going to cry, he felt like he was going to throw up until Lamont or somebody slapped him on the butt and said, "Good shooting, baby." And his mind slid right back from the dreadful horror of it all, like a snail sliding backwards in its own mess, and he thought, *What the fuck, I'm doing this for my country, for Odessa and for our kid, that motherfucking gook didn't have no business with his head sticking up like that anyway.* Besides, there was a good feeling about killing a man. You shot him through the head, you felt like throwing up. But you felt good, too, all down in the crotch. Warm and very pleasant there. Like God might feel. A man wouldn't keep on killing in a war, not even to save his own life, if killing didn't feel like God. The patrol moved on.

Next day was New Year's Eve, and they returned to base camp. A so-called New Year's truce was in effect, and there was a feeling of jubilation everywhere. But there was also tension underneath the sudden and somehow deceitful calm of the New Year's truce.

Joe felt it himself, and he could feel it in the other guys in the barracks as they horsed around and got ready to go to town. But Joe lay on his bunk, quietly smoking a cigarette.

He was in a somber, restless mood because he could not forget that he had killed. That was the kind of fucked-up war this was, where everybody flipped just because you shot somebody in the head. Even if you didn't mean to. Hell, everybody was treating him like a hero, and all he wanted to do was forget it. But pricks like Lamont and that big wop Sgt. Martucci wouldn't let him. Lamont came on like Pearl Bailey about to receive the Oscar for being last year's best man. "Joe, that was *marvelous*! You saved all our lives, you know that, baby?" Joe didn't know any such thing, but he did know that Lamont had to exaggerate the danger of the incident in order to make himself feel more important. Lamont said he was going to the service club to write his mother about it; and he gathered up his writing kit and left the barracks with a proud, wide-legged walk, drying his hands on the seat of his uniform to a kind of silent applause.

Sgt. Mike Martucci, who had never been a friend of Joe's, invited him into Saigon for a drink. "You did a good job yesterday of killing that gook," Sgt. Martucci said. "In fact, my patrol's the only patrol I know of that killed a gook this week." He was tall and broad and always smelled like garlic. Joe had the top bunk over his, and he watched Sgt. Martucci posing in the mirror, combing his greasy black hair. "Why don't we go into town and get some chicks?" Sgt. Martucci said. Joe looked at him in the mirror, and Sgt. Martucci nodded and drew one eye together into a lascivious wink. "They got some hot broads here, man. We could wipe out one together. Would you like that, man? Would you like that?" Joe shook his head. The idea didn't even interest him, doing a Triple-S scene with a prick like Martucci and some slant-eyed gook chick. "Thanks anyway," he said, forcing himself to smile. No sense antagonizing the jerk. "I think I'll stay here and write a letter to my wife." Martucci shrugged, obviously disappointed. "Yeah, well ... some other time," he said, half-jovially. Settling his cunt cap at a precise angle slantwise on top of his greasy pile of hair, he left the barracks whistling *Yankee Doodle*.

Joe tried to concentrate on a letter to Odessa; but his mind kept wandering until he finally gave in and went outdoors. Although the sun was about to set—purple and pale-red colors were already gathering over beyond the airstrip—it was still very hot. Joe felt sweaty and a little dizzy from the heat; he stood awhile in the shade down between the barracks, then he started walking. When he came to the supply area, he saw a warehouse there with the doors wide open and full of lightweight aluminum coffins stacked from floor to ceiling, waiting to be filled. Joe took out a joint and smoked it. Fifteen years ago his father Titus had bought a dozen whores at the same time for the two of them together. "It's always wiser and cheaper to buy in quantity," Titus had told him, either before or after the orgy, Joe didn't remember which. But that event had probably been his first most important lesson in economics; and he thought now how very wise it was of America, buying coffins wholesale like that.

As far as he was concerned, those coffins were another sign of how America was lying to them. He'd found that out soon enough, even if it did take a war to open his eyes to the fact that America was two-timing them all. Like a woman would, like a dirty white bitch, that's what he thought of America now. She told the white man that he had to protect her against the black; she told black and white alike that they had to protect her from the Viet Cong. Were those little men in black pajamas really all that dangerous to America? Or was it just another excuse for getting men to fight over her? She was never happier than when she had the whole fucking world fighting over her, dying for her, some of those dead being buried away in those modern efficiency aluminum coffins. With the dying sun falling on them through the open door, they seemed to be almost palpitating in time to the tympani of distant mortars. Joe's ears perked up. Man, if there was a truce on, then there shouldn't be any firing. But there was firing, which meant that truce was just another lie somebody was telling somebody else.

Joe walked on, very high. A squadron of jets was coming in now from the day's kill, moving in over the humped and sluggish mountains. Joe stood near the extreme end of the airstrip and watched some of the jets land, shrilling and whining like angry bees. He skirted the airstrip until he came to a secluded corner of the camp near the barbed-wire fence. A dusty road ran on the other side of the fence. From time to time, a Vietnamese man or woman plodded along barefooted and in rags, with or without family, doubled over under the weight of ceaseless war, without hope, seeing nothing but the ground. On the other side of the road, a rice field fermented underneath a blanket of water and manure. Joe took off his clothes. The heat hit him like a shock. Later on, after sunset, it would cool off some; but the heat held him now like smelly hot hands. Scratching the damp, curly hair in his crotch, he flexed his muscles like a lion and took a leisurely leak. Then he lay flat on the ground in a cluster of fragrant weeds and stared straight up at the sky while he smoked a whole joint.

He thought, *It's the last day of the year. I thank whoever I'm supposed to thank that I'm still alive.* The sky was red now, streaked with slivers of white and blue. The colors of the American flag. Shit. That Viet Cong guy had made it almost to the end of the year, too. And then he'd died. Joe shifted in the weeds. Hell, he might as well tell the truth right now. He hadn't killed that guy yesterday for either his country or his family or his flag; he had killed that guy accidentally, the same way you might accidentally kill somebody with a car, something like that. Shit. And the fact that he had killed that Viet Cong marked an important turning point in his life, he knew that. For one thing, it had changed his whole attitude toward America from naive love to solid suspicion. If America was the greatest country in the world, then why were Americans dying here in this mud puddle, this dust bowl? Shouldn't the greatest country in the world concern itself with greater matters and more beautiful things? Shit, man. Shit.

Looking down his belly, he saw that his dick had stood straight up; and he forced his mind onto the subject of Odessa, because he didn't like his dick getting hard while he had been thinking about death. Man, he wanted to wallow down in Odessa's black thighs now, to guide her lips down to his throbbing dick, to have her drink his come. . . . *Christopher, you beautiful motherfucker I wish I was double-jointed, I wish I could suck you myself, baby.* He spit on his hand; then he reached down and grabbed Christopher around the head and neck and helped him fuck his fist while he prayed inside his own head to somebody for that other Christopher that was growing inside Odessa's belly. *Let him grow up clean and strong and without fear. Let him never have to lie down in weeds in Vietnam and beat his meat. Let me do all that is right for him and none of the wrong that my father did to me. Let him show Odessa that the world is still all right to have babies in. . . .* He shot come all over his belly and thighs. He stayed there in the weeds until night fell and the come had dried in delicate crusts, so as not to goop up his pants. Then he put on his clothes and walked back to the barracks.

The full moon began its slow, steady ascent behind a bamboo thicket. Farther out across the field, Joe saw an old man plodding along behind a water buffalo. Going home. Joe started whistling. He felt just fine. He still had him eight months left in Vietnam; but Odessa had written him that the baby would be born next month, January of 1968, and that began at midnight. Eight months wasn't too long after that. He felt proud now that he was over here helping to defend America, like Odessa said in her letters. Because, in spite of all her shit, he still felt something big for America, he wanted to wallow down in her green thighs until she sang *The Star-Spangled Banner* backwards and admitted that a man who could make her do that didn't deserve all the shit she was giving him just because he happened to be black. Or deserved to get killed and to be buried in the obscenity of cold, lightweight aluminum. He had never really felt free in America; he hoped his son Christopher would, that he had somehow bought a part of America that his son would feel free in.

As Joe neared the flight line, he smelled the powerful odor of high octane seeping from the quiet hangars. No-smoking signs were posted every five feet. Joe could hear the sound of a radio and the drone of voices coming from Base Operations where the early night crew put in its shift and waited to get off. From the top of the control tower, searchlights stabbed the dark blue underbelly of the sky.

Suddenly and dramatically, the searchlights converged on a jet fighter that dropped screaming from the sky and angled for a landing. Sirens went off; crash trucks and ambulances raced down the runway behind the fighter. Joe ran with them.

Part of the plane's fuselage had been shot away by ground fire. Joe could see the pilot doubled over the controls, the small jerk of his body as he braked the plane and killed the banshee engines. Firemen stood ready with hoses; rescue personnel scrambled to the jet and lifted the pilot out. The crowd drew together in a tense little knot when it saw the blood staining the pilot's belly and between his legs. *You see?* the crowd seemed to be saying. *I told you the truce was a fake. The war's still on, men are still dying.*

The pilot removed his helmet and dropped it on the ground. He was a Negro lieutenant. Somebody picked his helmet up and handed it to him; he dropped it again. Medics with a stretcher elbowed through the crowd and hustled the lieutenant into an ambulance. The crowd started babbling as the ambulance sped away.

He got his balls shot out. The shell came through the bottom of his plane and exploded almost in his lap.

A good-looking guy, one of those colored pilots, I hear they're really good pilots, they don't give a damn for nothing.

What was he doing up anyway? Isn't that truce still on?

Pressure, man. We're putting the pressure on them, I read it in the paper.

Joe had to pass the dispensary to get to his barracks. He started to go another way, he didn't even want to go by the dispensary, knowing that somebody was in there all shot up like that lieutenant. His heart was racing with a combination of excitement and fear. He walked on, right to the dispensary. There was no one outside at all, and that surprised him, because he had expected to find another crowd of curiosity seekers. He went in.

There was a doctor, a major, who tried to give him a hard time. "You lose something in here?" he said. Joe started to walk out right then; he didn't even know why he came inside in the first place. But the colored lieutenant made a kind of pleading noise in his throat, and they all looked at him. He was looking at Joe. His skin seemed almost white underneath the outer layer of tan. The major went and tried to cut his flying suit off him; another doctor, a captain, was busy with injections in his arm. They had him half-lying on an operating table in a kind of grotesque sprawl. He made that noise in his throat again, and his parched lips cracked in a smile. "Hey, man, stick with me," he said around the rasping in his throat. He was talking to Joe, but everybody in the room got the message. They were the only two Negroes there. *I don't want to die with all these white people here, I want at least one of my own people here if I die.* His eyes were saying that. He reached for Joe's hand and tugged him with enormous strength to his side. "I guess you can stay," the major said.

The Negro lieutenant nodded, and closed his eyes in a slow half-wink. His eyes had the dazed look that comes with deep injury. The pulse in his throat swung in and out like a small bellows, stopped, started again, slowed down. The major cut off the last of his uniform and bent down between his legs with clamps and cotton. Joe looked, then looked away. *He don't have no dick and no balls. The red down there is oozing like a pussy opened for the first time.*

The lieutenant turned his head and peered at Joe, as though he could detect the shock and the unsaid question in Joe's eyes. *What the hell you doing out here dying for that white bitch for?* Joe was asking him that with his eyes; and the pilot's lips started moving, he was trying to tell Joe something. Joe leaned closer, but the lieutenant straightened him up with urgent pressure on his hand. The answer was couched in the eloquence of his wounded eyes. *I love her. She done me wrong, but I love her. I fought for her, baby, so don't you let nobody call you nigger when you go home.*

"Don't die," Joe said. "You going home, too." His voice was little more than a whisper. "Man, please don't die!" He was sorrier now than ever that he had killed that Viet Cong. How could anybody do something like this to somebody else? And there was nothing that he could do. . . . Frantically, his mind searched for some way to save the lieutenant. And he remembered the words that Mr. Cobb had read from the Bible at his mother's funeral down in Burnside. Beautiful, soothing words said by the real Saviour, powerful enough to keep any man alive. *I am the resurrection, and the life: he that believeth in me, though he were dead, yet shall he live: And whosoever liveth and believeth in me shall never die. Believest thou this?*

The lieutenant's eyes glazed over like marbles. Then the breath rushed from his chest in a long rattling sigh. The pulse in his throat bounced and lay still. "I think he's dead," Joe said. But nobody seemed to hear him. "I think he's dead," he repeated, louder this time. He uncurled the lieutenant's fingers from around his hand.

The major was working desperately between the lieutenant's legs. The second doctor, the captain, tapped the major on the shoulder. "Ken, it's no use. He's dead."

The major looked up, blinking. "Who the hell told you? He can't be. . . . It's not a mortal wound. . . ."

"He's dead," the captain said kindly.

"Who the hell told you?" the major said. There were tears on his bony nose; a strand of blond hair was matted against his forehead.

Joe left the dispensary. He could still feel the pressure of the lieutenant's hand on his own. *Don't you let nobody call you nigger when you go home.*

Before he went to bed, Joe looked out the window and saw the full moon, a magnificence of silver shimmering like the glass eye of God. *Fuck you*, Joe thought. Now it filtered through the window like a silver mist. "Fuck you, you white bastard," Joe said bitterly.

"What's eating you?" Sgt. Martucci asked drowsily from the bottom bunk.

But Joe hadn't been talking to Sgt. Martucci. Around him, the other soldiers slept sprawled out in gentle unconsciousness, as though building up their energies for the fact of dying, whenever that might be. Angrily, helplessly, Joe flopped over on his back.

"Joe baby, you all right?" That was Lamont now, talking to him in a worried whisper from the other row of bunks. "I'm all right," Joe said. He wrapped his hands protectively around his dick and balls and rolled over on his belly. It was well after midnight; they were already into 1968, and nobody had even wished him Happy New Year. On the contrary, that bastard Martucci in the lower bunk was getting ready to cuss him out if he moved another inch, he could feel that wop fuming down there, waiting to pull rank. Joe lay very still and fell asleep. And dreamed very clearly of his mother laughing at him, of his father's wet, devouring mouth. It was the first time he'd had that dream since he got married.

Next day, the Viet Cong mounted their major offensive. Except for the air base at Tan Son Nhut, which was the only Allied point that remained outside their perimeter of operations, they effectively ringed in Saigon. Some of them sneaked into town and took over the American Embassy for seven hours. After several days of hard fighting by U.S. and Vietnamese soldiers, the Viet Cong were routed from the vicinity of Saigon.

At the same time, word filtered down that some bigwig from Washington, probably the Secretary of Defense himself, had dropped in for a conference at the air base. Regrouping, as though they knew about or sensed the presence of some very important person at Tan Son Nhut, the Viet Cong dug themselves in like fleas around the air base and launched a rare frontal assault. Joe's regiment had orders to provide a buffer between the base and the Viet Cong until the Secretary got to safety. The Viet Cong were without air support, but they hit the forces at Tan Son Nhut with everything their ground crews could muster, and the Allies responded in kind.

It was the first time that either Joe or Lamont had been in full combat. Keeping their heads low, they lay side-by-side on their bellies behind anything that served for cover and fired their rifles until they ran out of ammunition. Then they reloaded and emptied their rifles again. Sometimes they wondered who was winning, because you really couldn't tell, everything seemed to remain the same. It was just like being at a shooting gallery, Joe told Lamont. He smoked so much pot that he really thought so, too, until the Viet

Cong moved their forward lines closer. Then he had a clear view of how a man died on the battlefield. Sometimes in bloodied bits and tattered pieces. Sometimes with a surprisingly small hole bored in the center of his forehead, or marking his uniform, hardly larger than a pencil insertion would have made, except that it was always large enough to let the life out of a man, so that he died like a punctured tire, pitifully deflated, the air oozing out black at first, then shameless red, thick, spurting, curdling fast to stickiness like raspberry jam to the touch, if you had balls enough to touch them after you or somebody else shot them down. Joe smoked pot and kept emptying and reloading his rifle. It was a shooting gallery, all right; the only difference was that those moving heads belonged to real people. He hoped to God that none of his bullets killed any of those people. He smoked more pot.

Shortly before sundown on the fourth day of fighting, a blue-and-white jetliner took off from Tan Son Nhut air base and banked sharply east. The Secretary, or whoever he was, was going home; they had held the airstrip long enough for that. Now the Allies would make a strategic withdrawal into the hills under cover of night and let the Viet Cong have the airfield until the Americans, reinforced, took it back again.

But before night came, Joe got shot. He felt the bullet eat through him like a white-hot knife. *My balls my balls!* he thought. *They got me in the balls!* He threw his M-16 as far away as he could, and fell down holding his groin. He heard Lamont shouting in a high, scared voice. *Medic! Medic!* Crying just like a baby, he had a very strange and lucid thought: *Man, Odessa was right, I don't want my son to have to go through no shit like this.* For a pain-filled moment, he was overcome by horror that he had helped bring an innocent baby boy into this motherfucking world. Now he knew how that colored lieutenant felt. *Medic! Medic!* And that Viet Cong dying. . . . *Medic!* A pleasant, dream-like sensation passed over his whole body, as though he was being immersed in lukewarm water. *Dear Holy God in heaven Jesus Christ Mama Odessa I don't want to die . . . !* Then his mind turned red all over, and he passed out.

———

Four months later, Joe Market stood at a urinal in Penn Station in Newark, taking a leak. There was a queer watching him from two or three urinals away; and the truth was that he had finished taking a leak and he was digging that queer looking at him. His duffel bag was on the floor beside him. He had been discharged from the Army and he was going home to Decatur Street. To his great relief, that bullet in Vietnam had only severed a tendon in his left leg, rather than shooting away his testicles. After surgical repair and four months in the hospital, Joe had been discharged from the Army. He limped sometimes now after a lot of walking. It was a small limp, barely noticeable to anyone; but it had made Joe unfit for the Army. And he was very glad of that.

With that queer looking at his dick, it got hard as a rock, because nobody had sucked him off since he went to the Army a year ago. Some of the orderlies in the Saigon hospital used to play with his dick and jack him off whenever they had the chance; but nobody there wanted to suck him, like they had some kind of scruples about taking come from a sick man. Lamont had visited him in the hospital two or three times a week, and Joe had been on the verge of asking Lamont to suck him, because he needed somebody to suck on his dick from time to time the same way that a fish needs water or a bird needs air in order to be complete. But he hadn't asked Lamont, he'd only thought about it; because the fact that he'd got shot had made Lamont into more of a sissy than he was before he joined the Army. "When I saw you fall down, man, I thought you were *dead*. And I had the funniest feeling then, and I asked myself, *What we doing over here in Vietnam? We belong back in Decatur.* I thought you were dead, man . . . I really thought you were dead." He just couldn't stop talking about it to Joe. "Man, I don't want no more of this Army bull-shit. All I want to do is go home." He told Joe that he had asked to be transferred to public relations after all. But the transfer had never been approved, and Lamont was still out doing patrols with Sgt. Martucci when Joe left Vietnam. "Give my mother a telephone call when you get home," Lamont had asked Joe, "just to let her know I'm all right." His eyes were tired and full of misery. "Although she won't care whether I'm all right or not."

Joe had called Mrs. Jones as soon as he got off the train in Newark, he wanted to keep his word to Lamont. But Mrs. Jones hadn't seemed interested at all in what Joe said about Lamont. She was trying to find out instead who Joe was and what his relationship was to Lamont. "We were in Vietnam, in the same patrol, Mrs. Jones. I knew Lamont in Decatur. We joined the Army together, it's been exactly a year ago this month. . . ." Mrs. Jones cut him off with a sound of malicious satisfaction, as though he'd confessed that he and Lamont had eloped together. "I know you, I've seen you around Decatur, always wearing them tight white pants. . . ." Joe smiled. Man, that old bitch really did think Lamont was queer. He hung up before she even finished talking. Fuck all that noise.

He was sorry that he couldn't remember the number of the phone in the hallway of his building so he could let Odessa know that he was in Newark. He thought about calling China at the laundry next door and having her tell Odessa; but then he decided not to tell anybody and to surprise them all. Maybe he'd sneak up on Odessa fucking some other nigger. But he knew that was out of the question, because Odessa was too hung up on him. Still, he toyed with the idea of Odessa fucking another nigger, somebody he could put the blame for that baby Christopher on. He'd pat that nigger on the ass, he'd say, "Man, you *keep* her, I don't want the responsibility of no wife and baby, not now, not after what I've been through. You keep her, man, that baby, too, you'd be doing me a big favor because I ain't even got me no job that's worthwhile talking about."

With Mr. Yen dead, he had thought about trying to get rid of Odessa and marrying China Doll, she was just as hung up on his dick as Odessa was. And he knew that Mr. Yen had left China all kinds of money. But underneath all her soft-sweet pussy and put-on airs, China was a bitch on wheels, she wouldn't take half the shit off him that Odessa took. Naw man, he'd better stick with Odessa, settle down again to the same old routine—if he could—and try to forget some things. Because he'd been through a lot in that goddamned Army. He had spent all of the last four months in that Army hospital in Saigon. Then airlifted to California, discharged, and a train from there to New Jersey. Man, after all that, he was glad that he still had some kind of dick to show; he felt highly complimented that the queer was looking.

He stood at the urinal for a minute or two more, letting the queer admire Christopher. When the queer licked his lips, Joe nodded and smiled. He put Christopher away. Sure, he'd dig a blow job right now, but first he wanted to get rid of his uniform. He put a quarter in one of those little rooms where you can wash up and change clothes. He had bought some sneakers, jeans and a tee shirt that he was going to change into, man, he was sick of that Army uniform. When he left the room, the queer was still waiting. Joe checked his duffel bag in a coin locker and followed him out of Penn Station, hell, he wasn't in that big a hurry to get home to misery.

Martin Luther King had been shot down in Memphis about ten days before, and the queer was still talking about that. Feeling Joe's dick with one hand, driving with the other, he shook his head somberly. "Lord child, all that rioting, they even had guards with bayonets on the White House steps. Who knows what this country's coming to? The next thing you know they'll be electing that asshole Nixon president. And won't that be something? Child, if that Nixon gets in, he's going to start shooting niggers down in the streets like dogs."

Joe wasn't the least interested in politics, and when he told the queer so, the queer seemed very surprised. "What are you interested in, sugar?" Joe took out his hard dick. The queer smiled. "Baby, I'm for that." He carried Joe to his apartment in Newark.

Sprawling back while that queer worked on Christopher, Joe found himself wondering what that other Christopher looked like. Because the baby had been born shortly after Joe had been wounded, when the Army had been trying to patch up his leg. Joe had felt like he was giving birth, too, being in the hospital at the same time that Odessa was. "You owe me five dollars," he'd written her, because he had bet that it would be a girl. Some of the nurses and patients had given him cigars, and he had felt real good about that. He'd even sent Odessa some blue silk material to make herself a new dress, she said that none of her old ones would fit her after the baby was born. But that had been four months ago; the novelty and excitement of having a baby had worn off now, and Joe didn't feel like he could be father to anybody or anything. Or even that he wanted to, so much misery in the world, just like Odessa and Miss Lavinia used to tell him. But he thought that he'd known every-thing then, that's what he got from going to college. A swelled head. And the stupid idea of joining the Army to fight for his country. Man, he'd really been a prick, he'd gone to the Army looking for gold, and he'd come back with a gimp tendon in his leg. And he hadn't been able to save even a nickel out of that little chicken feed they'd paid him every month. He'd have to go back to hustling again if he ever wanted to make any money.

When the queer got through, he gave Joe fifteen dollars and some change, that was all the money he said he had. Which Joe thought was a good enough hustle, his first time back selling dick. He let the queer kiss him and drop him off in Decatur, he said he had some business there himself. "Look me up again some time when you're in the mood," the queer said. He drove down Hickory Street to the corner of Decatur. It was around seven o'clock on a Thursday night in the middle of April. The streets were almost empty and the sky was gray-black, like bat wings sweeping every-thing. Pee Wee's cab was also gone from in front of Cheap Mary's. If Joe got out quickly and ducked up the alley beside the old Jewish woman's store, he was sure that no one would see him, and he could surprise Odessa by coming home the back way. He thanked the queer and got out of the car. Without even breaking stride, he zipped up the alley.

He stood there beside Cheap Mary's and smoked a joint. The backyards between him and his home farther up Decatur Street seemed like some jumbled and tangled abyss between what he was now and what he had been before that colored lieutenant had died. Before, he had been very high and hung up on life; and living itself had been like smoking pot on a bright day slanting down through a half-open door that opened wider every day onto newer and better things. He hadn't been bullshitting Tony Brenzo last year when he'd talked about making a future for his son; and he had gone to the Army with the picture in his head of himself forging a future for him and Odessa and their son, like someone carving down a piece of granite into a pleasant and agreeable shape.

But that had all been before he'd actually joined the Army, before Vietnam, before that lieutenant died and sent some dead thing creeping from his own fingers, to ferment and fester in Joe's belly. He could feel it there now, like a stillborn child sending the canker of its death throughout the living body, a dead but somehow growing fetus waiting some other definitive act of death so that it could be born again and die again at the same time.

Joe threw away the roach of the joint and wiped his hands on his thighs. Man, you can't get away from death, it narrowed down to that. By the same token, if death is all you can expect out of life, it hardly makes life worth living at all. And he was going to tell Odessa so, that he'd finally understood what she and Miss Lavinia had been trying to tell him before about why he shouldn't have a son. *In Vietnam*, he would say, after he had seen his son and all the greetings were over, and maybe they had even fucked once or twice, *In Vietnam, honey, first I killed this gook and that didn't bother me too much. Then I saw this colored lieutenant, he got killed, they shot his dick and balls out. Something happened to me then, honey, like there's a strange kind of raging anger inside me and I feel like I want to kill somebody with my bare hands anybody because I'm so motherfucking mad about seeing a man made into a woman and dying like a woman without any dick and balls at all up there between his legs. . . . You keep your eye on me, honey, you make sure I don't kill me somebody because the next person that calls me nigger and means it, I'm going to kill him with my bare hands.* That's what he wanted to say to Odessa; and as he hopped first one fence, then another, he wondered if his wanting to surprise Odessa by coming home the back way a day earlier than she expected him might not have to do with the fact that the front way reminded him of the old way, and had to be undone. As quietly as a cat, he dropped down into his own yard.

The locust tree there was budding. He snapped one of the buds off and chewed it so that the bitter flavor would hide the pot smoke on his breath. Odessa wouldn't like him coming home high, as though he had to smoke pot to give him courage enough to come home at all; and he didn't want to piss her off right now, he had too many important things to tell her.

Chewing on the bitter bud, he went up the back stairs and into the kitchen. He tipped through the kitchen, grinning as he thought of how surprised and delighted Odessa was going to be when she saw him. She must be sleeping, she and the baby both, that's why he didn't hear a sound from the bedroom. He went through the living room and into the bedroom. Odessa wasn't there at all. "Odessa?" He half-turned, thinking that she was in the bathroom; but the bathroom door was open, and he could see that no one was there. Then he saw the pale blue crib in one corner of the bedroom. His heart started thumping. He tipped over and looked down into his sleeping son's face. Man. He felt so strange. His baby looked just like Martin Luther King.

Joe sat on the bed and smoked some pot. He smoked very quietly so as not to wake the baby up, because he wouldn't know what to do with that child with its eyes open wide awake, he couldn't call it Christopher, somebody like that who looked like Martin Luther King. Cautiously, he got up and inspected the sleeping child again. This time it looked like him, some resemblance that he saw around the mouth and eyes, and that made him feel better. Then he wondered where Odessa was, why she wasn't home with the baby. She had quit her job at the laundry just before the baby was born, she'd written him that, so she couldn't be over there. He bet she was down at her fucking mother's house, he bet that was where she was, although he couldn't understand why she hadn't carried the baby along with her.

His head was reeling, and he staggered back and flopped on the bed. Man, he'd smoked too much pot, that sometimes happened; and he lay there with his eyes closed while his heart swelled and contracted with a noise in his head like steel bass drums. At the same time, his mind made slow and orderly revolutions as he speculated about the fact that he had seen his son and he didn't even like him; and that didn't surprise him, because he'd lost interest in having a son as soon as Odessa had written him that she'd had one. After that, he'd been curious and excited about seeing what Christopher was going to look like. And now he knew. *He's the only come my dick didn't throw away.* He eased up the bottom of the blanket and looked at the sleeping child's dick. It wasn't even big, not the kind of dick he'd expected his son to have, considering that big dicks ran in their family. Roosevelt, Titus, himself—all of them had big dicks; it seemed to him that his son's dick ought to be much bigger than that, it didn't matter that he was still a baby.

Half-disgusted, Joe lay down again on the bed. He wondered where the fuck Odessa was. Lord, he hoped he didn't die here on the bed and have her come in and find him dead. A man shouldn't die flat on his back looking at a blank white ceiling. That was the way women ought to die, but not men, flat on their backs with their pussies full of big dick and hot come the same way his mother Ramona had died looking past a man's cheek at a ceiling, the last thing that stood between her and Jesus, that water-streaked black pine ceiling, black from soot and age, that had kept her from seeing heaven all her life until she died on that bed back in Burnside, fucked to death poor Ramona faith intact pussy full of come emotions and complaints both too large and uncontrolled like a rose that petals open too wide and loses sweetness and perfection . . . and her soul went filtering right up through that ceiling like smoke through a chimney, *I am the resurrection and the life*. Shit. After Titus had told him that Ramona was dead, Titus had sucked his dick. He had liked it all right, but he didn't think he'd do that to a son of his, not as a habit, because it does something to a child's mind, like wearing down the edges between the sexes so that sometimes it's hard to distinguish between a man's mouth or a woman's pussy or just a random hole bored somewhere in a fence or a wall, and the dick gets hard indiscriminately as soon as the eye makes out the contours of a hole, it doesn't matter who or what the hole belongs to, all the dick knows is that it's a hole.

Shit. As far as he was concerned, a man shouldn't have to make distinctions any way. Like saying, *This is a man and this is a woman and this is a man's hole and this is a woman's hole. . . .* It was the same mistake he saw in having to say, *This is life and this is death* or *This is my body and this is my blood*, things like that, while he was interested in the inseparables, the things that could not be castrated and deprived of their essential identities. . . .

He stirred on the bed. He wasn't making sense, he knew that. If a man shouldn't have to make distinctions, then was there any such thing as *essential identities*? Shit. He needed some more pot, fuck Odessa finding him high. He took out another joint and smoked it. In a little while, his mind whispered to him, *The fact that your son's crib is blue and his blanket is blue, that means he's a boy, the blue does.* So, distinctions are important, like a boy is a boy and a girl is a girl, and by saying that, we're distinguishing them according to their essential identities. The evil thing then is when you make a freak out of a man, like making him a black man in an essentially bigoted white man's country . . . like shooting his dick and balls out over Vietnam so that he dies not a man and not a woman either.

Bitterly, Joe ground out the joint. At some entertainment that the Army had arranged for them in Vietnam, he'd gone with Lamont to hear a choir of young Catholic boys singing patriotic songs in high-pitched voices that had sent chills through him, they seemed so unnatural. *O beautiful for spacious skies for amber waves of grain.* Almost like the shrieking of smooth, featherless birds. Two or three days after that concert, Joe had got into an argument with Lamont about America. "I know I got wounded over here in Vietnam," Joe had said. "But America ain't done nothing to me . . . I mean, to me as an individual." Lamont had smiled like a smug sissy. "Man, you remember that choir we heard the other night? Well, the Catholic Church used to castrate little boys like that to keep their voices pure. And America has damned near castrated us, the black people, and all we can do is sing her praises. It's what you call the *inevitability of love*, I intend to write a book about it some day. Hell, what else did those boy sopranos have to love except the Church? She took their balls and buried them somewhere under the altar, and those boys sang their hearts out, they were so glad to be that close to their balls. It's what you do to a dog, cutting off his tail so he'll stay at home. It's the same thing with Negroes in America . . . what else do we have to love except America . . . ? Obviously we can't love our parents, because we're such a burden to them in one way or another. Man, we've got to love our country, because there's not a damned thing else we can love. . . ." Lamont had said that; and it had surprised the hell out of Joe, Lamont talking like that, because he hadn't known that Lamont had so much sense. Joe got up now and looked at Christopher again. The boy did look like him, he had to admit that; although he'd looked like Martin Luther King, too, a little while back. King had loved America, the way Lamont said we ought to do, and America had shot him down like a dog. Not just some sick, isolated white man acting independently. No. It was America herself who made such dreadful distinctions that a man's essential identity often gets him killed, which is what happened to King. Or gets a man twisted and maimed and destroyed sexless, which is what happened to his grandfather Roosevelt and to that Negro lieutenant in Vietnam. *The inevitability of love. Man, we got to be patriotic.* Lamont had been saying that he and all other black people are freaks, that's what he was saying. Locked up inside the church called America, singing in high-pitched voices, singing in gratitude for the fact that we have been castrated *for purple mountain's majesties above the fruited plain*; balls buried beneath the White House or shot off in Vietnam and Memphis and niggers keep on saying *I love America I do I do* and get their balls shot off or chopped off by mothers like Mrs. Jones or government axes and keep right on having babies with more balls to be shot off or chopped off while somebody stands around in the background singing in high sissy voices *America! America! God shed His grace on thee!* "Odessa?" He thought he heard her coming down the hall. "You was right, Odessa, you and your mother both." But when he realized that he hadn't heard Odessa, some trick of the imagination that had made him believe he heard her high heels in the hallway, he also realized, with a profound sense of sadness, that he would never be able to tell Odessa what he understood and what he had to do. He wouldn't be able to explain to Odessa, not to anybody. He almost thought he smelled peas burning, another trick of his imagination, because that had happened when Titus was killing his mother. He had a stone throbbing hard-on now he couldn't help it he remembered how his dick had jumped hard when Titus told him *Your Mama's dead Joe baby*, and he was higher and more disgusted now than he'd ever been in his life he'd given them a son for somebody to cut his balls out man now he understood why he hadn't liked the baby in the first place he was going to cover its head up now hide it now so that nobody not even Odessa would know it had been born and come with their scissors or knives, so, bending over he pulled the cover up from Christopher's dick it was bigger than it was before but bigger not hard or getting hard just big the way he wanted his son's dick to be big and he kissed Christopher on his dick and sucked it once or twice and then when the boy stirred and acted like he was going to open his eyes and look at the fucked-up world *look at him* Joe pulled the blue blanket over Christopher's head and held it there man somebody in this building sure was burning the shit out of peas . . . as he suffocated his son, looking into infinity with a marble-eyed glaze, he held the blue blanket down and realized that what that nearbaptism of death in Vietnam had taught him was . . . he felt Christopher getting hard rising struggling in his strong hands fighting against the blue blanket his white jeans struggling and hard like a motherfucker . . . that *evil* is not something you do to other people or that other people do to you—it is something horrible and sinful and hateful done to man and forced on man by God. Like that lieutenant. And his mother. And that Viet Cong. That is evil and of course some kind of Redeemer is needed to save us all from the capriciousness of God *slaughter* of death like he was saving his baby *You never going to know horror like I know horror* from all the horror and evil, it does exist in life he knew that now, of this life, he certainly wasn't *killing* this baby that was for sure because this black baby born in dark places was already dead when he was born. . . . Nearly screaming now, he felt himself caught up in the crushing hand of God. And inside all that pure clean and purifying agony, he felt the tiniest of tiny bones snap inside his head like a brittle silver twig, a delicate kind of ornament to adorn memory *I'm not going to get involved with anybody else ever again* he thought *screaming inside his own head* because it hurts too much *silently. . . .*

"Baby, don't you want a blow job?" Early the next morning, he was standing at a urinal in Penn Station in Newark, taking a leak. Smiling, he put Christopher away. "Thanks just the same man, but I ain't got time now. I just got back from Vietnam, I want to get home and see my wife and baby." The queer looked at him regretfully. Still smiling, Joe zipped his pants and went outside with his duffel bag. He was in uniform again, and he stiffened his legs and strutted with his butt pinched together and thrusting out his groin. Arrogance and invitation at the same time. A spade's walk, the walk of a war hero coming home. He got in a cab. "I want to go to Cousinsville," he said. "To Decatur Street."

The driver was a little guy wearing an old-fashioned chauffeur's cap. The name on his identification plate seemed to be an Italian one. "I've got a good friend by the name of Brenzo," Joe said. "He's from here in Newark. You happen to know him?" The driver shook his head, squinting into the mirror. "There're a lot of us dagos named Brenzo. I don't happen to know any." He sounded like he didn't want to talk, and Joe sat quietly awhile.

The downtown commercial section of Newark hadn't changed a bit in the year he'd been away. If anything, it just looked a little uglier, that was all. The real damage to Newark in last year's riots had been done primarily in the Negro ghettos. But here in the downtown area, lively and bustling even this early in the morning, there was no evidence at all of the scarred sections surrounding the downtown business core.

Joe's leg hurt a little, and he eased it out straight in front of him. "I just come back from Vietnam," he told the driver. "That buddy of mine I was telling you about, he's a cop here in Newark. I haven't heard from him for a couple of months. I just wondered whether you might know him, that was all." The driver nodded, a little less frigidly this time; he turned off Raymond Boulevard and started the long climb up Central Avenue to Cousinsville. "That war," he said, shaking his head. "When the hell's it going to end?"

"I don't think it's ever going to end," Joe said. There was something so final and sad in his voice that he and the driver both kept quiet all the way to Decatur Street.

Joe was in his gabardine cunt cap and uniform. A tailor in Vietnam had cut the pants and shirt to hug the contours of his body. He'd spent the night with that other queer from yesterday. That queer had a steam iron, and he'd pressed Joe's uniform. The crease in his pants was so sharp that it seemed to be sewn in, and there were two parallel creases running down the front of his shirt and three down the back. The queer had also polished his combat boots, and they shone like molasses. He had the bottoms of his pants bloused over the tops of his boots and held in place with dick rubbers from the PX. When the cab pulled to the curb in front of his house next door to the China Doll Hand Laundry, Joe got out, dragging his duffel bag. He stood there awhile after the cab had departed. He hoped desperately that someone would see him, because he dreaded going into his house alone. But it was just now about eight o'clock and there was practically no one on the street at that hour of the morning in Cousinsville; most people were at work by now, or still sleeping. A sudden terrible fear crawled in Joe's belly. Suppose Odessa still wasn't home? He didn't know what he'd do if Odessa wasn't home yet. He dropped the strap of his duffel bag. He unzipped his gabardines and arranged his dick so that it hung prominently down his injured leg. Then he went into the house.

He heard a voice like the dry whisper of rats. "It's Joe, Odessa. Joe's home, honey." That was Miss Lavinia talking.

"Oh my God!" Now it was Odessa's voice. He smelled the stench of candles and death, as though he had entered a tomb long unopened. He stood in the doorway. There were at least a dozen women in the room. He saw old Miss Lavinia looking at the floor, and China Doll dressed all in black, looking at him with a kind of naked and greedy desire shining in her dark eyes. For the barest of seconds, standing there, Joe felt as much woman as any of them. It had something to do with the smell of death, his feeling so feminine; and he hitched up his pants to show the true print of his own sex. Then Odessa came from the bedroom and stood in the door there. She was dressed in black, too. He could see that she had run to the bedroom to try and do something to her face. Her eyes were all puffed up and red from crying, he could see that. And there were candles burning in the living room, and all those people sitting there at this hour of the morning with sad faces. "What's the matter, Odessa?" Joe said. "Public Service cut the lights off, didn't you pay the bill?" She just stood there for a while, her eyes glazed over, liquid looking. Then she moaned and stumbled, like she was going to fall down. Her mother, old Miss Lavinia, who was sitting on the sofa near her, caught Odessa's hand. She said, "You might as well tell him, Odessa honey. He's going to have to know sooner or later, and you might as well tell him now."

"Mama! He's going to blame me!"

"Ain't nobody to blame," Miss Lavinia said. She kept her eyes firmly cast to the floor. "We can't even blame the white man for this. Most of the time, we can blame our misery on the white man. But not now. We got nobody to blame at all for this terrible thing that happened. It was just God's will, that's all. You tell him now, honey." Beside her, China Doll's eyes seemed to be swimming in a dark void. "Hi, Joe," China said. "Welcome home. You can have your job back at the laundry whenever you want it." She sounded very nervous.

"Go ahead and tell him, Odessa," Miss Lavinia said firmly.

"Tell me what?" Joe said. Then he walked into the room. He knew all the women there, the one or two men. He kept pulling at the belt of his pants to make sure they could all see his dick. He didn't know why that was important, except that he kept feeling like a woman for some reason. At the same time, there was a sensation down there like a smoothing hot hand over the tight gabardines; and he was ready to fuck Odessa right then and there if all those people hadn't been sitting around. He nodded to China Doll and then walked over to Odessa and put his arms around her. She crawled up against him, whimpering like a scared dog. Her body was hot and damp, like she'd been running. His dick jumped hard the minute she touched him, and he rammed it against her belly, just so she'd know he was home. "What you want to tell me, Odessa honey? I'm home for good now. I come to see our son Christopher. You know I ain't never seen him. I'm back from the Army, honey. Ain't you glad to see your sweet man Joe?" He kept ramming his dick against her, but she backed away so that they were standing half in the living room and half in the bedroom. "Where is our son, Odessa?" She swayed on her legs, and she would have hit the floor if he hadn't been holding her up. "Where is our son, honey?"

"Tell him, Odessa," Miss Lavinia said, almost crossly now. "He can't blame you for what happened."

"What happened?" Joe said. "Odessa, did something bad happen to Christopher while I was over there in Vietnam fighting for my country?" He felt her nod against his shoulder. "Where is he?" Joe said. She took a deep breath. "At the undertaker, Joe. He's at the undertaker. He got tangled up in the cover yesterday while I was out looking for a pair of red shoes. I wanted some red shoes to go with that blue silk cloth you sent me from Vietnam." Behind him, he heard all the women sigh together, as though they were glad it was over, that Odessa had finally told him the news.

He let go of Odessa, and stood at an angle so that they could all see his dick. That goddamn thing stuck out a foot in front of him, almost bursting through the thin gabardine. That was Christopher, the real Christopher; nobody could ever kill that. "Our son's dead?" His voice sounded high and unnaturally shrill to his own ears, like some of those sissy boy sopranos. "How come our son's dead?" For a second, he saw himself as a boy, standing naked in a creek, asking the same question about his mother.

"We been sitting up here all night praying for the baby's soul, and for your understanding," Miss Lavinia said. He wondered what the hell it was she kept looking at on the floor. "You certainly can't blame my daughter. It was an accident, Joe, plain and simple."

He didn't know what to say to Odessa's mother. He knew that he wanted them all to go. Odessa was standing behind him now, with her head against his back and her arms wrapped around his waist, as though she was prepared to restrain him from doing violence. He was standing in the bedroom facing the rest of the people in the living room. His body burned all over, like some kind of awful heat rash. His dick throbbed in his gabardines now, and he remembered how he had got like that when he had been The Naked Disciple and all those people were looking at him. He wanted to fuck Odessa something terrible. "I wish you'd all go," he said. "My son is dead, I'd like to be alone with my wife."

"I certainly hope you won't blame my daughter," Miss Lavinia said, dragging all her bulk from the sofa, her eyes still on the floor. China Doll was the last one to go. "Like I said, Joe, you can have your job back whenever you want it. That's the least we can do for our veterans." Joe nodded. "Thanks, China. I'll see you tomorrow." Then he was alone with Odessa, and she came on right away with that stupid goddamn whine that he just couldn't stand. "Oh Joe, I'm so sorry for what happened! I just went down to the corner to Cheap Mary's, looking for a pair of red shoes to go with that dress I made from the material you sent me. But Mary didn't have any shoes my size. So I decided to walk to Main Street. The baby was sleeping when I left; he always slept for two or three hours at a time, I didn't think there'd be any harm in going to Main Street. When I got back, he was dead."

Joe asked her if she found the red shoes. "No," she said, with a bitter laugh. He didn't say a word. He threw her back on the bed and beat the living shit out of her. He tore off every stitch of clothes she had on. Then he took his time and undressed. He took off his combat boots and stuffed his socks inside of them. He hung up his pants and shirt. He folded his cunt cap and lay it on the dresser. All this time, Odessa was drawn up in a little ball on the bed, whimpering and looking at him from wide eyes. "What you fixing to do, Joe honey?" He laughed. "What the hell you think I'm fixing to do? I'm fixing to *fuck* you, you dirty black bitch." He slapped hell out of her again and then he plowed into her with Christopher. The real, live Christopher. He worked on her all that day and half the night. Whenever he gave her the chance, she ran to the toilet, and he heard water running there in the old, ominous way. He bet she was taking those pills, too. Well, that was all right with him. When he got through with Odessa, she was so sore she could hardly walk. He was sore himself. Next day, they buried Christopher in a white coffin the size of a shoe box, and that was the end of that. A couple of weeks later, Odessa threw her big leg across him one night and whispered, "Joe, do you forgive me for the baby?" She was definitely taking those pills, and there was no chance at all of them ever having another baby. So when Odessa asked him that, Joe's sweet dick jumped hard like a motherfucker. "I forgive you," he said. He rolled over, swinging his black ass. "Swing your black ass like I swing mine," he said. She did.

After a while, when it seemed to be safe to do so without arousing suspicion, he stopped fucking Odessa and everybody else. Odessa didn't complain, even when he started sleeping in the front room on the sofa. She actually seemed relieved, and she went back to church, although she gave up trying to get him to go. Shit man, all he wanted to do was to smoke pot and be left alone. That was all he wanted to do. He'd gone back to driving the truck for the China Doll Hand Laundry. China Doll even tried to get him to go to school again, but he didn't want to. "I'm just lazy, I guess." That's what he would tell China Doll whenever she pushed him to finish his education. He started hanging out more and more with Pee Wee, letting Pee Wee rub him down.

One morning in October of 1968, after he'd finished making his first deliveries, he went to Pee Wee's place on Center Street for a rubdown. From time to time, as Pee Wee's hands worked on his body, he thought about the dead Christopher. And he was honestly glad that the baby was dead. For one thing, it meant that he'd never be able to do to Christopher what his own father had done to him. Also, it gave him a good excuse for not fucking anybody. He'd been fucking even before he was twelve years old. He was twenty-nine now; that was a long time to be fucking people you really didn't care two cents about. So, he'd gone on this clean kick. He didn't even masturbate. He even stopped talking and thinking dirty most of the time. He talked about people "having sex" and "making love" instead of saying that they fucked. He felt clean, sometimes he even felt good.

As for Odessa, she could have had her job back at the laundry, but she stayed home now. Sometimes she tried to get Joe to talk about the Army, but he told her very little. As far as he was concerned, the whole Army thing had been a bunch of crap; and he halfway blamed Odessa for not putting up more of a fight when he had told her that he was going to enlist.

After the baby's death, Odessa had sworn that she'd never wear another pair of red shoes, and she hadn't even worn that silk dress that she'd made from the material Joe had sent her from Vietnam. Then, he'd gone home one day just last week and saw that Odessa had had the dress cleaned and pressed. She was looking at him with a kind of fear and defiance in her eyes, but he didn't say anything. "Things change," he thought. First it was yesterday, now it was today. Things changed like that. Besides, it was a damned good dress, that material had really come from Bangkok where the best silk was, and he didn't see why Odessa shouldn't wear it. He decided to hustle ten bucks in some kind of way and buy Odessa those red shoes to go with that dress, she'd been hinting around for two or three days now.

Pee Wee had been massaging him for over an hour. Now, Pee Wee slapped him warmly on the butt. "Hey man, I got to go down to Newark on some business. Then I got to go to work. I'll see you later, O.K.?" Reluctantly, his hands left Joe's butt. Joe nodded. Sometimes he thought that Pee Wee was the best friend he had. The only friend, because he hadn't seen that damned Tony Brenzo since he'd come back from Vietnam.

He got up and dressed. "Man, it's nearly noon, I didn't realize it was so late," He'd promised to meet China Doll in her cellar way before this. He and Pee Wee smoked some pot together, and then Joe left.

Three

AFTER HE LEFT PEE WEE'S, Joe was walking down Decatur Street smoking pot when one of the Decatur Daredevils thrust a pink circular into his hand. It was an announcement about the electrocution in Trenton of the Reverend Winston Cobb for the murder of a young colored girl from the Decatur section of Cousinsville. The murder in 1965, and the resultant trial and sentencing to death, followed by a series of appeals, had caused a sensation in Cousinsville. Because most of the people there were from Virginia where Mr. Cobb had pastored before he burned his house down with his wife Mae in it, and escaped to the North. Here, he'd killed a 16-year-old girl right from Cousinsville. Now, all appeals rejected, Mr. Cobb was to be executed for his second crime, the first one being outside the jurisdiction of New Jersey.

The Negroes of Burnside were in an uproar, not only because Mr. Cobb was a black preacher, but because he was a black preacher whom most of them had known "down home." Joe also remembered Mr. Cobb, and it didn't surprise him at all that these many years later, Mr. Cobb was going to die in the electric chair for being a murderer. He expected anything from nigger preachers; but others in Decatur were less cynical, and the execution of Mr. Cobb had become the burning issue of the day.

With the traditional summer riots over and the November elections close at hand, the legal execution of a Negro preacher was welcomed by all political parties as being almost too good to be true. Democrats and Republicans alike blamed each other for the fact that Mr. Cobb had murdered that girl, whose body he cut up, wrapped in brown paper, and threw into Passaic River. Demagogues and rabblerousers from the other persuasions—those who favored Cuba, Russia, Nixon, Humphrey, black power and integration, and those who didn't—variously saw the execution as being either for or against their own ideologies. For their part, the Daredevils, a violent group of black young hooligans that was always in favor of somebody dying, had printed and was passing out handbills that announced the electrocution and encouraged attendance at the event. "You going to the execution?" the grinning Daredevil asked Joe. "Sure man, sure," Joe said. His eye swept the handbill. GO TO TRENTON! SEE JUSTICE DONE! There was also a notice that snacks would be served en route on chartered busses, Adults $3.50, Children $2.75 round trip. "I'll try to make it, man," Joe said. "Sounds like it might be fun." He and the Daredevil smoked some pot together, and then the Daredevil ran away.

Joe stuffed the handbill into his shirt pocket and walked on. It was late October, and the oaks and maples along Decatur Street were dropping leaves in furlongs by the curbstone. Several people looked at Joe like they wanted to make it with him; and it was strange, he thought, how people seem to sense when you're off the sex kick. Because nobody really tried to make him, they just looked at him. He could see the way their nostrils wrinkled when their eyes fell on him, as though the presence of all that seed inside him gave him the special musk of a stud in heat that attracted the attention of men and women alike, and at the same time told them that Joe Market was no longer putting out.

Sometimes while he was making deliveries for the China Doll laundry, customers would invite him for a drink or a stick of pot these warm October days. He didn't mind that. But if it went any farther than that, like them grabbing for his dick and trying to hustle him off to bed, he called a halt to all that shit. "I'll take off my clothes and you can look at me naked," he'd say. "But that's all . . . you can just look at me." A lot of people did pay him just for that, to see him naked. It was as far as he would go with anybody since about a month after the death of his baby. It depressed Joe very much to think about his baby, and he dug a joint from his sock and smoked it. He was still trying to find a way to hustle ten dollars to buy those red shoes for Odessa; but every time he made a little money on the side, he spent it for pot. He stayed high most of the time now. Sometimes it was just too hard trying to face the world as it really is.

Sometimes when business was slow, China Doll asked him to do odd jobs for her. He had picked grapes for China most of yesterday, and she was waiting for him now in her cellar. She had asked him to come down and mash the grapes. That meant he could get naked with China Doll. He had left the laundry truck parked on Center Street in front of Pee Wee's. Because Odessa was home, and Joe was walking down Decatur Street now instead of driving so that Odessa would think he was still making deliveries. Odessa was all right in her own way, but there were some things that she didn't cotton up to. Like China Doll, for instance.

He had come to the laundry now. Keeping his head low so that Odessa wouldn't see if she was looking out the window, he went up the alley between his house and the laundry next door and hopped the fence into China Doll's backyard. He pinched out the joint and put it back in his sock. Ducking his head, he went into the cellar.

China Doll was waiting for him there. "Hi, Joe. I thought for a while that you might not come." She saw the handbill sticking from his shirt pocket, and she took it out and read it. "You going to the execution? I'd need me a new dress if I went. I didn't know that just any old body could go to an execution."

"This is a big deal," Joe said. "Everybody's all excited about it. Maybe they decided to let everybody in."

China laughed. "That's the silliest thing I ever heard. How could everybody fit in just one small execution room?"

Joe was taking off his clothes as they talked. The pot he had smoked and the musk of wine and grapes in the cellar made him slightly dizzy. "Maybe they're going to electrocute Mr. Cobb five or six times so everybody can have a chance to see." He pulled off his socks and flexed his muscles in the sweet liberation of nakedness.

Because he denied her the sex she wanted, China sometimes reminded him of when they used to make love together. She came over to him now, and he saw the old hunger in her eyes. "When you going to make love to me like you used to?" she said.

Joe grinned. "One of these days I'm going to make your pussy sing, just like I used to. But not now, China. I've got other things on my mind."

China snorted. "You been promising that for the longest kind of time. And you ain't done nothing about it yet."

"I will," Joe said. "One of these days, I will. Right now, I want to get these grapes mashed."

There were four large barrels filled with grapes. There were five barrels in all, but the fifth one was sealed over—full of last year's wine, according to China Doll. Joe didn't really feel like mashing grapes, but he did feel like being naked. And he loved the yearning in China's eyes. Making a big show of his nakedness, he climbed into the first barrel.

He trampled steadily for about an hour, going from one barrel to the next, until his genitals were swollen purple from the juice. Finally, he climbed from the fourth barrel. "I've got to go back to work now, China. Why don't you get Pee Wee or Lamont to come down here and mash some more?"

China Doll frowned and shook her head. "Pee Wee? Lamont? Put their black asses in my wine? Joe Market, I asked you to mash my grapes because you taste good, honey, you keep your body clean, you make my wine taste good." He was dripping grape juice from his waist and between his legs down to his feet. "Get over in that corner there," China said. She hosed him down with water and tossed him one of her monogrammed towels. Joe finished drying and looked around for his clothes; but China Doll was holding them behind her, and she laughed and shook her head when Joe asked her for them. "You don't have to go running back upstairs to work. I'm the boss lady, I asked you down here to do a job of work for me."

"China baby, you know what a hard time Odessa always gives me when I come down here with you. She's a jealous woman, Odessa is. I don't want her throwing lye and molasses on my body, not in my face."

But China would not give him his clothes. "I don't see why you want to go running back to Odessa. I'm a whole lot prettier than she is, she looks like a little wet mouse to me."

"Girl, you just trying to get me excited. Why don't you give me my clothes and let me go to work?"

Pouting, China made a pillow of his clothes and sat on them. "Odessa wants to hog you all to herself, just because she happens to be married to you. Besides, I was very surprised when you married Odessa, a good-looking guy like you."

"I was surprised, too," Joe said. He propped himself against a wine barrel so that she could get a good look at him. He felt like The Naked Disciple again.

"Then why'd you marry her?"

"Because I loved her," he said simply. "You think I'd marry somebody I didn't love?"

China Doll shrugged. "Sometimes it happens. Take Mr. Yen and me. I married him, but I didn't love him. Everybody knew that . . . he even knew it himself. *That don't matter none*, he used to tell me. *That don't matter one bit.* He was a funny little guy, Mr. Yen. I never could call him anything but Mr. Yen. His full name was Chiang Chung-cheng Yen. But I couldn't picture myself calling no husband of mine something like that. *Chiang Chung-Cheng, you want some more hog maws, some collard greens?* He was crazy about colored food. Although he had to have his rice." She smiled, remembering.

"I liked Mr. Yen," Joe said. "He was a great guy." China smiled. "Is that why you stole his turkey Easter before last?" Then she laughed at the mask of innocence that Joe spread over his face. "I caught a glimpse of Lamont high-tailing it over the fence," she said. "When I had a chance to, I went and asked him about the turkey. He told me the whole story. You fooled me, Joe, by hiding in the cellar. But I knew you'd been there, because I saw the roaches and cigarette butts you left behind. And there were some turkey feathers, too."

"China, you talk too much," Joe said feebly. And China laughed again. "Oh come on! I'm not accusing you of anything. I think it was sweet of you to help Lamont out. He certainly needs somebody to help him. . . ." Her voice grew wistful, and she shrugged then. "But, like I said about Mr. Yen . . . I didn't love him. And I wasn't sorry when he died. Does that make me evil, Joe?"

Now Joe shrugged. "I don't know. I never think about those things any more. My motto is live and let live. You know that, China."

She gazed at him shrewdly. "You don't fool me, Joe. I know that your indifference is just a big act. *Joe Market, he don't care for nothing but a piece of tail.* That's what people say about you. But I know different, Joe. You might fool other people, but you don't fool me. I know that underneath your so-called coolness, you're eating your heart out because your baby's dead. And you can't stand the thought of death. . . ."

"Bullshit!" he said harshly. "You talk things that don't make sense. I was in Vietnam. I killed men."

China's gaze bored into his. "I'm talking about your baby," she said. "For example, how did you really feel when you came home and found your little boy dead? You might talk about that sometimes. Any other man would, if he wasn't putting on a great big act."

Joe's hands dropped to his groin. "There's nothing to talk about," he said. His voice had grown hoarse; he cleared his throat. "There was an accident, the baby died. It happens every day to somebody. Now give me my clothes." He went over and tried to pull them from under her, but she pushed him away. "Man, you're not fooling me. It hurt you. It hurt you to the quick. I know you blame Odessa, too. That's why you won't have sex with her, with me, with anybody. You're trying to get even with all women because Odessa killed your baby."

"Shut up!" He slumped to the floor like she'd kicked him in the belly. "Odessa didn't kill it. It was an accident. The baby got tangled up in the covers and suffocated." His hands were trembling. He dug in his shoes and brought out a stick of pot from his socks. "Give me a light," he said.

"That's no good," China said. "You can't keep on trying to escape the truth forever. Why you so scared of feeling, Joe?"

"Give me a goddamn light!"

She fired her gold, monogrammed lighter and held it to the end of the cigarette. He sucked in the smoke, closing his eyes and letting the fumes carry him high up and away from the cellar and Decatur Street. He thought of green gardens and wine-colored birds, each one with a ruby in its throat. *Fly away, Joe. Fly away, Joe baby.*

Now he was relaxed. The knot in his stomach was gone. Death, pain, fear, they were the unreality. *Their world, their pot, their law*, he thought, meaning the white man's. He was Joe Market, he was colored, he was beautiful—didn't people pay just to see him naked?—and he was high out of it all, leaving it to "them" to squabble about questions like right and wrong, evil and redemption, like white curs around an old, old bone. The garden and the ruby-throated birds were real.

He looked up and saw that China was taking off her clothes. He handed her the joint. She lay down. He stretched out on his back and lay his head between her legs. He could smell the fertile, fleshy ooze of her pussy, but he wasn't interested in that now. He could tell that she was already high. It only took a little of the shit to get her high. But he was on it so regularly, sometimes it took three or four joints for him to really blast off. "We're both naked," he said, as if noticing it for the first time. "Yes," China said. She placed her hand flat on his chest. The impact startled him. "Your heart is beating a mile a minute," she said.

"It's the pot." He was looking up at her, underneath her breasts. From below, they seemed to be sharp-pointed and unlovely. He thought that if they came loose they'd fall on him and mash him to death. He reached up and touched them, the round swelling where they grew into her body. "Why do you like to hurt me, China? You're soft and pretty, but you like to hurt me. Why're you like that, baby?" She was quiet such a long time that he thought she would not answer him. "I guess I am cruel," she finally said. "Like talking about Odessa that way. . . ." She jammed her hand over his heart. "And your baby. . . . Joe! Your heart nearly jumped out of your body when I mentioned your baby! Man, what you *scared* of? What you trying to run away from?"

He sat up and leaned against the wall. It was hard for him to breathe. "It's the pot," he said. "This is real good shit. From Panama. You know how some of that Panama shit affects the heart."

China looked at him with a knowing smile. He was sitting with his back propped against the wall and one leg crossed over the other. She parted his legs. "Lay back," she said. "Lay back and tell me how you really felt when the baby died. Joe, you got all that hurt in you. It's eating you up inside." She reached under him and cupped his butt in both hands. She coaxed him toward her until he was flat on his back with his legs slightly bent at the knees. "It's like a snake bite inside you, Joe. Somebody's got to suck the poison out. . . ."

"Quit, China," he said weakly. "You know I'm off that kick. . . . China, quit that . . . you hear . . . ?" Sliding away from her, he lighted another joint. China kept very quiet while he smoked it. He couldn't survive without pot. It was floating in his blood, the need to smoke pot, to stay high. There was so much to forget, and so much more not to forget. He took a long, slow drag, sucking the acrid smoke into his lungs. A dazzling light exploded behind his eyes, somewhere in the area of his brain, and set his head swimming. He felt China's cool hands twine again down between his legs. "Ah . . . China. . . ." He closed his eyes and sprawled back, farther and farther back, like sliding off stairs of velvet light, deeper and deeper into the luxurious warmth of another afternoon long ago in Burnside, Virginia. *Joe baby, your mammy's dead.* And then his father had touched him, like China was touching him now. He remembered the snake, the sun, his father's hot hands. For half a second, he felt an overwhelming panic strike the center of his heart. He was surprised that his mind had flown that distance, like an arrow winging down to the red dirt hills of Virginia. He sucked on the joint, once, twice, again. . . . Dragging his leg up cruelly, he kneed China Doll under the chin. "Goddamn it, I told you to leave me alone."

China was holding her throat and trying not to cry. "Joe, you didn't have to do that. All I wanted to do was help you."

"All you wanted to do was help yourself," he said bitterly. He was mad with himself for enjoying it so much, giving in that way. "All you women the same, you just out for what you can get."

They heard footsteps on the outside stairs leading down to the cellar, and then Odessa's voice as she rattled the door and said, "China Doll, you down here? Somebody up here wants to see you."

China Doll cleared her throat. "I'm here, Odessa. I'll be right up."

They heard Odessa move away from the door. Then she stopped. "Is my Joe down here, too?"

"Ain't he out making deliveries?" China Doll wrapped her arms around Joe, holding back laughter. "That's certainly what I pay him to do."

Odessa grunted; they heard her angry footsteps going back upstairs.

"She knows I'm down here," Joe whispered. "You can't fool that woman."

China Doll shrugged. "I ain't married to her, ain't nothing she can say to me." They hosed each other down quickly. "You'd better sneak out the same way you came in," China said, "so your wife won't know what's shaking. I don't want her throwing no lye and molasses on *me*. I'm going up to the laundry now. I wonder who wants to see me . . . ? Joe . . . I want to go to that electrocution tomorrow night. Will you take me? Her eyes were bright with excitement. He breasts rose and fell rapidly. Seen from above like this, they were lovely. "I'll take you," he said. He figured that he owed her something for kicking her under the chin. "But why you want to see that preacher killed?" She was putting on her clothes. Eyes downcast, stepping carefully into her panties, she seemed almost like a little girl. "Don't you want to see him killed, too?" Joe didn't answer that, and China finished dressing and then went up the inside stairs to the laundry. Joe pulled on his clothes and crept up the back cellar stairs. He sneaked the door open and looked out. Odessa was waiting for him in the backyard. "You dirty sonofabitch," she said quietly. "I knew you were down there all the time."

"Now Odessa, don't get the wrong idea. China Doll asked me to help mash her grapes. That's the only reason I went down there."

Odessa was puffed up like a thundercloud. "You won't even touch me, you won't even sleep in the same bed with me. Now I know why. It's because you been messing around with other women. Well, I'm going to cut that thing of yours right off you. I'm going to cut it off right down to the roots. . . ."

That scared him. She didn't have a knife or anything, not that he could see. But it scared hell out of him. He took a quick step and slapped her across the mouth. "Don't you ever talk about doing a thing like that to me. You tell me anything else you want to, but don't you ever talk about cutting off my dick. You hear?" They had moved down the alley, and two or three people had stopped in the street, hoping to see a fight. Joe grabbed Odessa's arm and hustled her up to the back of the laundry. "I ought to stomp hell out of you," he said. "I ought to stomp you down in the dirt." He was more angry because she had caught him with China Doll than he was about what she had said.

Odessa was shaking all over. "I was only kidding, Joe. You know I wouldn't do a thing like that to you." She had lost all her anger, and her eyes were frightened and filled with tears.

He was suddenly contrite. He took her in his arms and pressed her hard against the gray wall with his body. "Odessa, I don't know how you put up with somebody like me. All I ever do is hurt you. . . ." He could tell that she was surprised by the abrupt change in him, and that she intended to take advantage of it. They'd had only a few tender minutes like this since the baby had died. "Let's go in and go to bed," Odessa whispered into his shoulder. "It's been a long time, Joe, and I been needing you a whole lot here recently."

But he didn't want to have sex with her. He had the feeling that she might really castrate him after all. "Let's do it here," he said. He knew that Odessa was far too middle-class to screw outdoors. "The weather is warm, the sky is so blue. We could go over there on that pile of leaves under the grapevines." He was laughing at her all the while; and she seemed to know it, for she pulled back and made a hasty inspection of his eyes. But even as she looked, he knew that his body was working its magic on her. He ground her against the wall and she went limp in his arms. "Joe, don't do that, honey. Honey . . . you going to make me wet my pants." She was breathing like a racehorse. "Get wet," he said. "They'll dry again in no while, all this heat." He eased his hands underneath her blouse and squeezed her breasts.

"It just ain't fair," she moaned. Her voice sounded like she might break out into a scream any minute. "It just ain't fair the way you turn me into nothing like this. You just playing with me . . . I *know* you just playing with me. And I still get limp as a dishrag the minute you touch me. You like a drug, Joe, like some of them drugs people shoot in their arms." She was very close to screaming now. "Joe . . . it's been a real long time. . . . Let's go inside and make love."

He shook his head. "Let's make love out here." Her eyes rolled back, like a windowshade sprung up over her eyeballs. There was a thin line of sweat over her lips. He saw the muscles of her throat tighten up, and he lowered his head leisurely and swallowed her big mouth with his, scream and all. He had her pinned against the wall, her fists beat a helpless tattoo against his back as he corkscrewed brutally against her. In a little while she would reach her climax. He unlocked his mouth from hers and rammed his tongue into the bitter cavity of her ear. He was always surprised that she could have a climax from just this amount of love play. Now he felt nothing but contempt for her, she was so easy to excite. He felt a tremor run through her body, and she jerked both legs up and locked them in a scissors around his waist. She threw her head back and gave a muffled groan that reminded him of a dog in agony. There was something about her that always reminded him of a dog, the way she whimpered, the way she whined. Now she was gritting her teeth. "Get it off, baby. Go ahead and get that nut," he said kindly. But he could not help but feel contempt for her, the way she responded to his least touch.

After a while, Odessa pushed him gently away. He could see the pulse in her throat beating like a piston. He tried to kiss her, but she turned her head. She was ashamed now. "You make me feel like a dog," Odessa said. "You're so *uninvolved*. It wouldn't be so bad if I thought you felt the same way I did—if I thought you felt *anything*." She looked away. "Is it because of another woman? Is that why you don't feel nothing for me anymore?"

"There's no other woman," he said. She seemed relieved to hear that. She drew a deep breath. "Is it because of the baby, then . . . because of what happened to the baby?"

Joe grinned like a fox, showing all his teeth. "What's the matter with you today, Odessa? A pretty day like today. You hear the birds singing? Besides . . . I thought we agreed not to talk about that. . . ." He grabbed her hand and held it to his dick, but she pulled away with a sharp little laugh.

"You see, Joe? You trying to excite me again. And the terrible thing is I *do* get excited. I'm like a junkie where you're concerned, Joe. You're a habit I'm going to have to break."

"How come you talking like this?" Joe said.

"Because you been sleeping in the living room all this time. Because of you and China Doll, that's why. You think I don't know what you and she were doing down there in the cellar? Don't play me for a fool, Joe. You ain't ever seen me really evil. But I'm warning you, nigger, I can be evil as hell. You try me, you'll see."

The fury in her eyes made him uneasy. He was desperate to neutralize her, to seduce her anger away with his body. But she evaded his touch, crouching against the wall with her claws out like a cat. "I'm warning you, nigger. You want that face of yours scratched up, you keep on."

"Odessa, what's come over you?"

"I caught you with another woman, that's what come over me. I know what you and China Doll were doing in that cellar. And you won't even sleep in the same bed with me."

"I was mashing grapes," he protested lamely.

"I know what kind of grapes you were mashing. Pussy grapes, that's the kind." Then a strange look came over her face. "I hate you," she said suddenly. And it was true, for just that moment. He could see a sharp, blazing hatred crouching in her eyes. "You ain't nothing but a big dumb nigger," she said. "My God, what a fool I've been! I thought my Joe was a beautiful man!" Her voice lashed him with scorn. "You ain't nothing, baby. You got a nice body, I grant you that. And a nice something else too, if you ever do decide to use it again. But *you*? You ain't shit, nigger. I'm all of a sudden finding that out."

"Odessa." He grabbed his groin protectively, as though the sharp scorn in her voice would castrate him on the spot. "Odessa, I *love* you, baby. China Doll and me were just messing around, smoking a little pot. But I love *you*, Odessa. I've always loved you. . . ." He was maneuvering, trying to get in position to grab her and let his body work. He wanted to reduce her to nothing. *This black bitch, I'm going to make her suck all over my dick right here in this backyard with everybody watching.* But she seemed possessed with a new knowledge and a new strength. She rushed suddenly into his arms. He heard giggles smothered against his chest. "Take me, make me, Joe, baby. Here I am, in your arms. Make me do whatever you want, honey." When she pulled away, her eyes were bright with malice. "You see, baby? You can touch me now all you want to, I don't feel a thing. It's like something went dead inside me. You killed something inside me, Joe. From now on, we're not going to have any more of this one-sided bullshit. From now on, you got to love me the same way I love you. You got to get *involved* with me. If I ever do again."

"I'm going to kick your ass," he said. Now he was whining.

"Go ahead!" She flounced around and poked her butt out toward him, pulling her dress up over her hips. "Kick it, if it'll make you feel any better." She wiggled it at him, inviting. But he didn't kick her ass, and she wiggled it some more. Then she turned around with a dreadful smile. "Well, Lawdy me! All of a sudden little dumb, whining Odessa done come to her senses. I've been hung-up on you for a long time, Joe. But no more, baby." She almost stood on tiptoe to gaze into his eyes. "Don't you understand, Joe?" Her voice dropped to a gentle register. "Something's dead in me now. It died a little while ago, when you come sneaking from that cellar. From now on, honey, you got to love me like I love you. Our marriage is going to be a fifty-fifty proposition. What I'm saying is that I'm kicking the habit. I'm no longer addicted to Joe Market."

He felt tears sting his eyes. He cupped his groin, hanging on to the only reality he understood. If Odessa no longer desired him, if no one desired him, then what was there left? And if something was dead in her, and something was dead in him, hadn't they somehow made a death of marriage? "The red shoes," he said. "I'll buy you them red shoes you been wanting."

"You do that," Odessa said. There was pity in her eyes. "I'm going back home now. There's something on TV I don't want to miss."

"Odessa?" She was going down the alley.

"Yeah?" She didn't even turn around.

"Baby . . . I *love* you. I really *do*."

"I know that, Joe," she said over her shoulder. "I know you love me. It's just that you don't *respect* me. That's what I'm mad about. You don't respect me, you don't respect anybody. The worst part is, you don't even respect yourself."

"I'll buy you those red shoes," he said miserably.

"You do that, baby."

He felt weak in the knees. Closing his eyes, he slid to his haunches beside the house and listened to the sound of her heels receding down the alley, the slamming of the door as she went into their house. He probed in his sock for another joint, but then he remembered that he had smoked the last one with China Doll. He threw his head back and howled at the top of his lungs. He sounded like a dog chained to a stake that will not yield. Then he rested his head on his hands with his elbows propped against his knees. He felt a sickening lurch inside his head, as if his mind had suddenly vomited. *I need some pot. Pee Wee would have some pot, if he's come back from Newark.* He tried to come to his feet, but his body would not respond.

For a terrible moment, he thought that he was dying. *O Lord, I've always wanted to die in winter. Please don't take me now, the sun is so warm, the vineyard smells like purple perfume. Take me when no bird is singing, when the weather is bad, when the street is wet and nasty. Besides,* he thought, with an irreverent grin, *I've got an awful lot of loving left to do.*

Now he felt better. This time when he stood up, a magnificent surge of power ripped through his body. *Fuck Odessa. She's just a spiteful bitch.* She was inside the house now, watching television. He opened his jeans and relieved himself against the house, as if by doing so, he was pissing on Odessa inside. He heard a footstep in the driveway. *Shit, I ain't finished yet. Who the hell could that be?*

It was a white man. "Hi, Joe. Put your pecker away before I run you in."

"Tony Brenzo!" He put his pecker away, and shook hands. "Man, where you been all this time? How come you didn't answer my letters? How come you didn't write to me?"

"Hey, hold your horses, man!" Tony Brenzo backed away, laughing. Joe had not seen Tony since last year before he joined the Army. They had written each other regularly for a while; then Tony had stopped answering Joe's letters. "I been busy, man," Tony said. Joe thought that he looked older and sadder. But still beautiful, Tony was. And still white. Squinting, Joe stepped back. He felt that he had to size Tony up to see whether Tony had come back with attitudes that belonged to the white world. And he could sense that Tony was trying to find out the same thing about him and the black world of Decatur. They sniffed around each other now like two dogs meeting, testing each other for danger.

"How you feeling, man?"

"I feel O.K."

"What you been up to?"

"Been talking to the President."

"What that Texan say?"

"Not much." Tony scratched his balls and spat like a nigger would. "His old lady talked all the time through her nose. She wants to beautify America."

Joe threw back his head and laughed. Everything was still all right between them. "Man, I bet she do!" He grabbed Tony and almost picked him off the ground in a massive bear hug. "Tony, I *missed* you, man!" They squeezed the sweat out of each other.

Tony had really been down in Washington, he told Joe. "They put me on a special commission investigating riots here in the Newark area."

Joe looked at him sharply. "Still being a crusader?" He sounded sarcastic, because he always resented Tony's being able to become so involved with other people. Like all those white people in the civil rights movement, arms locked, singing *We Shall Overcome* with Negroes. What did white people have to overcome? They seemed out of place to him, too. "I bet you asked to be assigned to that commission," he said accusingly.

Tony didn't deny it. "Listen, Joe. Newark was damn near torn apart by that riot last year. And rioting like that is evil, desperate, ugly. Somebody's got to do something about it, because it takes all the guts out of a city. Lord knows, Newark never was a paradise, racially speaking; but now it's even worse. It's a hollow shell with all the insides gone. Man, everybody's suspicious of everybody else. Colored and white people both walk around with guns. It's not even like America any more. As soon as the sun goes down, everything closes up." He seemed tired now; his eyes were dark and disillusioned. "I've been in special training," he said. "That's why I was down in Washington. What we want to find out is the real reason behind these riots. We think that somebody from outside is stirring up trouble between the races here."

Joe sounded very surprised. "Somebody from *outside*? Man,

those riots you're talking about were started by colored people who got tired of being stepped on by white people. They didn't need any help from outside." He sneered grandly. "And by help, I suppose you mean *communist* help. Tony baby, why you talking like this? What'd them people do to you down in Washington?" They were sitting on the pile of leaves under the grape arbor where Joe had wanted to make love to Odessa. Around them, the ugly houses of Decatur squatted with the October sun high over their heads. Tony was quiet for a while, playing with a twig. Then he said, almost angrily, "These slums are an insult to God." Joe laughed. He really didn't see that much wrong with Decatur. For one thing, a guy could do pretty much as he pleased and nobody gave a damn; there was a lot more freedom in the slums than anywhere else. "Man, what *did* Lady Bird do to you down there in D.C.? I bet you want to beautify America, too." Tony stood up, brushing off his pants. "Let's go to Roscoe's and get a couple of drinks. I want to tell you what they did to me in Washington. But I've got to get you drunk or you're not going to believe me."

Joe got up, too. "If it's going to be that unbelievable, then we ought to get some pot from Pee Wee and turn on. I bet you became a Texan, I bet that's what you want to tell me." Tony laughed, and they walked down Decatur Street to buy some pot from Pee Wee. That was one of the things that Joe liked about the slums. Where else could you get that kind of action, except in the slums? Everybody knew that Pee Wee sold pot; most of the heads in Decatur scored from him. But nobody cared. That's the way it was in the slums. Nobody gave a damn about anything.

Walking down Decatur Street, Tony exchanged greetings with some of the colored people they met.

"Hey, Tony."

"What's happening, baby?"

"Tony Brenzo, you old dog! Where you been hiding, boy? My old man went up side my head the other night, I thought about calling you to put him under peace bond. How you been doing?"

"I been all right. How you been doing?"

"Fine, Tony. Just fine. It certainly is a pleasure to see you."

Being with Tony Brenzo enlarged Joe in the eyes of the people on Decatur Street, and he gloried in their envy and admiration. *Tony talks just like a nigger when he wants to,* Joe thought. *Just like I can talk like a white man when I have to.* He stuck his chest out and swaggered. He noticed that Tony was doing the same thing. *He likes being seen with me. Who the hell cares about Odessa, with a buddy like Tony Brenzo?* The fear that had covered him with her rejection lifted now from his shoulders like a weight. He was with Tony Brenzo, and for the moment that was love and admiration enough.

Then he remembered that the laundry truck was still parked on Center Street at Pee Wee's. But he had completed the morning deliveries. Besides, he figured that China Doll owed him something for that scene in the cellar. Especially since he hadn't been able to ask her for any money. "I'm taking the rest of the afternoon off," he said to Tony. "I'm going to get stoned out of my mind."

"Hey Tony, what you say, man? You want some pussy? We got a new girl just come in from Alabama. She something else, man. She something else."

Tony laughed. "I bet she is, man. But not right now. I'm going to get stoned with my pardner Joe here."

"O.K., man. But any time you want some pussy, you know where to buy it. We'll give you a special price. How you doing, Joe?"

Joe nodded. He was doing just fine. He started thinking that there might be something to integration after all. Except that he thought that neither he nor Tony could be this swinging together in a white neighborhood. Were whores and pot so easy to come by in a white neighborhood? Probably not. And he thought there was something very sad about that.

Pee Wee had come back from Newark and was dozing in his cab at the front of Cheap Mary's. Cheap Mary herself was arranging the window of her store. She was one of the few white merchants who had stayed on in Decatur after the riot there last year. She was a big, raw-boned woman, and she stared at Joe very hard now, as if daring him to chase *her* out. But when Joe grinned at her, she nodded, then shrugged and went back to her work. Joe reached in the cab and shook Pee Wee. "Hey, baby," Pee Wee said. He yawned two or three times until he saw Tony Brenzo. "What's happening, Tony? Man, you looking good. Ain't seen you in a coon's age." Pee Wee still didn't care too much for Tony, but he could come on like he did.

"I'm doing all right," Tony said. "Dig, man. I need us three or four sticks of pot. You holding?"

Pee Wee rolled his eyes at Joe.

"It's O.K.," Joe said. "He's not a cop today. He's a spy."

"Yeah. I'm Culp, you're Cosby," Tony said. Pee Wee sold them two joints for three dollars.

Cheap Mary took a pair of red pumps from a box and placed them on a stand. There was a sign reading AUTUMN RED IN ALL SIZES—$9.95. Joe stood a moment, looking at the shoes. *I got to hustle me ten dollars and buy them shoes for Odessa*, he thought. He and Tony crossed Hickory Street and went into the toilet at Roscoe's and turned on. The pot seeped right into the marrow of his bones. When they had smoked down to the roach, Tony put it out; and they went into the bar and took two stools near the window. Tony ordered a fifth of Old Crow, one hundred proof. Roscoe served them and went back to the other end of the bar where he could watch television away from the widow's glare. There was a sports special on Channel 2. "Cheers," Tony said. They drank a quick one.

There were three winos at the bar, trying to combine their pennies for a bottle. A young, fat black woman drank beer in a booth and squinted at television. She was wearing a red kerchief, bedroom slippers, and a red dress pulled back over her knees to show her plump thighs. Joe wondered if she was the new chick from Alabama that the pimp had tried to sell to Tony. She certainly looked like it. Man, Aunt Jemima, Aunt Jemima, that's what she looked like, watching television like it'd get up and run away if she took her eyes off it. She was all lard and loose pussy, he knew that, he could tell from the way she sat. He bet she was that chick from Alabama.

Joe had a clear view of the street over the half-curtain at the tavern window. Cheap Mary was still in her window. Joe thought she was looking at him. What the hell was she looking at him for? He raised his eyes and saw a solitary bird rising and falling over the rooftops, the indication of a white-hot sun farther beyond that. "Cheers," Tony said. "Like I told you, man, you're not going to believe it. But listen anyway." Tony filled the glasses again; Joe sipped from his while Tony talked.

What Tony said was that the government suspected that at least some of the summer riots were financed and instigated in part by international communism. According to the government, drugs and money were being channeled into certain ghetto areas to finance and embolden the acts of professional rioters. "What we're looking for specifically," Tony said, "is a Chinese guy who entered this country by way of New York back in November of last year. We call him Cindy Lou. He checked into the Hotel Vendôme on Forty-ninth Street and left a parcel with the clerk to keep in the safe there. A couple of hours later, Cindy Lou left the hotel walking. He never came back to the hotel; and insofar as we know, he has neither been seen nor heard from since. The simple truth is that somebody goofed. Cindy Lou was being watched from the time he left the ship. But he led our boys all over Chinatown, and they finally wound up following some other guy to a Chinese wedding. By the time they realized their goof, Cindy Lou had disappeared. We went over his room, through all his personal things. But there was nothing to help us. Then we looked at the parcel he'd checked with the desk clerk. And what do you think we found?"

"Mary Poppins," Joe said sarcastically. But when he saw that Tony really wanted him to be serious, he relented. "O.K., so what was in the bundle?"

"Heroin," Tony said. "Cindy Lou was carrying something like a half-million dollars' worth of prime heroin stashed in that bundle when he left the ship. We'd been alerted that he was part of a big smuggling operation. But we decided to let him pass and try to find out who his contact was on this end."

Joe swallowed his drink quickly. "Man, you shucking me?"

"Naw man, I ain't *shucking* you. Aside from that, we're pretty sure that dope was headed for places like Newark and Cousinsville. You sell it, you can finance a lot of riots. You get enough people to shoot it in their arms and they're just right for rioting. Joe, somebody somewhere wants to keep trouble stirred up in ghettos like this. We're trying to find out who that somebody is so we can put a stop to it. So far, we haven't had much luck. Man, we've had two officers working that hotel desk day and night, waiting for somebody to show up and claim that package. It's been there almost a year. As far as I'm concerned, you don't check a half-million dollars' worth of dope and then not have somebody try to pick it up. But so far, nobody has." Frowning, he toyed with his whiskey glass. "Another problem we have is that all those damn Chinamen look alike. . . ."

"A prejudiced statement," Joe cut in, and Tony laughed and shook his head. "Not prejudiced, not really. Have you ever gone hunting a Chinaman in Chinatown? Anyway, like I say, everything that I'm telling you happened around last November while you were still in Vietnam. Then, just this week, I was going over Cindy Lou's file when I saw something that seemed very important. Cindy Lou was a first cousin of Mr. Yen."

Now Joe was all ears. "Mr. Yen? China Doll's husband?" He felt the hairs on the back of his neck crawling. "Man, you *got* to be shucking me!"

"Not at all. Cindy Lou was sponsored on his trip to this country by another cousin in New York. But the fact remains that China's husband was related to him, too. Another interesting fact is that Cindy Lou entered this country on November 15th of last year. On November 16th, Mr. Yen died of a heart attack. There's no doubt about the cause of death. China Doll called the police emergency squad. I've talked to the medical examiner on duty that night and the death certificate is as good as gold. So, our problem is really three problems. One—what happened to Cindy Lou? Two—who was his contact here in the States for the dope he was carrying? Three—why has no one made an effort to pick up the package he checked in New York?"

Joe poured another drink. "What about China Doll? Did she ever see the guy?"

"Never heard of him, she said. I just talked to her. We thought there might be an odd chance that Cindy Lou showed up here and asked Mr. Yen for help, or even tried to bully Yen into helping him. That sort of violence could account for Yen's heart attack. But I'm willing to take China's word that she never saw Cindy Lou." Tony filled his glass again. "By the way, did you know Yen was cremated? I guess I never thought about it much when I heard he was dead. But China told me today that he was cremated. It was in his will."

"I know," Joe said. "I sort of liked Mr. Yen. Everybody was surprised, his dropping dead that way."

"He had a bad heart for several years, according to the autopsy report. He could have been expected to go at any minute."

"I didn't know that," Joe said. And he decided not to tell Tony anything at all about him and Lamont stealing Mr. Yen's turkey, because he didn't want Tony to know he'd done something that could have caused Mr. Yen to die of a heart attack.

Tony was pouring himself a refill. "Listen, Joe . . . the reason I told you all that about Cindy Lou is because I want you to keep your eyes and ears open. If you find out anything that might help me, let me know, O.K.?"

"Sure, Tony. You know me." And he promptly forgot all about it. He didn't know yet what those people down in Washington had done to Tony. But whatever it was, it wasn't good. Joe was feeling depressed now, and he was getting very tired of Tony's bullshit, even if they were friends. "Man, I sure don't understand you," Joe said, getting up suddenly from his stool. The pot and liquor had his head spinning. "If these slums are so bad, then they ought to be changed, right? And the riots are changing them, right? Then why you worried about who's starting those riots?"

Tony's eyes were black slits. "Because any change that takes place in America has to be done *the American way*, that's why!" They were almost shouting at each other; some people had begun to stare at them. The Alabama chick kept cutting her eye, as though *she* knew that black and white could never agree on anything.

Joe grunted. Cheap Mary was still looking at him from across the street. He felt very strange from the combination of pot and liquor. And he thought that Tony must be stoned out of his mind, too, talking about the American Way. Mrs. Tate in her history class had talked about the American way of change—slow, ponderous, legal, and unequal. Riots were quick and light-footed. Not legal, but certainly equal in the way they scared the shit out of everybody. Maybe America needed more of that, not less. Joe told Tony so, and Tony frowned into his drink. "Now it's time for me to ask what these people here in Decatur have done for you. You fought in a war, Joe, for the very things I'm talking about. What happened to you? You even wrote me that they'd put a plastic tendon in your leg. Doesn't that mean anything?"

Joe turned away. "It don't mean nothing. It just hurts some-time, that's all."

Cheap Mary had disappeared from her window for a while, but now she was back again, looking directly at Joe. *Why the hell does she keep looking at me?* Just then, he realized what Tony had meant about keeping his eyes and ears open. *He meant China Doll. He wants me to spy on China Doll for him, he thinks she's mixed up in that thing some kind of way. That's why he came to Decatur Street.* He felt a bitter taste in his mouth, like he was really Bill Cosby, or some kind of informer for the Nazis in those old pictures he watched on TV. He looked into Tony's face, and Tony grinned, as if reading his thoughts. "Yeah, baby," Tony said. Angrily, Joe slammed his hand on the bar. "Man, you were right! That's the most unbelievable thing I ever heard in my whole life!"

Tony slid from his stool and picked up a pink sheet of paper from the sawdust floor. It was the circular announcing the electrocution of Mr. Cobb. GO TO TRENTON! SEE JUSTICE DONE! "More unbelievable than this?" Tony said. His jaw was set in a firm ridge. "Actually, they're both part of the same thing—this circular, and what I've been talking about. Somebody's trying to keep trouble stirred up in Decatur. All I'm asking you, Joe, is that you help me find out who it is."

Joe just couldn't see how Tony could think all that junk he was talking about was the same as Mr. Cobb being electrocuted. Hell, Mr. Cobb was a murderer! And so what if the Daredevils were running excursion buses to Trenton tomorrow? That seemed like good business to him. "I don't know what you're talking about," Joe said stubbornly.

Tony stood up and wrapped his arms around Joe so violently that they both almost fell to the floor. They were very drunk. "Joe, you're a good American. I know you are, I don't care how corny it sounds or what you say. And you love America. I know that, too. Help me, Joe. These riots could mean the end of America, of everything. . . . That's what I found out down in Washington. Joe, will you help me? Like a good buddy?" Tony's fingers dug into Joe's shoulders like steel tongs.

Joe felt a lump rise in his throat; he couldn't speak. He was way up on a mountain again, he and Tony together, like two gods high in isolation, looking down on the world. The Alabama woman looked at them like they had to be two queers, no other reason for a white man and a colored man with their arms around each other in broad daylight. "Sure man, I'll help you. I'll keep my eyes open." He wondered what that Alabama bitch would have to say about that, he said it loud enough for her to hear. "Man, I believe you if you say something's going on." He guessed he always had believed it; but in some perverse way, he had been waiting for Tony to reach out and touch him again in order to make the whole thing real. He clinked his glass against Tony's and emptied it like water. "Speaking of that electrocution, you ever been to one?" he said to Tony.

"Naw, man. You?"

"Naw. Let's go to that one tomorrow. I can get real sharp. I ain't been real sharp in a long time. Besides, I promised China I'd take her. It's not everyday you get to see a preacher fried." He was thinking about his own father.

Tony was reading the circular again as they left the tavern. "All right, we'll go," he said. "I just might be able to pick up something valuable there. Although I think there's something grotesque about electrocuting a minister. It's almost the same feeling you get when a whore dies. It's just too much." Shaking his head, he got into Pee Wee's cab and took off for Newark.

Cheap Mary was still in her window. She looked Joe straight in the eyes, and smiled this time. She had broken, dirty teeth. Why the hell was she smiling at him now? *I bet that old white bitch wants some of my sweet black dick*, he thought. The sun was going down now, the sky overhead had turned the color of blood. The Alabama woman left the tavern, swinging her Southern hips ready for work. High over the roof tops, Joe saw birds soaring in black spirals. He staggered home and passed out. Odessa was still watching television. She didn't even look up when he came in.

You'd have thought they were going to electrocute God, the way everybody was excited and running around in Decatur on the morning of Mr. Cobb's execution. Or if not God Himself, then certainly one of his more favored representatives. For the office of preacher among black people is their most sacred totem; and while Mr. Cobb was a self-confessed and convicted murderer, he was still a minister of the Gospel and therefore a messenger of God to the minds of most people in Decatur. They didn't think he'd done so much wrong, killing that Dolly Anderson girl, she wasn't nothing but a little fresh something anyway. Black preachers are forever doing wrong, and are forever being pardoned by their people, since it is thought that preachers have some kind of special mandate from God to be less restrained than even Roman Catholic priests, and everybody knows how *they* are, wearing dresses and everything. This mandate for libertinism among black preachers is thought to express itself in his enthusiasm for fried chicken, free pussy and chocolate cake, in that order of edibility.

In the neighborhood of free pussy, the black preacher is especially fortunate, since devoted sisters of the church have long ago convinced themselves that to fuck their preacher is one and the same with fucking their God, which they consider the insanest and sweetest kind of love. They are the ones who make totems out of preachers; and a delegation of just such good black Christian women had gone to Trenton yesterday to ask the Governor's pardon for Mr. Cobb, but of course the Governor, a Catholic, had refused. When this word got around Decatur, everybody fell into a state of mounting excitement. Some of the more practical church sisters began preparing shoe boxes full of fried chicken and chocolate cake to send to Mr. Cobb, they guessed he'd have to go to Redemption without any pussy, they certainly couldn't fit *that* into a shoe box. Although some of the more faithful sisters, who would never, never admit this to each other, did dip their fingers between their legs from time to time and then rubbed their fingers—they called the damp stickiness there *love juice*—on the chicken and the cake. If Mr. Cobb was as big a pussy hound as people said, he'd recognize the flavor of love juice and know that somebody somewhere still loved him.

Joe was musing over this on the sofa the morning of Mr. Cobb's electrocution. The sun was shining. He felt an initial sense of surprise that the sun would be shining on the same day that Mr. Cobb was supposed to die. He took a shower and went into the kitchen, where Odessa was fixing breakfast. "Good morning," he said; and Odessa nodded. She seemed to be in a better mood than yesterday, although he could detect a new reserve about her. She had heard about the Governor's refusal, and she told Joe. When he told her that he was going to the execution with Tony Brenzo, she only nodded again. She fed him warmed-over pluck for breakfast. He mashed cornbread down into the stew. There were pieces of pig heart, liver, lungs and windpipe in the thin, rich gravy, flavored with pepper and sage. He had heard some white people describe Negro food as filth, and that had almost turned him against it. He usually ate meats that came from the A & P in sanitary cellophane wrappers, the same way white people did. But sometimes Odessa rebelled and cooked what she called "our" food. In truth, Joe was crazy about it. But he ate it now hunched over and almost secretively, as if the whole white world was spying over his shoulder. He swallowed some of the pig heart and wiped gravy from the corner of his mouth with a delicate forefinger. Odessa sat across the table from him, drinking tea. "It's a shame they're going to kill Mr. Cobb," she said. "I mean, so soon after Martin Luther King got shot down the way he did."

Joe took a swallow of good hot coffee. "One thing don't have nothing to do with the other. Besides, Martin Luther King's been dead and buried over six months now. And they ought to kill Mr.

Cobb. He killed that Dolly Anderson. He cut her body up and threw it in Passaic River." He did not tell Odessa that he'd known Mr. Cobb down in Burnside a long time ago, because with Mr. Cobb being a murderer like he was, he didn't want anybody to know that they had known each other.

Odessa sniffed. "From all I heard about that Dolly Anderson, she deserved killing."

That was the way it was all over Decatur. Everybody had taken one position or another. Joe went to work, and felt the excitement growing as the day grew hotter and then cooled some. "You going to the electrocution?" He must have been asked that a hundred times as he made his deliveries for the laundry. When he turned the truck in and went home, China stopped him at the door. "Tony called. He said to be ready about eight o'clock." Joe nodded, and went home to supper.

For the execution, he chose his lightweight gray suit, a plain white shirt, dark blue tie, and black shoes. He had thought about wearing his black suit, but then he decided that he wasn't going to a funeral after all. He kissed Odessa on the cheek when he left the house. She had her ass up on her back again, she kept on watching television.

There was still about an hour before Tony would arrive, and Joe decided to walk around Decatur and let them niggers see him when he was really sharp. He was walking down Decatur Street when he heard Odessa call him. He turned around, and she was running down the street behind him like the house was on fire, or something. "What's the matter with you?" he said. She stood on tiptoes and kissed him on the mouth. She had been eating pluck, and he could taste it on her lips. "I ain't mad no more," she said. "You go ahead and have yourself a good time." That made him feel good. He patted her on the behind. "You go on back home. When I come home tonight, let's see if I come in there and get in bed with you." Her eyes turned clear as creek water. "I'll keep your side warm," she said. She walked back home swinging her hips because she knew he was watching her, and everybody was watching them, and she wanted to show all them niggers that Mr. Joe Market was her man, he looked so good in his thin gray suit. Whistling, Joe walked on.

"Hey, baby."

"How you doing, man?"

"I'm sharp, baby."

"You sure is, man. You sure is."

There were old people squeezed on porches, fanning with sweaty handkerchiefs or cello-shaped fans from funeral parlors. Those children who were not going to the execution played shrill games in the shadows between houses, where the dying sun hovered above in a slanting, burnished mist. Joe walked past grocery stores where open barrels of salt mackerel and hot chitterlings squatted like funky women lazing under the onslaught of flies. Smoked sausages hung in russet links over the meat counter, like the guts of somebody from upstairs. Baskets of kale and collards, cabbages and sweet potatoes formed a row along the sawdust floors, a row of watermelons against them. Joe never bought at these stores. He preferred going to the A & P and pushing that little wire cart with white women, it seemed more elegant to him.

"I bet you going to that electrocution, man."

"Yeah, I'm going. You going?"

"Naw. I'm going to stay home and watch television. The old lady bought a watermelon. I'm going to eat that and watch TV."

Joe saw men and women with their children dressed up, going out to catch the busses for Trenton. He turned the corner of Hickory Street. Pee Wee wasn't there dozing in his cab, he must be working the graveyard shift tonight. And Joe was glad of that, because if Pee Wee had been there, he'd just tell him how sharp he looked. But Pee Wee always thought he was sharp, and Joe was in the mood for fresh admiration now. He went on down to the corner of Barrow, where the busses were parked.

"Man, look at that Joe Market. I bet he going to that execution. Some people have all the luck." Joe grinned crookedly, and walked on.

There was definitely a holiday feeling to Decatur. Even old Miss Lavinia had got sharp in her dreary black and stopped looking at the ground long enough to get to the busses, as though there was some possible relief in sight for all the suffering God had put her through. As the Daredevils had advertised, there were two busses waiting at the corner of Hickory and Barrow Streets to take people to Trenton. And there was a crowd of people milling around now—the electrocution was scheduled for the ambiguous hour of midnight, and the trip to Trenton would take about three hours—with shoe boxes of chicken and chocolate cake for Mr. Cobb, and portable radios, baskets of food, and thermos jugs of Kool-Aid for themselves, as though they were going to a moonlight outing at Coney Island. All of the Daredevils were there, slicked and greased like peeled onions, two of them with shirt sleeves aggressively rolled above their thick black biceps, selling tickets at each bus door.

Tony came for Joe and China Doll just before eight o'clock. He was very disturbed about the busses going to Trenton. "They're never going to let all those people in," he said. China Doll wore an amazing new beige miniskirt; it stopped just midway of her thighs, and rose even higher than that as she slid into the car. "Joe says they're going to electrocute Mr. Cobb five or six times just to accommodate everybody," she said. The three of them sat in front. Tony drove, changing from time to time with Joe. Around eleven-thirty, they reached the penitentiary at Trenton.

The two busloads of people from Decatur were already there, and the passengers were swarming around outside in a kind of sullen anger. Somehow catching sight of Joe, Miss Lavinia waddled over to him, her eyes completely downcast as though she was picking her way through the Forty-Year Wilderness. "Those Daredevils gypped us out of our money and now they just laughing at us. That man on the gate won't let us in, he say we need a special pass. I bet those Daredevils knew that all the time." She raised her eyes long enough to look hopefully at Tony; but when he showed her the passes that he had managed to wangle for China Doll and Joe and himself, Miss Lavinia sighed, and picked her way back to the busses where the Daredevils had locked themselves in until the crowd cooled off. "We ought to electrocute *them*!" somebody shouted. A Daredevil stuck his head through the window. "If you all don't act right, you all going to have to walk back to Decatur." Somebody threw a thermos bottle, and he yanked his head back inside the bus.

Parading back and forth in front of the penitentiary were pro-Cobb pickets and anti-Cobb pickets. Joe was surprised to see white and black people both, some of them women pushing baby carriages. "Now you know them babies ought to be home in bed," he whispered to China Doll—there was something about the whole situation that inspired secret voices—but she was looking at the imposing gray walls of the penitentiary like she was on her way to screw somebody inside, that's how she looked. Her lips were parted, and Joe could see slivers of her teeth where she held the tip of her tongue firmly between them. That miniskirt was so short she might as well have been naked; and she kept rubbing her hands over her breasts, almost as if in invitation to the prison itself, the almost unholy musk of maleness that permeated even here beyond the outer wall, the bright, unyielding spotlights that glared down on everybody.

Joe could feel the jealousy of the other people from Decatur as they loaded back on the busses now, and he stepped smartly through the prison gate after the guard had inspected their passes. He felt a certain pride at being the only colored man from Decatur who was going to see the spectacle. Some of the guards were colored, as well as some of the other spectators; but none of them had the scrubbed, self-assured aspect of Joe Market as he followed China Doll and Tony Brenzo into the small execution room and sat down with them on the stiff metal chairs. After all, it wasn't every day that one nigger had the chance to see another nigger burn.

The room was painted white, like the inner chamber of some public clinic. "When they going to burn him?" Joe said to Tony in a solemn undertone. Tony checked his watch. "Soon now. It's a quarter to twelve." So, they waited until the very last minute of the day to kill a man. True, it did give Mr. Cobb the whole day to enjoy, if you could call it that, a man waiting to be fried to death in that shiny chair. They had it set on a platform, and a dais on top of that, so that you almost got the idea that it was a throne and that pretty soon the green door would open and a king or a queen would walk in, or maybe even a pope to bless the tense little crowd. Joe thought that electric chair looked somehow like judgment seat, the broad arms for God to rest His arms on while He meditated, the coils rising high from that silver dome overhead like a kind of modified hair dryer. Man, he hoped Mr. Cobb had a lot of good insulation. Tony nudged him. "What you chuckling about, man?"

"I'm just nervous, that's all." He got control of himself, but something inside him still giggled.

China was chewing gum so hard that Joe could hear the bones in her jaw crack every time she smacked down on it. He moved his lips carefully to her ear, the way people whisper in church. "China, this ain't no time to be chewing gum, honey." She took the gum from her mouth and preserved it in a ball on the back of her hand. It looked like a large and ugly wart there. "I'm going to need something to chew on the way home, I know I can't find no Juicy Fruit at this hour of the night. Man, I sure wish they'd get started. If there's one thing I can't stand, it's waiting." Her eyes were so bright and shiny he wondered if she might have a fever or something.

The other people in the room seemed to be getting restless, too. Joe could feel a kind of tension that seemed to move from one person to another like the leisurely crawling of chinches in bedcovers, biting here and there as one person twitched, another rubbed his ear lobe, another moved in a beautiful slow grind down on his buttocks, as though to mash the tension to death. This whole room could be a part of Lady Bird's program to beautify America, a beauty parlor where ugly things were put to death. Stolid and upright, that silver dome overhead, the chair waited for its next client.

Mr. Cobb seemed to appear almost unexpectedly. A shock went through the room, as though everybody had forgotten for a moment why they were really there. Mr. Cobb was escorted by half a dozen guards and a *black* chaplain mumbling something from the Bible. Joe almost expected to see Mr. Cobb wearing a suit and tie, but he was dressed in a thin gray prison outfit that seemed to have been especially pressed for the occasion. The pants, like a scarecrow's, flapped around his ankles where they had slit them to fit the electrodes.

Joe was surprised to see how old Mr. Cobb had got. The last time he'd seen Mr. Cobb had been in 1951—seventeen years ago, that was true. But still, he didn't expect to see them kill an old man here today. He bet Mr. Cobb was at least fifty years old, maybe older. He wondered if Mr. Cobb recognized him, or even if Mr. Cobb could see him. Because those spotlights were so strong in his eyes that he had them drawn together into slits, like a tired old lizard, as he turned to face the spectators. Joe thought it was a damned shame that they should be killing somebody as old and tired as Mr. Cobb seemed to be.

But his strongest impression was that seeing Mr. Cobb was like seeing his own father brought back on stage after an absence of some twelve years. It was not the physical thing that made him compare Mr. Cobb to his father. For Mr. Cobb was shorter than Titus Market had been, and far blacker. He looked ashy now underneath his black, but that could have been due to the bright lights. His head was completely shaved and round like a basketball, whereas Titus Market's had been shaped like a football about to be punted. But what really reminded him of Titus Market was the fact that both of them had killed their wives. In a different way, that was true—Titus Market had literally screwed Ramona to death—but Joe thought it was important that two men who claimed to be preachers of God had each killed his wife, as though the practice of loving God left no real room for the loving of women.

"Does the condemned man have any last words?" The nigger prison preacher said that. Between him and Mr. Cobb, there existed a stiff formality as they carried out their separate roles in front of the white officials. But Joe wondered how he really felt, that other preacher, getting ready to watch another nigger preacher get electrocuted. *Does the condemned man have any last words?* It was almost as though the prison preacher was saying to Mr. Cobb, "Man, the fact that we're both colored preachers means that you dishonored me by killing that girl. Now the white man suspects all black preachers. I've got to help them kill you, man, if I want to stay alive myself."

Mr. Cobb took a broad step and mounted the platform like he

was going up into a pulpit to preach. "Yes, I have prepared some last words," he said. His voice poured out in round, ministerial tones. "I found out a long time ago that the duty of the church is not to save sinners, but to make a man sin. It is fear of the example of Christ that causes good men to turn bad. *Follow the example of this man*, the church says, *and you'll wind up on the cross just like he did*. The promise of heaven is pale indeed when a man has to die in order to achieve it. That is all I have to say." Almost majestically, he stepped back and sat down in the shiny chair. The attendants moved in and strapped his arms severely, testing the bonds to make sure that they were secure. When Mr. Cobb spread his legs so that they could strap his ankles, all of his manhood fell in a fat round pile to the chair seat. *He's going to get his balls burned*, Joe thought. He felt his own balls cringe inside their sac and, at the same time, the slow growth of his dick down his leg. He looked, and saw China's hand resting on his thigh. "Move your hand," he whispered. But she opened her fingers and spread them all around him.

The attendants put a mask that looked like a black rag over Mr. Cobb's face and head; then they placed that metal dome on his head and came down from the platform. Mr. Cobb shifted in the chair, trying to find himself a comfortable position. He kept his head up straight. Somewhere above them, the prison clock began striking midnight. Mr. Cobb gripped the arms of the chair, and the nigger chaplain raised his voice in satisfied prayer. "Receive, O God, the soul of this Thy son who has gone astray."

The lights dimmed then, and Mr. Cobb jerked in the chair like he'd been stung by a snake. Joe felt a jagged shock zigzag through his own body. Every time the lights dimmed, Mr. Cobb jerked and his legs snapped wide open. Incredibly, Joe saw that Mr. Cobb had a hard on. He guessed the electricity did that. He had a hard on himself, China was squeezing it half to death. He smelled, or imagined that he smelled, the foul, subtle odor of fried flesh. Then the lights dimmed for the last time and a little white man stepped forward with a stethoscope. He bent over Mr. Cobb, then straightened up. "I pronounce this man dead," he said. Angrily, Joe knocked China's hand away from his dick. The nigger chaplain picked up his praying. "Receive, O God, the soul of this Thy son who went astray. . . ." The crowd got up and left. Joe was almost crying. Shit, he hadn't thought that watching somebody get electrocuted was going to be like that. He was so angry and disgusted that he felt like killing somebody himself, he'd certainly kill with more mercy and dignity than that motherfucking electric chair. As they moved out of the tight passageway into the prison yard, Joe grabbed China roughly by the shoulder. "What the fuck's wrong with you, China? You sick or something, grabbing my dick like that when somebody's getting electrocuted?" China's eyes and lips were swollen as though she'd been making love. She bit the ball of gum from her hand and went back to chewing it. "How come your dick got like that?" China said. Joe let go of her shoulder. He felt like shit. "And what about you?" he said, hissing at Tony now like an angry goose. "Did you see your goddamned conspiracy?" Tony was unusually pale under the strong lights in the prison yard. "I saw it," he said. "If you didn't see it, you're blind." But Joe was looking now at ten or twelve shoe boxes stacked up in the guardhouse at the gate. One of the guards checked them out while another one kept his eyes on those shoe boxes full of fried chicken and chocolate layer cake that some of the good sisters had smeared with love juice for Mr. Cobb. And he hadn't even had time to eat any of it. "I pronounce this man dead." I pronounce this man *murdered* was more like it. One guard checked the visitors out while the other guard kept an eye on those shoe boxes, nigger women always do cook real good when they cook for a nigger preacher.

Joe, Tony, and China Doll were very quiet on their way to the parking lot, each occupied with his own thoughts. After Tony had backed his car out, China slid into the front seat between him and Joe and fell asleep almost at once. Her miniskirt had slid up to her belly button, but she kept her legs virtuously glued together, even as she slept. Joe rode with his head half out the window, letting the cool air blow in his face. In a little while, he felt better. Shit, he didn't care about Mr. Cobb. He didn't care about anybody who was stupid enough to let himself get killed like that.

It had been nearly eight hours now since he'd smoked pot, and that was the longest single period he had been without pot in almost a year. His mind felt extremely clear. And different somehow, as though there were really two of him—the one riding with Tony and China Doll in the car, the other floating somewhere over the car and watching him as he rode. He often had this feeling of being twins, one of him invisible but quietly active; although he had thought sometimes that the thing flying above him was something wicked and consuming, like a kind of shrill, mindless bird that would peck his brains to pieces if it ever got to him. But the presence tonight was as soft and smooth and soaring as swallows; he felt comfortable about it, like one feels about a following pet, and a kind of relaxation that is very kin to love. He remembered when he had been The Naked Disciple and he had been ignorant of love while at the same time he had wondered whether he might not be a god. But the years in between had taught him differently. Now, he saw himself as possibly more human than any other person. And weaker or stronger, depending on whether it is weak or strong to kill one's own son to save him from death at the hands of less merciful murderers. . . .

His head jerked at that. For it was true that he was a murderer in the eyes of society. Although God—and there *had* to be a God— would certainly understand and forgive him for everything; for God had killed His own son, or, rather, had turned Christ over to the more merciful Romans, rather than subjecting Him to the cruelest divine wrath. Titus had preached a sermon on that once, how God's anger could only have been appeased by God Himself in sacrifice. Surely dying at the hands of Romans was more merciful than dying in the awesome hand of God. . . .

The New Jersey Turnpike ran smooth as glass, and Joe rode on with a feeling of great confidence and satisfaction. *Christopher baby, you ought to thank your Daddy, sweetheart. Just look what he saved you from.* Vietnam. Castration. Electrocution. Assassination in Memphis, or in Los Angeles, like Robert Kennedy. And saved from the indignity of being black in a white world, of white boys on Southern twilight roads, and white men lynching niggers wearing women's dresses, his father had told him about Roosevelt, how he'd died wearing one of Madame Eudora's flowered dresses. *I saved you from all that, Christopher. Ain't you glad?*

It was nearly four o'clock in the morning when they got to Decatur Street. Mumbling her thanks and yawning, China Doll went up to her apartment. Joe and Tony sat in the car for a last cigarette. "I'm in the mood for a Triple-S scene," Tony said. "Why don't we go up and make China?" Joe shook his head, and Tony looked at him sharply. "Man, you pissed or something?"

"Naw. I'm just tired. Tony . . . dig . . . what did you mean about a conspiracy at that execution? What kind of conspiracy?"

Tony ground out his cigarette in the ash tray. "It was like everything in that guy's life was destined to lead him to that particular place at that particular time. I believe in law and order, but killing a man that way seems to be an insult to human dignity."

"He died with a hard on," Joe said proudly. He thought it really meant something, a Negro preacher dying like that. Like some old western cowboy dying with his boots on. "I didn't tell you this before," he said, "because I was ashamed for anybody to know. But now I'm not. When I was a little boy in Burnside, Virginia, I played the Christchild in a Christmas tableau. Mr. Cobb was the preacher there." He got out of the car and closed the door.

"Mr. Cobb died like a real man," Tony said, leaning across the seat. "They would've had to drag me to that damned chair. And, like you said, he died with a hard on."

Joe nodded. When they killed him, however they killed him, he hoped he'd have a hard on, too. He said good night to Tony and went into the house.

He could tell from the cadence of Odessa's breathing that she only pretended to be asleep. She was covered by a sheet, and the contours of her body excited him for the first time in months. He was a man, and he was still alive; he wanted to thank God for that. Bending down, he kissed Odessa. "Odessa, baby. Wake up, honey." Her eyes opened and closed with the speed of a shutter. "You smell like a pole cat. Get away from me until you wash that other woman's smell off your body."

"Odessa, that ain't no other woman you smell. That's just me, honey. Sometimes I smell like that in this kind of weather." But the excuse sounded weak even to his own ears. Of course it was China Doll's perfume that Odessa smelled, some of China's pussy-and-perfume smell that had rubbed off on him. But he still resented Odessa reacting to him that way just when he'd decided to be nice and fuck her for a change. "Besides, I think you got your nerve, asking me where I been. I'm a man, baby. I don't have to explain to no woman where I been."

Odessa sighed. "I didn't ask you where you been. You must have a guilty conscience. I said you smell like a pole cat."

Man, that must be her own pussy she smelled. But he decided to enjoy himself. "It's the best smell in the world, honey. Soon as I wash this funk off me, I want to get some of yours. I ain't had none of your pussy in a long time, and I want some now." He turned on the light and started to undress, peeling the gray pants down his lean hips. He knew that Odessa liked to watch him undress, that it excited her the same way people get excited at a striptease show. She raised up on her elbow and reached for a cigarette. But that was just an excuse to get a better look at him. He pulled off his shoes, socks and T-shirt. Odessa sat up in bed now; and from the rapid rise and fall of her breasts he knew that excitement was getting the best of her. *She'll be begging for my dick in a minute*, he thought, watching it get stiff. Grinning, he flexed his muscles, making them ripple down the hard length of his body like a sleek black cat. Then he walked toward the bed. Odessa's eyes crossed and almost popped out of her head as she stared at his dick. *Like something in a trance*, he thought. *Like a lady bird charmed by a snake.* Deliberately, he took the cigarette from her hand and stubbed it out in the ash tray. Odessa didn't move. Her lips were swollen with passion. Fat and full of juice. *Like a blackberry*, he thought. *If I stick this fat pin in her lips, they'd pop wide open.* He tightened his leg muscles and flexed his but, arching his body closer to the bed.

Odessa groaned. "Go wash first, Joe. You still got that other woman's smell on you. . . ." Man, talk about imagination. He ran his fingers through her hair. Cool wire. "I'm your wife, Joe. Don't make me do something like this without washing first."

"I ain't making you do nothing, baby. You want me to go wash, then I'll go wash." But he did not move, except a slight shift of his body toward her. He massaged her skull gently with his fingertips, dragging her closer to him. "But if you love me, baby, you won't care whether I'm clean or dirty. Just go ahead and do what you want to. Show me you love me."

"Joe. . . ." Squirming frantically toward him, she made contact. The shock of it almost knocked him off his feet. One time he had gone fishing with Tony in the ocean, and the large-lipped dolphins took the bait with that same kind of electric impact, making a noise like a shotgun blast over the low-lapping waves. He fell sideways, moving carefully to bring Odessa with him. Her hair crawled all over his belly. Sticking out his leg, he dragged the cord from the table lamp out of its plug. Darkness swallowed him like a second black mouth. *Man, I ain't shit, making my wife do something like this when she don't really want to.* But the feeling of guilt was as quickly replaced by a mixture of power and contempt. She desired him, she loved him—it was the same thing. He grabbed her by both ears, tugging her away. "Odessa baby, I thought you said you hated me?" But she was moaning deep down in her throat. She fought his hands away. "You'll be sorry for this," she whined. He grinned in the darkness. Shit, he didn't care. She was far too gone to stop now, she was working on him like a madwoman. That'd teach her to say she didn't love him, to scare him the way she had yesterday. *Work baby, work on that good meat.*

Later on, Odessa raised up over him. "Kiss me now if you love me," she said, almost like a challenge, her stale hot breath dropping like dew into his face. He could have kissed her—the funk in her mouth was his own, the residue from his loins, and he loved that funk of himself. Instead, he turned away from her. "You must be kidding, baby. You go brush your teeth and rinse your mouth out, then I'll kiss you . . . if I ain't sleep by then. . . ."

She sat a long while hunched over him in the darkness. Finally, she gave a long sigh. "Is it because of the baby that you treat me like this? Because I let the baby die?"

A gentle tenderness in her voice touched him; but he clenched his teeth and forced himself to laugh. "You're real funny, Odessa. I don't even think about that baby anymore."

"A nigger man ain't shit," Odessa said bitterly. "All you niggers are the same. You think you know everything. And what you don't know, what you don't understand, you laugh at. Just like you're laughing now. But I know you're crying on the inside, I just drank from your body, Joe Market, and nothing came out but tears."

He was touched beyond pretending. "That was beautiful, Odessa, what you just said." He had been lying with his back to her. He rolled over and wrapped his arms around her.

"Oh Joe, you feel me *shudder* when you touch me? Don't that mean nothing to you, honey?"

"Odessa, I'm going to cry in a minute. You're going to make me cry, baby." He was kissing her face, her throat, returning to her lips, swallowing them with his own. The tears came. "I love you, Odessa. God, I love you so much! That's why I hate you sometimes. I think you got the hoodoo on me. I don't think a man's supposed to love a woman like I love you. . . ."

"Joe honey, talk to me honey . . . you ain't talked to me like this in over six months, I been keeping count. . . ."

"You scare me, Odessa, that's why I treat you mean. You know so much about me. Sometimes I hate you, knowing so much about me the way you do."

Odessa squirmed closer to him. "That's the way a good marriage is supposed to be. We ain't supposed to have no secrets from each other. I know everything there is to know about you."

She sounded so completely sure of herself that it annoyed him. "Not everything," he said. His mouth suddenly went dry, as though he had sucked a green persimmon; and he wet his lips with the tip of his tongue.

"What don't I know about you, Joe? You tell me right now." She was in a playful mood. She tickled his ribs and whacked him in the chest. "You tell me right now."

Fear formed a hard knot in his belly. "I can't tell you, Odessa." He laughed, to keep with her mood. But she detected the hollowness in his voice, and she grew serious at once.

"Is there something I ought to know, honey, something you've been holding back?"

He cursed himself for a fool. If he had been smoking pot, if he had been high, he'd never have made a remark like that, about her not knowing everything about him. About Christopher. The pot was important for that reason; when he was high, he could forget the terrible pounding of secret small fists at his brain cage. Also, if he'd been high, he never would have made such a fool of himself, crying all over Odessa that way, kissing her in the mouth after she'd gone down on him. And there wasn't a bit of pot in the house.

"Tell me, Joe. I'm not going to let you rest until you do."

He rolled from the bed and went to the window. Decatur Street was still dark; dawn was an hour or two away. He heard Odessa's feet hit the floor. Her naked body moulded against his from behind, and she wrapped her arms around his waist, holding him gently. "Tell me, Joe, whatever it is. I'm your wife. I got a right to know what's troubling you."

"Maybe it ain't none of your business," he said sharply.

"Everything about you is my business."

He could not avoid the heat of her hand, pouring from her fingertips like hot lead. She held him deliberately, as if knowing that the anger could not flow out as long as she loved his body that way, holding him now with one hand and smoothing the other down his chest and belly.

He felt like a woman, being caressed that way. How many women had he stood behind and caressed in the very same manner? It was an incredible sensation, that while his dick swelled and throbbed in her hand, the rest of him could tremble and respond like a woman to the smooth, caressing motion down his belly and chest. He felt helpless in her hands. And when she asked him again, "What is the secret, Joe?" he bit his tongue to keep from screaming out the truth that her fingers sought so eagerly. He had to get away from her. "I've got to get some pot," he said, tearing himself away from the pressure of her body, the probing of her hands.

"At this hour?" She knew the panic she had struck in him, and she reached out to press her advantage.

But he was filled with terror, and backed away. "Pee Wee's at the cab stand," he said. "I think I'll go just like this . . . naked . . . I know a way over the back fences, nobody will see me. . . ."

Odessa turned the wall light on now. "You in such a hurry to get away from me, you'd go *naked* . . .?"

That was another error—his haste to leave—because it only sharpened her interest. "Joe, what is it? Your eyes are scared white! Joe Market, you tell me the truth, you hear? What you been holding back from me?"

She lunged at him in a fury, her two small fists ready to beat the truth out of him if need be, as though any secret of his so dark and frightening was also a threat to her. But Joe stepped quickly to one side, and went out the back door, naked in the warm October night.

Odessa was right behind him. "Joe, come in the house! You lost your mind or something? You come in here right now!"

But he had to get away from her. He halfway hoped that the police would catch him and lock him up so that he would never again be in danger of revealing his whole self to her. "You go on to bed, Odessa. I'll be all right. . . ."

"You done lost your mind! You ain't got no business being outdoors naked like that!"

He saw a way to get her inside. "You want to wake the neighbors up?" That had its effect; her voice dropped an octave and she scooted back inside the door, aware that she was also naked.

"I just want to get some pot, Odessa." He was calmer now that her fingers were no longer trying to milk the truth about Christopher out of him. "I'm going to hop these back fences down to Pee Wee, and I'll come back the same way. It's nearly five o'clock in the morning, there ain't a soul out to see me."

He could tell that she was still undecided. "The moon. . . ." she began. But he suddenly grew impatient, and whirled, taking the fence between him and China Doll's backyard in a beautiful vault.

"Joe, I won't be here when you get back." He looked over his shoulder and saw that she had smacked her hand over her mouth after saying that. Her noise, if anything, would give him away. She did not call again. The wind was warm and gentle on his body. He saw the faint blur of Odessa in the doorway, watching him. He tossed his hand in a light salute. Then, working close to the building so that she could not see him from her angle, he tensed his long legs and sprang the next fence.

There were perhaps six backyards now between him and the corner where Cheap Mary's store joined Decatur with Hickory Street. He took each fence in the same joyous way. Released from its prison of clothes, his body exulted in the naked play of power. His heart beat at a slow, restrained tempo. Crouching like some wild animal on the stalk for whatever prey, he moved easily from one yard to the next, always favoring the side closest to the rear of the houses, in case someone might be up and see him.

The full moon seemed a jungle moon, the expanse of backyards an African plain. Approaching Cheap Mary's yard, he saw a locust tree hooked over in the moonlight. He took the last fence and crept to the foot of the tree. He felt an overwhelming impulse to climb it, to stand tall and naked in its highest branch and beat his chest at the moon. The tree was short and stunted, but strong enough to hold him. He reached up and grabbed the lowest limb and swung into the tree. He heard the dry crackle of leaves as the tree took his weight, like the rustle of a woman's crinoline as he entered her.

Once, he thought, *a naked savage stood in every tree, but now I am the only man with balls enough to get naked and climb a tree.* He threw his head back and bayed silently at the heavens, tensing his legs to keep his balance. Suddenly, the tree shifted, and he fell to the ground. "Ouch!" he said, and he cursed some. His shoulder, which had taken the impact of the fall, was numb and throbbing. He stood up and shook himself experimentally, but nothing seemed to be broken. He crept across the yard. Just then, someone spoke to him from the darkened window above his head.

"What are you doing here naked in my yard at this time of night?"

It was Cheap Mary, sitting in her kitchen window. "I've been watching you all the while. Why did you climb my locust tree? Who are you?"

He was too surprised to move or speak. Suddenly, a light came on full in his face, blinding him. He realized that she had turned on the kitchen light in order to see his features. He stood with his eyes closed until the light went off again.

"I know you," Mary said. "You're that colored fellow that lives up the street. You work in the hand laundry. You married Miss Lavinia's daughter, Lavinia and I have been friends for years. She used to clean for me once or twice a week before my husband died."

Joe lost his fear. It occurred to him that if she was going to call the police, she would have done so by now. The tone of her voice was natural and unafraid, as if she surprised a naked man in her yard every night. His mouth felt dry from the initial fear. "Can I have a glass of water?" He moved closer to the window. When she stood, he saw that she wore a long white gown. He heard the running of water, and then she thrust a glassful out the window at him. He drank greedily, and gave the glass back.

"Want some more?"

"No, thank you, ma'am."

She was quiet awhile.

"Want to come in? Maybe you'd like a small drink?"

"No, ma'am. I think I'll be going on home."

He heard her shift position in the window, slowly, as if it caused her pain to do so.

"This isn't the first time I've seen you in my yard," Mary said. "I saw you when you came home from the Army, the time your baby died."

He was suddenly dizzy. The moon exploded like firecrackers in his face. Holding to the window sill for support, he whispered, "How you know about my baby?"

"Everybody in Cousinsville knew about that unfortunate accident." He felt her hand cover his, the dry, rough skin curling around his own. He was disgusted by the contact, but he was afraid to pull his hand away. "You'd better come inside so we can talk this thing over," she said. Mercifully, the pressure on his hand disappeared.

There was a low stoop leading to the kitchen door. He heard a latch withdrawn and then saw the white blur of her gown in the doorway. Her arm came up, beckoning to him. He let go of the window sill and almost fell. His knees seemed full of water. Mary opened the door wider. He staggered up the stairs and squeezed past her into the kitchen. For just an instant, she pressed her body against his. Then she turned and led him into the bedroom. She closed the kitchen door and locked it. They were sealed together in her bedroom.

Cheap Mary was a large Jewish woman of nearly seventy, almost as tall as Joe's own six feet. Her eyes were enormous black daisies, ringed by lashes that seemed to be painted on with a thin pencil. She crouched in front of him now with a fever burning in her eyes, letting them run slowly up and down his body. Joe was terrified of her, and he was at the same time intensely aware of his nakedness. "Ma'am, you got something I can put on?" He forced himself to grin. "I didn't expect to do no visiting, I was just taking me a little stroll."

Mary shook her head. "I sold all my husband's clothes after he died," she said. "The only clothes I've got here are some of mine." Her hair was yellow, streaming down her shoulders like twine; but as she ducked her head, gazing at his enormous dick, he saw that her hair was gray where it grew out from the part. She was bent over almost double now, inspecting his dick. Then she raised her head and he saw laughter working round her mouth in a light smirk. Age hung underneath her eyes in small satchels. Her skin was the color of ashes beneath the flecks of powder on her forehead. The rouge on her cheeks seemed like large red berries growing in the skin. "You wouldn't mind putting on some of my clothes, would you?"

"Ma'am, I'm a *man*, I don't want to be wearing no woman's clothes."

She seemed not to hear him. There was a chiffonier on tall carved legs in one corner near the bed. She dug in the drawers and came out with a thin orange negligee. "This'll do just fine," she said. She flung the negligee out until it billowed between them like a delicate cloud. "You put that on . . . it always has been too big for me. Then I'll make us a nice drink—I have a bottle around here somewhere—and we'll talk about the way your baby died. Your poor wife, why Miss Lavinia told me Odessa nearly lost her mind when the accident happened that way."

She prattled on, ducking into the closet and coming out with a bottle of whiskey and two glasses. There was a pitcher of water on the bedside table. She poured two large drinks and cut each one with a drop of water. "You're such a *huge man*," she said, "I know you can take your liquor straight. So can I. The water's a concession to morality. But, then again, you don't think much of morality, I gather." Her lips puckered in a girlish smile. "The negligee, haven't you put it on? Put it on, please. It's much too large for me, so I'm sure it will fit you. Besides, it goes well with your color." Although she smiled, there was a firm tone of command in her voice. Joe drew the gown around his shoulders and stuck his arms through the billowing sleeves. It fit him, as she had said. But the soft material offended his body, and he planted his hands on both hips and spread his legs, holding the gown open arrogantly to expose his dick.

"You see?" Mary clapped her hands. "I knew it would fit you. And it becomes you, too. Now we've got to do something about underpants for you. You look so . . . so *grotesque* . . . hanging out that way."

She scooted to the dresser and dug out a pair of large, baggy bloomers. "Yes, these will do fine. They'll cover that horrible part of you, that nasty man part."

He was determined not to put them on. "You got something on your mind about my baby, you tell me so I can go. . . ."

Mary shook her head. "It's not going to be that easy," she said harshly. Then she smiled, and her voice changed. "Oh, I'm not trying to hold you against your will. It's just that I get lonely sometimes, I need someone to talk to. You don't know how many times I've got up in the middle of the night and sat in that kitchen window, feeling so lonely I'd almost die. I'd pray for someone to come along and maybe have a little drink with me, a little conversation. When you came along, I knew my prayers had been answered." She took a drink, frowning in a ladylike way. "But, as I said, tonight isn't the first time that I've seen you in my yard. Now . . . why don't you put on those lovely bloomers? They're *expensive* bloomers, really. And they certainly will stretch. I bought them at Bamberger's three or four years ago, although they're still in very good condition. Now why don't you put them on and then sit here beside me on the bed? And it's not that I'm trying to emasculate you, degrade you, anything like that. . . . It's just that my husband . . . well, he was also a large man—I mean, sexually large, like you are, although he was physically rather small in the body . . . and he used to hurt me something awful in our more . . . intimate . . . moments. I wasn't very sorry when he died, he left me well off, there was insurance, the store to keep me occupied. . . ." She paused in her rambling and took another drink. "Have you definitely decided not to put my bloomers on? You were so handsome that night in your dungarees and T-shirt when you sneaked back through my yard—Oh, I saw you, all right—so *man* looking, I can understand your not wanting to put on my bloomers. It's just that you insist on showing me that ugly *thing*, it frightens me to see it. My husband was built the same way."

So, she had seen him. He hadn't doubted it from the first minute she'd spoken to him. But now he was sure. He was determined to find out all that she knew. Wrapping the gown around him, he stepped into the bloomers and drew them over his hips. Except for the elastic in the waist and legs, they could have been a man's baggy underwear. He was not nearly so offended by them as he was by the negligee. But she had seen him going through her yard the same night that Christopher died. He wondered how much she really knew. How much of what she heard—the gossip from Miss Lavinia and other customers who told white folks everything that happened in colored houses—how much had she been able to piece together from that? He threw his head back and swallowed all of his drink.

"My husband used to drink the same way," Cheap Mary said, filling his glass again. "He was a man of enormous appetites, my husband was. I suppose all real men have enormous appetites. We lived together for over thirty years before he died. He was a very strange man, I'd learned to expect anything from him. After a while, nothing he did surprised me. That's why I wasn't too surprised when I saw you naked in my yard a little while ago. Living with my husband taught me not to be surprised by anything. Living around colored people the way I do, making a small living off them, has taught me the same thing." She laughed, and raised her drink in a mock salute. "I bet you were a lot more surprised than I was," she said. "When I spoke to you the first time, you nearly jumped out of your skin."

"I thought all decent, respectable people would be asleep in bed," Joe said curtly.

Cheap Mary considered that. "An odd distinction. I mean, that you know what decent and respectable are, but you don't consider yourself a part of it. Obviously you don't, or you wouldn't be roaming around people's backyards naked that way. Don't you have any respect for the law? You know it's against the law to run around naked the way you were."

"The law is for weak people. I'm not weak. Why should I respect the law?"

"I've been here for thirty years in this neighborhood," Mary said. "I've noticed that attitude in all the colored people. I've even talked to my friend Lavinia about it, the idea colored people seem to have that they're somehow outside of so-called white morality. You look like an intelligent young man, do you know what I mean?" At Joe's nod, she continued. "I understand that attitude of the colored people. My husband was the same way. He wasn't colored—he was Jewish, like myself—but he also felt that the law was for other people, weak people. When you say weak people, you mean white people, don't you?"

He nodded without hesitating. She drew her knees up and wrapped her arms around them. "You do not consider yourself weak, you have contempt for weakness. Yet, you've allowed yourself to be weakened by putting on my negligee and bloomers. I can only surmise from this that I know something about you that you'd rather I kept to myself. For instance, you don't want Miss Lavinia to know that you were on Decatur Street the night your baby died . . . at approximately the same time the baby died. You don't want her to know that, do you? You wonder how I know? Well, I'll tell you. But first, I want another drink. Pour me one, pour one for yourself, too." He did as she ordered. "What is your name?" He told her. "Joe Market. Listen well, then, Joe Market. Do you believe in fate? You don't? Well, you certainly should and perhaps you will when I finish telling you my story. You see, I remember that night very well for several reasons. It was early evening when your wife Odessa came into the store. Around supper time it was, because I was broiling a steak and baking a white potato in the kitchen when I heard the bell ring on the door outside and I wondered who it was coming into the store at suppertime. It was your wife Odessa. I've known her since she was a little tot, her mother and I have been friends for years. She was very excited that night. *Miss Mary*, she said, *my husband's coming home from the Army tomorrow, isn't that wonderful? I've saved me ten dollars, and I've just got to have me a pair of red shoes, Miss Mary. He sent me the most wonderful blue silk material, and I made me a dress out of it. Now I need some red shoes to go with it.* She told me her size—it was a size five, which is very small, most of the women around here have much larger feet—and I was really very sorry when I couldn't find her a pair. She was so disappointed, poor child. Then I remembered that I had some more shoes stored back in the kitchen closet. They were old styles, but Odessa was so anxious to buy some red shoes that I told her to wait a minute, I'd check in the kitchen to see if there were any. Besides, I was worried about my steak and potato in the oven, and so I went back to the kitchen." She shifted position on the bed and motioned for Joe to pour her another drink. "That's when I saw you go through the yard. It wasn't very dark then, so I hadn't turned on the light in the kitchen. I checked the oven—the steak and potato had a while yet to cook—and I was standing by the stove with the window open to let some of that heat go out when I saw you duck through the yard and jump the fence, going up toward your house. At first, I was annoyed about that. I don't like anybody cutting through my yard, trampling down my flowers and what little grass I have. But you were gone so quickly, I didn't have time to even yell out the window. So I decided not to let it worry me. I didn't know that you were Odessa's husband then, although I would've recognized you if I'd seen your face, because Miss Lavinia has showed me all the pictures Odessa had taken at the wedding. Anyway, all I knew then was that it was a tall colored man who'd jumped my fence. Living here in Decatur like I do, I've come to expect anything from the colored people. So, I looked in the closet, but there were no red shoes there at all. And your wife wanted only red shoes, although I suggested that pink, or light blue, or black, or silver shoes, or even navy blue shoes, would go nicely with a blue dress. I had all those colors in stock and in her size, you understand, but she wouldn't hear of it. *My husband likes me in red shoes, I was wearing red shoes when he asked me to marry him.* That's what she said. It was a Thursday night, I remember. I told her the stores on Main Street were open until nine o'clock. *Why don't you take a quick walk out there?* I said. *I'm sure you'd find something nice in your size.* She seemed undecided at first. *I left the baby home alone,* she said. *He was sleeping, though . . . I guess he'll be all right. . . .* That's what she said. And then she left. I looked out the door and saw her running toward Main Street. I was sorry I didn't have what she wanted. I've known Odessa since she was a little girl. She was happy that night, and I was happy for her."

Somewhere out over the city, a clock struck five. Joe had only been here about fifteen minutes, but it seemed far longer than that. He felt ridiculous, sitting curled next to Cheap Mary, dressed in her bloomers and negligee. But he was also very frightened, although he kept his breathing to an even tempo so that she would not notice his fear. Cold sweat formed under his arms and between his legs and slid down his body like thin, cold fingers.

Cheap Mary was talking again. "Odessa was here just a little after seven o'clock, I remember. I always eat supper at seven thirty and I had my steak and potato about ten or fifteen minutes after she left. The hour or so between seven thirty and nine o'clock is the best time here in the store, and I was relatively busy then out front. Odessa came back at about a quarter to nine. She had found a lovely pair of red shoes on Main Street, but they cost more than the ten dollars she had. *Would you like me to loan you some money?* I said. You see, everybody calls me Cheap Mary, but I'm really very generous. Besides, Odessa's such a sweet, lovely girl. She was disappointed, but she wouldn't take any money. *I just came by to let you know, Miss Mary*, that's what she said. I told her I was sorry she didn't get the shoes, she wanted a pair so bad. But she smiled and said she'd be able to get them when you came home, she'd just have to wait, that's all. She didn't stay long because she was worried that the baby might be awake by now, and she rushed home almost at once. I went to the kitchen then and put the kettle on for some tea. That's when I saw you again. The light was on in the kitchen this time and shone full in your face. *Why, that's Odessa's husband*, I thought, remembering the pictures Miss Lavinia showed me and that I'd also seen you around. *He must have come home early and wanted to surprise her.* That explained why you had gone home through my backyard and over all those fences. You wanted to surprise Odessa." She gazed at Joe shrewdly. "But now you were coming back the same way, without seeing Odessa, because she had no more than left the store when I saw you on your way back." Her large black eyes seemed to glow, holding him almost in a trance. Now he was the lady bird charmed by the snake. "There was only one reason for you to go home and then leave without seeing your wife. I didn't know what that reason was until Miss Lavinia told me about the baby being suffocated. You did it. That's why you left and came back the next day."

He couldn't resist speaking. "It was an accident." His voice came out in a hoarse croak.

Nodding, Cheap Mary smacked her lips with heavy satisfaction. "I wasn't too sure about the facts, but I knew that you had killed that child. And for all these months now, I've been waiting in my kitchen window for you to come hopping back across that fence. I'm a patient woman, I knew that some day you'd come back. All things come back." She moved across the bed and pulled her dress above her wrinkled knees. "Now, there's a favor I want you to do for me. It's my price for keeping quiet. You do want me to keep quiet, don't you?"

He turned his head and looked at her thin legs with the blue veins imbedded in the freckled skin. "You want me to fuck you?" he said bluntly.

Cheap Mary shook her head. "Not that. I hate that. It hurts too much."

She kept her legs stretched out and pulled the dress a little higher up her thighs. He noticed for the first time that she wore high-buttoned shoes, the old-fashioned kind with high heels and pearl buttons studded in the gray suede material halfway up her leg. "They're a special kind of shoes," Mary said. "I wear them for the support. I'll take them off if they bother you."

"No, they don't bother me," he said.

"Then, you'll do me the favor?"

The idea of crawling between those mottled thighs disgusted him. He stripped the negligee and bloomers off and sat back on the bed. "What'll you do if I don't?" he said.

She studied a while. "Well, there are two possible alternatives. First, I could notify the police about what you did to the baby. They'd try you for murder, you know. You'd have a hard time convincing them it was an accident, considering your silence all this time."

Joe nodded. He had thought about that before. "And the other alternative?""

"I could tell Miss Lavinia. Which would be almost the same as telling the police. Especially since her daughter is involved."

"You don't leave me much choice," Joe said quietly.

"I know. That's because I'm a desperate woman." She leaned forward and lay her hand on his arm. Involuntarily, he pulled away from her touch. It was like a hand from the grave touching him.

He burst into tears. "Please don't make me do it."

Her eyes were full of pity, but he saw that she would not relent. "I *need* it, don't you understand? I'm going to die soon . . . it may be the last time before I die. Don't you have enough love in you for that . . . to satisfy another human being before she dies?"

"Please don't make me do it."

"And why not? If it's something I need, and something you're quiet capable of doing . . . ? I assure you, it requires a whole lot less energy than murder. . . ." Her voice was full of contempt. "You're so much like my husband was. A great deal of self-love, an equal amount of self-pity. He felt that no one loved him—he was certainly right about that as far as I was concerned—and he thought that gave him the license to love himself. And to pity himself at the same time." She shook her head and lectured him like a schoolteacher. "Self-love is perhaps the greatest sin of all. It stifles the basic drive of man, which is to search for love *until he finds it*. Self-love is simply the easy way out; self-pity is the justification for it."

Now she leaned over and peered into his face. "You don't know what I'm talking about, do you? I'll bet you didn't even listen. My husband was the same way. He was good for only one thing. I've missed his doing it so much. . . ." She pulled her dress higher. "Do you supposed you could do me the favor? It's the only price I'm asking for my silence."

She reached out and clutched him firmly by the head. He was in a panic. . . . How many times had he done the same thing to men and women, grabbing them by the head and tugging them with a slow, cruel smile into the nest of his sex? He resisted her pull, but desperation gave her strength, her fingers seemed made of wire.

"Come, dear child . . . you'll find it's not so unpleasant as it seems."

He held his breath. "That's right," Mary said, inching toward him, ". . . that's right . . . just one more time before I die. . . ." Like ecstatic horns of Satan, the gray suede shoes dug into his butt.

Daylight was rapidly approaching when Joe left the back door at Cheap Mary's and crept into the yard. A brisk wind had risen; pale gray against the backdrop of dark houses, the locust tree nodded as though it, too, knew all his secrets.

Joe fell against the house and vomited. He was still naked, and his body was covered with cold sweat. Man, he needed him some pot right now. He was sure that all this shit had happened to him because, right from the execution on, he hadn't smoked any pot. If he could make it down the alley to the street, and if Pee Wee happened to be at the cab stand there, he could whistle to Pee Wee to bring him some pot. But he doubted that he had the strength to move, much less to whistle.

Man, that white bitch did me in. He pushed himself up straight, leaning against the house for support. *She waited six months to do me in.* He found himself grinning, because he admired that kind of determination in anyone, even if he did come out on the short end of the stick.

Now he felt better. One of these days, when he had gotten over the shame of it, he would tell Pee Wee and Tony and Lamont how he had gone down on Cheap Mary. *Man, that old white woman is something else!* He grinned in a sort of proud way and padded down the alley to Hickory Street. He snaked his head around the corner of the house, and saw Pee Wee's cab parked up the street.

Joe felt very daring. Hell, there was no one around. He might as well walk to the cab instead of whistling for Pee Wee. This was certainly his lucky day, because he had faced exposure and overcome it. Boldly, he walked from the alley and strolled down Hickory Street to the cab stand.

Pee Wee was sleeping on the back seat with his short legs stuck out the window. Joe got in the front seat and shook Pee Wee by the shoulder. "Wake up, man. I come to get some pot."

Pee Wee was alert at once. "Hey, Joe. How come you out here without a shirt on? You that hot, man?" He was still in the back seat, and he couldn't see that Joe was naked.

Joe laughed. "Man, I ain't hot no more. I had me a rough time yesterday and last night. All I want to do now is to get high and crap out. You got about five joints on you?"

"They in the dashboard." Pee Wee crawled from the back seat and got in the front. "Man, you *naked*! What you doing out here naked like that?"

Joe liked the way Pee Wee's eyes bugged in surprise. It would be all over the block tomorrow, another example of Joe's don't-give-a-damn attitude. He could hear Pee Wee now telling his friends, "Man, you know that stud Joe Market? Sure you know Joe Market, everybody know him. Well man, he walked *buck naked* to my cab at six o'clock in the morning, looking for pot. That stud got big balls, baby, ain't *nothing* that stud won't do." Stud was the highest compliment you could pay a man on Decatur Street. It referred to his courage as well as to the size of his dick. In Pee Wee's mind, the name of Joe Market was synonymous with stud.

"Here. Stud, you *crazy*, baby. I don't know what I'm going to do with you." He gave Joe five joints and lighted a sixth one that he puffed on and handed to Joe. Then he started the cab motor. "I'm going to take you home, man. It's damn near sunrise, somebody'd see you for sure now."

Joe was agreeable to that. Pee Wee had seen him naked, and others would soon know. Joe was tired of the whole thing now, but still he slumped in the front seat and propped his foot against the dashboard, throwing his legs wide open in invitation. It had been a long time since he had offered his dick to Pee Wee in those Louisiana woods. And Pee Wee had refused then. But would he refuse now? Joe didn't know, but he had a feeling that one of these days soon, he'd find out.

Pee Wee sucked on the joint and handed it back to Joe. "Stud, you the *craziest* nigger I know." His voice was filled with admiration as he drove slowly up Decatur Street with the dignity of someone chauffering a royal personage.

It was very light now. Joe thanked Pee Wee and hopped from the cab. "See you around, stud," Pee Wee called warmly after him. Joe raced up the alley to his back door and stepped into the kitchen. Tony Brenzo was sitting at the table drinking coffee.

"Where the hell you been, Joe? Odessa called me, she was almost out of her mind. Jesus Christ, you must be out of *your* mind, Joe! Why're you running around naked like that?"

Joe grinned, and looked in the bedroom. "I'm all right. Where's Odessa?"

"She went over to her mother's. I told her I'd call her if and when you got home. She was worried to death, Joe."

"You call her. I'm going to take a shower and try to get some sleep." But Tony didn't move. "Look, man . . . I don't know why I went outside naked. I just had to, that's all. You understand what I'm saying, Tony?"

Tony shook his head. "I'm confused, Joe. I don't know what to make of you when you act like this. I mean . . . well, shit, man! Horsing around with me is one thing. But then you've got a wife and a home. You've got *responsibility*, Joe. You're not only responsible to your wife and your community, you're responsible for their good opinion of you. That's the whole basis of law. Suppose somebody arrested you running around bareassed naked like that?"

Joe laughed. "You'd get me off."

"Would I, Joe?" His faced turned hard as steel. "You say that, it makes me think you don't know me very well."

"I know you, man. You're a freak, you like to make weird scenes, you're all fucked like I am."

"I think it's time we had a serious talk," Tony said. "You go take your shower. I'll call Odessa and tell her you're all right. Then we got to have a talk."

Before Joe could say anything, Tony went into the hallway to call Odessa from the phone there. *I wonder what's bugging him?* Joe thought, as he went into the shower. And he was drying himself when he heard Tony come back into the kitchen. He wrapped the towel around his waist and went into the kitchen combing his hair.

"What'd Odessa say?"

"She was relieved you hadn't got into any trouble." Tony dragged out two chairs. "Sit down, Joe. There's something I want to talk to you about."

"Let's get high first. I picked up five joints from Pee Wee."

"Let's wait a while, Joe. What I've got to say won't take long. Something you said before—about my getting you off if you got into trouble. Well, that's not true, not now. I gave you a break when I found you hustling in that room in Newark. And I'm glad I did, because you deserved a break. You didn't know anything then, Joe. But you've grown up now. You've got an education, a family, personal responsibility. In other words, you're on your own when it comes to you and society. We're friends, yes. And I dig the same things you dig. But I'm still a cop. I'm supposed to arrest anybody who does a criminal act. Anybody, Joe. That means my mother, my sister . . . my buddy. You understand what I'm saying?"

Joe nodded. "You're saying that you're a cop first, my friend second. I understand that. But will you always be a cop, Tony?"

"Always. As long as I carry this badge."

"Even when you're smoking pot with me? When we're balling chicks together? And all that other shit?"

"Even then," Tony said. "Look man, I don't claim to be perfect. Sure I do things I shouldn't. Everybody does—which is more a justification than a reason. I guess it's human to do wrong. If I was really a good cop, I'd turn you in right now for possession of narcotics, I'd turn myself in as a habitual user of narcotics. The fact that I can't—or rather, *won't*—means only that I'm a bad cop. That is, as opposed to a really good cop, a cop who respects the law behind closed doors the same way he respects it when he's in the public eye. I'm not that kind of cop, Joe."

Joe grinned. "I'm going to get high. You bug me when you start talking like this, Tony. You got something on your mind? Say it, then, but don't keep beating around the bush." He lighted the joint and sucked in a lungful of the smoke. He handed the joint to Tony.

"Like I say, I'm a bad cop," Tony said. He took the joint and they smoked in silence until it was finished.

"Let me tell you one thing about white people," Joe said. "I'm high now—I don't think I'd tell you this if I wasn't high, Tony. But let me tell you something about the white man. He's a hypocrite, that's what he is. He pretends to believe in something that he really doesn't. Take all this bullshit about democracy, and everybody being created equal, and the right to vote, and the rest of it. The white man pretends to believe in all that stuff, but he really doesn't. He says one thing, but he does the exact opposite. That's what a hypocrite is. The white man can't make up his mind about whether to be a devil or an angel. That's part of what's causing all the trouble in this country right now, the white man's hypocrisy. America is a big masquerade party, with everybody pretending to be so pious, so full of brotherhood and virtue, that I could puke every time I think of it. That's one of the reasons I like you, Tony. You're the only white man I ever met who wasn't playing a role. Until this morning, that is. Now you got your ass on your back, you coming on like the rest of them white motherfuckers."

"Now let's talk about the black motherfuckers," Tony said lightly. "You deny there's any hypocrisy among the colored people?"

"Naw man, we're not hypocrites. We're honest, simple, fun-loving folk, filled with mischief and music. Not to mention that *natural* rhythm. Isn't that what white people say about Negroes?"

"Some of them do. Some Negroes say it about themselves. But what I'm interested in now is the hypocrisy of the black man. Isn't there a masquerade on your side of the fence too?"

"Sure. Everybody pretends. I'm not putting that down. What gets me is *the pretense of virtue*." He liked the sound of that. He slouched in the chair and scratched his belly. "What I mean is that the white man's hypocrisy makes him *pretend not to hate*. There's a big difference. The white man's pretense is designed to make him feel better than the colored man. Superior. On the other hand, a Negro pretends in order to keep from being destroyed. It's as simple as that."

"It doesn't sound so simple to me. Why does the Negro have to pretend? Why can't he just be himself? Nobody'd put him down for that."

Joe grunted. "Man, you coming on real dumb this morning. You remember you told me about the Italians going through this same crap? But now the Italians have become integrated into American society. All that means is that he became less Italian and more American. And to be American means *the pretense of virtue*. That's why the Negro can't be himself. The white man's efforts to make the Negro 'a real American' means that he wants the Negro to pretend that everything is peaches and cream in America. Is there equality here? No. *Pretend there is*, the white man says. *Pretend long enough and it'll come true.* Is there democracy here? No. *Pretend there is*, the white man says. *Pretend long enough and it'll come true.* That's why the Negro has to pretend. We're being injected with a virus that's unhealthy and ambiguous. We know it's no good for us, but we can't survive in the American atmosphere without it. So each day we take in a little bit more of the virus, we become more hypocritical, more white—*sick*—we even talk and think like white people more and more every day. But we don't like it, Tony. We don't like it one damn bit."

Tony whistled. "I've never heard you sound off like this before, man. You *are* ambiguous! You surprise me when you come on like a scholar, because I almost never think of you as a guy with a really good mind. . . ."

"That's because you're prejudiced," Joe cut in. "No, I really mean it. Not in the same way that other white people are prejudiced. But you do have an idea in your mind that I'm just a spade with a good body and a big dick."

"Not just a spade, Joe. You know better than that. You're a very special spade in my book."

"But still a spade."

Tony stood up and walked around the kitchen with his hands in his pockets. "I don't like this, Joe. I don't like this at all. What you're saying is that you're different from me, from all other white people. But then when I mention that difference, you become resentful."

"I'm sorry," Joe said. "I forgot to pretend."

"Cut the crap!" Tony said sharply, and Joe looked at him in surprise. "I mean it, Joe. You're talking about all this pretense bullshit. Well now I'm going to tell you something. I believe in *the virtue of pretense*. I believe that if we fake brotherhood long enough and well enough, it eventually will become a reality. Pretense is a kind of putting forth, a projection into the future, like a bridge from one generation into the next. Law, manners, and customers are all part of the general play-acting we call civilization. The better we pretend to be civilized, the closer we come to realizing the American dream. That's part of what I mean by *the virtue of pretense*. You said it the other way around. But either way, I think it's the only way we can ever arrive at the truth."

They heard the sound of seven o'clock striking. "I've got to go to work in another hour," Joe said. He yawned and stretched. "You talk about the American dream. I'm going to take a nap. If I'm lucky, I'll have me a nice wet dream in the next hour."

"Now you're back on that dumb spade kick," Tony said angrily. "Man, you bug the hell out of me."

"You're forgetting to pretend," Joe said dryly. "You love me, remember? I'm your great big black blood brother."

All the blood seemed to drain from Tony's face. "You've gone too far this time," he said quietly.

"Have I?" Joe said. "Do you really love me, Tony? Can you really love a spade, a nigger, a big dick black man? I doubt it. All you motherfuckers are the same. You hate me. I hate you. Let's cut this bullshit and tell the truth for a change."

His body was trembling. He reached for another joint to calm his nerves, but Tony grabbed his hand. "I love you, Joe."

"Let me go, you sonofabitch. I hate your white guts."

"You're lying, Joe. You love me."

"I hate you." He tore his wrist from Tony's hand. "You wop motherfucker." A red haze crept into his eyes. He felt his fingers curl into a fist, the powerful thrust of his arm as it came up and walloped Tony underneath the chin. He heard the dish cabinet crash as Tony staggered back and fell against it. Joe ripped the towel from around his waist. Naked again, he felt like a savage bent on destroying a long-time enemy. "Come on, you white bastard. Fight me if you got the balls."

Tony took off his jacket. "I got the balls, baby." He lunged at Joe and floored him with a flying tackle.

They grunted as they thudded to the floor together. Then they fought in silence as they attacked, parted, then attacked again. In trying to destroy each other, they destroyed the kitchen around them—tables, chairs, dishes, broken and scattered underneath the violence of their struggle. Like two athletes in a Roman arena, they fought cleanly with all the power their bodies could muster. And yet, they did not wound each other. It was like a fight in slow motion, the way their fists sped toward each other and then slowed before landing, as if arrested by their own desire to somehow destroy without disfiguring. Their clenches, too, were more like the violent embraces of love. Belly to belly, they grabbed and squeezed, melding torsos and grinding hips. Again and again the violence soared, then slowed to the tempo of a brutal caress until they finally collapsed side-by-side on the floor, aware that what might have begun in hatred had terminated on the edge of sex. Their heavy breathing was the only sound in the kitchen, except for the hissing of gas in the heater and dull whirr of the electric clock that marked the beginning and the end of their battle. They had fought thirty minutes without a victory on either side.

Joe's chest heaved like a bellows. His body was covered with dirt and sweat. He had torn Tony's pants and shirt almost off him. "Man, you can wear some of my clothes," he said.

"I love you, Joe."

There was a long silence.

"I love you too, Tony. You know that."

"Now you understand why we've got to pretend?"

Joe nodded. *We fought to keep from making love.* The fight itself had been a kind of perverse love-making; but it did leave room open for further contact. The act of love between two men or between two races, he supposed, would surely shut a final door. *Let us pretend that we love, but let us never love, let us fight to keep from loving. Future generations will benefit from our performance as we have benefited from the performance of the generations before. We cannot love now because we have lost the ability to love. To regain that ability is the search for Eden, a slow and painful process or reawakening.* That is what Tony was saying.

"I sure hope future generations appreciate all we're doing for them," Joe said dryly.

'They will. Man let's get up and wash this shit off. Then let's have breakfast. I'm starved."

The kitchen was a wreck. Joe laughed. "Odessa's going to have a fit when she comes home."

Tony put his hand on Joe's shoulder. "She's not coming home, Joe. She asked me to tell you, but I couldn't do it before. Odessa says she's had it . . . she's leaving you. She wants you to pack her things and bring them over to her mother's."

Joe stood a long while in the bathroom door. "Fuck her," he finally said. He went in and took a shower. He heard Tony scraping up wreckage in the kitchen. The water was scalding hot on his back, but he liked the torture of it. Odessa. Man, talk about pretending, he knew what it was to pretend. *Odessa, why did you have to leave me just when I was getting ready to tell you what really happened to the baby?*

She could die and go to hell now believing she was really the cause of the baby's death, he didn't care. The burden of guilt was on her soul, for as long as she believed herself guilty, then she was so.

Belief. Another form of pretense. Another mask put on for the ball.

I'm not guilty at all, he thought. *As long as Odessa thinks she's guilty, then I'm innocent.*

Now he could deny Cheap Mary's hollow accusations. Who would believe her if he denied it strongly enough?

"Hurry up, Joe. What're you doing in there, whacking your whang?"

"Yeah, baby." It seemed a good thing to do. He mixed cold water with the hot and formed a rich lather in his hand. He whacked his whang.

Let us pretend that we are just and noble men. Tomorrow, somewhere in the future, black men and white men will not have this perverse need to degrade each other. But in the present atmosphere, degradation and perversion is our only mode of love. Tony had said that. Was it true? Joe did not know, but he thought, *Thank God for white people like Tony Brenzo, for without them, we would never know the beauty of being black.*

When Joe left the house on Decatur Street, stuffing his T-shirt into his white jeans, it was nearly eight thirty in the morning, but he had the distinct impression that it was closer to three thirty in the afternoon. The cool morning breeze seemed to be hot; the pale sun seemed desert red. Cars traveling down Decatur Street at fast speed seemed to him to be going slow, and those which crept along registered in his mind as going extremely fast.

He went down the front stairs—the steps seemed to be a league apart from each other—and entered the China Doll Laundry. The small bell tinkling on the doors sounded to him like the striking of cathedral bells. He covered his ears to drown the music.

China Doll was working behind the counter. She looked fresh and rested, considering how late she must have gone to bed after they got back from Trenton. "I don't pay you to get here late," China said. "And what's going on with Odessa? She just called a little while ago to say that I could have you all to myself. What you and she been up to now?"

"We had a fight." His voice sounded very loud in his ears. He blinked, and banged his head with his fist in an attempt to lessen the effect of the pot.

"You're high out of your mind," China said. "Did you and Odessa fight about us being in the cellar?"

"She got over that. This was about something else."

China started checking off the list of that day's deliveries. "I saw Tony Brenzo leave your house a little while ago. He looked like he was high, too."

Joe laughed. "High ain't the word. He was way out in space."

"Tony's a good guy. If you see him before Friday, tell him I'm giving a little Halloween party. You're invited, naturally. Tell Tony I want him to come, too. Tell him to wear a mask. It's supposed to be a masquerade, but you have to take off your clothes at the door." She smiled. "The mask is for the benefit of bashful people. That certainly doesn't include you and Tony. But wear a mask anyway. I think it might be fun." She handed him the delivery slips. "Lamont came by to get his shirts. I had him load the truck for you. It's parked in the driveway. You think you can make those deliveries without bumping into somebody?"

"I feel better now," he said. "This is bitching pot I scored from Pee Wee." He gave China a joint. "I'll be back around noontime," he said, inspecting the sheaf of delivery slips. "You turn on about eleven thirty, I'll take you swimming naked in one of those wine barrels, now that Odessa ain't around to bug us."

"You do that," China said. She stuck the cigarette in her dress. "Run along now, Joe. I still got a business to look after."

The sun seemed to fry his brain. He stood awhile, measuring the distance between him and the delivery truck. It seemed to be parked at the end of a mile-long alley. He took three steps and climbed into the driver's seat. The steering wheel was the size of a dime; he gripped it with both hands and squeezed it to its normal size. *Damn, I am too high to drive, too high to make deliveries.* He needed to sleep for an hour or so; but he knew that China would get pissed if he went to sleep right here. He started the motor and backed from the driveway. The houses on either side of him seemed to race along in the opposite direction, but he knew that that was just another effect of the pot. He kept a gentle pressure on the accelerator and eased the truck into the street. China Doll waved to him from the window and patted her breasts, where she had stored the joint, to remind him of their noontime date. He shifted to second gear and drove slowly down Decatur Street.

With his concentration on driving, his head cleared a bit; but the buzzing behind his eyes, like an angry bee trapped there, told him that the marijuana was still having its effect. He wondered if Tony was still high, how he was making out.

Cheap Mary's store on the corner of Hickory Street was still closed. *Probably sleeping off the effects of that tongue-lashing she made me give her.* He laughed to himself. Maybe he'd go back some night and make her do the same thing to him.

Pee Wee was parked in his usual spot, and sleeping as usual.

Joe honked his horn until Pee Wee woke up. "Hey, Pee Wee. I just stopped to tell you what a motherfucker that grass is. You got any more, man?"

Pee Wee looked uncomfortable. "I got some, Joe. Dig, man, I'm not putting you down or anything like that. But you owe me thirty bucks for pot already. When you expect to pay me, Joe?"

"Friday, baby. Don't I always pay you on Fridays?"

"You missed the last two," Pee Wee said glumly. He palmed ten joints from the dashboard and handed them to Joe. "I'll let you have these for five bucks. But that's all I can let you have, Joe, until you pay me some bread."

"I said I'd pay you Friday." He kicked the truck into gear, but he did not pull off. Pee Wee always backed down after coming on strong like that.

"You mad with me, stud?"

Joe flashed him a dazzling grin. "Naw, baby. You all right by me, baby."

"I'm glad to hear that, Joe. Because I value your friendship, I really do."

"I know, baby." He pretended to check his watch. "I've got to split now, Pee Wee. I got a screwing date at noontime, and I want to make these deliveries before then."

Pee Wee's eyes popped. He always got excited when Joe talked about sex. He looked up and down the street. "Stick around a minute, man. I'll turn you on." He lighted a joint and handed it to Joe. Joe smoked leisurely; he finished nearly all of the joint and handed Pee Wee the small roach. "Thanks, baby. I'll dick her a couple for you."

Pee Wee's gaze flashed toward Joe's crotch, and away again. "All that dick you got, stud, I envy the hell out of you."

Joe laughed. "Baby, you getting me hard." Which was not true, he was teasing Pee Wee. He jerked his foot off the brake and moved out before Pee Wee had a chance to see for sure. *All them cats hung up on my dick*, Joe thought, as he continued up Hickory Street. *They just jealous of me.*

Suddenly, the full force of the pot hit him between the eyes.

For a moment, he was blinded. He jerked his foot off the gas and swerved toward the curb. The truck climbed up on the sidewalk and stopped there when Joe hit the brake. Joe blinked; and when he could see, he was relieved to find that he had blacked out at a clear spot. Trembling, he backed the truck off the sidewalk and maneuvered it into the curb. *God, I'm blasted out of my fucking mind.* He slumped in the seat.

Man, he was scared. He was aware, too, that the pot was making him overreact to what was probably only a small incident. But he couldn't help it. Suppose a car or another truck had been coming from the other direction? He'd be a dead black nigger right now. Or if not dead, then certainly injured, because he'd hit that curbstone full force, he was surprised that none of the tires had blown out.

He got out and looked at the truck. It was all right, and the tires, too. A few people looked at him with little or no interest as he climbed back into the truck. He certainly didn't feel like working any more; and he drove very slowly to the park and sat there awhile. Man, he did almost get killed. That scared the shit out of him. He didn't want to die now. He didn't ever want to die, but he certainly didn't want to die right now. Not with China waiting for him in the cellar at noon. Because he made up his mind right then that he was going to fuck China Doll to death, he hadn't fucked anybody in nearly five months.

Then he wondered what Odessa was doing with her mother Miss Lavinia. Man, he could just picture how Odessa and Miss Lavinia would react if Cheap Mary did happen to tell him that he had killed the baby Christopher, instead of Odessa being the guilty one. He bet Odessa and her mother would hang him up and cut his balls out. Man, you get nigger women mad enough, they're capable of anything.

That scared him. He started the truck up, he was going to do him some hustling right now and protect his vital interests. Even if Mary did tell Odessa and Miss Lavinia what she thought she knew, all he had to do was deny it. In the meantime, he'd buy Odessa those red shoes and slip some sweet dick into her. She'd tell Cheap Mary to go and suck lemons, that's what Odessa would do. And with

Odessa on his side, back with him again, Miss Lavinia could talk all she wanted.

Slowly, Joe drove down Hickory Street. The first thing he had to do was to hustle him ten dollars. Hunched over the steering wheel, his eyes swung from left to right. But he didn't see a single person he could get ten dollars from.

Then he thought of Lamont. Shit man, why not? Lamont had come home mysteriously discharged from the Army about a month ago. He probably still had some bread. Lamont lived with his mother in a small apartment on Pierson Street. Joe went there and punched the bell, and Lamont opened the door at once. "Hi, Joe," Lamont said.

Joe threw his arm around Lamont's shoulders. There was no mistaking the tremor that went through Lamont's body. "Hey baby, what's happening?" Joe said. He looked Lamont straight in the eye. *This guy wants me real bad*, Joe thought. *I can get ten dollars here with no sweat at all.*

Lamont invited him in. "How's Odessa?" He seemed very nervous; his eyes looked everywhere now except at Joe.

"Odessa's fine, Lamont. I just came to thank you for loading the truck this morning. Man, I was too far gone, I appreciate what you did. China told me about it."

"That's all right, Joe. Anything for a friend."

Joe smiled and sat down. Lamont had been writing on some pages attached to a clipboard; he picked the clipboard up and sat on the opposite end of the sofa. "What you been writing?" Joe said, just by way of making conversation. Lamont shoved the clipboard behind him. "Oh . . . nothing. . . . I was just fooling around with something . . . Actually, it's an essay for a contest sponsored by the American Legion. You're supposed to write something about America." He squirmed, trying to hide a kind of fierce pride. "Of course, you're not supposed to be older than seventeen. And in high school. But I thought I'd enter anyway. I mean, who's to find out?"

Joe nodded. "And what if you win?"

Lamont looked bewildered for only a minute. Then he fluttered his hand in a gesture of disbelief. "Me win? Not in a million
years." But Joe could tell by his voice that he sincerely wanted to
win, he wanted to be able to brag to his mother about something.
Joe recalled how Mrs. Jones had sounded when he talked to her on
the telephone about Lamont; and he realized now how bitterly disappointed Mrs. Jones must have been when Lamont had come
home alive from Vietnam. And Lamont? Hell, he looked like a bigger sissy now than before he went to the Army. He was wearing a
pair of faded blue jeans that fit him in the crotch like a woman's
tight slacks, forming a fat V there. *He keeps himself strapped down
now*, Joe thought. *He's ashamed of his dick.* That was something
new with Lamont. Before this, he'd always been showing off his
tiny little dick. It was as though he had finally made up his mind to
stop fighting being queer. His white T-shirt clung to his chest and
showed the sharp points of his titties. Man, he looked just like a
queer if Joe ever saw one.

"Why you staring at me so hard, Joe?" Lamont asked, with a
nervous little laugh. He still sounded like Pearl Bailey, only tired
now, without any use for life at all.

"Was I staring? I wasn't aware . . . my mind was a million miles
away." The dusty apartment was crammed with large pieces of
overstuffed furniture, lamps with tasseled shades, velvet ottomans
and religious pictures in broad gilt frames. An old woman's
apartment.

"I bet you're trying to figure out why the Army discharged me
early," Lamont said defensively. "Well, I guarantee you that it had
nothing to do with *homosexuality.* That's what my mother thinks."

Joe was watching Lamont with his eyes half closed. "Then why
did they discharge you, Lamont? Frankly, I was as surprised as
everybody else when you got discharged so soon." He scrunched
down into the sofa and stretched out his legs so that Lamont could
get a good look at the print of his dick.

But Lamont looked away. "I got a medical discharge," he said
petulantly. "I got ulcers over there in Vietnam. Six months after I've

been discharged, the Army starts paying me a monthly disability pension. Now, would they do that if I was discharged for being queer?"

Joe shrugged. He had come to expect anything of the Army. It wouldn't surprise him a bit if they were pensioning off queers. "Lamont, I think you worry too much," he said amiably. "I got some real good pot here. You want to turn on?"

"Well, I really don't like to," Lamont said hesitantly. "It makes me lose control. . . . I start thinking about death, unpleasant things like that. . . . I'd rather not, Joe. . . ."

But Joe had already lighted the joint. "Come on," he said, as if trying to persuade a girl. "Take one or two drags . . . for me."

"I'd rather not, Joe."

Joe moved over closer to Lamont. He could smell the faint odor of perfume that filtered from Lamont's body. *How come I didn't notice before?* Joe wondered. He could tell that Lamont was frightened, and it excited him, like the pure fear of a virgin. "It won't hurt you, Lamont. You'll hardly feel it." The same lie you tell a virgin, the same warm, coaxing voice.

"Please don't make me do it, Joe."

"Do it for me, Lamont. For me, baby."

Lamont took the joint. He knew how to suck the smoke in and hold it there until his eyes bulged and his heart fluttered like a frightened bird's underneath the thin T-shirt. He smoked rapidly, with a small frown creasing his forehead and his pink lips puckered in distaste.

Joe took the joint back. "There. That wasn't so bad, was it?"

Lamont made a face. "I just don't like it . . . it makes me lose control."

Joe finished the cigarette. "Maybe you ought to lose control some time, Lamont. It's good to let go every once in a while. It helps relieve the tension."

Lamont laughed in a shrill way. "That might be true for some people, but not for me. I know myself . . . I *really* get carried away. . . ."

He's high, Joe thought with satisfaction. "What times does your mother come home? She come home for lunch?"

"No, she doesn't get here until after six. And speaking of my mother, she'll have a fit if I don't do what she asked me to. She's sending a trunkful of clothes to her mother down South. She wants me to tie it up and call the express people. I've been trying to get the energy all morning, but it's been so hot. . . ." His hand fluttered like a fan.

"It is hot," Joe said. "You want me to help you?"

"Oh would you? The trunk's in her bedroom. Maybe we can drag it out here."

"Let's leave it in the bedroom."

Lamont gazed at him a long while. Then he shrugged, and went into the bedroom. Joe followed him.

The mother's bedroom was long and narrow. A large double bed was jammed into one corner. Next to it stood a chiffonier. In the opposite corner was a television set on a mahogany stand. All the furniture was covered with thin sheets of red plastic. "Sometimes in this kind of weather, those water pipes leak," Lamont said, indicating a double row of rusty pipes running across the ceiling. "They drip and mess up Mama's things."

Joe sat on the bed. The plastic crinkled under him. "That trunk?" It was a tall, fat trunk standing on one end. The hasp and lock were shaped like two ears joined together.

Lamont uncoiled a ball of rope and threw it around the trunk. "Help me," he said to Joe.

"Come here," Joe said.

Lamont's face turned a sickly yellow.

"Come here," Joe said.

"Please, Joe. . . ." His voice was a high squeak.

"Come here, motherfucker!" The plastic crackled as Lamont sat down beside Joe.

Joe lay back and closed his eyes. He waited for what seemed an eternity, but Lamont did not touch him.

"I won't tell anybody," Joe said.

"I'm not *queer*!" Lamont cried. "Everybody thinks I'm queer, but I'm not! I've never done a queer thing in my life!"

"Sure, I know," Joe said patiently.

"Joe, I thought you were my friend . . . why are you coming on to me like this? I respect you, Joe. I *admire* you. You remember when we stole that turkey from Mr. Yen last year? I thought you were the greatest guy in the world, doing something like that for me and my mother. I thought you liked me, Joe. I'm not queer. I swear to God I'm not. I've even got a girl friend now. . . ."

"*You* got a girl?" Joe said.

"Well . . . a woman, really. Listen, Joe, I'll tell you something. You know, I never had sex with a woman before, I never even fooled around with a girl the way I hear you and Pee Wee talk about it. My mother . . . well, you know how my mother is. She told me a lot of things about girls. She frightened me. But just the other day, this woman I've been knowing for a long time, she said to me, *Lamont, you ever been to bed with a woman?* I was surprised as the dickens, but I told her no. *Poor baby*, she said. We started fooling around drinking some wine, and then I *screwed* her, Joe. Oh, it was fabulous! I never knew how great it would be, it's like something out of this world. When it was over, she asked me to do a favor for her— something dangerous, Joe, I'll tell you about it some time. *Yeah baby, I'll do anything in the world for you*, I told her. And I meant it. So you see, Joe, I can't be queer. Can I? I mean, I made it with a woman, I enjoyed it, I've never made it with a man. . . ."

"But you wanted to," Joe said cruelly. "You remember when we used to go swimming together in the Army, how you used to look at me in the shower, at my dick? Like it was something good to eat? You remember? You think I didn't notice, but I did, baby."

"I made it with a woman," Lamont said miserably.

"Lots of queers do. They're convertible, that's all."

"I'm not queer, Joe."

"Sure, I know," Joe said patiently. He reached out dragged Lamont down beside him, rubbing his rough cheek against Lamont's smooth face.

Lamont sighed like a woman. He was whimpering.

"You remember how you used to look at me in the shower?"

"I remember, I remember." He kissed Joe on the lips. "What do you want me to do?" His breath was coming in little spurts.

"What do you want to do?" *Queer bastard. I knew all the time you were queer.*

"You sure you won't tell? I mean, I think I'd kill myself if anybody knew, if my mother ever found out. You won't tell anybody? You won't treat me like I'm queer later on?"

"I promise."

"That's not enough. I want you to swear on your mother's grave."

"I swear on my mother's grave." He felt Lamont's hands light on him like two birds come to roost, the thin fingers fumbling at his belt. He gave a contented sigh and closed his eyes.

It surprised him how easy it had been. *Queer bastard.* He felt that Lamont had betrayed him, being queer all these years without letting him know. They could have been balling together all these years.

He knew just how long to wait. With queers, the ones you had to con money out of, you waited until they got carried away, then you took your meat from them. You made them whine and beg you to give it back, and then you asked them for your price. Joe waited just long enough, and then he flopped over on his belly. His knee knocked Lamont to one side.

"What's the matter, Joe? Didn't you like it? Joe, please turn back over."

"I need ten dollars," Joe said.

Lamont didn't make a sound. Joe peeked at him from under his arm. Lamont was crying, but he didn't make any noise.

"I need ten dollars," Joe said.

"I'll give it to you, Joe . . . I'll give you anything you want."

Joe rolled back over. After Lamont finished him off, he got up at once and went into the bathroom. He was disgusted. Leisurely, he relieved himself. Then he lit a joint and smoked it, sitting on top of the commode. When Lamont tapped a few minutes later on the door, Joe reached up and locked it. "I'll be out in a minute, Lamont."

"Take your time," Lamont said. "I'm going out for a while. I just wanted to give you the money. I'm pushing it underneath the door." Joe looked down and saw the corner of a ten-dollar bill. "I see it," he said. But he did not pick it up. *He's going out because he's ashamed to look me in the face. Well, he should be, pretending to be my friend all these years.*

"Joe?"

"Yeah."

"I never did anything like that to anybody before. I swear to God."

Joe said nothing.

"Joe, do you hate me?"

He remembered trying to explain to Tony Brenzo how the Negro pretends not to hate. And that whole bit about the white man's hypocrisy, his pretense of virtue. *I don't hate you, Lamont, you're a good guy, a real man, all my good friends go down on me.* That's what Lamont wanted to hear, something like that. *Fuck him,* Joe thought. He was glad the bathroom door was between them, closed and locked.

"I think I do hate you, Lamont. I might get over it. But the way I feel now, I hate you for what you did."

He heard Lamont sob. "Don't talk like that, Joe. You don't know what you're doing to me. . . ."

"Don't I? You're queer, baby. I'm surprised at you, Lamont, doing something like that to me."

"You made me!" His voice was almost a shriek now. "You promised you wouldn't put me down! You swore on your mother's grave!"

Joe flushed the roach down the toilet. He stood watching the swirling water collect in a whirlpool and sweep the roach down the commode. "Baby, a man must do what he must do," Joe said softly, resting his face against the door, talking with his lips close to the place where he knew Lamont's ear listened.

Was that true? Was it true that all the evil in a man must express itself, as well as the little bit of love in him? How long must a man pretend? It was true that he hated Lamont for taking his seed that way, for draining the life out of him just to flush it down the toilet along with his other waste.

"Yeah, a man has to do what he has to do," Joe said. "For example, you had to find some way to get out of the Army, Lamont. You think I believe that ulcer shit? That bullshit about a pension? And you think your *mother* believes it? Man, that old woman's sharp as a tack. Can you prove it, Lamont? You got a paper from the Army saying you got ulcers?" Lamont was very quiet. "Have you?" Joe cried. He was aware that the pot was making him overreact again; but he was also filled with indignation, Lamont telling a lie like that. "Have you got a paper saying you got ulcers?"

"No." Lamont's voice was a faint whisper through the door.

"I thought as much," Joe said, with grim satisfaction. "They discharged you because you're queer, didn't they?"

"I'm *not* queer! I just couldn't stand that Army any more! I *had* to get out! That's why I pretended I was queer!"

"Yeah . . . like you pretended with me," Joe said nastily. "You ought to be ashamed of yourself, Lamont. Just imagine what your mother would say if she found out."

He sat in a terrible, heavy silence, waiting for Lamont to speak.

"Joe?"

"Yeah?"

"Can I have another joint? Please? Shove it under the door."

Joe hesitated. "You sure you want one, Lamont? You know how it makes you lose control. That's what you said."

Lamont laughed bitterly. "Don't play with me, Joe."

Joe pushed the joint under the door. He heard Lamont strike a match, and then his soft inhaling. He picked up the ten-dollar bill and stuffed it in his jeans. He realized, now that he had the ten dollars for Odessa's shoes, that he had used that as an excuse to justify making it with Lamont. *I don't give a damn about Odessa any more, let her stay with her mother. If she does come back, she's going to start asking a lot of questions I don't want to give the answers to.*

"Joe?"

"Yeah."

"I've got something else to give you."

"More money?"

"No . . . well, yes, there's money involved. A lot of money. More than you ever dreamed of. But listen first. I'm involved in this thing . . . I can't tell you what it is. But I'm afraid, Joe. Or I was afraid. But I'm not now. I know just what to do. There's only one thing, Joe. I'm not queer. I never have been. You believe that, Joe?"

Joe said nothing. He heard Lamont sigh. Then, the slow whisper of something else shoved beneath the door. He stooped and picked it up.

"Goodbye, Joe. Tell China goodbye, too."

It was a claim ticket from the parcel room of the Hotel Vendôme on Forty-ninth Street in New York City. The ticket was dated November 15th of last year.

Cindy Lou's claim ticket. He knew it had to be that. His scalp prickled, and a slow excitement crept along his body. *Lamont must be the Stateside contact for the dope that Tony was talking about.*

Joe waited five minutes more in the bathroom. Dropping his jeans around his ankles, he soaped himself down and dried on one of the fluffy pink towels with *Mother* embroidered in thick blue curlicues. Then he unlocked the bathroom door and stuck his head out.

"Lamont?"

The apartment was deathly still. His heart beat like a sledge-hammer.

He went into the bedroom.

Lamont was hanging from the water pipes. He had climbed up on the trunk and then stepped off to hang himself. The rope was looped in a crude noose around his neck. His face was the color of ashes and his head hung at a funny angle to one side. Eyes staring at nothing, he twirled round and round at the end of the rope, like a plumb tied to a string.

Joe sat on the bed. His body was shaking so hard that he had to sit down. *Lamont, Lamont . . . you died with my seed in you. Like my mother died with Daddy pouring his seed into her. Like I suffocated my son, the seed from my body, I covered his head up and killed him. . . .* Did he smell peas burning, or was that just his imagination? *I did good when I killed my son, Lamont, this ain't no world for him to grow in, this ain't no world for you, Lamont, for nobody, the way we live like dogs and we die worse than dogs. . . .*

After a while, his body stopped shaking and he felt very calm. He went to the telephone in the living room and dialed a number. "Can I speak to Tony Brenzo? My name is Joe Market." A second later, he heard a voice in the receiver. "Tony?"

"Yeah, Joe baby. What's happening, man? You sound sad."

"I found out who the contact man was for that Cindy Lou guy you talked about, you remember?" He waited for Tony to say something; but Tony kept very quiet. "Anyway, it was Lamont. He went down on me . . . he gave me the claim check in payment . . . as partial payment. Then he went into the bedroom and hung himself from the water pipes."

"I'm sorry, Joe. I know how you must feel."

"I don't feel anything. I guess he was trying to get even with me for what I made him do. He must have known the cops had a stakeout, waiting for somebody to pick up that package. Dirty fucking queer."

"You wait there, Joe. I'll be right over."

Joe hung up the telephone. He couldn't go back into the bedroom. He sat instead on the sofa; and when the clipboard that Lamont had been writing on poked him in the behind, he picked it up and read the essay that Lamont had been writing for the American Legion contest on America:

In America, the colored people and the white people are like a man and a woman who gave grown used to each other in marriage. Love makes us hate the faults of the one we love; it also makes us magnify those faults, and hate the weakness that creates them. In a marriage, it is not unusual for one partner to deny important rights as a means of controlling the other partner. This is a real and harmful thing. But it is not based on hatred. However blind and misguided, it is based on love. For in the final analysis, we in America do somehow live together in peace and suffering. And in certain rare moments, we respect each other, we love each other, and die side-by-side, not because we believe that America has yet become a perfect union, but because we believe that America can become a perfect union. Each crisis between us at home brings the people of our country closer to the realization of that ideal. When we face the enemy, we are Americans first, and we can forgive the thoughtlessness that persecutes us in peacetime. For if we are to awaken a sense of justice and decency in the hearts and minds of all Americans, then we must continue to fight our battle in the farms and villages and cities of America. Because in this way, we preserve the heritage of America, which is our yoke and at the same time our salvation. Let no enemy think that he can exploit this quarrel, or no friend think that he can settle it. For our argument is a conflict between brothers; and the man who interferes in a conflict between brothers is always the one who loses first blood.

Lamont's essay for the American Legion competition. Joe put the clipboard on the arm of the sofa where Lamont's mother would see it. She worked at St. Mary's Hospital, in the diet kitchen there. Joe got the hospital number from Information, and asked to speak to Mrs. Jones. When she finally came on the line, he said bluntly, "Lamont just killed himself, Mrs. Jones." There was a long silence. Then Mrs. Jones said, "Who's calling, please?" Joe told her, and she said, very nicely, that she'd remembered seeing him around. "Was you one of Lamont's *men friends*?" she asked. Joe said yes, he was. "He was one of those funny people, wasn't he?" Mrs. Jones said. "Yes, he was. He was queer," Joe said. She gave a sigh of infinite satisfaction. Another pause. Then, "How'd he kill himself?" Although she didn't sound very interested at all, even when Joe told her. "Well, I've got to go back to work now, you know how these white people are," Mrs. Jones said. "Thank you so much for calling me, Mr. Market." Joe hung up. He couldn't wait for Tony any longer; and he went outside, leaving the apartment door wide open. The heat rushed up and scalded his eyeballs. He started the truck and drove back to the laundry. There was a sign on the front door: CLOSED FOR LUNCH. He went around the side and into the cool cellar.

China Doll was waiting for him. He smelled the acrid stench of pot. Her eyes were dreamy slits in the pale halo of her face. She was stoned out of her mind. She had spread a blanket on the floor, and was lying there.

"Lamont killed himself," Joe said. "He was a great goddamned writer, and he killed himself."

China didn't seem surprised at all. "Poor Lamont." She stretched out and raised her arms to Joe. "I'm high, Joe baby. I got other things on my mind. . . . Make my pussy sing, Joe . . . it's been such a long time. . . ." He took off his clothes and went to her, because it had been a long time.

Shit man, Lamont would have loaned me that ten dollars. Or Pee Wee, or China or Tony. Even Miss Lavinia would have. Or any one of a hundred other people, if I'd just asked them. But I went up there and made Lamont kill himself. Although he didn't feel too bad about it, because Lamont was a queer, and nobody had told him to go hang himself, he felt nothing but contempt for Lamont, hanging himself like that. Every other nigger in the world is fighting to keep from being hanged, and Lamont does it as a matter of course.

Hooking his arms under China's thighs, he lifted until nothing of her was touching the floor except her head and shoulders. Now he was getting pure pussy, he could feel all of China's insides mashing like hot, fat, wet maggots around his dick. Well, that was that, he wasn't going to have anything else to do with queers as long as he lived because a woman's pussy is so good. . . . "Man . . . you . . . got . . . a . . . devil . . . in . . . you . . ." China grunted. He had already come with Lamont, so there was nothing inside him except tears. He held those back, though; and he used China brutally, tearing her open with savage thrusts. He made her pussy sing, all right. When he got through, she tried to get up from the blanket, but she was too weak to move.

"You say Lamont killed himself?" She had come down off the pot now and she sounded like the news had just registered.

"Yeah, he killed himself. He hung himself from the water pipes in his mother's bedroom."

"Poor Lamont." She watched Joe as he pulled his jeans up over his hips, stashing his dick liked a bloodied weapon. He had drawn blood from her pussy as though she'd been a virgin; and she seemed very pleased about that. "Did Lamont say anything before he died?" Her voice sounded drowsy, and she cleared her throat. "You know, like famous last words?"

"He said he wasn't queer. He was, but he swore he wasn't. He told me to tell you goodbye."

"Anything else?" She was nearly asleep now.

"He said he wasn't afraid."

"Well, that's nice," China said. She rolled over and fell asleep.

Joe left the cellar and went home. And it was while he was standing under the hot shower that he realized that Lamont hadn't been Cindy Lou's contact at all.

Man, Lamont was in Vietnam with me last November. And that's when Cindy Lou came here to Decatur. So Lamont couldn't have got that claim check from Cindy Lou, because Lamont didn't even get back to Decatur until last month. He changed the hot water to cold, rubbing himself briskly. *Then where did Lamont get that claim check from? Because it doesn't stand to reason that Cindy Lou mailed it to him all the way over there in Vietnam. Or that Lamont would keep it all this time without trying to pick up that heroin.*

Drying himself roughly with a large, red towel, Joe felt very much alive. His body tingled with a cold, clean new life, and he didn't care how Lamont had come about having that claim check, it certainly wasn't any business of his. That was business for the police. Besides, he was sleepy like a motherfucker, he needed to get him some sleep. Although he was sure that the only reason Lamont would ever get mixed up with something like pushing dope would be to make money for his shitty mother. To impress her. To buy her love. Lamont Cranston Jones. Queer. His body was probably already on its way to the county morgue. Poor dumb bastard, that really might have been his first time sucking a dick, because he sure Lord didn't know how. Joe stretched out naked on the bed and went to sleep.

Four

"Tonight's the night of Halloween
When all the witches can be seen. . . ."

China stopped singing. "How does the rest of it go?" she said.

Tony shrugged. "I don't know. I haven't even heard it since I was a kid. You know how it goes, Joe?"

Joe was drinking wine from a sauce pan, holding it by the handle like a dipper. He emptied the pan and jammed it on his head like a cap, the handle sticking out over his face. "How does what go?" he said. China sang the song again. "Naw, I can't remember. I don't think I ever knew." He collapsed between Tony and China Doll on the floor. "Shit, I'm bugged. Where are the other people, China?"

"They'll be here. I invited some friends from New York. They said they might be a little late. But they'll be here for sure."

China's party had begun at nine o'clock; it was now close to ten thirty. Tony and Joe had arrived promptly at nine. The three of them were naked now, and China had been trying to talk up a Triple-S scene before the other guests arrived. But Tony had noticed Joe's reluctance, and he persuaded China to wait until later.

"What's eating you, Joe?" Tony said. "You're not yourself, that's for sure. You still brooding about Lamont?"

"Partly that, partly something else," Joe said. "Look, Tony, let's you and me put on our clothes and go outside awhile. You wouldn't mind that, would you, China?"

"You promise we'll make the Triple-S scene later on?"

"I promise," Joe said. "Come on, Tony. Let's take a gallon of China's wine and split."

Tony started to dress, but China would only give them their pants. "So you'll come back," she said. "I know you guys. You'll get drunk out there and forget all about me."

"I couldn't forget you, baby," Tony said. He wrapped his arms around China and kissed her. "Tony, don't go just yet," China said. Tony nodded to Joe. "I'll be down in a little while," he said. Joe grabbed a gallon of wine and went downstairs. There was a slight chill in the air that he found refreshing. He went up the driveway and sat in the moonshade with his back against the wall, drinking now and then from the bottle of wine.

Two days had passed now since Lamont's death. When Joe went to Police Headquarters with Tony to make a statement about what he knew of the suicide, Tony had told him not to mention the queer part. "Some of those guys at headquarters might not understand. Just tell them you stopped by Lamont's to borrow some money. Tell them you went to the bathroom and he slipped the claim ticket under the bathroom door. When you came out, you found him hanging in the bedroom. You tell them that, I'll take care of the rest." Joe followed Tony's instructions, but he had caught the policemen looking at him in a way that made him feel uncomfortable in his tight white jeans and the form-fitting T-shirt designed to show off his chest and biceps. *Do they know I'm a queer hustler? Or do they think I'm queer?* He left the station and went across the street to a diner. Tony came a while later and told him the case was closed as far as they were concerned.

"What about that Cindy Lou guy? You think he's still hiding somewhere?"

Tony nodded. "That's what we figure. And hiding somewhere not too far away, either. Or close enough for him to have given that claim ticket to Lamont." Joe's ears perked up at that. He hadn't thought that Cindy Lou might have given the ticket to Lamont *after* Lamont came home from Vietnam. Which meant that Lamont was Cindy Lou's contact after all. "Anyway," Tony said, "that Cindy Lou guy is Immigration's headache now, not ours. And I want to thank you, Joe. You helped us a lot."

"Tony, what did you tell those other cops about me?"

"The truth," Tony said. "I didn't want it in your written statement, so I explained it to them off-the-record."

"You told them I made it with Lamont?"

Tony placed both hands on Joe's shoulders. "I had to, baby. This is serious business. I had to tell them the truth."

"I wish you hadn't done that," Joe said. "Those fucking cops looked at me like I was a freak." Indignantly, he had walked out of the diner and went home.

Now, sitting in the driveway on Decatur Street, looking at the moon, Joe turned the wine bottle to his head and drank. He had got over being annoyed with Tony almost as soon as it happened. Shit man, he *was* a freak, he was honest enough to admit that. But not Lamont's kind of freak, that was for sure.

He drank some more wine, because for the first time since Lamont's death, he felt a genuine sense of regret that was very close to guilt. He had been in a great party mood earlier tonight until Tony had told him that Mrs. Jones had donated Lamont's body to the Newark Medical Center. "In the interests of science," Tony had said. Which was just a high-sounding way of saying that Mrs. Jones had turned Lamont over to experts to find out what kind of freak it was that she had produced. They were going to cut Lamont's body up and preserve some of it in alcohol and maybe burn the rest. In the interests of science. And in the interests of Mrs. Jones, who was wiping out the last traces of her son in whom she had not been well-pleased worth a damn. . . . Just that morning, Joe had seen Mrs. Jones on her way to work. In her white hospital uniform, she had walked with a lighter step than usual, brushing aside the condolences of her neighbors by saying that she appreciated that, honey, but she was already late for work. She seemed very well-pleased then.

Shit. Joe almost felt like crying. At least for his own dead son there was a grave and a tombstone where Odessa went every May with flowers in memory of the child Christopher, who had survived, however briefly, inside the holocaust of life. But Lamont had no grave, no tombstone. A part of him would remain in jars of alcohol, the rest of him would be burned up.

Joe's insides cringed at the idea of that, and he took a drink of wine. Man, the human body was sacred to him. He had learned that lesson from Titus, and he had learned it well, all those years he had been The Naked Child and The Naked Disciple. He didn't understand how Mrs. Jones could have done a thing like that to her son, how anybody could do something like that to their own flesh and blood. But he didn't want to feel sorry for Lamont, he didn't want to feel sorry for anybody. *Shit, Lamont was a fucking queer, and queers ain't human as far as I'm concerned.* Although he got a certain consolation from that, he still wondered what parts of Lamont that medical center would keep and what parts of him they would throw away. . . . Just then, a car stopped in front of the alley. Joe looked and saw Pee Wee climbing from his cab.

"Hey, Pee Wee. Come on and have a drink of wine, man."

"That you, Joe? Man, I come looking for you. Dig, Joe . . . you promised to pay me some money tonight, remember?"

"I remember." He gave Pee Wee the ten dollars he had made off Lamont. "China hasn't paid me yet," he said. "She'll pay me later on tonight. I tell you what, Pee Wee . . . Odessa's at her mother's house. You go get Odessa for me and bring her back here. I'll give you the rest of the money when you get back. O.K.?"

"O.K., stud. You dig, I'm not pressuring you, man. It's not that I need the bread before I can score anything more from my contact. You understand, don't you?"

"I understand."

Pee Wee took another drink and gave the bottle to Joe. Joe wiped off the bottle before drinking. "You hear about Lamont?"

"Yeah, man. Wasn't that something? The newspapers made Lamont sound like a really big-time pusher, they certainly do like to exaggerate. I was surprised, though, Lamont killing himself that way. Some kind of pressure really got to him."

Joe took another big swallow of wine. "Go get Odessa for me, will you, Pee Wee? I ain't seen her for a couple of days now, I'm dying to see her."

"O.K., stud. You'll have the rest of the bread when I get back?"

Joe nodded, and Pee Wee pressed three joints into his hand. "That's very special shit," he said. "Hashish. It'll make you walk on your head." He took the bottle from Joe and drank deeply. "You know, it's a funny thing, Joe. I been a cabbie on that corner for years. But tonight's the second time I'll be bringing a fare here to Decatur Street in all that time. I brought Mr. Yen here one night just before he died. It was raining something terrible. I guess that's why he didn't want to walk. It's funny how most of my fares are for outside of this area." He popped a white eye at Joe. "You going to pay me for bringing Odessa, ain't you, Joe? Man, I *hate* to keep mentioning money, you and me being such good friends. But my debts been piling up lately."

"I'll pay you," Joe said. "Please, Pee Wee, go get Odessa now. She's at her mother's. Tell her I said to come." His voice broke in his throat. "Tell her I need her. . . ."

"Sure, stud, I'll get her. I know what you mean."

Do you, Pee Wee? You cheap sonofabitch. Bugging him about the fare like that. He lit a stick of hashish to quiet the anger he felt growing in him. Pee Wee hung around to get a couple of puffs, and then he left. "You a good stud, Joe, I hope you don't put me down because I asked you for the bread, and for that cab fare. But man, my expenses been growing in leaps and bounds. You dig, stud?"

"I dig, baby." He filled his lungs with the hashish—it was sweeter, subtler than normal pot, the way it insinuated itself into the mind—and held his breath until Pee Wee drove off with an impressive gnashing of gears. *Black bastard. One of these days I'm going to make him eat my dick.*

He did not hear Tony Brenzo come out of the house and up the driveway. He was thinking of his mother smothered by the weight of love, and his son smothered by ignorance, and the lieutenant who died with his boots on and his balls shot out, and Lamont, and cheap Mr. Yen taking a cab to avoid getting wet. . . .

"That pot, Joe? Give me a drag, baby. Some of China's friends got here from New York, the party's just starting to swing."

Joe gave him the joint, and Tony sat down beside him. He smelled of wine and sex. He smoked some pot, then he took the bottle and drank, and gave it back to Joe. When Joe drank, the bottle was still warm from Tony's mouth. "You know, I was just thinking," Joe said. He was higher than he'd ever been in his life; that hashish was something terrible. "I was thinking that we certainly been through a lot together."

"A hell of a lot," Tony said.

"I think it's coming to an end."

"Why you think that, Joe?"

"I'm not sure. Just a feeling I have. Like I've come to the end of the road. I've done everything, I've done nothing. It's as simple as that."

Tony half-twisted and stretched out on his back alongside the house with his head in Joe's lap. "What the fuck was in that cigarette?" he said thickly. "I feel like I'm going to blow my stack."

"It was hash. Hashish. You ever had any before?"

"No." Tony's head was soft and warm, pressing on his dick. "You?"

"No. But it's a motherfucker. You feel all right, man?"

"I feel all right. Like somebody poleaxed me, that's how I feel." But his voice sounded normal now. They were quiet a while, then Tony said, "What about Odessa, man?"

"What about her? I sent Pee Wee to get her. But I don't know whether she'll come or not." He drank, and passed the wine to Tony. "Nigger women can be pretty shitty, once they get their asses on their backs."

"I know," Tony said. He sat up and drank, then put his head back in Joe's lap. They were both aware that Joe almost never used the word nigger around Tony, although Tony easily referred to himself as a wop or dago. To show Tony that he had made a definite step forward in their friendship, Joe decided to use the word again. "Man, what you know about nigger women?" he said warmly.

"I was married to one," Tony said. "She was beautiful. The marriage was beautiful. Everything was beautiful until she died of cancer."

Joe felt awkward and confused. He lit the hashish and took a long drag, then handed it to Tony. "Man, you should have told me before."

"Why? Would it have made any difference?"

"I don't know. Maybe. Maybe not. Your wife . . . she taught at that school in Newark you took me to?" He felt Tony's head nod in his lap; and he detected a kind of pain in Tony that made him wish he was with Odessa right now. "Man . . . I'm going back to Odessa, if she'll have me, you know that?" He was going to lead a good life, too, he certainly was.

"I'm glad to hear that, Joe. I think you'll feel better once you and Odessa get back together." They smoked the last of that stick of hashish, and then Tony stood up. "You going home now, Joe, or you going back to the party?"

The hashish was doing very wild things to Joe's head. And there was something important he tried to remember, but it eluded him. He stood, too, and threw both arms around Tony. "Shit man, I'm going to the party. Where else but to the party?" Tony's naked chest was warm against his own, and he really loved Tony then because Tony had married a nigger woman, that's what he'd been trying to remember. But he decided not to tell Tony that, it was enough just to think it. "Who're we going to Triple-S tonight, Tony?"

"What about China? She's crazy to have it happen. You in the mood, baby?"

"I'm in the mood, baby." They went inside to the party.

Around two dozen people were there now. As China had promised, everybody was naked except for masks; and Joe and Tony checked their pants at the door and put on their masks. China had softened the lights and was playing Ray Charles on the stereo set. Pot smoke hung like a cloud over the party. Some people were dancing, some talking, some kissing. On the center table, China Doll had set up several gallons of whiskey and wine and a huge platter of fried chicken. Except for three or four guys who already had stiff hard-ons, it seemed an ordinary party scene.

China was baking hot biscuits in the kitchen, her naked round butt turned upside down now over the oven door as she inspected the bread. A pot of turnip greens bubbled on the fire. "This might not be party food," China said, taking the glass of wine that Joe brought her, "but it certainly tastes good after an orgy." Her body was flushed from the heat; her breasts jiggled as she stirred in the greens with a chicken fork.

Joe winked at Tony. "I don't know if I go along with the idea of an orgy," he said, threatening China with his body. But she fended him off with the chicken fork. "Boy, I'm going to pluck that thing of yours out and fry it in hot grease. Besides, there's nothing you won't go along with, I know you."

"Amen," Tony said. Now he tried to grab her, but she swiped at him with the fork. Laughing, Tony jumped back into the living room where another group of China's friends were involved in the ritual of arriving. "Joe, you watch the biscuits for me, baby," China said. Breasts bouncing, she rushed to the door with a handful of masks and some pot to put the newcomers in a party mood.

China had lived in Greenwich Village for a while before she married Mr. Yen, and these were some of her bohemian friends she had invited to the party. One of them was a red-haired poet with a red beard and red hair all over his body. When all of them were naked, he read a poem about Malcolm X, the slain Black Nationalist leader:

> To sum up his life,
> which is all our lives,
> is to say that being torn
> and buffeted by the wind,
> capriciously to be denied
> the ordered free flight
> of even the least elm leaf,
>
> rather, to be chased like
> miaowing cats before
> the hot-jawed hound,
>
> what man would not climb
> the pole of hatred
> and there sit and hiss
> curses at his clumsy pursuers,
>
> rather than to turn tail
> and be devoured
> by the ambiguous lips of love?

He bowed self-consciously to light applause and joined a group of his friends in a corner.

There were two Negro girls with the Village group. One was light-skinned; the other had a sleek, blue-black complexion, with fine limbs and tight breasts. Obviously intellectuals, the girls argued incessantly with each other, as though they were strangers; but they came together in a hard core of indignation when anybody tried to interrupt them.

"The trouble with you, honey," the light-skinned girl said, "is that it bugs you to admit that maybe black people are not ready for integration. Mind you, I said *maybe*. Just for the sake of argument, let's say that blacks really are different from other people, less human, unequal. . . ."

"Nonsense!" the black girl snapped. "You sound like Richard Nixon would sound, if *he* had the balls to come right out and say what he thought. Now, if it *is* true that we've been ignorant and unaware during three hundred years of segregation, then George Wallace is right when he says we're not ready for integration. But I don't think this has been the case. I think the black man has enjoyed living in America. Like every other American, he has always been loyal to this country's lies as well as to its realities. You say that he is less human, unequal. . . ."

"Only for the sake of argument," the light-skinned girl interposed.

The black girl nodded. "All right, for the sake of argument. But you remember what Thomas Jefferson wrote in the Declaration of Independence?" A small group of people had gathered, and she recited to them all, flashing her white eyes and touching her breasts for emphasis. "*All experience hath shewn that mankind are more disposed to suffer, while evils are sufferable, than to right themselves by abolishing the forms to which they are accustomed.* Well, this is the greatest proof of the black man's humanity—not that he has done *something* to right the wrong done to him, but that he has done *nothing*. If he had successfully rebelled against slavery 350 years ago, he would have been a superman indeed. Good Lord, it took free white American colonists over 150 years to rebel against

British domination! And you expect more of the black man? The fact that he is only now rebelling is proof of his being like everybody else."

"I disagree with you completely," the light-skinned girl said. "Each man rebels according to the authority that he is resisting. There is no more Britain to rebel against, and that's why nowadays we have black power, and long, hot summers, and student riots. I am *not* saying that the black man is unequal; but I *am* saying that what he is rebelling against makes him unique in America." But the black girl did not agree. And they argued violently, but in whispers now, because China Doll had asked for attention on the other side of the room. The hairy red poet was reciting another of his works:

> He'd been watching the moon
> all the while.
> Just at the moment of orgasm,
> he slid out of her and shot cum
> at the Shakespeare moon,
> lying there in the grass
> with his toes pointing skyward,
> spending on his belly.
>
> Of course she didn't understand.
>
> Great is the man who finds
> even one small husk
> that he can feed on from the
>   whole kernel.
> In this chaos of confused
>   and ever-changing winds
> The only truth is confusion.

That was the signal for the orgy to begin. Like a game of musical chairs when the tune is suddenly stopped, there was a general scramble for chairs, sofa, and clear space on the floor. Some couples squirmed against the wall. A young blonde girl was arrested by the red poet and impaled in mid-stride. After a few minutes, the room was filled with writhing couples; and the essence of sex filtered upwards like a soundless prayer to the God of fucking and formed a delicious miasma with the pot smoke that floated over everything. Joe and Tony tried to make the two spade chicks who were still arguing politics; but the light-skinned girl announced with a sneer that *she* preferred women, while the black one flashed her large white eyes behind her mask and said that she thought it was too early for sex. "Look me up later, baby. After midnight. I'll give you a ball." She went back to arguing with her friend.

Hungrily, Joe and Tony looked around. "Looks like we're out in the cold," Tony said. "Where's China?"

Surprisingly, she was in the kitchen stirring in her pots. She laughed when they came in. "You got to be quick around here," she said. "And don't be looking at me with them great big hungry eyes. When I wanted to make it, you guys didn't."

"Only Joe," Tony cut in. "Not me, China."

"Not me, China," she mocked him. "Go away now, can't you see I'm cooking? And next to sex, I love food best of all."

Joe grabbed a chicken leg and chewed it; but Tony would not be put off. "I want you, China . . . I want you now. . . ."

"Tony . . . honey . . . you're *greedy*! You just had me before I started cooking these turnip greens. . . ."

"I want you again, China. I didn't get enough before."

But China still teased. "I sure do appreciate your interest," she said, patting her hair like a real cool bitch, "but you got to convince me that I ought to, baby. I mean, it's so soon and everything. . . ."

Tony stretched and turned off the kitchen lamp. The only light came from the gas jets on the stove, flickering blue eyes in the heavily shadowed kitchen. Gently, Tony caressed China's breasts while she shielded her eyes with an over-flung arm. "Tony . . . Tony . . . Tony. . . ." Her soft skin was the faintest of gleams beneath Tony's fingers. "Eat me, baby," Tony said. "Eat me right now." Slowly, but firmly, he forced her to the floor, guiding her head to his crotch.

Joe was on his way out of the kitchen when China called him back. "Joe, get some more wine from the cellar, please. Everybody's going to want some wine when this is over."

"Sure," Joe said. He thumped Tony on the butt. "Whale, baby

. . . and don't let them turnip greens burn." His pants were hanging in the hall closet; he found them and took the other two sticks of hashish from the pocket. Then he went to the cellar.

There was an inside stairway that led from the third floor apartment to the cellar, and Joe went down naked as he was. *Damn, that Tony's a stone cocksman, the way he took China Doll.* He knew that China didn't really want wine from the cellar, that she just didn't want him around while Tony was fucking her. A woman was funny that way; she didn't want another guy around unless she was fucking him, too. *Well, I'll get China later on, with Tony. And that black girl, too. She's a pretty intelligent bitch . . . I wonder if that light-skinned chick is making it with her?*

The cellar funk seemed to be the rich atmosphere from another century, the heavy aroma of wine dominating the lighter fragrance of damp walls and soggy timbers. There was a medieval musk that made him think of monks and cloisters. Like a disturbed snake, the water heater hissed steadily at its own pilot light. Joe fired a stick of hashish from the pilot and smoked it on the bottom step. Then he took off his mask and looped it over his arm. Solemnly, like the swishing of black silk dresses, an array of ideas lifted themselves and began a stately witches' dance inside his head.

The only truth is confusion. The red poet had said that; and it did not take any kind of genius to see that confusion certainly was the truth of America in these latter days of 1968. Far from being a seductive white bitch now, crippled by political murders, riots, civil disobedience, and the war in Vietnam, America 1968 reminded Joe of a tired and befuddled old woman—some of his new attitude had come from his contact with Cheap Mary—awaiting the impeccable order of death. Because America in the Age of Johnson was so jumbled and disarranged that the current Presidential contest lay between a happy little bumpkin like Hubert Horatio Humphrey and a less-humorous travesty in the person of Richard Milhous Nixon. The black people of Decatur had already decided that Nixon would win the race, just because Humphrey seemed to possess such a jocular ignorance of what America needs and wants that, elected President, he would certainly require Americans to laugh all the time as the solution to every disagreeable situation. On the other hand, Nixon would find some sly way to increase the confusion in America—if those shrewd, stubborn jowls of his were any indication—while he pretended to be looking for a way to put an end to confusion altogether. He would stop the war in Vietnam in order to step up the wars at home. Which meant that America soon would be returning to one of her more amusing and less-expensive recreations—that of destroying black people—since yellow people are so numerous and so distant from the American motherland that they are a hundred times more costly and more troublesome, and certainly a great deal less fun, to kill.

Joe smoked some more hash. He was aware that the narcotic had expanded his ability to think; and he found himself excited by the fact that the American government and the American people are not and probably never have been representative of each other. Also, he understood for the first time how little real differences there are between white people and black people. The fact that Tony Brenzo had loved and married a black woman, and still mourned her, had shown him that. He saw very clearly now that the basic conflict in America is between her people and her government, and that much of the hostility between blacks and whites is a direct result of the government's practice of reducing democracy to the level of nonsense in order to raise big business to the level of government. Spurred on by these money merchants, black and white Americans alike sell their souls to the most attractive devil; and the people of whatever race who are riotous and discontent all over America are people who have resurrected themselves and are asking for their souls back.

Inside such a climate, then, what can a man do to keep from selling his soul? Joe's ethics teacher at Seton Hall had told him that the soul is that quality in man which applauds good and recoils from evil. Specifically, how does a black man go about saving his soul? He certainly cannot accept the white man's God, his Bible, his *good*, when the black man himself is the definition of evil in these philosophies. By the same token, neither can he reasonably accept the promise of the Messiah and salvation, since the Bible dooms

the black man to be a servant to his brothers. And salvation becomes the most insidious posture of all, because it flings us into the
jaws of bondage and terror while it blinds us to the monster's teeth.
The soul might recoil from evil, but does not reject it. All too often
it applauds as it recoils, like *white* ladies who snatch their skirts
back from the monstrous mouth, but grind their hips in time to the
writhing black figures there. Civilization marches on to the crunch-
ing of black bones, accompanied—incredibly—by the sanctimo-
nious harmony of psalms.

Joe went to the heater and lit the hashish again. The ruby eye
of the automatic fire alarm glared hypnotically at him as he
smoked, like a sacred and disembodied jewel in the surrounding
darkness. He leaned back on the steps and closed his eyes. *And he
said unto them, this is my blood of the new testament, which is shed
for many.* A sharp pain that pierced the seat of his brain caused him
to remember the long-forgotten ritual of communion in Mr. Cobb's
church in Virginia, before Titus Market had started his own religion. *And as they did eat, Jesus took bread, and blessed, and broke
it, and gave to them, and said, Take, eat; this is my body.*

Was it possible that Christ did know something of truth, although he was not divine? *One of you will betray me.* He had certainly known that. Perhaps it was in such a room as this—cool,
musty with wine. But an upper room, with beams. The desert outside, bursting with springtime. And Christ surrounded by his
twelve disciples, saying with joyful satisfaction, *One of you will betray me . . .* saying, really, *One of you will ask me to prove that I am
flesh and blood and not a god at all. That is why you will betray me.*
Judas smiled secretly, knowing with a great rush of love that it already had been done. . . .

This is my body, eat; this is my blood, drink. The hustler and
the Biblical hero command alike, squirm their thighs alike inside
the hot jaws of terrible Life that sucks and sighs and tears with its
teeth, drinking the body's ejaculations. *This is my body which is
given for you, this do in remembrance of me. If any man eat of this
bread, he shall live for ever, and the bread that I will give is my*

flesh, which I will give for the life of the world. But the sacrifices of warm flesh provide a tenuous footing as the sun swirls, herding her family with her; only a truth of great proportions can light there. None alights; therefore, no truth is of proportions substantial enough to matter and be remembered. *Verily I say unto you, I will drink no more of the fruit of the vine, until that day that I drink it new in the kingdom of God.* The only truth is confusion.

Shit. That stick of hashish was done. Joe turned on the cellar light. Man, that hash was a motherfucker; he had one stick left, and he was going to save that for later. Now he wanted to get back upstairs and fuck. The wine casks squatted like five fat women along one side of the cellar. Near them was a row of shelves where China stored the bottled wine. Joe took down four gallons and started upstairs.

Suddenly, on an impulse, he decided to fill a jug from the fifth barrel. China said it contained wine for special occasions. Well, an orgy was going on upstairs, and there was certainly nothing more special than that.

He turned the spigot and watched the purple liquid pour into the glass bottle. When the wine slowed to a bare trickle, Joe decided to take the top off the barrel to increase the flow of wine. He found a hatchet and lifted the wooden head from the staves. Then he just stood there staring with his mouth hanging open. Because a dead man's naked body was in the barrel.

Mr. Yen. China's dead husband. Stuffed and crammed down backwards inside the barrel like garbage crammed into a can, stuffed feet first and then his small torso jammed backwards down on top of him and his arms squeezed to his sides. China's dead husband who was supposed to have been cremated, crammed down here in a wine barrel, his body curved back like a statue. . . . A small bullet hole grew like a blemish in the center of his forehead. *Somebody shot Mr. Yen and stuffed his body down here in this barrel.*

Round yellow face . . . glassy white eyes . . . mouth grotesquely open like a fish gasping for air . . . thick tongue the color of grapes.

The wine came only up to his knees, and Joe could see the pale head of Mr. Yen's dick, solid between his legs like a fat sausage. The organ itself was enormous even in death, the head resembled a fat, peeled chestnut. *He was hung almost like me, the little bastard. No wonder China married him.*

Joe was shaking, and his stomach churned sourly. He remembered that China had drawn wine from this very same barrel, she had thrown it on him and licked it off his body that day he came down here to mash grapes. *China, you dirty bitch, you knew his body was in there all the time, throwing that wine on me.* He turned away and tried to vomit, but nothing came up, although he stuck his finger down his throat. But nothing came up, and he stopped trying after a while. *You didn't love him, China, you admitted that. But you must have really hated him to use him so miserably in death.* For it was surely China Doll who had shot Mr. Yen and stuffed his small naked body down here in the wine barrel.

Joe turned out the lights again. He lit the third stick of hashish. At Seton Hall, he had toyed with the idea of becoming a scientist, although he had suspected that the only place inside of science for a black man is to sweep its floors. Except for the science of ignorance and superstition, which is religion. Now, he felt greater than a scientist, like a man who has seen through heaven, as if, from a vantage point in the universe, he had been privileged to see the spinning sun and all her young, swinging in wider and wider circles through an ever-increasing infinitude. Now he could make an exact science of speculation.

He knew, for example, that China Doll had suddenly become the central portion of this particular puzzle. Revolving around her, like the planets in their system, and with the same unshakable attraction to exactness, rotated answers that were, for the first time, precise ones. It is rare indeed for a man to have this chance of answering with *exactness* . . . to have the end product of speculation so nicely packaged and preserved as Mr. Yen was . . . to slim the chance of error to such a delectable hairsbreadth. The prospect excited Joe, almost like the surging excitement of sex. He sat down to formulate his dissertation.

The man China had had cremated had to be the mysterious Cindy Lou that Tony had talked about. Mr. Yen's cousin. The drug peddler. Cindy Lou's body, not Mr. Yen's, had been cremated.

It was obvious, too, that China Doll had given the claim ticket to Lamont. She was of course the woman Lamont had raved to Joe about. Somehow or other, China had gotten the ticket from Cindy Lou and given it to Lamont.

Once examined, the pieces fitted together perfectly. Joe remembered Pee Wee saying he had brought Mr. Yen home one night in a rainstorm. But Mr. Yen had been too cheap to take a cab for the short walk from Hickory Street to his house, rain or no rain.

Then it must have been a Chinaman who didn't know Decatur well enough to find Yen's house by himself. A Chinaman who didn't want to arouse suspicion by asking for information. A Chinaman called Cindy Lou by the police.

Pee Wee wouldn't have known the difference. Besides, even Tony Brenzo had said that all Chinamen look alike. Joe thought there was beautiful irony in the fact that Cindy Lou had slipped through a police dragnet to his death here in Decatur because of the blind eye of prejudice. Who had actually looked closely at the living Cindy Lou and seen the unique features of an individual?

The police following him had followed only a yellow skin—small wonder he had led them to a ghetto of yellow faces and given them the slip so easily. Pee Wee had seen the same yellow face here and assumed it belonged to Mr. Yen, the Chinamen he knew. When China called the police, they hadn't bothered to check the corpse's identity for the same reason. They had taken her word that the man dead in her living room from a heart attack was really her husband. And why not? If all Chinamen looked alike, why not trust the word of someone who claimed to actually know the vital statistics of just one of those familiar faces?

Cindy had to tell China Doll and Mr. Yen about the claim ticket for the package with the dope in it before he died. But China was too smart to pick it up herself. So she had waited until she thought the heat was off. Then she had seduced Lamont and talked him into doing it. "Did Lamont say anything before he died?"

China had asked Joe something like that when he told her about Lamont. He realized now that she wanted to know how much Lamont had revealed. *Lamont, hanged by the neck like Judas from the water pipes, you betrayed your queerness and that's why you died. You fucked China Doll, and that gave you the balls to make it with me, and that's why you died.*

Then, another thought struck him. Why couldn't China claim that Cindy Lou had shot Mr. Yen, then died himself of a heart attack? She could say that she hid Yen's body and had Cindy Lou cremated because she didn't want trouble with the police.

Joe grinned in the darkness. None of that would hold up. First of all, if Cindy Lou had really killed Mr. Yen, wouldn't it be logical to assume that he would kill China as well?

Second, if Cindy Lou really did shoot Mr. Yen, and then died himself, what was there for China to fear from the police? The only answer seemed to be that Cindy Lou died first and then China had shot Mr. Yen. The other way around would have left her completely in the clear; she could have called in the police and still have gotten away with the claim ticket.

The fact that she called the police meant that she didn't want Yen's own doctor involved, because Yen's doctor, at least, would have recognized his own patient. It meant that China had already killed and concealed Yen's body, and needed the *police* to confirm a false identification of Cindy Lou's body. If not that, then why hadn't she called a private physician, or even Yen's own doctor, for surely he must have had one.

Obviously, then, China had killed Mr. Yen *because of the claim ticket*. Perhaps they disagreed about getting involved in something so dangerous as dope peddling. Rather than the big-time operator that Tony had made him out to be, Cindy Lou was obviously very small fish. A guy with the idea of bringing dope to America and selling it for a lot of money. Which would explain the amateur way he had tried to smuggle the dope into this country. And would explain why he had come to Yen's in the first place. He needed an accomplice, someone with knowledge of America's ways. Someone trustworthy. His cousin, Mr. Yen.

But, suppose that either China or Mr. Yen was Cindy Lou's syndicate contact for the dope? No, that didn't hold up, either. First of all, if Yen had been the contact, then there wouldn't have been an argument with China about the dope. With Cindy Lou dying of a heart attack, and if Yen had been a part of the syndicate, he would have been smart enough to turn Cindy Lou's body over to the syndicate for them to dispose of. And if China herself had been the contact, then she would have given *Yen's* body to the syndicate for them to get rid of, rather than taking the risk and going to all the trouble of hiding it down here. China was a strong girl, and Yen hadn't weighed more than a feather. Still, it must have cost China a lot of effort to get his body down here.

Yes, China was certainly guilty. She would be excited at the prospect of danger and easy money; Mr. Yen would be reluctant, determined to call in the police and tell them about the dope. China had to kill him.

Only she could have given the ticket to Lamont, because she was the only logical link between Lamont and the dead Cindy Lou. There was no big dope syndicate involved here, just the fear and greed of a woman who was given a golden opportunity for getting rid of her rich husband, and took advantage of it.

Joe smacked his mouth over the deliciousness of knowing, finally, all the facets of a single problem; and he hugged his groin in delight. The privilege of knowing even a small truth is a privilege reserved for only a few men, he knew that. *I'm not just a dumb big dick nigger, I can reason, I got knowledge nobody else got.* Still, he felt a kind of fatal kinship with the dead Mr. Yen, because any man hung like that deserved a better death.

Then he realized that for knowledge to have real value, it must be used. And he felt a great sadness. Because if he revealed China's crime, it would mean that he cared about it one way or another. And he really didn't care, except as an intellectual exercise. China meant nothing to him, other than that she was a damn good fuck. But so were a dozen more women he knew. And Mr. Yen had meant even less. What did he care about China murdering her husband? Once again, the familiar phrase: their world, their law, their morality . . . meaning the white man's. "Fuck it," he thought. "I don't give a damn."

China, like every other criminal, was asking him, the onlooker, to prove that he did care for somebody, some thing—or that he didn't. He could prove the former by talking, the latter by keeping quiet. *China, by your act, you are trying to make me show that I am a thinking, feeling, sensitive individual.* Shit. *Well, I'm not,* he thought. *I don't want to get involved in no more of this shit. I don't want nobody else dead because of me.*

He turned on the light and gazed a long time into the unseeing eyes of Mr. Yen. Then he smiled, because he felt very proud of China Doll. She had committed the perfect crime. Perfect, because now he knew about it, and that was like nobody knowing at all.

He closed the lid over the barrel and sealed it. Yen was dead, his big dick with the fat chestnut head would never fuck again. That was all.

"Fuck it," Joe said. He was not dead, he would fuck right now. He put his mask back on and went upstairs with two gallon jugs of wine clinking in each hand, frantic for the Triple-S scene with Tony and China Doll. *The only truth is confusion, but some truth is certain fact. And it's a fact that I don't give a damn about any of this. All I want to do is fuck.*

"Let me get on the bottom," Joe said. He lay flat on his back; China took her position, then Tony. Joe brought his butt off the floor. He was glued to China and Tony, they were suffocating him with their bodies, he was his mother and son rolled into one, powerfully male and female at the same time, dominating in sex and being dominated by it. He knew that Tony Brenzo was not making love to China Doll so much as he was making love to him, Joe Market, who, until now, had always insisted on being top man in the Triple-S scene.

Tony had looked surprised when Joe had asked for the bottom position. He didn't know why he had asked for it himself. He had always avoided it because it seemed to him to be the position of death and femininity, lying on his back like that. Now, as China and Tony collided over him in heavy cadences that ended like the tail of a shock wave always at the base of his spine and in the roof of his mouth—for China seemed determined to ram herself headfirst down him that way as well—he heard the plaintive twang of a guitar and his mind registered the fact that only six people remained at the party. The red-bearded poet squatting in the corner with his guitar was one of them. "I got a feeling, man, like, something *great* is going to happen, and I'm not talking about sex either, I've had enough of that." Sated in one respect, he rested on his haunches and waited, watching the three of them locked together, strumming a sad accompaniment to their undulations.

Joe moved in a kind of slow fury; China squirmed to meet him. Tony said over and over through his teeth *O goddamn goddamn goddamn* sending China back into the sweatiness of Joe who rigidly repelled their double attack on his underbelly, sending the shock waves again that fused them together somehow with the solitary string that the red poet plucked, a single string plucked incessantly by one finger, piercing Joe's brain with a maddening insistence, like the slow and repeated insertion of a sharp needle.

He remembered, too, that the black girl and the light-skinned girl were making love together in the bedroom. They had announced their intention of doing so shortly after Joe's return from the cellar with the wine. "I meant it, man, when I told you we'd have a ball," the black girl had said, by way of apology to Joe. "I mean, I've never made it with a man before. You appealed to me, I thought it might be nice to try. . . ." All the while, with a triumphant grin on her lips, the light-skinned girl was tugging the black girl toward the bedroom. It was obvious that the black girl would play the passive female role—the other girl was too openly butch for it to be otherwise—but Joe still objected to the idea of her sinuous body thrashing under the onslaught of another woman. "Maybe some other time," the black girl had said, just as the door closed with a resounding slam in his face.

Then, Tony and China had tagged him for the Triple-S scene. "Man, this Tony Brenzo is hot as a firecracker," China had said, laughing, eating from the pot of turnip greens. Looking at the disarray of empty bottles and chicken bones and dirty glasses and plates on the table, Joe realized that the party had reached its climax and then subsided while he had been in the cellar. Had he been there that long? It had not seemed so long; but the fact that the black-skinned girl was having sex implied that it was at least after midnight, he supposed she had really meant it when she said she never fucked before midnight. . . .

"Here, baby." The poet was squatting over him now with a drink in his hand. He held the glass to Joe's mouth gently, like someone administering to a sick or wounded man. He served China and Tony in turn. "I know how it is, man. I always get thirsty in a scene like this, but I never want to break the contact, either. I'm just doing for you what I wish somebody'd do for me when I'm making a three-way scene. By the way, you guys are beautiful, real poetry in action. . . ." He said that, and then he went back to his corner and the single string on the guitar.

Once again Joe was being suffocated, and he was surprised at how peaceful the sensation felt. There was no other word to describe it. For perhaps a full minute, he could not breathe— China's mouth plugged his own, Tony's forearm dragged him closer around the neck, cutting off his windpipe—nor could he see, China's hair coming undone suddenly and tumbling into his eyes, so that he shut them. The double sensation of choking and blindness filled him with an almost overpowering elation. *I cannot love, I do not deserve to live.* The thought flashed once like a faulty neon in the midnight of his mind—his air was still cut off, surely death was the next step, a tumbling over into the abyss of eternal night —and then the miracle of air sucked into his lungs as China released him—only then did he realize that her own heart had been still against his chest—and he looked up blinking around white stars into the beautiful, cruel face of Tony, the full lips curved in a diabolic smile, the weight of Tony's balls grinding against his own, the hairy forearm tightening around his neck *Tony don't choke me man* then his neck performing the remarkable feat of lifting his head from the floor without breaking under the pressure of Tony's arm sending his lips closer to Tony's closer closer until his mouth met Tony's hot red lips in suction so powerful that it felt to him as if the very marrow of his brain was pulled down to the tip of his tongue. Then incredibly China's mouth was also on his, her tongue filling his mouth so that they were sharing his lips, Tony's possessing the left side looking downward and China's the right, his neck twisted around like that at such a sharp angle that he must surely die from a broken neck if not from the exquisite pleasure of being so ecstatically close to death while at the same time to be so glued together in sex three tongues now twanging the single tragic string of the red poet's guitar Joe heard a moaning rise in his ears all three of them melded together at mouth and crotch legs flailing together in frantic desperation to be freed and yet avoiding the possibility of untwining by twining even tighter ... his throat full of juices his dick full of pussy and ramming the head of Tony's dick inside of China's pussy, the saliva of two mouths pouring with a special kind of sweetness into him ... his hands full of flesh, perhaps China's perhaps Tony's ... and meat full of pussy hairy balls to hairy balls knees locked around two bodies riding him with the measured desperation of solid waves plowing an ever-mounting evermoving sea so that now his thighs tightened his butt came together his spine tingled as the spume collected in a squall-ing spout at the base of his skull and leisurely blew the top of his head off. . . .

Tony grunted and came, too; China bore down and arched up simultaneously, holding them together in a delicate balance, receiving and blending their juices with her own.

The single guitar string quivered and subsided.

"O God I love you, both of you!" It was China mashed between them; she fell asleep almost at once.

Tony reached underneath Joe and dragged them closer together. Joe ran his hands up and down Tony's smooth back, the ivory feel of it, until drowsiness overtook them both. . . .

———

. . . so that Joe did not know how much later it was that he looked up and saw Odessa and her mother staring down at him with shocked faces. Pee Wee was there, too, looking somehow like an upside-down water pitcher when viewed from the bottom.

Joe had been dreaming; he thought at first that this was part of the dream, Odessa and her mother, and Pee Wee . . . until Pee Wee squatted beside him radiating the real funk of cruddy socks and pants pressed too often, and said, "Odessa's here, man. Her mother come with her." So that he knew it was not part of the dream—he would remember it later, an insane dream of redemption that had somehow seemed prophetic, foretelling an end which seemed to be waiting for him just around a familiar corner. Miss Lavinia's bristling indignation was real and present, the ridiculous straw hat making an aureole of yellow around her wealth of black hair and the matching fat cheeks, looking somehow like Sojourner Truth poised on a rock or the late blessed Bethune, but ugly in a less angelic way, the round cheeks puffed up like oversize black walnuts, the heavy handbag suspended now directly over Joe's line of vision, as if holding a bomb which she would drop momentarily to destroy him and China Doll and Tony, for they were still locked in the Triple-S, remaining together somehow even in their sleep, China asleep on Joe's chest, Tony sleeping on her and in her. . . . From the corner of his eye, Joe saw the red poet squatting against the wall, using his guitar as an oversize fig leaf, grinning from ear to ear. It was obviously the beginning of the something great he had waited for to happen.

"Three dogs," Miss Lavinia said. "Nothing but three dogs."

"Mama, I told you not to come," Odessa said meekly. Her voice was weak and trembling, and Joe felt that same old familiar disgust for the weak part of her, although he knew she could be incredibly strong when she wanted to.

He decided to get up. Pee Wee was still squatting near him; the smell of the man was almost overwhelming, those damned dirty socks he wore, all of the stench of him seemed to accumulate there and aim itself at Joe's nose.

"Pee Wee, old buddy . . . move back a bit, man. Wake Tony up for me, will you?"

Pee Wee was glad to comply, Joe could see that, the way his round little eyes devoured the three naked bodies, the lump that started to grow in his smelly pants so that he jammed his hand into his pocket and played with himself there while he half-prodded, half-caressed Tony Brenzo awake.

Tony did not notice Odessa and her mother at first, and Pee Wee was standing behind him, admiring the rear view. Tony opened his eyes and smiled down into Joe's face. But something he saw there must have warned him, for he looked up and saw Miss Lavinia, with Odessa wilting behind her. "Hi, Odessa. Miss Lavinia, what a pleasure to see you," he said politely.

"Dirty dog," Miss Lavinia said. "Nothing but a dirty dog."

Tony grinned and looked at Joe. "What we going to do, baby? I can't stand up right now."

"I can't stand up either," Joe said. He was enjoying this. Shit, nobody told Miss Lavinia to come sticking her fat nose where it didn't belong. China slept contentedly between them, the juices of love dried in a sticky mess around her mouth. "Miss Lavinia, Tony and I are sorry," Joe said, "but we can't stand up right this minute. If you'd give us two or three minutes, maybe we'll be ready to. But if we stand up right now, well, you're going to see something very embarrassing. . . ."

"Odessa, bring me a bucket of cold water," Miss Lavinia ordered. "That's what you do to dogs when they get that way."

"Mama . . . *please*!" Odessa wailed.

"Bring the cold water, child." She looked down into Joe's face, addressing him through clenched teeth. "I couldn't prevent my daughter from coming, but I'm glad now that I came along to protect her. She told me about your running out in the street buck naked. I don't know what kind of man my daughter got herself married to, but it's certainly my duty to protect her."

"Mama," Odessa said helplessly.

"Hush, child," Miss Lavinia ordered, swelling out her breasts. "Bring me the water."

"How's throwing cold water on us going to protect Odessa?" Joe said. He felt Tony's body move, and he saw that Tony was red in the face from trying not to laugh. "You pour cold water on us, Miss Lavinia, all you going to do is mess up China's nice floor, get her rug all wet. . . ."

When it was obvious that Odessa would not bring the water, Miss Lavinia went to the kitchen herself. They heard her fussing in a loud voice as she tried to find the light switch. The red poet put on his shirt and trousers; he went to the kitchen door and helpfully fumbled with Miss Lavinia. "Now, you're what I'd call a gentleman," Miss Lavinia announced, "even if you are barefooted, at least you're not completely *nekkid* like them three dogs out there. . . ."

Tony was laughing quietly in great gulps. Joe reached around and tapped him on the butt. "You still hard, man?" Tony nodded, still laughing. "Me too," Joe said. "The damn thing won't go down." He looked up into Odessa's face. "Hi, honey," he said, as if seeing her there for the first time. "Why don't you take off your clothes and join the fun?"

"Joe . . ." she began severely, and he thought that some of the old spark had returned. But then her voice soared to that high whine he detested. "Joe, honey, I hope you don't think Mama's coming here was my idea. I wouldn't have come if I'd known this was going on. . . ."

Pee Wee squatted beside him with a lighted joint in his hand. "Looks like you're going to get wet up," he said, rolling his eyes toward the kitchen. "You want to turn on?"

It was more of the hashish. Joe and Tony killed it rapidly, sneaking glances toward the kitchen where Miss Lavinia and the red poet could be heard hard at work. It seemed, from the sounds she made there, and snatches of her talk, that the only pot suitable in size for the baptizing, as she called it, was the one in which China had cooked the turnip greens. From the scouring sounds they heard, it was also apparent that she was scrubbing it out. Then, ominously, they heard the sharp *pinnnnggggg* of water in the pot, and Miss Lavinia thanked the poet loudly as he left the kitchen and came to where the three of them lay. China slept peacefully on.

"I hope you guys don't get the wrong idea," the poet said. "I had to help her, you understand. But that doesn't mean I'm putting you down. I mean, I'm interested in *events*, you know what I mean?"

"I know," Tony said.

"I mean, man, you guys strike me as being the same way. Like, all you have to do is get up and put some clothes on, then the old lady won't throw water on you."

Joe and Tony pretended horror. "Put our *clothes* on?" Joe said. "And miss the fun?" Tony chimed in. "Man, you sure you dig events?"

"I see what you mean," the poet said, and he went back to his corner.

Odessa circled him helplessly, wringing her hands. "Joe, please get up, honey. I think Mama means what she said."

"I know Mama means it," Joe said, laughing. They could tell from the fat swirl of water now that the pot was almost full.

"Sounds like she's filling a goddamned tub," Tony said. "Pee Wee, why don't you help her bring it in? I mean, she's an old lady and everything, she might get a hernia or something."

"Good idea," Pee Wee said, and he went to the kitchen.

"I think we ought to wake China up," Joe said. "After all, if she's going to get *baptized*, she ought to know something about it."

"I think you're right," Tony said.

They called China, and nudged her until she woke up. "You guys ready for another set?" she said accommodatingly, and it was obvious that she wanted to make it again from the way she squirmed between them.

"No, honey," Tony said gently. He gave her the rest of the hashish and waited patiently until she smoked it. "You high?" he said, when she stubbed out the roach.

"I'm high," she answered, twisting her neck back trying to see into Tony's face. Then she saw Odessa. "Odessa, *honey*, what you doing here all dressed up like that for, sugar?"

Tony started laughing again. Joe tapped China on the shoulder. "Baby, listen. You better get something waterproof to put over them naps you always patting down. Odessa's here with Miss Lavinia. Miss Lavinia's in the kitchen filling up a pot of water, you know that pot you cooked the turnip greens in? Well, she's filling it up with water, and she's going to pour it on us."

China considered that. "You say the pot I cooked the turnip greens in? What'd she do with the turnip greens?"

"I think she threw them out. And she scrubbed the pot, too."

"My good greens. And she's going to pour water on us? Why?"

"Because she says we're dogs."

"Hot or cold water?"

"Cold water, I think."

China shivered. "Man, the cold water in this house is the coldest in New Jersey. I think it comes from Alaska right to my kitchen."

"Then it ought to be invigorating," Tony said.

"It's invigorating all right," China said, just as Miss Lavinia and Pee Wee came into the room lugging the big pot between them. Miss Lavinia was sweating and tipping on her toes; Pee Wee slunk along, showing his gold teeth in a big grin.

"When I count to three," Miss Lavinia told him, "you pour."

China held up her hand. "Just a minute, honey," she said lazily. "I want me something to put on my head. I just had my hair done yesterday, and I don't intend to get it all kinked up again already. Odessa sugar, I know you carry one of them plastic kerchiefs with you. Loan it to me, please."

Odessa dug in her pocketbook and gave China the kerchief. China took her time and tied it around her hair, tucking in all the ends. "All right, Miss Lavinia, I'm ready now."

The three of them bunched close together.

"One . . . two . . ."

China raised her head. "That water hot or cold?"

"Cold," Miss Lavinia announced. But her voice sounded bewildered, as though she had come to doubt the wisdom of her plan.

"Lawd, the cold water in this house is enough to give me pneumonia," China said.

That seemed to encourage Miss Lavinia. "Three," she finished counting, and she flung the water on them.

But she had caught Pee Wee by surprise, and she threw him halfway across the room when she heaved the water. He landed on his belly and skidded against the bedroom door. Almost immediately, the door opened, and the black girl was standing there stark naked, saying sleepily, "I wish you guys would keep it quiet in here, we're trying to sleep."

She seemed not to notice the three drenched figures on the soggy rug, Miss Lavinia holding the empty pot, Odessa cowering against the wall, Pee Wee half-dazed on his belly at her feet. Only the red poet seemed to interest her; she smiled at him and closed the door. He picked up the guitar and ran his fingers softly over the strings.

Joe and Tony and China began laughing at the top of their voices, kicking their feet against the floor. They still did not separate, although the water had been ice cold. Even Odessa started to laugh, and that surprised Joe. He smeared the water off his face and looked at her. "Take off your clothes, honey," he said warmly.

She stopped laughing suddenly, and a strange look came over her face. "Go home, Mama," she said. "I think you've made a fool enough of yourself."

But Miss Lavinia was furious. "Child, you don't know what you're saying! You stay here with these people—these *perverts*—and you're doomed, sugar! Come on now, go home with mother."

Joe admired Odessa like she was now, the firm lines of resolution around her mouth, the way she stood erect and defiant, all her meekness and whining gone. "Mama, *go home*. Joe's my husband for better or worse, that's what the marriage vow says. Maybe things got to get even worse before they'll get better. I don't know." She kicked off her shoes and reached behind to unzip her dress. "I just want you to go home, Mama. I'll be all right. You're interfering where you're not concerned."

It was a tense moment as Miss Lavinia tried to stare her down, but Odessa's gaze did not waver. Finally, Miss Lavinia gave a deep sigh down in her bosom and shook her head. "That boy has a sickness, he's passed that sickness on to you. I've done all I can do, I'm going to church now and pray for you." She waddled to the door and opened it. "You'll get yours in hell, Joe Market," she said bitterly. "God will take care of you." She closed the door before he had a chance to answer. They listened to her heavy footsteps clump down the stairs as if she was being pursued by demons, then the angry slam of the downstairs door.

"Well, China said, "now that Miss Lavinia's gone, I guess we might as well get up, there's no other reason for staying down here." She slid from between Joe and Tony, and, for an instant, Tony was sprawled face down on top of Joe. "Take it easy with Odessa," Tony whispered. He sounded worried. "I'll take it easy," Joe said. He wrapped his arms around Tony and squeezed him, savoring the hard muscularity of their naked bodies pressing together. Then he slapped Tony on the butt, and Tony bounced up like a boxer, flexing his muscles and scratching his hairy belly.

Odessa was naked now. She stood near the bathroom door, holding her clothes in front of her, as if still undecided about showing herself completely.

Pee Wee sat with his back propped against the bedroom door, rubbing his injured knees. From time to time, he glued his eye to the keyhole, but it was obvious from his disappointed look that nothing was going on in the bedroom that he could see.

The red poet strummed his guitar in a sort of half-trance, but his eyes were alert and his ears stuck out like two antennae.

China had brought the mop from the bathroom and was sopping up the water from the floor into a bucket that Tony squatted over and held steady for her.

And yet, as they went about their individual tasks, Joe was aware that every eye was watching him and Odessa. He liked being the star of the show. But at the same time, he felt a subtle anger kindle in his heart, like a secret fire eating away at the understructure of reason. That fucking Odessa. Coming here with her mother. Making a fool out of him in front of everybody just when he'd decided to go back to her and lead a good life, the kind of life that she'd enjoy. And here she'd showed up with that fucking Miss Lavinia and spoiled everything. Well, he'd show Odessa who was boss. Fuck a good life. He strutted over to her on stiff legs and slapped her full in the face with his open hand. "That's for bringing your goddamned Mammy up here." He snatched her clothes from her hands and wiped off the rest of the water that Miss Lavinia had poured on him. "What do you think of that?" he said arrogantly.

Odessa's eyes dampened, but she did not cry. "I don't think nothing, Joe." Her voice was clear and steady, as if she were, in truth, reading from a script, as if the camera had now focused on her over Joe's shoulder. "I'll be whatever you want me to be, Joe. I just don't think I can live without you, away from you. Whatever you want me to do, I'll do. . . ."

Joe snorted in disbelief. "You bullshit! You trying to put me on, honey? *Me?* This is the kid, remember? No broad puts me on." His voice was a cruel, grinding monotone. He wrapped his fingers in Odessa's hair and snatched her head sideways. "Who you trying to bullshit, bitch? You always been pretending you didn't approve of the kind of life I live."

"I don't approve," Odessa said clearly.

"Then why you say you'll be what I want you to be? I want you to be like China, like the other girls I know. I want you to smoke pot, dig orgies, fuck my friends. . . ." He squinted into her eyes, but saw no fear there. What he did see surprised him by the nakedness of it, and he jerked his hand from her hair as though her head had suddenly sprouted serpents. "You love me?" he said, although he had seen the answer in her eyes.

"That's why I'll do whatever you want me to."

Her assured calm frightened him. "Well, we'll see about that," he said, and he swaggered over to Pee Wee and asked him for a joint.

"I've only got the hashish," Pee Wee said. "That stuff's too strong for somebody like Odessa. She don't smoke that much pot."

But Joe insisted, and when Pee Wee gave him the stick of hashish, he lighted it and paraded around the room taking large puffs. He felt like a performer in a circus arena, and he was aware of the looks of curious interest in the eyes of the red poet, who had laid aside his guitar, and of Tony and China where they kneeled together over the mop bucket. *They dig me*, he thought, *they dig what I'm doing to Odessa, her and all her pure airs.* He filled his mouth with smoke and stopped in front of Odessa. He grabbed her brutally around the waist and kissed her with his mouth open, forcing the smoke down into her lungs at the same time. It was a cruel but sure way of getting her high. Odessa's eyes grew round as saucers; she gulped and swallowed the smoke three more times when Joe repeated the operation.

He posed in front of her and finished the joint, blowing smoke at her until he saw a strange expression come over her face and he realized, with a feeling akin to sorrow, that she had really gotten high for the first time. Behind him, he heard a sigh from the spectators, as though they had all been holding their breath to see her reaction.

"How you feel?" Joe said.

She leaned against the door for support. "I feel fine, Joe." She talked in a thick-tongued way; the hashish had eaten up all the fluids in her mouth.

"You still love me?"

"I love you, Joe."

"You know what I like, don't you?"

For a second, he thought he saw a spark of defiance break the glaze of her eyes; but when he looked again, they had clouded over with that same dull luster.

"You know what I like you to do?" he said again.

She nodded. "I know." Her legs buckled at the knees, and she slid down to the floor with her back to the wall, reaching out at the same time and grabbing him by the cheeks of his butt. He parted his legs and let her work.

Behind him, he heard the red poet solemnly pluck a single string. He could not see Tony or China, but Pee Wee had a clear picture of what was going on. His eyes bugged almost out of his head. "That's right, baby, you work on your lover man, I love you when you work on me like that," Joe said.

He heard a door open. He screwed his neck around and saw Tony Brenzo at the closet, rapidly putting on his clothes.

"Where you going, Tony baby?"

Tony's face was a cold mask of anger, but he said nothing. He pulled on his shirt and stuffed it into his pants.

Joe shrugged, and winked at Pee Wee. "He can't take it," he said, nodding toward Tony.

China came up behind him, laying a calm hand on his shoulder. "Joe, I think this has gone far enough."

Joe whirled, pulling himself away from Odessa with a loud, popping noise. "*You* think it's gone far enough? Who the hell asked you? This is my wife. I treat her any kind of way I want to."

"Not in my house you don't."

"And what's so goddamned special about your house? Look, baby, I knew you when you didn't have a pot to piss in, who the hell you think you are anyway?" He was shouting, and he tried to stop, but he couldn't. "And don't be coming on so goddamned high and mighty with me, China. Because I saw something downstairs, baby, and I know you don't want me to say what it was!"

China turned pale. She locked eyes with Joe; her eyes seemed to cross, she was looking at him so hard. "Fuck you," she said calmly. "This is still my house." She helped Odessa to the bathroom, talking to her softly. But Joe lunged like a bull and broke them apart. "I'm not finished with this bitch yet!" He slammed China against the wall, and shook Odessa roughly by the shoulders. "*Do you love me?*" He was screaming now.

"I love you, Joe."

"*Then suck my motherfucking dick you black bitch!*"

She nodded as if her head was too heavy for her small neck, and he caught her by both ears as she got back on her knees and sucked him. Joe smiled, swelling his chest in triumph.

Tony was fully dressed now. Standing with his hand on the doorknob, he looked at Joe like he was looking at shit. Joe looked away. *Tony baby it hurts me when you look at me like that Tony stop me baby before I kill somebody I think I'm losing control.* But Tony just stood there looking at him, and China was knotting a housecoat around her waist that she had taken from the closet. The red poet's

hand seemed frozen in mid-air over the guitar strings. The bedroom door opened a crack and the black-skinned girl stuck her
head through and stared without saying a word.

"Everybody's against me!" Joe cried.

"Not *me*, stud." It was Pee Wee, standing underneath his elbow, Pee Wee seemed right now to be that short. "I'm with you,
stud, all the way. You dig that."

Joe laughed, and kissed Pee Wee on the top of his head. "Good
old Pee Wee, I knew I could count on you. You want to do me a favor, Pee Wee?" Odessa was still working on him, and he leaned
back comfortably.

"Sure, Joe. You know me. Anything for a friend."

Tony, stop me, baby. I don't know what I'm doing.

"I want you to make Odessa for me. Would you like that?"

Pee Wee's eyes popped. "How you mean, man? You mean I can
dick her?"

"Sure, man."

"Suppose she won't let me?" He had never liked Odessa; his
eyes were happy and shrewd at the same time.

"She'll let you. She loves me. She'll do it for me." He squeezed
Odessa under the chin. "Won't you do it for me, baby?" She nodded, still sucking; and he grinned with satisfaction. "You see what I
mean? Go ahead, Pee Wee. Do her in."

Casually, he moved back; he went and stood halfway between
Tony and the red poet. Odessa slumped in front of Pee Wee; China
stood near them, a look of complete disgust on her face. The black
girl stared gravely from the bedroom door. Joe heard the whisper of
a zipper being undone, and then Pee Wee moved forward on his little short legs and wrapped his arms around Odessa. Joe fell to his
knees. He looked at Tony. *Help me baby I think I'm cracking up.*
But Tony's gaze seemed to bore through him.

Joe covered his eyes with his hands. He was terribly afraid.
There was a constant movement inside his brain, like the scurry of
mice in an upstairs room. His heart seemed to beat at twice the
normal pace, squeezing great waves of blood through the narrow
passage of his temples. *That hashish has me all fucked up, I smoked*

too much of it too fast. He felt a bitter sickness start at the pit of his stomach; and sudden terrible lights exploded on the blank screen of his vision. Then he opened his eyes and looked straight into Odessa's.

She was staring at him over Pee Wee's shoulder where he hunched in front of her with his little black hands all over her naked body like spiders and his stubbled face pressed sideways against her breasts in an ecstasy of enjoyment, his baggy pants swinging in and out, in and out, a sodden mess hanging between his legs as if some time in the past he had shit in his pants and never cleaned them out.

"Joe. . . ." Odessa's lips moved thickly around his name. She lifted one arm and held it out in a mute appeal to him. He saw the gold flash of the wedding band on her finger.

Joe shook his head and blinked, like somebody coming back from a trance.

That dirty motherfucker, what's he doing to Odessa?

He roared at the top of his lungs. Every fiber in his body seemed alive. He felt his muscles tense, spring forward, then the hard impact of both hands around Pee Wee's neck. He twisted his body violently and slammed Pee Wee halfway across the room.

"What you doing to Odessa? You dirty black sonofabitch, what you doing to my wife?" He advanced slowly on Pee Wee, crouching like an ape on the rampage.

Pee Wee was still in a daze from the suddenness and fury of Joe's attack. He scooted away on his behind.

"You *dare* put your hands on my *wife*?"

"You told me I could, Joe! I didn't mean no harm! *Joe!*"

Joe leaped ten feet and landed flat on Pee Wee. His fingers seemed to have a life of their own, finding Pee Wee's neck and closing around it like a vise.

"Joe. . . !" He recognized Tony's voice now.

"O my God, get him off, Tony! He'll kill Pee Wee!"

China was pulling him from behind, clawing his shoulders, his hair. But it only excited him more, those hands all over him, the struggling body underneath him on the floor. For an instant, the red haze pulled back from his vision, and he saw Pee Wee's mouth stretched open like a tunnel, his fat tongue lolling drunkenly against the yellow and gold teeth. Joe felt his dick getting hard. He knew what he must do, what he had always wanted to make Pee Wee do. . . . Moving so quickly that neither China nor Tony knew what he intended, he scooted up Pee Wee's body and rammed the terrible swelling of his dick all the way down Pee Wee's throat. Oblivious to the teeth that clamped and tore him as he entered, his mind jumped back over the years to a dark box car and a train rattling north, when he had just met Pee Wee and somebody was collecting on him in the dark. He knew now that it had been Pee Wee, he suspected all the time that it had been Pee Wee. Collecting on him then and never doing it again so that Joe wouldn't think he was queer. All those years Pee Wee could have been sucking him, and didn't. Getting him excited with massages and then not sucking him because he wanted to come on like a man. Angrily, Joe rammed his dick even harder, he was trying to ram Pee Wee's tonsils down his goddamned throat with his dick. *This is my body eat motherfucker this is my blood drink this is my body which is given for you this'll teach you to fuck with Odessa you fucking queer. . . .*

"Good God, he'll kill Pee Wee! Tony, he's choking Pee Wee to death!"

It was Odessa's voice, he was glad she was all right. He fought the tugging hands on his head and body with broad swipes of his arm, and held Pee Wee impaled with the other, palming the back of his head, thrusting brutally.

Yeah, I just might kill Pee Wee he's got enough dick in him to choke an elephant he's always been hung up on my dick his face is all gray his eyes popped out. . . .

Man. He *wanted* to kill Pee Wee, he wanted to kill *somebody* with his dick. He humped like he was inside the resiliency of a woman's pussy . . . one, two, three times . . . and drove Pee Wee up into a corner.

"Joe, cut it out, goddamn it!" Somebody was dragging the two of them out backwards. *That's Tony pulling us back. He wants me out in the open where he can get to me.* Joe flexed his legs and drove Pee Wee deeper into the corner.

"Hit him in the head, Tony!"

He waited an eternity for the blow to come. When it did, it was a slow, glancing wallop, he knew Tony wouldn't hurt him. But the blow seemed to liberate the come boiling in his loins. Pulling Pee Wee's throat all the way up on his dick . . . it was tighter than any pussy he'd ever had . . . he gave a last vicious thrust and let the come flow.

Half-dazed, he fell to one side. He felt Pee Wee being dragged by the heels past him. *I hope the bastard's not dead, I want him to remember this as long as he lives.*

"You all right, Pee Wee?"

"Get your hands off me!" Pee Wee shrieked like a woman. Joe smiled in his half-coma. Pee Wee was all right; he was actually better now than he'd ever been in his life, because he'd had him some good dick, some good come, too.

"I want you to arrest him, Tony! You saw what he did to me! I got witnesses . . . ! Ughhhh . . . I think I'm going to puke!"

Joe lay wrapped in a wonderful haze of contentment. Voices and other sounds came to him now as though from a faraway distance. The scrape of a nappy beard against his cheek caused him to open his eyes. The red poet . . . a virile whisper in his ear—"Man, you were magnificent! Poetry in action! Man, wow!"—and then he felt the gentleness of hands that could only be Odessa's lifting his head to the soft material of her dress and smoothing his brow simultaneously with her fingers. "Joe, did they hurt you, honey?"

He opened his eyes and closed them quickly. *Honest to God, Odessa, I don't know why I treat you the way I do. It's not because of the baby, you don't even know the truth about the baby. It's because of something in me . . . something that's been in me since I was born. . . .* He wanted to say that, but he couldn't bear to be so nakedly exposed before Odessa. He couldn't even bear to look her in the face. Tears seeped through his lids and stained his cheeks.

"Where are the others?" he said.

"Gone." It was China's voice.

"And Pee Wee?"

"He's all right," Tony said. "He'll just be gargling his throat for the next couple of years." He felt Tony's cool hand light on his thigh. "What got into you, baby? You were like a madman there for a while."

"I guess it was the hashish. That was strong stuff." But he knew it hadn't been the hashish, for the effect of that had worn off; and yet, he felt the same uneasiness in his brain, as if suddenly and without adequate warning, it would slip its cogs again and tilt him inside of insanity. He knew that if it happened again . . . *when* it happened again . . . he would be beyond recovery. A terrible urgency seized him; there were so many things left to do.

"Let's go home, Joe."

He kept his eyes closed. "I'm rotten, Odessa. I'm no good for you. You go home, you'll be better off that way."

She drew his head to her breasts and cried. "Joe, honey, I *love* you! There ain't nothing you can do I can't forgive!"

"I'm no good," he said. He opened his eyes and saw Tony and China watching them with concern. "I got too many secrets, Odessa. They're cracking me up. They'll crack me up if I don't tell them, they'll crack me up if I do."

"Tell them," Odessa said. "You'll see, Joe. I'll still love you. You'll see."

He wondered. Was love capable of such unbridled forgiveness? If so—if anything was acceptable to love, and forgivable— could love be trusted? He felt that there was something *immoral* about that kind of love, and he could only feel contempt for it, the same way he'd feel about a whore who could fuck anything that walked. Love, like anything else, had to pick and choose, not swallow any and everything. If Odessa learned nothing else from their marriage, it seemed important to him that she should learn that.

Sitting up, he propped his back against the wall. Tony, Odessa and China were all dressed; he was the only one naked. "Listen,

Odessa . . . the reason I'm no good for you is that there's nothing *sa-cred* to me. I can't think of a thing that I wouldn't do, or put up with. You saw what I did to Pee Wee, what I let him do to you? I smoke pot, I chase other women, I hustle queers. . . ."

But he couldn't go on, because she was looking at him with such love shining in her eyes that he had to look away. "Odessa . . . you don't understand what I'm saying, honey."

"I do understand, Joe. But none of that matters, what you're saying. I love you, Joe. That's all that matters.

"Big deal," Joe snorted. He felt like slapping her. Jesus Christ, how could anybody be so goddamned blind? He didn't *want* her to love him; but the more he tried to tell her that, the more she talked about love. He was filled with anger and disgust. Shit.

"Let's go home, Joe. I *know* you love me. You *told* me so."

She twined her fingers in his; but he pulled his hand away, shaking his head. "I was lying, that's all. I'm no good for you, Odessa. I'm really not. Listen . . . you want to know just how bad I am? Well, I'll tell you about me. . . . I wouldn't even turn somebody in for *murder* if I knew they'd done it. That's how bad I am." He couldn't look at China now. She was sitting next to Tony with her legs crossed, and she didn't say a word.

Odessa laughed like a stupid little bitch. "Is *that* all, Joe? I don't even see why you're talking about something like murder. But I don't think that makes you bad, honey. It's what *anybody* would do." Her lips were drawn back in a tight grin; her eyes burned like somebody with a sick fever. "People just don't want to get involved in things like murder. Isn't that right, Tony? You're a policeman, you ought to know." But Tony shrugged without committing him-self; he seemed very interested in the outcome of this byplay be-tween Joe and Odessa.

Desperately, Joe turned to China. *You know what I'm talking about, China. You know I saw Mr. Yen's body in the cellar. But I won't tell on you if you help me get rid of Odessa. You help me do that, and I'll give you the best fucking you ever had in your whole life.* He was sending her the message with as much intensity as he knew how, pleading with his mind, his eyes. *Odessa's going to be destroyed if she keeps on loving me. She's going to destroy me, too. Because I can't love any woman, China. Not since my mother died, and I was down in the creek playing. I should have been up there in the house with her to protect her from my father, I knew the kind of dog he was. Ramona wouldn't have died if I'd been there with her. She was the only woman I ever really loved, I know that now. When she died, love died, too. I got married to Odessa just because I thought I was turning queer. And that's the honest-to-God truth. Help me, China.* But she returned his gaze very calmly, while Odessa went on talking. She was almost hysterical now, trying to convince Joe that he was good, that she loved him no matter what, that nothing he or his friends could do would ever change her love for him. *China . . . goddamn it, you can love me, I don't mind that because we're the same kind of people, you and me. But not Odessa. If you love me, China, help me get rid of Odessa. I'll fuck you the best you ever been fucked. But help me send Odessa back to a clean, normal life, where her kind of love can survive. . . .*

". . . why, Joe is the sweetest person alive when he wants to be," Odessa was saying.

"Look, China, I'm not bullshitting!" Joe said bluntly, cutting Odessa off. "If you don't tell them, I will."

China jumped up and started pacing the floor. She still seemed calm, however. Only her pacing, and the way she held her hands tightly together, gave her away. "I thought you believed in live and let live?" she said to Joe. "When did that change?"

He shrugged, almost apologetically. "A little while ago," he said. "You going to tell them?"

"Tell us what?" Tony said. "What the hell's going on here? I think all of you have cracked up."

"Not me," Odessa said serenely. "I'm in my good senses, I know what I want. I know all I've ever wanted, and that's Joe."

"China, you tell them!" Joe cried. He leapt from the floor like he was going to hit China. Alarmed, China shied away. "Tony, nobody's crazy," she blurted out. "I just have a small confession to make, that's what Joe is so shook up about. Oh, it's no big thing, really," she said, laughing, holding herself in firm control. "But these two love birds here have convinced me that honesty might be the best policy after all." She looked at Tony gravely. "What I'm trying to say, Tony, is that Mr. Yen's body . . . well . . . it's downstairs in the fifth wine barrel, the one against the wall. . . ."

Tony's mouth dropped open. "You kidding me, China?"

She shook her head. "No, I'm not kidding. Ask Joe. He saw it there tonight when he went to get the wine. Didn't you, Joe?"

"I saw it." *God bless you, China. I'm going to give you the sweetest fucking you ever had as soon as I get the chance.* "I saw it, and I wasn't going to say anything about it." He shook Odessa by the shoulders. "Don't that convince you, Odessa? I didn't *care*. It didn't make any difference to me. You see how evil I am? I'm rotten, Odessa . . . I'm no good for you. Will you please go home now?"

But Odessa tossed her head stubbornly. "Did China kill Mr. Yen?" She seemed horrified, but determined to stick to her guns. "The fact that his body's downstairs doesn't mean that China killed him. Maybe somebody else did."

"Somebody else did," China said smoothly. "I might as well tell you the whole story. I'll make it brief. You see, one night last November, this cousin of Mr. Yen's showed up here. He said the police were after him on some kind of a dope rap, he demanded protection. When Mr. Yen refused, this guy shot him. He was the man you asked me about, Tony, that guy you called Cindy Lou. Anyway, he shot Mr. Yen. I was terrified, as you may very well understand. I thought that was really the end for me when he turned toward me with that gun and aimed it. Then all of a sudden, this terrible look came over his face. He grabbed his chest and dropped dead right there on the floor. . . ." She pointed to a coffee table. ". . . right there near that table, he almost fell on top of it. Well, you can imagine how upset I was, seeing my sweet husband killed, and then his murderer just dropping dead when he's about to shoot me as well. I was in a terrible panic. I knew the police wouldn't believe me.

That's why I decided to hide Mr. Yen's body in the wine barrel, and to pretend that the other gentleman was my husband. After all," she said blandly, "all Chinamen look alike anyway."

Tony stood up, cracking his knuckles. "What about the claim ticket Cindy Lou was carrying? Why'd you take that? How'd Lamont happen to come by it?"

China's eyes grew large and innocent. "Claim ticket? Lamont? Tony, what *are* you talking about? I've told you exactly how things happened. I just don't think you want to believe me."

"You said Yen was shot. What happened to the gun?"

"Well, as I said, I was in a *terrible* panic. I hid the gun overnight. Then, next day—it was a Sunday—I got all dressed up and went to New York by myself. I took the ferry boat to Staten Island. Somehow or other, right in the middle of the bay, my pocketbook came open . . . the gun dropped into the water before I could catch it."

Tony's eyes were hard and unbelieving; he was all cop now. "I think you're lying, China. I think you killed Mr. Yen. That Cindy Lou guy probably did have a heart attack—our medical examiner confirmed that, before you had his body so conveniently cremated—but I think he gave you a claim ticket for a package full of dope he had checked in New York. You and Yen got in an argument about it, and you shot Yen. That's what I think."

China smiled sweetly. "Can you prove it, honey?"

Tony groaned. "No . . . and nobody else probably can, either. Not without the gun, without some evidence linking you with the claim ticket. . . ."

"What claim ticket?" China said.

"The one you gave Lamont."

"Did Lamont say I gave it to him? In front of witnesses? He's dead, remember? And dead men can't testify."

Tony threw up his hands. "Get dressed," he said. "I've still got to take you in. And I want to see that body you're talking about."

"All right, Tony. But you can understand, though, why I didn't say anything before. I mean, my being so young and Mr. Yen being so old, and rich . . . well, you know how people always get the wrong idea when something like this happens to a rich old man. . . ."

"I know," Tony said dryly.

"You *see*?" Odessa clapped her hands. "I *told* you China didn't kill anybody! Isn't it wonderful, Joe?"

Yes, it is wonderful, he thought. China had managed to fabricate a story that kept her believably in the clear. Or, rather, she had been given a chance to recite the story she had rehearsed a thousand times in her mind since killing Mr. Yen. Yes, it was wonderful. But where did it leave him? Right where he was before, if not worse. Because now it seemed more than ever that he *did* care, making China turn herself in that way. How could he convince Odessa that it was dangerous to love him? That only disaster lay in store for her if she persisted in not seeing the evil in him?

I'll tell her about Christopher. I'll tell her that I killed Christopher.

The answer had been nagging him all the time, as though the earlier act itself had foreseen that the time would come for Odessa to deny him.

"Tony, I got something to tell you, too."

Tony frowned impatiently. "Is it important, Joe? I've got work to do now."

"It's important." He put his arms around Odessa, because he wanted to feel her reaction. That seemed very important to him. "I guess you'll have to arrest me for murder, too." There was a dull throbbing in his temples, and alarm bells were going off inside his head—*Cool it, man! Cool it!*—but he refused to pay attention to them. "You see . . . I killed our baby, Odessa's and mine. I came home from the Army earlier than anybody expected, and sneaked up to the house over those back fences. Christopher was there alone, and I started thinking about things, about how bad things were going to be for him here in this fucked-up world. So I killed him." He felt perfectly calm. "I pulled that blue blanket up over his head, and I killed him."

A long shudder wracked Odessa's body before she drew away

from him. "You?" Her voice was so low he could barely hear. "You killed Christopher?" She reminded him of himself down in that creek in Burnside, saying almost the same thing to Titus after Titus had told him that Ramona was dead. "You killed Christopher?"

"I saved him," Joe said. For some reason, he felt like grinning. "You said yourself that this was no kind of world for a baby to grow up in."

She started crying. "But you convinced *me* that it was all right. . . . Joe . . . honey . . . did you really kill our baby?"

"I saved him," Joe said doggedly. Tony and China were frozen like statues near him, but he would not look at them.

Odessa wandered around in a small circle, staring first at the floor, then at the ceiling, folding and unfolding her hands. "*You* did it? I thought *I* was the one. . . ." She began laughing hysterically, holding her stomach as if in great pain. But Joe put his hand over her mouth, silencing her. "Listen," he said. "I'll tell you exactly how it happened."

He told it brutally, leaving out no single detail, watching Odessa's eyes grow wide in horror as he talked. She looked so funny, he thought about grinning; but he controlled himself. When he was finished, Odessa threw her head back and howled in a long, drawn-out cry filled with anguish and pain. That frightened Joe—"Odessa, I *saved* him!" he cried—and he tried to put his arms around her again.

But Odessa pulled away, and shoved him at the same time. "Don't you touch me! Don't you ever touch me again! You're *crazy*, that's what you are! You made me think I did it! All this time, you had me believing I did it!" Caught unawares like that, Joe stumbled backwards and fell against the wall. He slid to the floor and stayed there.

Odessa bent from the hips and beat him in the face with her fists. "*You're crazy . . . you're crazy . . . you're crazy . . . !*" The blows hurt; he felt blood trickle from his nose down to his chin and chest. But he did not try to defend himself. A lot of people had thought Jesus Christ was crazy, too. And he was also beaten. *The soldiers plaited a crown of thorns, and put it on his head . . . and they smote him with their hands.* Madame Eudora, Roosevelt, Titus Market—he felt the burden of all of them on his head. He couldn't help it, he couldn't hold it back anymore, and he started grinning like Titus Market while Odessa beat him. *So that it might be ful-filled according to the Scriptures.* He heard her breath coming out in heavy gasps. China and Tony both stepped in to stop her, but she fought them off and kept on beating Joe.

Finally, she stopped beating him. He was sitting with his legs apart, his back to the wall. Stained with blood from his nose, his dick and balls fanned out like a devilfish between his legs. He knew what Odessa was going to do. *When the chief priests therefore and officers saw him, they cried out, saying, Crucify him, crucify him!* Tony and China knew, too; he heard China suck in her breath as if to warn him, saw Tony's body shift as he moved closer to Odessa. Joe spread his legs.

"Don't do it, Odessa. Please don't do it," Tony said.

But Odessa shoved him away and brought the sharp heel of her shoe down between Joe's legs . . . once . . . twice . . . three times. . . . He doubled from the pain, but he made no sound. Although his mind stirred with satisfaction under a great mist of pain. He heard the door slam and the staccato beat of Odessa's heels as she ran downstairs. He knew that he would never see her again, and he felt a great sense of relief.

Now, soothing hands moved between his legs. *Dear China. You got away with murder, and I owe you a good fucking in the bar-gain.* But when he opened his eyes, he saw that it was Tony Brenzo kneeling beside him, tenderly holding his dick and balls.

"She damn near castrated you," Tony said. His voice was very strained, and there were tears in his eyes. *Now there was leaning on Jesus' bosom one of his disciples, whom Jesus loved.* Joe reached out and pulled Tony's head to his chest. "It's all right, Tony baby. I can still use it. . . ."

China came from the bathroom with a wet washcloth and sponged the blood from Joe's body. He held Tony's head to his chest all the while, refusing to let it go, making China leave the blood there under Tony's cheek, covered by his black hair. When China went to change clothes, Joe took the washcloth and wiped the tears from Tony's cheeks. Then Tony cleaned the rest of the blood from him.

He riseth from supper; and laid aside his garments; and took a towel and girded himself. After that he poureth water into a basin, and began to wash the disciples' feet. . . .

"I've got to take you in, Joe."

"I know." He fought very hard to keep a straight face.

"Don't worry, buddy. They'll let you off with a light sentence. They'll understand. They might even give you a suspended sentence. Man, I'm sure you were suffering from being in Vietnam, and that's something in your favor." His eyes were full of tears again. "Joe, I don't think I could stand seeing you locked up. Not you, Joe. . . ."

I am my Father and my Father's Son. I shall pray the Father, and he shall send you another Comforter that abide with you for ever. He started grinning again, he couldn't help it.

"What about China?" Joe said. He couldn't stop grinning, as though the muscles in his jaw had become unhinged. "You think she'll get off?"

"Probably. There's not very damn much we can prove."

"I'm glad," Joe said. "She's a great chick."

China came from the bedroom, dressed for the street now, carrying a small suitcase. She twirled, showing off her dress. "I'm ready, Tony. Is this what the well-dressed woman prisoner wears?"

"You'll do," Tony said. "Joe . . . I got to take you in too, baby. You better put on your clothes. . . ."

They'll let you off with a light sentence . . . they might even give you a suspended sentence.

His whole body cried out for punishment. *Oh where can the heart of man be comforted?* And then, he knew.

"Give me an hour, Tony. Will you do that? Just an hour. There's something I have to do."

"O.K., Joe." Tony checked his watch. "I'll be at your place in an hour. For God's sake now, put on your clothes, do what you got to do, but don't get into any more trouble. Like I say, you'll probably get a suspended sentence, maybe a year or two at the very worse."

"Tony?"

"Yeah?"

"I think I love you, Tony. You're the only person in the world I think I really love."

"I dig, Joe." He cupped Joe's chin in his incredibly cool hand. "Everything's going to be all right, baby. You got to believe that." Joe grinned. He felt just like that prince disguised as a frog in that fairy tale. Oh, it was so funny! *I am the resurrection and the life: he that believeth in me, though he were dead, yet shall he live: And whosoever liveth and believeth in me shall never die. Believest thou this?*

Tony looked at him strangely. "You all right, Joe? Why you keep grinning like that?"

Joe turned serious again. "I'm all right," he said.

China kissed him goodbye. "Take care of yourself, honey. Thanks for not telling on me. Thanks for giving me a chance to tell on myself." She smiled, but her eyes were troubled. She kissed him deeply, as if trying to transfer some of her strength to him. "I'm sorry about the baby. But I understand you, Joe. Don't worry because you can't love. The important thing is that people love you." She left with Tony. Joe knew that she would be back soon, here in these familiar rooms, downstairs at the laundry, checking packages for delivery.

The silence closed in around him. *I have given you an example, that ye should do as I have done.* The clock on China's mantel said it was after three o'clock in the morning. Joe went downstairs and up the driveway. Then he began for the last time the journey over the back fences, hopping and grinning and racing in a kind of joyful frenzy.

Cheap Mary was sitting in her window. She got up without a word and let him in. They went into the bedroom. "I've been waiting for you," she said.

He sat on the bed and let his hands drop between his knees. "They know about the baby," he said. His voice carried a tone of bewilderment, like that of a small boy recounting a tragedy to his mother. "They don't understand that all I did was save him."

Mary nodded. "And have you come to save me, too?"

"I've come to save you, I've come to save the world."

"Really, now?" She seemed very amused. "So many people make false claims nowadays. Can you prove that?"

He thought he could. But first, he was very concerned for her comfort. "Would you like me to put your bloomers and things on, like I did before?"

"No. Your being naked doesn't bother me at all now." She was smiling very graciously. "And would you like me to fix you a small drink?"

"No, ma'am. Thank you just the same."

"Very well, then. Go ahead with what you have to say."

So he told her about that day twenty-three years ago when he had played the Christchild in the Christmas tableau. "That woman named May Jones, she was my mother in the Christmas tableau. She was the first woman I ever fucked. She gave me my first cross, too."

"A perfect mother," Mary said sarcastically. She seemed bitterly disappointed. "All that's nothing but *sheer nonsense*! I expected something real from you, something *concrete*. The next thing you'll be telling me is that you're Bonaparte as well. When did you start to believe all that nonsense?"

Her voice was so full of scorn and disbelief that he felt like crying. "I told you. Ever since I was six years old, the year World War II ended."

Mary seemed even more doubtful. "That's a very long time," she said. "If it had started then, you certainly would have done something about all this by now."

"About all what?" He started wondering whether she was crazy. Up until now, he had thought that he was the crazy one. Abruptly, he stopped grinning. Now he wondered about Mary.

She sighed. "It *couldn't* have begun then. That's too far back.

Are you sure it started then? Think as hard as you can. I bet you'll find that it started later on."

"What started later on?" Instead of answering, Mary turned her head and smiled slyly into her collar. And he realized then that she was a whole lot crazier than he was. While at the same time, he knew exactly what it was that she had been talking about the beginning of—although she still had not given it a name—and when it was that she was talking about.

"After we met those white boys on the road," he said, and his voice seemed to be coming through him, as though his face was a mask behind which another person spoke hidden lines, "we went on into New Orleans. I remember that Daddy was pretty upset about those white boys . . . you see, they wanted to fuck me . . . and he started talking to me about going home to Burnside and farming again. . . ." Mary shifted beside him, restlessly, he thought. "Is this what you want to hear?" he said.

"Yes, that's what I want to hear. The beginning." But how did she know that it was the beginning, when he had only realized it a short while ago himself? Looking at her slantwise, he wondered if she might not be some kind of white-skinned witch. "Go on with your story," Mary said; and Joe fell back into his narrative. "Anyway, we met this whore and fucked her. Then I went back to the boarding house. Daddy stayed with the whore. The next day, I went across the river. And met this white woman. She made me fuck her through a fence." He told her about that in detail, about the sign, and how the woman put it back up after he fucked her. "On the way home, I saw an eclipse of the moon," he said.

"And what else happened?" Mary said. He could feel a surprising new tension in her that transmitted itself to him from where she crouched on the bed.

"What else happened? Nothing much. I just thought about that white woman before I went to bed. I hated her. Suppose I had got caught? Lord, I'd be dead right now. I hated her, I wanted to kill her. The way she'd used me for her own pleasure, and then wouldn't even talk to me. And putting that goddamned sign back up." He bit his lips, but Mary looked at him sharply, urging him to go on. "I made up my mind then that I was going to kill me a white woman, one day. . . ." Ashamed, he ducked his head; he couldn't go on. "That's all," he said.

"I remember that eclipse," Mary said. She sounded almost happy. "My husband had died just that summer, so you can see how many years I've been alone. But I wasn't used to it then, not at all. And I was sitting in my window when I saw that eclipse. There had been stories about it in the newspaper, so I was sitting up to watch it. And I thought, *Somebody watching this moon right now ought to kill me*. That's how lonely I felt."

He looked at her sharply, and he felt like slapping her right in the face. Because he knew she was lying, he could feel it in his body, her lie, as though she had sprayed him with a poison that was seeping into his every pore. She hadn't seen that eclipse; she hadn't thought any shit like that about somebody killing her. Then why was she lying?

"Oh, I didn't just want to *die*," Mary was saying. "That's so mundane and uncertain . . . so *haphazard* . . . not knowing how you're going to leave this world. At least we deserve this one final choice after putting up with life as long as I have. And I'm tired of it—all the sadness, the little traps that are set for us to fall into, the tragedy of men and women trying to love one another." She stared at him intently. "I am nearly seventy years old. Do you understand what I'm saying?"

"Yes, ma'am." He got up and started walking the room again. And truth tumbled down in his brain like an avalanche of burning stones. Because he realized that Mary's lying to him was a terrifying act of love. She knew his need, she was willing to sacrifice herself for him, so that the prophecies might be fulfilled. *You want to kill a white woman and I am a white woman who wants to be killed.*

When he turned, she was staring at him from the bed, nodding slowly. "I believe that you are my Saviour," she said softly, "just as you were your son's Saviour."

He smiled. "I lied when I told you I killed my son accidentally. It wasn't an accident. But Tony says there's a good chance they won't punish me for it."

"And of course you want to be punished," Mary said. "The human condition—sometimes it carries us to salvation in strange ways. And it requires so many sacrifices, so many. . . . It's the only proof that we love, when we sacrifice. If the sacrifice is strange enough, *great* enough, we say that a man—or a woman—is a hero. Are you a hero, my son?"

She might have been his mother, Mary in her white nightgown, the fat ruffles at her throat, her gentle voice lulling him into a strange and wonderful new world of contentment.

"Are you a hero?" she said again; but he did not answer. Smiling instead, he admired himself in her bureau mirror. He remembered clearly now the dream that Miss Lavinia had awakened him from. In his dream, he had been killing a white woman with his dick. *To this end was I born, and for this cause came I into the world, that I should bear witness unto the truth.* Sick, desperate, reviling—but yet the truth.

His body seemed like a magnificent work of bronze, the pale lamplight outlining the lean ripples of his muscles, the slow maddening rise of his dick as he prepared for Mary's ultimate sacrifice.

O Lamb of God who taketh away the sins of the world.

He felt a terrible pain knife through his brain. He was redemption and redeemer in one.

He dropped spit into his hand and greased himself. "Your husband just didn't know how to do it," he said to Cheap Mary, approaching her with his dick straight out. A wild grin tore his lips.

"Call me nigger, you white bitch." She looked deeply into his eyes. "Nigger," she said, with almost delicious delight, although her eyes were dark with fear. "Nigger," she said. She stretched out her bony arms and pulled his dreadful weight upon her as he parted the dried old lips of her pussy and waded on up inside her. "*Nigger.* . . ." His nostrils were filled with the smell of burnt peas, and Mary's violated pussy.

She died, as was her wish. It was the way his own mother had died, so that he became, again, his father, and somehow, his son. . . . He wondered if the Holy Ghost had finally entered him, or if it would only enter him when he was punished for this act of love. Be-

cause he knew now that each—and himself more so than most—
finds his own discipline, looks for the Redeemer in his own way—
the Comforter, the Holy Ghost—to complete the trinity with Father and Son.

Satan himself is transformed into an angel of light.

He went to the kitchen and called Tony Brenzo. "Come get
me, Tony. I've saved myself. You understand, Tony? I've saved
myself."

"Where are you, Joe? What the hell have you done?"

"I'm at Cheap Mary's. I saved her . . . I saved myself. . . ."

He hung up the telephone and walked back to the bedroom
mirror. His body seemed to glow with an unearthly beauty now. He
stared at his reflection a long time. *You did this yourself, Joe Market. Nobody else did it but you. I know somebody is going to say the
white man did it. But you found your own way, Joe, you followed it
without faltering.*

A terrible, flaming spirit entered his being, almost stifling his
breath with the onslaught of its coming.

I am the Holy Ghost, I have come to redeem the world.

He heard the divine words plainly inside the captivity of his
mind, and he knew how he would die.

Strapped in that devil chair like Mr. Cobb, insanity denied, all
appeals exhausted, prayed over by that nigger chaplain in the
death room.

Does the condemned man have any last words?

Yes. The condemned man does have last words. The very fact
of being human panics us into the most grotesque play-acting
imaginable; and we deal in absurdities to keep life from being a total waste, like one constant jacking-off party. Now please suck my
dick. All you slimy motherfuckers, black and white alike.

He had refused to see Tony. And Odessa hadn't come to the
trial, she hadn't even come to the prison. Legally, though, she was
still his wife; and she was his only relative. He wondered if she
would give his body to the Newark Medical Center when they
turned it over to her. *Odessa honey, don't do that please. Or at least
save my dick, don't let them destroy that too.* But he knew that she

would have all of him destroyed, she was just that pissed off with him still, she didn't give a damn.

They had him strapped down now. And blindfolded. But he couldn't get his dick hard, damn it. And then he heard the humming of a distant generator. Inside his last second of life, he had a long exhaustive look into heaven. Man, God was a *black woman*, somebody that looked like his mother Ramona. Sucking him off. His dick jumped hard then, yes it did. He spread his legs. *Father forgive them, they know exactly what they're doing.* He died.